THE BOROUGH BOYS

BOOKS 1-4

TAMSIN BAKER

CONTENTS

GRAYSON'S MATE

AARON'S MATE

BRAD'S MATE

MEGAN'S MATE

First Box Set E-book Publication: April 2018

Edited by: Avril Stepowski

GRAYSON'S MATE

THE BOROUGH BOYS SERIES BOOK 1

CHAPTER ONE

The sun was setting, on an early winter day in Melbourne. The red and orange hues faded in the sky, darkness nestling in.

"See you back at the 'Borough. I've gotta make one more stop, then I'll follow you."

The Betas nodded their understanding and Grayson jumped into the cab of his truck. He drove to the computer shop to pick up his new laptop, then returned to the truck with one destination in mind.

Home.

He put his hand on the keys, but a familiar scent caught his attention and he faltered.

"What the hell...?"

It couldn't be.

He got out of the truck and pocketed his keys, after locking the doors. There were wolf shifters nearby and they were on the hunt. He could smell their adrenaline, their excitement.

These wolves had been members of his pack, he recognized

their distinctive scent. Or they had been... until they'd gone rogue. As Alpha, it was his responsibility to make sure they weren't up to no good.

Grayson moved through the streets, following the tracking instincts in his blood, as old as time.

He turned and kept moving up the street until he saw a recreational reserve, with a playing field, a car park and a clubhouse all surrounded by trees.

A good, quiet rendezvous point. But a hunt was on, and this would be a perfect spot for an ambush.

He moved around in the shadows and watched as the scene unfolded. A car pulled up to the reserve, turning into the main entrance. The driver stopped and switched the lights off.

Grayson inhaled the air, scenting the excitement of the wolves' hormones increasing.

Then he spotted them. Two men, behind the parked cars.

Suddenly he saw whose scent had caught his attention. Tollie stepped out into the carpark, under the main lights, to greet the men who got out of the cars.

Thugs, definitely. And human, too.

What was Tollie up to?

And who were the two others setting up the ambush?

Probably Alexander and Ned, Tollie's brothers.

Tollie was talking to the humans in leather jackets and one wore dark glasses. Who the hell wore sunglasses at night?

He needed to stop this now. Tollie and his brothers could literally eat those humans for breakfast.

A wolf-shifting male was twice as strong as a human, and it was obvious Tollie's brothers were going to ambush these humans.

Grayson couldn't stand by and let his old pack-mates shred

anyone, it was not only unethical but it had too many ramifications for his kind.

With the stealth of his wolf, Grayson went wide and then snuck up behind the pair, who had their full attention on the encounter in the car park. It was obvious from their poised position that they were about to spring their trap and he needed to stop them before they did.

He'd nearly reached them, when Alexander spun to see Grayson, taking away the element of surprise.

Grayson leapt forward and hit the Beta's jaw, pushing it sideways across his face, short-circuiting the Beta's nervous system all the way to his knees.

Grayson turned towards the other brother, who was swinging a haymaker towards his head. Grayson's fists lifted up to his scalp, creating a protective shield with his arms that absorbed the blow.

Grayson brought his fist down in a punch he'd been taught by an old boxer, like the action of a fast-bowler, right into the middle of the brother's unprotected face. The brother was unconscious before he hit the ground.

Shouts erupted from the car-park meeting in response to the noise of the fight. Now it was time to screw up Tollie's meeting properly.

The humans shouted out to them and Grayson called back to the meeting beneath the lights.

"Hey, Moe...Larry and Curly can't make it to the party. They've got a bit of vertigo at the moment."

The humans jumped in their car and took off.

Grayson smiled as he grabbed the two Betas by their belts and hefted them forward.

Tollie came barreling up. "What the hell is your problem, man? Grayson! What the fuck are you doing here?"

"I could ask you the same thing, Tollie. What was the plan,

huh? Take whatever the humans were selling you? Or kill them before you paid them?"

Tollie scowled at him and bent down to attend to his brothers.

"Grayson, what the fuck? Seriously. You kicked us out of the pack. You have no rights here. Fuck off and leave us alone."

Grayson glared down at the Betas. He'd done everything he could to make these men a welcome and happy part of their community.

"You left, and that was your choice. That doesn't mean you can come down to Melbourne and cause trouble. If you attract attention from the human police you know that'll bring down a whole new hell on all of us."

They'd been family when they lived in the Borough. Now the three brothers looked like a group of street urchins.

"Fuck off, Grayson," Tollie spat, his spine straightening until he was at his full height—till three or four inches shorter than Grayson. "It's your fault we're here."

"Listen here, Tollie. You can't look after yourselves, let alone a pack. So, either come back and accept the hand that fate dealt you, or fuck off entirely and leave here and the 'Borough well alone."

Grayson's wolf rose to the surface as Tollie's eyes flashed with his shifter.

A growl rose and vibrated through him and the men stumbled backwards.

"Just go, Grayson!" Tollie yelled as the brothers slowly got to their feet.

"Tollie, by the looks of your boys, you need to return to the pack. Accept reality, and stop being such a pain in the arse."

These stupid wankers might have already attracted the wrong attention. The last thing they needed was to have the police on their doorstep.

"Fuck off, Grayson, and leave us alone."

Tollie grabbed his brothers and they stumbled away.

Grayson watched them go, ambivalence tearing him apart. He knew those Betas would need guidance to get back on the right path, but he had a pack to protect.

So he returned to his truck and drove away.

It was time to kick their pack's security up another level. With those rogue netas still around, and as stupid as ever, the pack needed to be protected.

Luckily their predecessors had been vigilant in regards to safety of the pack and their family, and had built a town that would protect the weakest of them.

They'd built tunnels under the homes that were used as an escape route if the houses were ever under attack. But the humans had evolved their weaponry significantly since the days of pitchforks and lighted torches.

Each house had triple-thick brick internal walls, bulletproof glass and automatic locking systems.

But they could do more. He had to speak to his father about installing motion sensors and security cameras on the perimeters. And some of the outlying farms needed a lot more up-to-date technology.

Rain splattered on his windscreen and grew heavier the further out of the city he drove. He turned the wipers up to the third tier, focusing hard on the white lines on the road so he didn't swerve near the other traffic.

In Greensborough, they were lucky it rained so much. Their fields were green and lush, their crops abundant.

He rounded the small hospital on the corner and said goodbye to Melbourne for another couple of months, heading home, alone. To a house that was empty, like his heart.

He'd never expected to still be single at thirty-five. Male

shapeshifters were born with a birthmark that was distinct to each individual. Baby girls of the pack were born with no birthmarks, however, a mark appeared on their skin once they turned twenty-one.

The woman's perfect mate would have the same mark on his body, in the exact same place. It was a straightforward and easy way to know who Fate had decreed for you.

It was a system that had worked for their pack for centuries, and everyone in their town believed wholeheartedly in it.

Grayson had turned thirty-five on his last birthday, and he still hadn't met a woman, wolf-born or human, who had his black, gnarly tree shaped mark.

When he'd been younger he'd been glad to have the extra time to live without the responsibilities of a mate, children.

Now? It was frustrating as hell. Not to mention, extremely lonely.

A small, red car ahead of him swerved into oncoming traffic, narrowly missing a white sedan that swung out of the way.

"Hey, buddy, be careful. Whatcha doing?" Grayson muttered to himself.

The car suddenly sped through a huge puddle and spun out. Grayson slammed on the brakes, though he knew it would be in vain. The weight of his truck would be impossible to slow down enough as the smaller vehicle slammed into the passenger side door.

It hit with a loud bang and sickening crunch, then ricocheted off and headed towards a tree like a runaway train, smashing into the trunk.

"Holy crap!"

Grayson's heart pounded so loud in his ears it sounded like a bongo drum and sweat broke out on his brow.

He stomped on the brake and managed to pull the heavy truck

to a shuddering stop. His gaze flew to the mirror, watching the small car he'd inadvertently run off the road.

Was the driver okay? Were they drunk? What the hell had happened?

He put the truck into park and jumped out of the cab, the cold rain pouring down on his head and soaking him in seconds. He cursed as his heart raced with adrenaline. This was the sort of stuff you saw in the movies, not on empty roads in country Victoria.

"Hey! You okay?" he called out to the car that had smoke billowing from the bonnet and glass shattered over the bonnet and ground.

A soft moan sounded from the car, and Grayson's heart rate began to gallop.

"Fuck."

They were alive. Barely though, by the sounds of it.

He walked across the road carefully and reached the car's window. He reached for the handle and pulled open the car door. That was when he saw the driver for the first time.

Grayson's whole core tightened and burned, and he grabbed for his chest, feeling his heart burst and flame.

What the fuck was that? He gasped for breath and opened his eyes. He hadn't even realized they were shut.

In the mashed up little red car, sat a stunningly gorgeous man. Probably in his mid-to-late twenties.

His light brown hair held a red tinge to it and sat loosely around his face, almost to his shoulders. Blood poured down one side of his face from a gash just above his right eye.

And it wasn't stopping.

"Oh, shit, I'm going to help you out, okay?"

. . .

He tore his wet t-shirt off and ripped it into several strips with shaking hands. It looked so much easier on TV.

He wrapped two strips around the man's head wound and jumped as something sparked under the hood of the car.

"That's going up. I've gotta get you out."

The man's head lolled around on the head rest as though he understood what Grayson was saying and was trying to reply.

"Good. Let's go."

He reached into the car and put his arms under the man's slight body, lifting him out of the car and pulling him back towards the truck.

He had to get this guy out of the rain, away from the car and somewhere safe.

He didn't smell like he'd been drinking. In fact, a scent unlike anything Grayson had ever smelled reached his nostrils. He inhaled sharply, getting even more of the tangy orange aroma.

His cock hardened in his jeans and he gasped at the strength of the reaction inside his body. His knees shook as he staggered to his truck, pulling open the door and hoisting the man in the passenger side.

Blood soaked through the makeshift bandages, and the young man was getting paler by the minute.

Despite his superhuman strength, the power fled Grayson's body like a vampire was draining his life source.

His arms were barely strong enough to pull himself around to his side of the truck and climb in.

When he'd finally managed it and pulled shut the door, he let out a massive sigh.

He didn't really know what was going on here, but as he shook off the water streaming down his face and thrust a hand through his long hair, he assessed the situation further.

His body was weak but aroused, despite the cold and the danger. How was that possible? Unless...

No. It couldn't be, could it?

The man next to him wore a black t-shirt and Grayson gasped as his eyes spied a strange mark beneath the cotton.

No way.

He pushed the sleeve up, groaning aloud when he saw the mark he'd been looking for his whole life. The black, gnarled tree that he carried on his own arm, imprinted on a human male!

"Oh, fuck!"

Grayson pinched the bridge of his nose and squeezed his eyes shut.

It was almost unheard of for an Alpha male to have a human mate at all, let alone a person who was most certainly... not female.

What sort of cruel twist of fate was this?

The man beside him gasped and spluttered awkwardly, blood dripping down his chin. His breathing had changed, a raspiness that hadn't been there before now appearing.

He had two choices, take this man to a hospital in town, or take him home to Greensborough. They had a great doctor and several nurses at the hospital.

Grayson twisted around and groped beneath the seat for the Red Cross first-aid kit. His fingers found the cold handle and he pulled out the metal box, relief winging through his terrified heart.

He removed the strips of shirt that he'd wrapped the man's head in to stop the bleeding. Hopefully there wouldn't be an infection.

He opened the packaged bandages from the first-aid kit and

dressed the wound properly, his heart racing in his chest so loudly he could hear it beating above the rain pelting down on the truck.

As he patted the gauze, pulled the edges of the gash together, wrapped and held the wound tight, his whole body ached with the need to gather this stranger up and keep him close.

“Focus,” he muttered to himself He taped the clean, white bandage into place. That would hold for now.

The man moaned and rolled his head again, making Grayson’s heart leap and do a virtual dance.

“Holy shit...” He leaned away, his breath coming in painful gasps. Of all the people... in all the world.

He swiped a hand over his mouth and let his hand clench into a fist as it lay against the dashboard. What in the hell should he do?

He blew out a long breath and gripped the steering wheel. He had to get his mate back to safety. Now.

My mate... Oh fuck, the possession shit was happening already.

The truth of the thought made him cling tighter to the steering wheel while the man beside him grew whiter by the minute.

Grayson reached over, his balls throbbing with lust at the scent curling up into his nostrils. Even half dead, his mate aroused him like no other. Damn.

He lay the passenger seat as far back as it would go and frowned at the blood now soaking the bandage.

As he started the truck, a single dribble of red liquid slid down the stranger’s cheek.

“Oh, to hell with it.”

There was no choice. He had to take the man home with him. The very idea of letting him go and perhaps never seeing him again made pain course through Grayson like a sharp knife sliding into his guts.

He turned the engine back on and glanced over to his mate.

"No, I'm not letting you go."

He shook his head at his own possessiveness and pressed his foot on the accelerator.

He'd never even been attracted to another male before, let alone had sex with one. Why would Fate choose a man as his mate?

The gorgeous stranger beside him moaned a little, and his head dropped forward.

Grayson reached across and gently pressed his head back, his heart leaping at the softness of his mate's tousled hair and smooth skin. Even pale, bleeding, and unconscious, he was fucking beautiful.

"Bloody hell." He turned off the main road and pushed the truck harder up the hill into the mountains.

He wiped his palm across his forehead, sticky with sweat. His heart thumped like crazy with purpose, his brain whirling with the implications of what he'd done, and what he was about to do.

Greensborough was the only place for them both, but the question was—what the hell was he going to do with his little human when he woke up?

Someone was pounding on Reagan's head with a sledgehammer. Heavy, insistent, and downright unbearable.

When the fuck did I have time to go out and get drunk?

The throbbing continued and seemed to get worse as Reagan forced his eyes open and a bright light hit his eyeballs.

"What the..." He blinked rapidly as he brought his arm up to press his palm to his forehead, searching for a way to dull the pain consciousness had brought.

"Ow!" Pain sliced through his ribs, and he hissed as his respiration increased and his heart beat a steady, heavy rhythm in his chest.

Reagan tried to get up from his supine position, but the nausea that accompanied the wave of pain proved too much to bear.

"Please don't try to get up. We haven't given you anything for the pain yet as we weren't sure of your medical history or allergies."

Reagan looked towards the mature female voice that was coming from somewhere within his room. He narrowed his eyes as he stared, his brain frowning over the lack of sense this was making.

His vision was clearing finally, and everything around him looked legitimate. The doctor in a white coat, a sterile hospital room. He'd obviously had an accident of some sort. Why didn't they have access to his medical records in the hospital?

"Where am I?"

The brunette woman smiled at him with practiced warmth.

"Can you tell me if you are allergic to any medications? I'll give you something for the pain, and you can sleep."

"What happened to me?"

The woman pulled his blanket up, and the lights dimmed a little. His eyelids were so heavy it felt like they were weighed down by lead weights.

"You were in a car accident and sustained a few broken ribs and a moderate concussion from what I can determine. Do you have any pain in your body other than your head and ribs?"

Reagan let his eyes close and groaned as another wave of nausea hit.

"Can I prescribe some Endone? Can your body handle codeine or morphine derivatives?"

Reagan nodded, then wished he hadn't as his headache returned with a vengeance.

"Endone's fine. I'm not allergic to anything..."

He'd sort all this out when he woke up again. He was so tired.

There was rustling and some murmured words, but he couldn't stay awake a moment longer. He fell quickly into a dream filled sleep.

CHAPTER TWO

Reagan's mouth was so dry. Endone did that, of course. He'd forgotten.

But as he checked his once aching body and found sweet relief from the pain, it was well worth the cracked lips and parched tongue. His head didn't feel like it was stuck in a vise anymore either, and his breathing was easier now.

He blinked awake slowly, forcing his eyes to open and then focus by pure will. It took a minute longer than it should have, but when he achieved his goal, he could finally see everything around him.

He had a good look around the plain white room he'd been brought to. Nothing weird to report off the cuff, yet he knew in his gut that something wasn't right here.

Reagan clenched his abs for support and hefted himself up with effort, hissing as pain curled up and spread out through his chest in waves of heat.

"Fuck. That hurts."

"Of course, it does, you idiot. You ran your car head first into a tree!"

Reagan cried out in surprise and yelled again with pain as he twisted to see the man whose voice had thundered at him. Six feet five of hulking male stalked forward from the corner, glaring at him with as much menace as Reagan had ever seen on anyone.

"Lay down before you hurt yourself."

Reagan's heart leapt into his throat, and he gaped at the giant. He almost expected the man to physically push him back down, but as he waited, it didn't happen.

The man kept his distance while staring at Reagan with an intensity that was unnerving. Well, to be accurate he had to admit that it was *almost* unnerving, because the giant was too striking to be truly terrifying.

Reagan pushed the strong feelings of instant attraction down and focused on finding something ugly about the man in front of him. He searched the guy's grizzly face, square jaw, and piercing blue eyes. And yet he couldn't find any feeling, other than the urge to run his hands over the prickly skin of the man's jaw and draw him in for a kiss.

Reagan was gay, always had been. There had never been a time of experimenting to find out about his sexuality. He'd known who he was from the age of thirteen.

But his focus, for as long as he could remember, wasn't hot guys and sex, it was medical school. Getting through University on a scholarship and no parental help was bloody hard. Gorgeous men, or men of any kind for that matter, were a luxury he didn't allow much time for.

"Hang on a minute! What day is it?"

The grizzly bear's eyebrows rose, and he slowly crossed his meaty arms over his massive chest.

Shit. Could the man get any bigger or more substantial? He looked like some sort of lumberjack from Reagan's dreams.

"Ah, Thursday about two, why?"

"Thursday! Fuck! My exams start next Friday and I haven't even finished my study notes. I need to get out of here."

Reagan sat up and pushed down with his hands to get rise off the hospital bed.

The big man's reaction was extreme. He growled like a big dog, pushed Reagan down on the bed with two hands, and then jumped back as though he'd been burnt in the process.

"You stay there. You're injured and can't drive, and the doctor hasn't cleared you to get up yet, either."

There was something seriously weird going on. This guy wasn't giving off any gay vibes at all, and yet Reagan's nipples were as hard as ice chips. And the way the guy was looking at him... Reagan couldn't stop likening it to the way a hungry man would stare at a juicy steak.

He narrowed his eyes at the man towering over him.

"Who died and made you the boss of me?"

The man blew out a long breath, his gaze skittering all over the room like an embarrassed teenager. "I'm Grayson. I help run things around here... I..."

Grayson groaned and spun away, storming out of the small room, leaving only cold air in his wake.

What in the hell was that?

Reagan lifted the white sheet and glanced down at his naked body. His ribs were black and blue, but other than that, he didn't appear to have sustained too much damage.

From whatever the hell had happened.

Grayson had said something about a car accident...

His hand crept up to his face, and he winced as his fingers touched swollen, tender, hot flesh, and stitches covered with plastic. "Great...a head injury. There goes the last two weeks of study."

A chuckle entered the room as an older woman walked in. "Study? What are you studying, Reagan?"

Oh, they know who I am. Thank God.

"Medicine. Exams start next week. Where am I?"

The doctor nodded, making a note on his chart. "I assumed you were a student. I found a hospital I.D. badge on you. Congratulations on almost finishing. How are you feeling?"

You didn't answer my question.

"I'm okay. Vision's fine, bilateral temporal headache, and my ribs hurt, but I think I can stand up and go home soon."

She smiled at him with that look they'd been taught, the one that said, "I'm listening to you, but I'm in charge, not you."

"We'll decide that in a few hours. You've only just regained consciousness, and it would be remiss of me not to monitor you a little longer. I'll get the nurse to come and give you some more painkillers."

"I don't need any more, I'm feeling fine. When can I be discharged, and you haven't told me where I am yet."

"You're in the mountains of Greensborough. Your car swerved off the road and hit a tree yesterday. One of our residents found you and brought you here."

"I swerved off the road? Shit, did I hurt anyone?"

"No, luckily the other driver managed to handle his truck, even in the rain."

Thank God for that.

"But, why did they bring me here, rather than take me back to the Whittlesea hospital? I work there and must have been driving home..."

His mind wandered, trying to remember finishing his shift. Had it been raining? Had he fallen asleep?

"Oh, shit. I could have killed someone."

The doctor leant over and squeezed his arm.

"I remember how hard university was. The long hours, the ridiculous hospital shifts. Get some rest, and I'll be back to check on you in a few hours."

He smiled back at the woman who'd apparently tended his wounds. He was grateful, of course, for her care, but the hairs on the back of his neck began to stick up. What the hell was he doing in Greensborough? He hadn't even realised there was a hospital here. It certainly wasn't listed on any Doctors reference guide he'd ever read.

She left with another professional smile, and he lay back as though he was going to do as she asked.

He waited another couple of minutes to make sure the doctor had gone before slowly swiveling around and sitting up in bed. His head spun like a top, but it was a lot better than it had been when he'd woken up earlier.

It was time to escape and work out exactly where he was. There was something fishy going on here and he didn't trust anything he was being told.

He pulled himself to a standing position and staggered across the small room, falling into the chair by the window when his tired legs gave out.

He heaved in a sharp breath around his fractured ribs.

"Holy hell."

That had taken more effort than he'd expected. Maybe he shouldn't be moving around so much. He shook his head at his weakness. He worked two jobs and managed a full-time course load at University, with very little support, family, or assistance. Now he was wondering if he could even dress himself. Wow, how things had changed.

Drugs. That was the short-term answer.

He fumbled for the small plastic cup containing more Endone and swallowed them down with some water from the bedside table. It wouldn't take long to kick in and should hold him for a few hours.

"Now...where the hell have they put my clothes?"

A nearby dresser looked promising, so he dragged open the top drawer from his seated position and let out a small whoop when he found clean black t-shirts. He pulled one out, loving the soft feel of the cotton on his skin as he slid it on. Pain splintered along his right side as he lifted his arm and twisted to get the clothing on.

He clenched his jaw and tightened his resolve. The next drawer revealed blue jeans and grey sweats.

Perfect.

Reagan glanced towards the window. Sunshine, yet it was May. Only a month away from winter in Australia, so the wind would be chilly.

He managed to stand on legs that wobbled and pull on the jeans that were a touch too big. No matter. He was up, he was dressed, and he was getting out of here.

"What the hell do you think you're doing?"

Reagan jumped and twisted, gasping as pain shot through his chest once again. It was the big gorilla from before. He lowered his eyebrows and glared at the guy standing in his doorway, lustful heat twirling through his traitorous body, completely at odds with the anger in his mind.

God, he's delicious!

"What does it look like I'm doing? I'm getting out of here!'

Grayson marched into the room, laying down a laptop computer and some magazines on the side table.

"I thought you'd be getting bored by now."

Reagan was struck with the thoughtfulness of the gesture, yet he couldn't get over how weird everything was around here. "I'd prefer to just go home." He began to edge towards the door, and Grayson shadowed him.

"You...can't."

Reagan stared up into the dark blue eyes of the six foot four giant. At exactly six feet, he was no midget, but compared to Grayson, he felt petite.

"What do you mean I can't? If this is a hospital, they have to let me go. I'm healing, I'm feeling well, and I have so many exams to study for, you have no idea!"

His voice had turned childish and sounded like he was pleading, so he cleared his throat in a rush. Panic was starting to infiltrate his system, and he wasn't sure whether to run or fight.

Grayson's incredibly sexy eyes scanned him then he nodded once.

"I'll take you around town, and answer your questions, but you've gotta promise to stay until tomorrow so we can sort out a few things."

Reagan opened his mouth to rebut the request, but thought better of it. He may not get a better offer than that, and what was one more extra day when he'd probably be dosed up on meds at home anyway.

"Okay, but are you going to tell me where I am?"

He wasn't sure he believed that doctor, but something about this big guy told Reagan he'd be honest. Grayson beckoned him with a hand, so together they stepped outside the hospital room and into a white corridor.

His heart pounded louder, blood thrumming in his veins with each step he took. After a turn and two doors, Reagan was led outside into the sunshine and fresh air filled his lungs.

He blinked rapidly, lifting his hand to shield his eyes from the heat and the light. Relief filling him with such intensity he realized he'd been feeling very claustrophobic in that white room.

Something to consider when talking to his patients in the future.

"You're in Greensborough."

So, the doctor had been telling the truth.

Then he was even more curious why he'd been brought here rather than back to the Whittlesea hospital.

"Isn't that a couple of hours north of the city Melbourne?"

Grayson nodded, his gaze darting around at the people in the street.

"Yes, northwest, to be precise. We're up in the hills and quite closed off, so we generally don't get many visitors."

Something in the way Grayson said no one came to visit made little prickles of unease rise on Reagan's skin. He grinned up at Grayson to keep the crazy at bay. "So, you guys are some sort of weird cult then? With sister wives and a prophet of some sort?"

Grayson shook his head and indicated a building in the distance. Reagan looked that way and noticed a church of sorts. "Most of the people in town are Christian. Presbyterian Church, or Catholic. And no, we aren't some weird cult. We just like to stay off the grid and live our lives away from Big Brother."

Reagan nodded in understanding. He got a bit creeped out by the way social media and cell phones followed your every move too.

He took this first opportunity to look around the town he knew nothing about, a little disappointed to see that his imagination had been creating something that simply wasn't there. What had he expected? Twenty-foot high fences and people in straitjackets?

Out here in the sunshine, there wasn't anything unusual at all.

It looked like any main street in a small country town. There was a post office, a general store, a pharmacy, and a pub.

But his curiosity still wasn't satisfied.

"Well, if there's nothing weird going on here, then how come I can't leave? And as a side note, you were the one who brought me back here, weren't you?"

No other scenario made sense. Why else would this exceptionally hot man be babysitting him?

Grayson nodded with a terse jerk of his head.

"Thank you for saving my life. But why did you bring me here when you should have taken me back to Whittlesea? That's where we had the car accident, wasn't it?"

Grayson nodded. "Yeah, I was down in town getting hardware supplies for the coming winter."

"Why didn't you take me back?"

Grayson shrugged, ignoring the question, making the tightness grow in Reagan's belly.

He tried again. "Tell me why I have to stay here an extra day. Why can't I just go back home now?"

Grayson rumbled a little, a strange growly noise that made Reagan jump back.

"What the fuck is going on with your throat?"

Grayson shook his head and turned away a moment before twisting back around, his dark blue eyes turning almost black. "Look, I'm asking you to stay one day. That's not too much to ask considering you almost wiped me off the road and died on the way back here."

What? Oh, damn.

"I didn't force you off the road. What are you talking about?"

Grayson growled again, the sound so visceral it caused Reagan's belly to tremble.

"You were swerving along the road, and even though you

slammed into my truck, I managed to keep it on the road and not run into a tree like you."

Reagan bit his lip and looked away. Shit. He could have done some major damage.

"I was coming home from night shift. I'm working two jobs on top of medical school. I must have fallen asleep—I don't know—I can't remember much before the accident."

Grayson stepped around him and gently ran his fingers through Reagan's hair. "You hit your head, so I'm not surprised."

Reagan didn't move as tingles of awareness and longing passed down his spine. He looked up and met this stranger's gaze, hearing the gentle tone of concern for the first time.

Reagan stared up at the man-mountain, letting the heat between them flicker and build. His skin tingled, and he bit his lip, their eyes meeting in a clash of need.

What on earth was happening here?

CHAPTER THREE

Grayson clamped down on his wolf, hard, who howled like the moon was at its highest. He used every bit of his self-control not to pull his mate in for a kiss.

What would his mouth taste like? Would it have the flavours that he'd dreamed of? Those special hormones or whatever they were, that he'd searched for in every kiss he'd ever had. Those flavours of ecstasy that he innately knew existed, had been hinted at through some of the best of those kisses that had always fallen short.

His heart had ached for years, waiting to feel the closeness of his mate. To have all those things that he would share with the one destined for him. The feelings that he would have, not for just one day but for all his life.

There was no denying the fact that Reagan was his. He'd heard the legends a thousand times since he was a child.

And unfortunately for him, his feelings for this human fit the stories like a glove.

The first sign, of course, was the almost painful attraction to

Reagan, despite the fact that Grayson had never been with a male before. The feelings were beyond his control, he knew.

Who or what attracted one person to another was not a chemical reaction they knew anything about. It was inborn. He'd met people all his life and yet no-one had ever caused his body this reaction.

Waiting another thirty-five years to maybe feel this again and forego all the joy in his life? Even if his destined mate had been purple with green spots, he'd rather a life of love than wander the earth alone. Reagan was definitely his mate—he could feel it in every cell of his body. That identical mark didn't lie.

The legends said that the attraction would grow stronger and stronger if they didn't fulfil the bonding soon. There was no denying the inevitable.

How was he going to explain the legends and the inevitability of it all to his human mate? He was pretty sure the soul mate ideal was not a very smart pick-up line to use in this case.

A loud noise sounded in the street and Grayson turned, pushing Reagan behind him to shield him in the case of any harm.

"What are you doing?"

Reagan struggled against Grayson's grip, and he let his mate go. It was just a ladder clattering off the side of a shop and onto the pavement.

"Nothing. What other questions do you have?"

"Who are you?"

Grayson heaved a massive sigh and tilted his head. That question was so much more complex than his little mate realised.

"Come, meet our council."

Reagan gave him a strange look, one eyebrow flicking up, but he kept his mouth shut. Grayson had a strange premonition he'd see that look many times in his future, and the thought made his heart perform that strange quiver it had been doing since he'd first laid eyes on Reagan.

A mate—his mate—for life.

They walked towards the town square and his father stepped out of the meeting hall unexpectedly.

Damn, he should have spoken to his dad first.

"Son, who do you have there?"

His father's sharp gaze narrowed in on Reagan, and Reagan looked back and forth between them. He had a good idea knew what his mate must be thinking. The apple hadn't fallen far from the tree with him. He was just a younger, slightly bigger version of his father.

"Dad, this is Reagan. Reagan, my dad. The head of our Council."

"You guys have a town council? I would have thought Greensborough would have been part of a larger shire."

Grayson nodded while his father studied Reagan with keen, blue eyes. It was an excellent observation of Reagan's, but they were completely independent. Always had been.

"No, we're self-governing in a lot of ways. The council is made up of five men. My father's the...mayor."

"Nice to meet you, son." Grayson's father extended his hand and Reagan just stared for a moment, then shook himself visibly.

"I'm Reagan."

"Jack." His father smiled with natural charm.

"Is that..." His dad pulled on Reagan's arm and brought him closer, staring at the birthmark curling down beneath his short sleeve.

"Hey, do you mind?" Reagan yanked as though to pull his arm back, but Jack had a tight hold on him.

"Dad, let him go." Grayson's voice growled out of him in deep waves. His mate was released.

Reagan rolled his shoulders and straightened to his full height, which was half a foot shorter than the men around him. "It's just a birthmark. Nothing contagious or anything. "

Jack stared at them both with wide open eyes. "Um...what do you do, Reagan?"

His dad's voice had gone strange, high-pitched, and strained.

Hold it together, Dad.

His father was having a harder time recovering himself than Grayson had. Discovering your soon-to-be son-in-law was human, and a male, would be a shock to anyone. Especially an Alpha.

"I'm a medical student. I just have to finish my last semester of exams before I get my license and can start practicing. Although, I would like to continue with a residency for a specialty, I think."

Jack's face lit up with a smile so wide it looked like it would crack. Then he began to chuckle.

"A doctor. Oh, son, your mother will be proud."

Jack slapped him on the back with a heavy whack, and Grayson pushed him back. Bloody smart-arse.

"Stop it. Bloody smart-arse."

Reagan held up his hands and took a step back, as though intimidated for some reason.

"Look, I don't know what's going on, but I need to get back to the city ASAP. I have eight days until my finals, and I haven't worked this hard for six years to miss them now."

Grayson's arms shook at his side. Why didn't Reagan understand?

"You can't leave!"

He reached out for his mate and watched Reagan's pupils dilate with fear as he stumbled away.

Oh, no.

Reagan took three steps back, his heart rate picking up with the adrenaline now pumping through his veins. He couldn't stay and fight these two goliaths, so his muscles began to tremble as he prepared for flight.

"Grayson, son..."Jack placed a calming hand on Grayson's shoulder, and Reagan took the opportunity the older man had given him. He spun on the ball of his foot and pain ricocheted through his ribs as he pushed off from the ground and began running.

Reagan pumped his arms to make himself move faster, his head was spinning like a top.

Oh crap, oh crap. Where in the hell should I go?

Grayson was closing in on him. Reagan could hear his breathing and the thud of his foot falls as he drew closer. The pain in his ribs was making him sweat and he could feel the faintness closing in on him.

"Reagan!" Grayson bellowed, and reached out to grab him. Reagan twisted out of his reach and turned right, heading for the forest line. If he could just get away from Grayson, he might have a chance.

"No!" Grayson's voice boomed through the air as he knocked Reagan sideways, tackled him, and together they rolled to the ground.

"Ow!" Regan grunted and cried out as pain coursed through his ribs, and his head exploded with black light. His shoulder was scuffed on the ground and his body became the pillow that lay beneath the huge bulk of Grayson's body.

"Let me go!" He screamed up at the man above him, and Grayson flipped him over and grabbed both of his hands, pinning them above his head with the strength of iron shackles. Reagan gasped for air, the blackness receding as the pressure on his ribs released.

"No. You have to listen to me!"

"Get off me!" Reagan fought against his captor, throwing back his head and flexing his spine, attempting to show Grayson how mad he was. When the man above him only glared down, Reagan finally let himself fall flat against the grass. He was never going to win this one.

"Fine. I'm listening."

A smile twitched at the edges of Grayson's mouth, then it was gone.

"I need you to stay, for just one night, then I'll drive you home myself tomorrow."

"Bullshit." There was no way Reagan believed that. "For all I know, you'll lock me up in some dungeon and throw away the key. I don't trust you for one second."

"I'm serious. Come on. If I let you up, do you promise to listen for a minute?"

With Grayson's heavy body crushing his pelvis, he didn't have much of a choice.

"If you get off me, yeah, I'll listen."

His ribs ached with fire, and his belly hurt from Grayson's weight, and something was sticking into his thigh.

As Grayson moved off him and stood up, sweet relief rushed through Reagan's body. He sat up carefully, staring at Grayson's crotch where his huge erection was now obvious.

"That was what was digging into me?"

Grayson flushed bright pink and looked away, breathing hard. "Blame the adrenaline."

Yeah, right. "Whatever you want to tell yourself. Anyway... What do you wanna say?"

No matter what Grayson said, it wouldn't measure up against the pressure of his university course.

"You said you'd stay for a day, why the change of mind?"

That was true, and he'd still need rest from his accident once he got home, but he didn't like feeling trapped.

He'd never liked it. And the lack of a choice was a hot button of his.

"You know you're freaking me out, right? We have a car accident and instead of driving me to the nearest hospital, you just take me home with you. It's weird, and you haven't given me any real answers as to why you did it."

Grayson frowned, and reached out, pulling Reagan to his feet. Pain split his ribs, but the warmth of Grayson's touch dulled it immensely.

"You won't believe me if I tell you the truth, and I don't want to scare you."

Reagan stifled the need to make a smart-arse comment. Horror movies taught you not to poke the crazy. But this really did sound like some sort of freaky place.

"Well, you've got me hostage. I'm two hours from home with no car and no phone. Shit, where *is* my phone?"

Grayson shrugged. "Don't know. In the car, still? I didn't have time to look for anything like that."

"Probably... Anyway, tell me what's going on. I think I can take it." If they were some weird cult, the last thing they'd want was a queer doctor, surely?

"Walk back with me, and I'll explain some of it."

Reagan nodded, his head whirling and making his stomach lurch. More painkillers were definitely needed. He began walking back with Grayson, a calm washing over him once again.

Something about this beautiful, big man completely unnerved him. He was pretty sure if he let his guard down properly around Grayson, he would be completely swept away.

"Talk."

"Okay. Well, let me tell you about Greensborough, first. Our ancestors built their homes here almost a hundred and fifty years ago. Five original families settled this town. Over the decades, more families have been added and we have grown as a community. As you know, we are self-governing and almost self-reliant. Our soil is very fertile, and we farm much of the land to the east. Our focus is on keeping our community strong and healthy, a bonded unit."

"I don't know Grayson... It's sounding more and more like a cult, but go on."

A weird hysteria was making a smile stretch across his face. He shouldn't be smiling, he knew he shouldn't be. But there was something strangely comical about all of this.

"We aren't a cult, we're a pack."

Reagan stopped walking. "Of what? Animals?"

Grayson stopped and turned towards him, his dark blue eyes hooded and showing concern. "Sort of. We have a... magical gene that runs through the males in our family lines. We shape shift. The females can't."

Reagan swallowed hard, his mind a blank. A magical gene? That did what, again?

"Um...shape shift? As in... you can turn into an animal? What sort?"

Is this some kind of joke?

"I'd prefer not to say at the moment, just keep up with me, okay?"

Reagan couldn't help but roll his eyes. He'd fallen into the twilight zone.

"There are many legends about our people, and we have great

faith in Fate. I believe I was meant to save you, meet you, and if you'd just give me one more day, I'll explain everything."

What choice did he have? Steal a car and run away? His logical mind pointed out that so far, they'd looked after him just fine. If they wanted to hurt him, they would have done it already.

"Okay, but you need to swear that you'll take me home tomorrow."

"If you want to go, of course, I will."

"What do you mean if I want to go? Have you not been following what I've been saying? I have exams. Lots of them!"

Grayson started walking once again, and Reagan followed. "I know. A doctor. Pretty impressive."

Reagan shrugged. "Yeah, well, I love it."

Grayson grunted in response and together they walked back in silence, the electrical attraction between them shimmering like light on a lake.

"It's almost dinnertime. Shall we go meet everyone?"

"What do you mean everyone?"

His shoulders ached and his ribs burned.

"I think I need some more pain meds."

He swayed a little as his vision began to darken at the edges. He stumbled, groping for anything to steady himself when Grayson grabbed him and swooped him up into his arms.

"Put me down. I can walk."

He could barely see, but this was getting bloody embarrassing. First Grayson had hunted him down, wrestled him to the ground and now he was holding him like a baby.

The massive hulk carrying him grunted. "Relax. I'll take you back to the hospital, then we can go eat."

Reagan closed his eyes and let himself relax into the arms carrying him. Not like he had much of a choice, anyway.

GRAYSON'S BODY burned with the heat of his mate in his arms. The man was as light as a feather and as fragile as one of their females. All males born in their community shifted form, and with that came speed, strength, and a vast superiority to heal.

Their females did not.

And thus, the men of their pack were very protective of their more fragile mates.

Grayson had never thought it would be possible to feel this way about another man. The desire to protect him, to care for him, even to fuck him until he passed out with exhaustion.

A strange warmth rose up his neck.

Sex with another man. Who would have thought?

Obviously, the Fates had. This man had been created for him. He needed to get used to the idea. His hormones were already adapting to the situation, so he better adapt his subconscious as well, because his body had intentions of doing things he'd never thought possible. And it felt damn hot and bothered about doing them.

He flinched and pushed open the hospital door, depositing Reagan safely with Doctor Sarah, and moving back to stand in the waiting room. Despite his little speech to himself, another part of him still hadn't come to terms with the fact that his mate was a man. It felt like something, or someone, had truly fucked up.

He'd have no children. And that was probably what annoyed him the most.

Why Reagan? Why a man at all? It made no bloody sense.

He shook his head and began pacing the hall. An acceptance of their fates was in their genes, but as an Alpha, one of only five born this generation, part of him wanted to buck the system. Marry someone else that wasn't his 'true' mate.

A woman, preferably.

Perhaps that would still be possible? Especially if Reagan was set on leaving.

Grayson could find a female whose mate had died, or never became known to her? It would mean no strong, true mate bond for them, but it would mean a family. A continuation of the bloodline for his father's Alpha genetics.

Reagan stepped back into the hall, a box of pills in his hand.

"I'm all good to go, although I think I'm going to need some new clothes. The doctor said mine were thrown out."

A shudder coursed up Grayson's spine as the memories flicked into his mind. "They were covered in blood."

Driving Reagan back to Greensborough had been the toughest two hours of his life. He'd known that the other hospital had been closer, but he couldn't bear the idea of potentially losing his mate to the human system.

Instead, he'd risked Reagan's life for his own selfish purposes. Now, especially knowing what he did about his life to come, a part of him regretted that choice.

"Let's go."

He marched out of the hospital and waited for his mate, who toddled behind him.

"Can I get some clothes now?"

Grayson flicked his wrist to check the time.

"Yeah, we've got about ten minutes before everything shuts down. We'd better hurry."

He strode down the path, making a few quick turns until they both stood in front of the only male clothing shop in the 'Borough. He pushed open the door and shoved Reagan inside. "Pick some stuff for today and tomorrow."

Reagan nodded and chose a couple of pairs of black jeans, checking their sizes, then selecting two t-shirts and a grey hoodie.

Grayson's eyes slid down his mate's thin body. Compared to the other males in their area, Reagan was small… So easily hurt.

He pushed the thoughts away. No one would dare touch Reagan while Grayson drew breath.

"Shit."

Reagan's face appeared stricken.

"What's up?"

"I don't have my wallet!"

"Don't worry about it." Grayson took the clothes from his mate and placed them on the counter. "Put 'em on my account, Sally, okay?"

"Sure, Grayson." The petite blonde gave him an interested look and began packing up the clothes. Sally was married to one of the Betas and was already expecting her first child.

"I can pay you back tomorrow, as soon as I can access a bank."

Grayson rolled his eyes and shoved the bags at his mate. "It's a few clothes. Forget it. Thanks again, Sal. See you at dinner."

Reagan gave him a quizzical look.

When they stepped out of the shop, he asked his mate, "What's wrong now?"

"Do you all eat together? Like a commune?"

Grayson groaned and tugged Reagan along the street. "I live a block from here. You can get changed there, then we'll go to dinner."

Why did his mate have to question everything? It would be so much easier if Reagan had been brought up in the pack and already understood everything.

He reached for his keys, stepped up to his new town house, and unlocked the door. "Come in."

Reagan stared at him for a minute as though weighing his options, then obediently came inside.

"Where's the bathroom? "

"Through there." He pointed to the downstairs bathroom, and Reagan went off to change, closing the door firmly behind him.

Grayson let out a breath slowly, feeling the darkness shifting inside him. His mate was home, in his house, where he belonged. A lightness filled his heart that he'd never experience before and as he realized what the feeling was, he let his head drop, defeated. Reagan was the one. There would be no other option for him now.

Damn it.

"All done." Reagan stepped back into the kitchen area, his lithe legs now encased in clothes that fit, his broad shoulders stretching the cotton tight.

Inside his mind, Grayson's wolf howled and pawed at the ground, tight with lust and need. *Kill that thought*! He couldn't take Reagan now, especially not against his will. Their mating needed to be done right. With full disclosure, and consent.

He clenched his fists tight, digging his short fingernails into his palms, tensing his muscles as hard as he could so his body would absorb the adrenalin. His body was way too into this.

The pictures of Reagan's naked muscles, his lean rump, the groans, the ecstasy, kept flashing up on his mind's screen. *Focus, Grayson, focus.*

"This is a really nice place."

Reagan glanced around the open-plan living area with awe in his eyes, and Grayson encouraged the tension out of his body and away.

Focus on the present.

"I built it last year."

He hoped Reagan didn't notice the robotic answer. He was proud to have gotten out those words, given the state of disarray of his mind.

He had to think about something different.

"Let's go eat."

CHAPTER FOUR

Grayson kept Reagan in sight at all times as they made their way to the hall. The whole pack ate together. It was how they were raised. Economical, easy, and good for bonding.

He pushed open the door and let Reagan step inside first. The noise and warmth of the gathering hit them like an oven door, and Reagan stepped back into Grayson's chest.

A growl rolled through him as his wolf reached for his mate, wanting to pull him closer and protect him from all those around them.

"Why do you keep making that noise?"

"Because you keep touching me." The retort was out before he could stop it and Reagan shot him a hurt look before glancing away.

G........."''I..."G.........."

"Grayson!" Megan's voice burst out, knocking any apology that was forthcoming from his mind. His bubbly baby sister could throw a storm off its path. Megan bounced up to him, her curling red hair flowing around her beautiful face. "Hi, I'm Megan. Grayson's sister."

She stared straight at Reagan, and Grayson watched as his mate fell under his baby sister's spell, his shoulders visibly relaxing as a bright smile lifted his face. "I'm Reagan. Nice to meet you, Megan."

Megan brought Reagan in for a very gentle hug, rubbing his arm to expose the birthmark she obviously already knew about.

She stared at it for a moment, her mouth dropping open. "Grayson! Is it..."

"Is it what?" Reagan's eyes narrowed as he looked from his arm to Grayson.

Grayson shrugged, not willing to answer that question just yet. "It's just a weird mark, Megan. Relax. Let's go sit down."

His sister stared at him with wide eyes before scowling and grabbing Reagan's hand. She pulled him towards the Alpha's table, where all five families sat at the center of the vast hall. There was room next to Megan, and she tugged Reagan down to sit next to her, everyone at the table staring at Grayson's mate with interest.

Heat crawled over his back, and Grayson stepped forward, a growl raising and vibrating through his chest as he wrapped an arm around Reagan's shoulders in a possessive claim.

"What are you doing?" Reagan hissed at him.

Grayson's wolf clung to his mate, the presence of so many unmated wolves around him making him anxious. But his human side could feel the weight of the eyes on him, and he knew he wasn't doing the right thing.

His father stood up, staring at him hard. "Grayson. Sit down."

His wolf had no choice but to obey and he let go, dropping into the seat next to Reagan.

Reagan glared at him, and Grayson's heart danced at the sight of his mate's strength and passion. Anger it may be now, but later on, that would translate into something so much more powerful. Life with Reagan was going to be anything but boring.

"Who's your friend, Grayson?"

Tony, the Alpha sitting next to his father, asked casually, picked up a chicken leg and began eating it with apparent nonchalance.

But the table was quiet, and everyone was staring.

Did he dare lie about the importance of Reagan to him?

"I'm Reagan Forster. Grayson saved my life last night when I smashed my car into a tree, but I need to get home, so Grayson said he'd take me back to Melbourne tomorrow." Reagan's voice was strong and steady, and pride blossomed in Grayson's chest.

Few men could withstand the energy of the table that currently surrounded him, and his mate wasn't missing a beat.

He cleared his throat and began introducing everyone. "Reagan, this table is for the five elders who run our Council. My father, Jack, you know. This is Tony, Charlie, David, and Ron. And their families."

The way their pack operated, there were only five Alphas in a generation, and all of them bore only one Alpha son. The rest of the community were ranked as either Beta or Omega males. The Betas were often sent to university, but the Omegas were put into more laborious or service type roles.

Grayson didn't agree with the rigidity of their hierarchy and believed all men were born equal, and able to determine their fates. But times were slow to change, and there were definite physical advantages born to the Alpha protectors of their group.

And he did have to admit that the Elders were right about one thing, they had not stayed such an active, vibrant community for no reason.

Everyone seemed happy within their role in the community,

except the Rogues—seven men, all born Betas, who bucked the system. They wanted nothing to do with learning a trade, nor educating themselves to further the betterment of the community. They were lazy and cruel, yet wanted to lead the pack as an Alpha did.

What they failed to understand was that an Alpha was the main protector of the pack. He would die for the pack. And the Rogues wanted nothing of that responsibility, and only wanted the status that came with the title.

It wasn't happening.

Never.

Not on his watch.

"Nice to meet you all. And thank you for allowing me to use the facilities at the hospital. Doctor Sarah did an excellent job of patching me up."

"My husband tells me you're a doctor?" His mother's sweet voice spread down the table, and Grayson couldn't help rolling his eyes. Of course, his father had gone straight home to brag about Grayson's newly found mate.

"Yes ma'am, although I haven't graduated yet. Six more exams and I'm done."

Ron, the elder sitting closest to them, his deep voice rolling down the table, said, "Another doctor will significantly improve the pack."

"What do you mean?" Reagan sounded surprised, and Grayson struggled not to groan. Could they be a little more subtle?

Grayson grabbed their plates and jabbed at Reagan to get up. "Ron probably wants you to stay. Take it as a compliment. Let's get some dinner."

Reagan looked confused, but followed him as they made their way over to the buffet table next to the kitchen.

"Get whatever you want, as much as you can eat." He began piling his plate with roast beef and chicken, his stomach growling with the aromas of their chef's offerings for the night.

"Wow. What a feast. Do you get this every night?" Reagan was cautiously taking some of the potatoes and Grayson scooped up some stewed beef and dumped it on Reagan's plate.

"Eat this. You need to regain your strength. And, yeah, this is normal. We eat well."

A werewolf's appetite was twice that of a human male and their chefs catered accordingly. Most chefs were Betas, and they had both strength and creativity.

"Okay." Reagan took a little more—not nearly enough by Grayson's standards, and then headed back to the table.

Grayson took more food, then he stopped. His belly tightened and pulled at him as Reagan moved further away.

Stuff this.

He abandoned the buffet and went back to the table, his body settling down the moment he took his seat next to his mate.

This wasn't a good sign of what was to come. This need to be so near Reagan would be his undoing.

Reagan was engrossed in a conversation with his sister, so Grayson let his gaze wander. His father smiled at him, and his mother's eyes were shimmering with tears.

His chest tightened with emotion. He'd never thought about how his parents would feel when he finally found his mate, but they were happy. More than that, they looked relieved.

He'd have to speak to his dad about Reagan being a male. How would that work with the succession plan?

"TELL ME MORE ABOUT YOURSELF, Reagan. Do you have a big family? I sooo want a big family when I get mated. Five kids at least!" Megan rambled on, and Reagan couldn't help laughing and smiling with Megan as she talked.

She was utterly enchanting.

"Mated? You mean, like married?"

She cocked her head at him. "Yeah, I suppose so. We have a slightly different ceremony than you do, I'm pretty sure, but that's me. Anyway...tell me about your family."

He swallowed hard. Family...what was that? "I...ah, don't have much family actually. Everyone's gone."

Megan waved at someone, and when Reagan turned around, he found an older woman walking towards them who had Grayson's bright blue eyes.

"Reagan, this is my mum, Katherine. Mum, Reagan was just telling me about his family. Go on."

The person next to Megan moved and Katherine slipped into his place. She had a kind face and bright eyes, and her aura was soothing. Just as his mother's had been.

"Ah, well, I was just saying that I don't really have any family. Dad was an only-child, and so was Mum. And they only had me. My grandparents died when I was young and then when I was eighteen, Mum and Dad passed away too. A car accident, actually."

He took a long drink of the water in front of him.

That had almost been him, too. Shit. If it hadn't been for Grayson, he may have passed away just as his parents had.

He stared at Grayson for a moment, gratitude spilling over him like a hot shower.

"Anyway...that's me."

Katherine reached over and squeezed his hand. "I'm sorry to

hear about your family. I'm sure your parents would have been very proud of you."

He choked on a sob, tears tingling in the back of his nose and throat. Ridiculous that after eight years he could still get so choked up. "Thanks...um, they knew I wanted to be a doctor and were very supportive of it. Dad especially. It was practically his dying wish, so I can't tell you how important it is for me to do well."

Katherine continued to hold his hand and smile at him. "It is so lovely to meet you."

Reagan stared at her, the tears in her eyes confusing him. Why was everyone acting like they'd been waiting for him, and he was meant to stay forever? It was very strange. "Thanks."

"Eat," Grayson growled from behind him, elbowing him in the side.

"Ow, yeah, okay." He reached for his fork, then elbowed him back, his arm ricocheting off solid muscle. "And quit poking and pushing me. I have several broken ribs, remember?"

Grayson grimaced and flashed him a smile in between huge bites of food. "Sorry, keep forgetting you take so long to heal."

"So long? It's only been two days. "

Although, surprisingly, he was feeling a lot better already. The painkillers Doctor Sarah gave him must be working.

Grayson shrugged like that didn't make sense to him, and Reagan shook his head, finally eating some of the amazing food on offer. Rich gravy swirled in his mouth, and meat so tender and juicy it made him moan aloud.

"Wow, this is incredible." Hospital cafeteria food and frozen meals at home didn't come close to this.

"Glad you like it."

They ate in companionable silence, the hall buzzing with energy and conversation.

"Grayson, Grayson!" An attractive young man ran up and grabbed at Grayson's shoulder.

Sparks of envy flickered in Reagan's chest, but he pushed them down. Ridiculous feelings.

"There's a problem with one of the farms. They think it's the Rogues. Please come."

"Shhh, calm down, Jimmy. You don't want to start a panic. I'll come."

Grayson pushed his almost empty plate aside and stood up, turning to him. "I've gotta go deal with this. Megan can take you back to my place and show you the spare room. You'll stay with me tonight."

There was no question in the statement, but Reagan found himself nodding anyway.

"Don't worry about it, Grayson, we'll show him 'round." Marcus, Tony's son, gave him a grin and a snarl ripped through Grayson's lips.

"Touch him and die, Marcus."

Marcus laughed and turned back to his food.

Huh? What in the hell was that?

"Pardon?"

Reagan stared up at Grayson, who looked like every muscle in his body was tense. His teeth were bared, and his hands were clenched into tight fists at his side. The boy, Jimmy, cowered beside him as though Grayson's anger was directed at him.

Reagan stood up, unafraid of the huge man in front of him. The need to comfort Grayson became an overwhelming feeling that he could not contain.

"Calm down, Grayson, it's fine. I'll stay with Megan and then get to bed early." He reached out for Grayson and laid a hand on his arm. Heat seared his palm, making a soft moan rise in his throat.

Grayson visibly relaxed, his shoulders dropping down from their high, tense position and his face lost its contortion.

What are you doing?

He didn't understand the connection he shared with the man in front of him, but there was more going on here than his conscious brain could decipher. And although he wasn't a big believer in fate and such nonsense, there was a lot to be said for instinct.

Grayson gave him a grateful smile and a single nod, then headed off with the younger man.

"You want to go grab some dessert? "

Megan had stood up and was indicating a newly filled table of sweets.

"Oh, for sure."

They walked over, and he gazed at the mountains of home-made eclairs, cakes, biscuits, and pavlova.

"Oh, my God. I would get so fat if I stayed here." He began picking things up and piling them on a plate.

Megan laughed at him, only choosing only one of the many sweet treats. "Nah, you get used to it after a while."

She stopped and looked out towards the room and Reagan paused next to her.

"What are you thinking?"

She chewed on her lip and gestured to the room. "I was just wondering if Grayson had explained anything about our community."

"You mean, your pack?"

Her eyes widened. "He told you? "

Reagan's stomach tightened. "Told me what?"

"About our family and the...you know, shifting and stuff."

Reagan bit into one of the chocolate chip cookies, fluffy biscuit and buttery yumminess exploding through his taste buds. He groaned and ate more. “Yeah, but I didn’t really believe him.”

She giggled. “I can imagine for you, it would be strange. But for me, having grown up with all of this, your version seems weird.”

“My version?”

“Yes. Where men aren’t strong, and super-fast, and shift into incredible, beautiful animals with the full moon.”

His heart jumped, pounding harder as he stepped closer to Megan. “Are you serious? “

“Of course, I am.”

“You’re...you’re...wolves?” Impossible!

He took a step back from her, and she laughed, moving forwards. “Not me, you idiot. Only the men shift. We women are just human.”

“Well, that seems unfair.”

She huffed. “Don’t I know it!”

Reagan took some deep breaths, surprised at how natural she made everything sound. “Tell me more about your...pack, then.”

“Well, there’s three rankings of wolves. There’s only five Alphas and they’re born to the Council. Occasionally, an Alpha can be born to a Beta, but they have to go through testing and stuff.”

He nodded, forcing his mind to go blank even as it churned up a thousand questions about this ridiculous story.

She continued. “The rest of the men are broken up into Betas and Omegas. The Betas go to university, generally do a trade or business management. The Omegas are designed to serve. A lot of them don't have mates, but they're essential for the growth and stability of the pack.”

Spoken like a true queen.

Reagan looked around the room and saw the truth in what she said, and the difference within the community immediately.

"Are the Betas bigger as well?"

"Oh, you noticed that? Yes, the Alphas are the largest. You can't tell now because most of them are sitting down, but they're all over six feet three. The Betas are still very strong and fast, but they only tend to hit about six feet."

There were several tables of thinner, shorter families and Reagan pointed to them. "And they're the Omegas?"

"Yep."

"Wow. It's strange being put into a box the moment you're born like that. It's ...discriminatory."

She laughed at him. "You're kidding, right? You don't think humans do the same thing? That children don't follow their parents in genetic similarity? That occupations don't run in families? We're an active community, pure and simple."

She had a point.

"But what if a son of an Omega wanted to go to school, or he was bigger, like a Beta? Could he change his path?" He hated the idea of a predestined fate that you couldn't change.

Megan grinned, eating some of the orange cake she'd chosen. "You sound like Grayson. He thinks anyone is capable of anything, and that there should be more flexibility."

Something surged in Reagan's chest, and relief followed strongly after it. Grayson believed in equality too. Fantastic.

"Well, Megan. What would happen?"

"He'd have to go into a testing ring with one of the Alphas, but it doesn't happen very often. "

"Yeah, but at least there's the possibility. Then I suppose I'd be a Beta."

He was six feet tall and not very muscular.

She shrugged. "You're an anomaly. You may look like a Beta,

but you're a doctor. Our Alphas are the most intelligent, and the only doctors in the past have been Alpha-born females, like me."

"Interesting."

And it was. Sure, he hated the idea of being judged and boxed at birth, but many people he knew tended to follow their parents in a lot of ways. Physically, personality types, and jobs—it just wasn't so obvious.

Nor categorised in such a way.

"Do you want to see any more of the town, or do you want to go back to Grayson's and relax?"

His ribs ached, and some of his headache had returned. He could use some more painkillers and sleep.

"I'd love to go back and rest if that's okay."

"Yeah, sure. Finish your dessert, and I'll walk you back. I have keys. "

They finished up, and he bade goodnight to the Alpha table. When each of the men stood up to shake his hand, he was dwarfed by their breadth of shoulders and towering height. Even the older fathers maintained their size with age

Amazing that, although, they supposedly weren't genetically related, they were all carbon copies of each other.

On the walk home, Megan and he spotted a loved-up couple, canoodling by the hall.

"Oh, they're so cute. Amelie turned twenty-one a few weeks ago, so she and Dylan have been preparing for their mating."

He stared at the young couple and tried to see what Megan was talking about. Cute wasn't really the word for it.

They both looked ravenously hungry as they kissed and pawed at each other's bodies quite awkwardly as they fumbled in the dark.

They were a bit young to be getting married by his standards.

Childhood sweethearts perhaps?

"Have they been together long?"

He looked again. They didn't look like it had been very long.

"Oh, didn't Grayson explain that either?"

"No, what?"

"Amelie barely knew Dylan a few weeks ago, but they're fated to be together. All of our mates are."

"Huh?"

Grayson said that they believed strongly in fate, but that was a bit ridiculous.

"So, what was it? Love at first sight or something?"

She shook her head, laughing. "No. All werewolves are born with a birthmark on their body. It can be big, small, dark, light—they're all different. Then, when a woman turns twenty-one, her mark develops, and it matches the werewolf she's meant to be with. This is mine."

Megan lifted her cotton tank top and Reagan looked down. There, where she pointed, swirled around her belly button was a crescent moon shaped mark.

"Wow. That's pretty cool. So, who's your mate, then?"

If what she was saying was true, it would make dating pointless and finding the love of your life, easy. Sounded perfect.

Megan shrugged. "There isn't a man in the pack with the same mark, but he could be a part of one of the northern families. We all meet once a year at a festival in April. My parents will ask around then"

She seemed so sure, so confident of the legends her people had taught her. How was Megan so accepting that her husband would be someone that the mystical Fate had chosen for her?

It couldn't be that easy, surely?

"That's pretty incredible. What about gay couples? Does that happen too? Or is being homosexual illegal or something here?"

"Gay?"She frowned as though she didn't understand the term.

Luckily, Reagan didn't look gay or effeminate, he never had. For all he knew, they could stone him for being homosexual here. Just like some backwards country town.

"You know, men who sleep with men. Women who sleep with other women. "

She giggled good-naturedly. "Oh, I know what it means. We don't worry about that sort of thing. Your mate is your mate, irrespective of sex. It's uncommon for two men to have the same birthmark, but when there's no corresponding person in their pack or they can't find them, it's quite common for people to pair up in same-sex couples."

A question hovered in the back of his mind. He knew he shouldn't ask. But as he bit the side of his tongue to stop the question, they stepped up to Grayson's front door step, and he couldn't help himself.

"Is Grayson mated? Or in a relationship with anyone?" It didn't look like it from the way his house was arranged, or his mannerisms, but you never knew with some people.

Megan stared at him, long and hard for a moment, then twisted away to open the door with the keys she held. "Ah, no. Not yet. He's been searching, but hasn't found his mate yet." She opened Grayson's front door and stepped back, not quite looking at him properly.

"Megan, you okay? You've gone weird."

"Oh, I'm fine. Just thinking. You all right to go inside by yourself? The spare room is just to the left of the bathroom. Blue doona cover. "

"Yeah, I'll be fine, I'm sure." His head was pounding with proper bass guitar quality now. He needed more of the painkillers the doctor had given him.

"Great. Good night. "Megan stepped forward and gave him a kiss on the cheek, the move as sweet as it was unexpected.

"Goodnight and thanks for all your help."

Reagan closed the door and stepped into the brand new house, taking his time as he looked around once again. It was lovely, and for some reason, his whole body relaxed the moment he locked the front door.

Home. The feeling was undeniable.

He scoffed at his own romantic notions.

It was simply... impossible.

He was getting delirious again, obviously.

Reagan found the pill packets from the hospital and took some more pain killers. He had a quick shower in the ultra-modern wet room and crawled between the clean sheets in the spare bedroom. Everywhere smelt like Grayson—strong, woodsy, sexy smells.

He fell asleep with his head full of erotic dreams and a body too exhausted to respond.

CHAPTER FIVE

Grayson pushed open his front door, his cold, dirty body longing for a shower. He sniffed the air and the fragrant orange scent of his mate filled his nose. His blood throbbed, lust surged, and his cock hardened within his jeans.

Damn. There goes a relaxing shower.

He walked towards the stairs, heading for his master suite, which was situated on the top floor of his house. But as his hand landed on the balustrade, his legs wouldn't move.

What the hell?

He tried lifting his foot, but it was stuck to the floor like someone had driven a nail through his boot. His brain screamed at him to go and find his mate, now.

He sighed out his frustration at himself and turned towards the spare bedroom. There was no point fighting the ridiculous notion, he knew he wouldn't win.

Because if he was truthful, he could understand his wolf's need to reassure himself that Reagan was okay. The bloody

Rogues had set fire to one of the wheat farms. An entire year's crop, gone. Luckily no one had been hurt, but it would weaken the pack, which he supposed was their purpose.

They'd need to pull money from somewhere else to provide for the farming family to make up the money they would lose from not selling their wheat.

Grayson stepped up to the guest bedroom door and peeked through the crack. He couldn't see Reagan in the dim light, so he nudged the door open a bit further and the head of the bed came into view.

Reagan, his tousled brown hair strewn across the pillows, lay there fast asleep.

Lust slammed into him even as a sigh of contentment vibrated along his veins.

He was safe.

Grayson turned away sharply and pushed himself quickly up the stairs and into the double shower he'd built with his mate in mind. Of course, back when he'd been designing his house with a draftsman, he'd imagined luscious curves and sweet feminine moans in his bathroom.

But now, as he stepped beneath the hot spray and wrapped his hand around his cock, Reagan's face was all he could imagine.

He pulled up the old mental files that would arouse him as an experiment of sorts. Would he really be able to adapt to this new world that Fate had thrown at him?

He focused on the old images that used to excite him, but no matter what he saw in his mind's eye, they were dull and meaningless in comparison to the life he had ahead of him.

This new awakening to a male was hot. Damn hot. And excerpts from his old library were only killing the mood. He wanted Reagan's body. Those mental pictures made him hot. Imagining the soft skin over those lean muscles, all different angles flashing at him. Reagan being erect and excited in front of him, pushing that rump back at him, tempting him.

Reagan's arse wiggling in front of him. What would it be like to be inside him and feel his arse grabbing his cock? And to feel his hard erection in front of him. What would that be like, that was the definitive question.

His groan ricocheted off the dark tiles as images of his mate's face, twisted in rapture, made his belly tighten. Reagan would be bent over in front of him, his tight arse squeezing Grayson's cock again and again.

No-one could say an arse pulsating on his cock wouldn't feel good. He'd felt it before, just not from a male.

But if couldn't be that different. Especially a tight muscular arse like Reagan would have.

Grayson's cock throbbed harder in his hand and it made him imagine what it would feel like, having Reagan's hard cock throbbing and pulsing in his hand instead. If it felt as good as his own did now, fuck that would be hot. Feeling him coming...

"Oh... fuck..."

He blew all over the tiles, hot cum pouring out of him as shivers of ecstasy washed over his skin.

"Wow." That had been far too intense for a self-induced orgasm.

He closed his eyes for a moment, enjoying the last zings of pleasure before turning his face beneath the spray. Well, it seemed that answered his question. The thought of a cock in the picture sure didn't worry him now, as long as it belonged to Reagan.

Grayson laughed. Life sure was strange.

He applied himself to washing away the grime of the night and when he finally stepped out of the shower, he fell asleep in his king-sized bed.

Alone.

Which to his wolf, and to his own better judgement... was now so very wrong.

Reagan could smell sizzling bacon, strong coffee, and fresh bread. Even as he stretched in his bed, blinking his eyes awake, his stomach growled for the food that had woken him.

He rolled onto his side and pushed himself up, the ache in his ribs much less painful than yesterday.

Which was incredible, and the doctor inside him also said, truly unbelievable. Most people couldn't move for weeks after such an injury.

He reached for the painkillers he hadn't taken since last night and stopped himself. Maybe he should test how he felt first.

He stood up and pulled on his new jeans, amazed to feel the stretch and pull of healthy muscle.

What the hell was happening here?

Was there something magic in the water up here? Nothing else could explain why he was healing so quickly.

Reagan inspected himself in the mirror. Some of the bruising on his head and ribs remained, but overall, he looked a hell of a lot healthier. It defied understanding. Everything he'd learned at University over the past six years told him what he was seeing was impossible.

His stomach growled again, and he shook his head to clear the confusion. No point worrying about something that was a gift. He'd be able to go home today and get back to his old life.

A coldness akin to grief crept into his gut and made him gasp. *What was that?*

He waited for the feeling to change, breathing in and out slowly as it eventually passed.

Something else to ignore.

He pulled one of the new t-shirts out of the bag and ripped off the tag. At least he was taking a few mementos home with him. He'd have to get Grayson's bank account details to transfer the money back to him.

"Oh, fuck..." This time the cold hand hit him straight in the gut, and he doubled over, unable to breathe.

"Hey, you okay?" Grayson's voice in his room eased most of the pain, and he pulled himself up to stand.

Their eyes met, and his knees gave out. Grayson lunged forward and grabbed him, pulling him tight against his body. "What's happened? Are you hurt?"

Grayson began running his hands over Reagan's body, and he moaned, the pure pleasure of Grayson's touch causing an immediate reaction in his groin.

"I'm fine"

Grayson stepped back and opened the door. "Oh, okay. Breakfast's ready."

He disappeared and left Reagan feeling bereft and lonely. So he pulled on the t-shirt quickly and walked out into the living area, anxious to be near the man-mountain, whose very presence made him feel better.

"That smells incredible. Can't believe how hungry I am."

"Eat. You're too small." The gruff words were barked at him through gritted teeth as Grayson slid a pile of bacon from the frying pan directly onto the plate in front of him.

Saliva pooled in his mouth as the aroma filled his nostrils. "That's a lot of food."

Another grunt and Grayson turned away.

"What's with the caveman routine? I don't get why you're looking after me if you can't stand the sight of me."He picked up a greasy piece of bacon with his fingers and bit down into it.

Grayson spun around, his brows drawn down low. "What are you talking about?"

"You." Reagan gestured to Grayson's stance with a pointed finger. The bigger man's arms were crossed over his chest, his jaw jutting out as though he were ready for a fight. "I can't tell if you hate me or ..."

"I don't hate you."

"Then why do you flinch every time I come near you?"

The words, *"Are you a homophobic prick?"* sprung to mind, but Reagan swallowed them before they could get a handle on his tongue. He had no idea how Grayson would feel about the fact that he was gay, but he didn't want to test the waters.

"Because I..." Grayson grabbed the frying pan and used a spatula to shuffle fluffy scrambled eggs on top of the bacon in front of Reagan.

"That's enough. Thanks." Reagan waved his hands, picked up a fork, and speared some of the food before Grayson piled on any more.

He tried to ignore the fact that Grayson wouldn't answer any of his questions, and instead focused on the flavors, the creaminess of the milk and the hint of cheese in the eggs.

But despite his best efforts, the question he'd asked still circled in his mind. Why did Grayson have such a strange and strong reaction to him?

"You want coffee?"

"No thanks."

He ate as much as he could until his stomach ached. "Thanks so much for that. Will you be able to drive me home soon?"

"Ah, yeah. I suppose." Grayson looked straight at him, lust pouring through his gaze like the heaviest cream. "I'll go get dressed. Wait here, yeah?"

Reagan nodded without thinking, swallowing hard against the lump in his throat.

Grayson managed to break eye contact and left the kitchen, treading up the stairs with a lightness that surprised Reagan. Grayson's steps barely made a sound for such a huge guy.

He sat and listened to the soft footfalls, a door opening, then a shower being turned on.

A shiver coursed down his spine. Reagan's cock took notice and throbbed in response.

Grayson was naked.

Right now. Upstairs.

Images of Grayson's muscular body swirled in his mind and he couldn't stand it.

Reagan jumped to his feet and ran his hands through his hair, tugging on the strands and enjoying the twinge of pain that followed.

However, it gave him no relief from the burning in his groin that came with it. What would Grayson do if he walked up those stairs and joined him in the shower?

Probably kick him out on his arse, thats what.

Reagan paced back and forth on the polished floorboards, the perfection of the new house mocking him. How could his environment be so calm, so relaxed, when inside he was a sea of turmoil?

His skin itched and throbbed and an awareness of himself, unlike anything he'd ever experienced, coursed through him. Igniting him, firing his arms and legs into action.

He couldn't stand it a moment longer. He had to find out if what he was feeling had any basis in reality or if he truly was delusional.

Reagan tore at his t-shirt and ripped his jeans down his thighs, kicking them away from him. His cock throbbed with a need he knew would only be satisfied in one way, and only one man could do it.

His legs moved, almost of their own volition, towards the stairs. He began to climb, his stomach tightening with nerves as he moved toward whatever future he was making for himself.

There was a strange sort of magic swirling around him, or he would call it that, if he believed in such things.

It was crazy. But so right.

If he felt this, surely Grayson did too? Why was Grayson holding back?

As he stepped into the huge, open bedroom at the top of the stairs and stood outside the closed bathroom door, a calm ran over him like a cleansing rain. His heart stopped racing and settled into a comfortable rhythm. Time to find out what all of this meant.

He lay his palm against the wood and pushed open the door. Steam wafted towards him in a billowing wave. The white cloud dissipated, parting for him like the Red Sea. His breath caught in his lungs as his eyes devoured the body before him.

Grayson was a god of a man. Even in his wildest dreams last night, Reagan's imagination had not done Grayson's body justice.

Dear God...

His shoulders were massive, his abs as defined as any eight pack Reagan had ever seen, and the legs on the man were like cut tree trunks. Reagan's eyes zeroed in on the organ between Grayson's legs as the water sluiced down his bronzed flesh.

"Holy shit."

Grayson's blue eyes snapped open, and he turned his back on Reagan, hiding his desire. Which was all too obvious in that amazingly long and gorgeous cock that had Reagan's blood pounding south.

He'd been hard walking into the bathroom, which he was sure

Grayson could see. But now his balls were drawn up, and he panted for breath. His wanted to know what it would feel like to have that cock inside him, splitting him in two.

"Get out. What the hell are you doing in here?"

Reagan licked his lips and stepped forward. Grayson's tone brooked no argument, but his erection told a whole other story.

As a doctor, not to mention, a horny male, he was listening to Grayson's body. "I wanted a shower, and I thought you'd like some company."

Grayson grunted and huffed, curling his body up even more as Reagan moved closer.

"Use the shower downstairs. I'll be out in two minutes, and we can talk then."

Reagan walked blindly into the shower and moved around to Grayson's side. Grayson turned away again, hiding what looked like a rock-hard erection.

Yum. Glad I wasn't wrong.

Reagan grabbed the soap from the tiled wall recess and made a good lather in his hands. Grayson wanted him, then? Good.

He was going home soon, so they only had a couple of hours left together. They may as well enjoy each other while they could.

"What's wrong, big guy? Afraid I'll like this amazing body a little too much?" He pressed his hands into Grayson's back, and half expected him to bolt right out of the shower.

Instead, Grayson groaned like he'd never been touched before. It was a combination of both sweet relief and painful intensity.

Grayson dropped his shoulders, his whole body relaxing as Reagan kneaded the tightly wound muscles.

"You've been avoiding me, Grayson. How come? You know we can have some fun before I go, right?"

Grayson didn't respond. Instead, he bent forward, placing both hands on the grey tiles in front of him.

More access. Hmmm...

Reagan slipped his hands over the lean hips in front of him and moved them around to the extended cock in front of Grayson.

"Oh...shit..." Grayson moaned and gasped, the sounds shooting right to Reagan's balls.

Reagan worked Grayson's cock with his hand, loving the thickness in his fingers as he held the big head, and then the hard rod of flesh.

Using both hands now, he stroked Grayson's cock faster as he rubbed his own erection against Grayson's firm buttocks.

He'd so love to top this incredible man, feel the tight clasp of Grayson's arse around his cock, but if he knew anything about an Alpha in an animal kingdom, that was never going to happen.

As though Grayson had heard his thoughts, he spun and grabbed Reagan, pinning him against the wall with one quick movement.

Cold tiles against his back made him gasp, but that discomfort soon vanished in the wake of the incredible feeling of Grayson's hands on his arms and his cock pressed against Reagan's belly.

"You don't understand what's at stake here." Grayson's deep voice echoed in Reagan's ears, the thrum of his heated blood barely allowing the words to register.

Reagan grinned, bumping his pelvis out against the huge man holding him. Nothing else mattered except satisfying this clawing need inside him. "I don't care. Just fuck me."

He grabbed hold of Grayson's biceps, expecting to be lifted against the wall when his eyes caught a glimpse of black ink. He narrowed his eyes and stared at the deltoid muscle above his fingers. That was far too familiar to be a coincidence.

No way, it couldn't be.

His stomach dropped, an icy cold washing away the heat in his blood. "What the hell is that?"

He stared harder, turning the flesh to his gaze with his palm. Grayson had a tattoo—a birthmark, identical to his.

Impossible. It couldn't be. No way.

Megan had explained what that meant in their world...but it wasn't possible. He wasn't a werewolf. Neither were his parents. How could he be fated to be with Grayson?

He slowly lifted his gaze, afraid of what truth he'd see there. Grayson's blue eyes stared back, and he swallowed, hard.

Reagan's voice sounded a little higher than it should be as he asked the strangest question of his life. "Why do you have a birthmark like mine?"

Grayson pulled back and shut off the water with a sharp flick of his wrist, the effect as rejecting and painful as a body blow.

Reagan grabbed a nearby towel, his erection now gone, as was Grayson's. So depressing.

He rubbed himself down and quickly wrapped the towel around his body. Why did he feel exposed now that the lust was gone?

Grayson still hadn't answered his question.

"That's just coincidence, yeah? Nothing to do with the shifter mate, thing...that Megan told me about?"

Grayson grabbed a towel and stormed out of the bathroom. The room was still hot and muggy, and Reagan struggled to breathe.

"Shit." Reagan ran a hand through his wet hair and took a deep breath. This just got freaky.

That would mean he was Grayson's mate. He'd have to stay in Greensborough. What about his life? His career?

He shook his head, trying hard to dismiss the strands of logic his brain had pulled together to create a picture. The facts Megan had explained about their pack sounded more like myths, stories to him. He hadn't thought they were actually... real.

They couldn't be.

It made no logical sense.

He took a step into Grayson's bedroom and Grayson was already pulling on blue jeans and his characteristic black short-sleeved shirt.

A pang of lust hit Reagan dead center in his chest, and he cleared his throat to distract himself. What was with his ridiculously lusty reaction to this man?

"Tell me what's going on, Grayson."

Grayson shook his head and pure instinct made Reagan move to the door and hold his hand out as the big man in front of him charged forward. "No! You have been holding me here for days! I have tried to be patient. I have been as calm as humanly possible, considering the circumstances. Now, tell me what the fuck is going on and why the hell we have matching marks when your sister said that was just a wolf thing!"

Grayson growled and spun back into the center of the room. "It doesn't mean anything!"

Reagan snorted and glared at the man in front of him. "Bullshit! Then you can just take me home right now. I'll get back to my life, and we can forget we ever met!"

Grayson paced up and down the room making weird, strangled, animal noises.

"Grayson, tell me or I swear to God..."

"All right!" Grayson stood in the center of his room and placed both hands on his hips, puffing up like a bloody peacock. "The matching marks mean we're mates. You're destined for me and I'm perfect for you. Now, are you happy?"

"Shit!"

He'd known it. From the moment he'd seen Grayson, he'd known there was something special about him. The lust between them, the safety he felt with Grayson nearby. It was creepy and perfect, and not possible!

No! This was not meant to happen. He let his arms drop, and the towel slipped to the floor. He hastily grabbed it up again, wrapping it back around his body, which was slowly going into shock. He could feel the cold, the shivering.

Stop! Concentrate!

"So, everything you told me...your sister told me...it's actually true?"He couldn't feel his legs anymore, and he staggered to the bed, landing with a thump as his arms fell to his sides like a deflated puppet.

Grayson groaned and threw his hands up in the air, still standing in the middle of the room like a monument to masculinity. "Well, I have no idea what my sister told you, but Megan's as straight as an arrow when it comes to honesty...so the simple answer would be yes."

"So...what does that mean? Am I a prisoner here now? Did you lie when you said you'd take me home again?"

Grayson shook his head and stormed to the door, flinging it open. "No, I'll take you home. Today, if you want. You can go back to your life, and we can pretend this never happened."

Reagan didn't move. He couldn't.

This wasn't happening.

Was he Grayson's mate... husband?

What on earth had he gotten himself into?

Grayson's heart thundered in his chest like a bass drum, so loud and profound he could feel the rush of blood in his ears pushing through his veins.

Boom, boom, boom, boom, boom.

Let his mate go?

Never!

His wolf snapped and howled inside him. Grayson had to push with all his strength to keep the shifter down.

Stop! Don't you dare break free. You'll scare the shit out of him.

"Fine, then. I'll go get dressed." Reagan's tones were quiet and hurt as he walked forward as though to move past Grayson and go back downstairs.

Not a chance in hell was Reagan leaving him.

Grayson grabbed Reagan and pulled him against his body. Reagan's towel fell to the floor and his mate's naked form was against him. Grayson couldn't wait a moment longer. He pressed his lips down onto his mate's and inhaled Reagan's flavour and sweet, orange scent. They flowed over him in an all-encompassing wave of pleasure.

A deep growl emerged as the perfection of the situation moved through him. Every cell is his body responded to the magic that wove through him with his mate's touch.

He stepped towards the bed and Reagan's hands frantically grappled with Grayson's jeans. He pulled open the zipper and tugged down the denim, then Reagan did something ridiculously hot.

He fell to his knees before Grayson.

Grayson's head fell back on a groan as Reagan took his cock into his wet, warm mouth, sucking hard. Pleasure exploded through his body in a cacophony of sound and light.

He could barely keep his eyes open, yet he forced himself to look down. Reagan's reddish-brown hair glistened in the sunshine that streamed into his bedroom.

Such a gorgeous boy.

My mate.

A contented sigh rumbled through him.

Never, even in his wildest dreams, had he thought he'd see a man in front of him like this. But now that he saw Reagan loving him in this way, he knew he'd never see another there.

Ever again.

Reagan continued to suck on the head of Grayson's cock with his perfect mouth, warmth and wetness enclosing him over and over again. Reagan lifted his hands to cup Grayson's heavy balls and the pleasure intensified.

He couldn't take much more. He needed to fuck Reagan. Now.

Grayson grabbed his mate under the arms and pulled him up, rubbing his hard, wet cock against Reagan's warm skin for a moment, savouring the electric zings of sensation. Then he threw his mate onto his king-sized bed.

Reagan bounced on the mattress and grinned up at him with sexy happiness. Then he arched like a cat in the sun, stretching out his long, lithe body for full display. Reagan's cock was already hard, red, and wet-tipped, lying against his belly.

Grayson ripped at his clothes, shedding his black shirt and the remains of his jeans in seconds. Then he stopped and stared at the feast before him.

The enormity of the moment hit him square in the chest like an axe to the sternum. He wheezed in a breath as the carved headboard caught his eye.

His hand-made bed. The one he'd ordered and then waited months for the craftsman to make for him. The bed he'd slept in every night, waiting for his mate to finally arrive. A bed he'd never shared with anyone.

That bed, his bed, their bed, now housed the man the Fates believed to be his real partner. His one and only mate.

Whoa.

CHAPTER SIX

Grayson prowled towards the bed, adrenaline zinging along his veins with the speed of light. Reagan rolled over and thrust his pert little arse up into the air, the perfect contours and muscled strength calling to Grayson for the first time in his life.

He groaned with the need flowing through his veins and crawled onto the bed, laying down on top of his beautiful mate. He covered Reagan with his body and bit down on Reagan's shoulder as his mate shuddered with pleasure beneath him.

His wolf sighed and vibrated with happiness within him. This was how it was meant to be.

"I need you," Reagan whispered, as he wriggled beneath him.

I need you, too. You have no idea how much.

Grayson pushed himself back onto his knees and reached over to the top of the chest of drawers looking for something slippery. Hair gel—that would have to do this time. He really wasn't set up for this sort of thing. "Push your arse back for me."

Reagan did as he was told, arranging himself onto his knees, then he turned his head and looked over his shoulder, staring at Grayson.

Those intense brown eyes met his and burned into Grayson's soul.

This was right. So right.

What ignited him was that he could see his mate in those eyes. That once-in-a-lifetime feeling went right through him.

He was proud of how his body had responded so powerfully to his mate. That was what a pair bond was about!

He could feel the heat and the electricity the moment generated. His whole being desperately wanted his cock in his mate.

He lubricated his shaft with the hair gel, readying it for Reagan's hot body.

Gasping at the strength of his arousal, he let go of his cock quickly, the heat of his orgasm already tingling at the base of his spine.

This was going to be volcanic and he couldn't wait.

He spread some of the lube over the winking star of Reagan's arse, pressing one finger into the tight channel to ready his mate for the thickness of his cock.

Reagan groaned, and his head dropped forward onto the bed.

Pride surged in Grayson's chest as desire wove through him. His mate was perfect. "You're... beautiful. So fucking hot!"

Reagan choked out a laugh. "I didn't know if you wanted me or not...if you were straight, or gay."

Grayson used more of the hair-gel and inserted a second finger, stretching Reagan's body, waiting until the tight muscles relaxed. Reagan would never be able to take him like this. He was way too tight.

"You're my mate. That's what matters."

He pulled his fingers out and moved his aching cock closer. He needed to know what sex with Reagan was like.

Would this count as their mating? Part of him hoped so, yet he knew it was too soon for them. The other part felt guilty for not explaining what it would mean to Reagan if they did mate properly.

They wouldn't be able to leave each other after this if their magic wove together, as he half-expected.

His wolf surged inside him, refusing to be denied now that they were so close. Grayson grabbed the shaft of his cock, rubbing the head on the outside of Reagan's body.

"Yes! Thank God. Just please fuck me."

"You know what this'll mean, right? I'll need you after this. We won't be able to go back to how things were before."

Reagan groaned and wailed, "What? Oh, I don't care. Please, just do it."

Grayson grabbed Reagan's hips and lined up his cock with Reagan's arse, pulling him back slowly. Reagan rocked on him, gasping and groaning, making the sexiest noises in the world, while Grayson stayed perfectly still. Sweat beaded on his brow as his cock got swallowed up by his mate's gorgeous, tight arse.

Heat flowed through his body, along his spine and down his legs.

Reagan's muscled arse hit his belly, and he felt, for the very first time, what it was like to be really home. The warmth, the closeness. If there was a heaven, he was there. Pure bliss flooded into his mind and descended over his earthly body. Every sense was in rapture. This was what it felt like to be deeply linked to his mate.

Time froze as he was immersed in color and sensation. He let himself fall into its ecstasy, surrounded by his mate. And Reagan confirmed he was there too.

"Oh, fuck... I think I'm going to come."

Reagan bucked beneath him, and Grayson just let it happen.

He didn't move, holding tight to his mate so that they were still connected, deep in Reagan's body.

Reagan's cry echoed around Grayson as his arse squeezed Grayson's cock tightly. His orgasm was literally pulled out of him, and he had no hope of stopping it.

Magic and heat slammed into him like a truck as he joined with his mate's groans—moaning, and crying out. He let go of what little control of his body he had, and his seed squirted into Reagan. Filling his mate up. Joining them. Blending their bodies forever.

Heat seared his birthmark. His shoulder was on fire. Reagan grabbed for his own arm, squeezing the birthmark with another loud moan. It appeared the same thing was happening to his mate.

Grayson embraced the pain and let his eyes roll closed as he held tight to Reagan's hips, keeping them connected. Wanting nothing more than what was to come.

Their mating. Their forever.

Exhaustion swamped him from nowhere, blindsiding him with a tremendous whack.

He fell onto his side, still deep within his mate, and passed out.

Reagan woke hours later, his arse now empty, but his whole body still nestled into Grayson's groin, the big man's arms around him.

He couldn't believe that he was so comfortable. So warm and safe. So perfect.

He'd slept so heavily.

How had this morning even happened? One moment Grayson

had slid into him and then next, his head exploded with an orgasm. The fastest and most intense of his life.

The next thing he knew, his birthmark was on fire, and then he was waking up.

Whatever this was, it was not normal.

He glanced down at his shoulder, half expecting the skin to show the remnants of charred flesh, but instead he gasped to see the change that had taken place.

There, standing next to the gnarled tree that was his birthmark, stood the image of a black wolf. The wolf's eyes glowed blue against the darkness on his skin.

An intense, amazing blue.

Just like Grayson's.

Had someone come in during their sleep and tattooed him?

"What the fuck?"

"Huh? What's wrong?" Grayson shot bolt upright, first staring at the door as though expecting to see someone or something. When he saw there wasn't anyone there, his whole body relaxed and he lay back down, rolling Reagan over so that he was cuddled into Grayson's side.

His breathing started to slow once again, and Reagan gave Grayson a push in the side, struggling to sit up. He couldn't go to sleep again! Grayson's arms were tight around him, apparently not wanting to let him go.

"Grayson, would you listen? My birthmark has changed. What did you do to me?"

"What the..." He grunted as Grayson practically flipped him right over as he jumped up, grabbing for Reagan's arm and gaping down at it.

"Is that my..."

Grayson turned his own arm over, and they both stared at the bronzed flesh.

"Where's your mark gone?"

Grayson's mouth was wide open, his eyes huge and bright. "I've never heard of this happening. I need to speak to my father. Can you stay here, please? Don't go anywhere. Actually, you can come with me."

Grayson sounded worried, his tones wobbly and confused.

Reagan relaxed back against the mountain of pillows. They were both still in one piece. It couldn't be that bad.

And in this world, it seemed that anything was possible. Even things his scientific brain was having a field day with.

"I'll stay here. It's fine. Those massive Alphas scare me a bit. I'll just have another shower, I think."

He smelled like sweat and cum. Dirty, dirty sex. Hmm....

"All right." Grayson stood up and began to dress, his brow furrowed. As he pulled on his shoes and took a few steps towards the door, he turned around. "But, don't leave. No matter what."

Reagan laughed and waved his hand at Grayson. Where would he go?" Go see your dad. I'll be fine. I don't know anyone anyway."

Grayson stalled another moment then with a twist, left and must have walked down the stairs, though Reagan didn't hear him go. Grayson's steps were still as silent as ever.

You sure you're a wolf? You could pass for a cat with moves like that.

Reagan laughed at his internal joke, happiness bubbling inside him with a strong potency. His head spun and his legs were wobbly.

Maybe his sperm was magic too? He outright laughed at that one, nestling into the warmth of the bed and closing his eyes for a minute.

He didn't know what had happened this morning, other than the most powerful orgasm of his life, but something had changed.

Something massive.

But with adrenaline and happy hormones pumping through his body, he couldn't bring himself to care about the outcome. Nor look too deeply at what it would all mean.

Reagan took another whiff of the cloud around him and cringed. Yep, time for a shower.

He pulled himself out of Grayson's huge bed and floated into the bathroom. He turned on the shower and re-lived all the moments since he'd stepped into this same room this morning.

And what a trip it was.

"But what does it mean, Dad?"

His father frowned, chewing on his lip and huffing. "I've only ever heard about this once before, from a story my grandfather once told us."

Grayson threw his hands up to the sky. Since he'd shown his father the spot where the missing mark had been, his father had been practically silent. Pale. Strange. Stunned.

"Well, what did he say?"

There was silence again, and Grayson collapsed into the armchair opposite his dad. He'd found his father at home, having lunch as he often did.

"Tell me again what happened to Reagan's mark. "

Grayson rolled his eyes. He'd already repeated this part twice. "Reagan's birthmark is pretty much the same, but it now has a wolf standing beneath the tree. Not that it's a tree, technically, but you know what I mean. It has blue eyes and everything."

"This is very unusual, Grayson, but we've always known that you would be special. Your mark is considerably rare. Huge and defined, a definite show of strength, growth, and stability."

Frustration brewed and boiled in his belly. Maybe he should have gone to one of the other Alphas for the answer. "Dad. Speak plainly please."

"It means you are destined for great things, son. As is your mate."

"What do you mean? Reagan's a man and human. What could he possibly do?"

"The only other coupling that I have heard this happen to was another all male pairing. Two strong, Alpha wolves that saved their pack from death and rebuilt, here, in Greensborough."

No... It couldn't be.

"Wait. Are you talking about the old legends? But hang on a minute." They'd been taught that the founders of their pack were two Alphas that bred the line of the original Council.

"Yes, the great Luc and Gray were mates. A legendary, strong, dynamic team who defeated all that stood in their way. It was said that when they mated, the two marks changed and linked."

But that would mean they weren't genetically linked to the Alphas as he had at first thought. How could they be?

"Does that mean Luc and Gray didn't father our lines?"

His father's eyes were distant as he shook his head. "No, they did. That part's true. They chose five women to birth the five new families, and Luc and Gray shared them all. We still aren't sure which male fathered whom. Although, Gray did have blue eyes they always said. That was the main reason your mother wanted to name you Grayson."

Grayson heaved out a sigh. "So, children are still possible for me."

"I can't answer that. We don't need children now as they did then. They were re-building an entire pack, and without their genetic lines there may never have been another Alpha born. But you and your mate can decide when the time comes."

Grayson frowned. He wasn't sure how Reagan would feel about sharing a woman, or impregnating her. Two hundred years ago it may have been different, but his mate was a modern man. A gay man. With all the jealousies and insecurities of the modern age.

He'd have to think about that one.

"There's something else I was thinking about, too. Your mate may be human, but unlike our women, I believe he will change from your mating. Does he know what being part of our pack will mean for him?"

Grayson looked away from his father for the first time and heard his father's gasp.

"You didn't tell him."

"No. I didn't think the mating would occur if we simply... you know. Anyway, it's done now, and I will live with the consequences."

His father made a reproving tsk sound. "Yes, you will."

Heat flushed his cheeks. He'd been irresponsible. Not at all like his normal self.

His wolf began to pace with impatience inside him. It was time to go. Return to Reagan.

Grayson stood up and his father embraced him, hard, in a way he hadn't done in a decade.

"This is an excellent sign, son. But, also, an omen of things to come. I believe danger is around the corner. We must band together and keep the pack secure. Something is coming."

Grayson gripped his father back, sharing the strength of the greatest man he'd ever known. A wonderful father, leader, husband, and friend.

"Yes, Dad, we will."

He turned and left, his legs restless and eager to get back to Reagan. He hated leaving him. His skin itched with the need to be close to his mate. He pushed his legs to move faster as he walked through the town, the streets lined with people, the sun shining on a beautiful spring day.

The door to his home was shut, and relief flowed through him. For some reason, a part of him expected someone to burst in and steal his mate when he wasn't looking. Something that could not happen, and would not happen. Ever.

He really should explain to Reagan about their security measures, and where the escape tunnel was, in the event he ever needed to use it.

He pushed open the door, and wonderful laughter filled his ears.

He stopped and stared at the picture before him, so perfect it was like a mirage. A dream.

There, sitting at the kitchen table were his sister and his mate.

His knees weakened as he gripped the handle.

His future had arrived. Finally!

"Hey, bro. I see you got down to business pretty bloody fast."

Megan's giggle made him frown. Was it so obvious already?

"What did your dad say?" Reagan asked, his smile warm and relaxed as he sat drinking something from a mug.

Megan's eyebrows rose high on her forehead in question. Obviously, Reagan had filled her in.

"He said he's only ever heard of it happening once before and it was also between a male, male couple."

"Oh, okay." Reagan seemed to accept that, and he turned back to Megan.

His sister, however, looked skeptical, giving him a hard stare. He probably should explain more to Reagan, but how and when?

"I'm not sure what you guys put in your food, but look at this. Did you pump me full of steroids last night or something?"

Reagan stood up from the stool he'd been sitting on, and the black t-shirt that fit him just fine yesterday now bulged and stretched at the seams. His pecs were bigger, his arms thicker, and as he stood up and opened his arms wide to accentuate the difference, he seemed taller too.

His dad had said Reagan would change. Boy had he been right.

"Ah, no, definitely not."

Reagan looked down upon himself with a startled grin, his voice happy and light. "Well, whatever it is. I feel fantastic. My ribs should still be healing, but they feel good as new, which is impossible. I'll have to get an x-ray to check, but I'm pretty sure I'm back to normal."

Megan ran a hand over Reagan's shoulder and down his arm, tracing the wolf in the birthmark with her fingertip.

"You seem to have taken on some of the characteristics of the wolf, Reagan."

Reagan grinned at her. "Again, impossible. But then again, should I really say that word around here? You guys live in a world of fates and magic. Not to mention, alleged shifting bodies. Are you ever going to show me that, by the way?" Reagan lifted an arrogant brow in a challenge and a growl rolled out of Grayson's throat.

His mate didn't believe them.

"I'm not sure you can handle it."

Reagan's laugh sounded musical. "After the crash, the birthmarks, us this morning, and everything Megan told me last night, I'm sure I can handle anything."

Grayson looked to his sister for guidance. Reagan was finally starting to sound relaxed and happy. He didn't want to ruin that.

"Damn, it's already two o'clock. Are you still driving me home today?"

Reagan's words seemed to jump out of nowhere, and Grayson

shook his head, unable to speak as his wolf clamped down on his jaws. Reagan leave? Never.

"Grayson, come on, that's not fair. You told me you would drive me back, and I have so much to do before my final exams. Please."

"Reagan, I don't think you understand..." He couldn't find the words to explain how important this was.

His mate didn't feel it. Something cracked within his chest.

He couldn't breathe, his heart hurt.

"What's wrong?"

Grayson choked out some words. "You have to stay, at least today. Until you understand what this mating thing means, to our pack and me."

"If I show you my wolf, if I prove that we haven't been telling you tall tales, will you stay, at least until you understand what you're giving up by walking away?" It was brazen and he wasn't sure it was going to work, but he had to try. There was only one thing he wouldn't do for Reagan, and that was let him leave.

"Sure. Show me."

Grayson took a few steps back into his lounge room, giving himself the space he needed. He stripped off his top and jeans, hearing Reagan's surprised gasp before he let the magic take him.

His powerful black wolf surged forth like a genie from a bottle, filling him up and demanding preference over the human form.

Fur sprouted over his body, and he fell to his hands, his fingers disappearing into paws.

CHAPTER SEVEN

"Holy shit!" Reagan jumped back, his leg catching the kitchen stool, causing it to clatter to the floor with a loud bang.

"That's a wolf. A real wolf!" He pointed at the animal standing in Grayson's lounge room, unable to believe he was seeing what he was seeing.

Grayson turned into an animal.

A real one.

His heart pounded dangerously fast in his chest, adrenaline rushing through his blood, making his arms and legs twitchy and ready to fly.

The wolf dropped to the floor, laying its head on its two front paws and looking up at him with eyes as blue as the sky outside.

"Relax, Reagan, he won't hurt you. It's still Grayson. He knows it's you. Even when they're in wolf form, they have full control over their bodies."

He took a few quick breaths, then saw white flashing spots on the periphery of his vision.

Slow down, or you're going to pass out!

He grabbed the extended hand Megan offered and squeezed it tight, concentrating on her warmth, her presence to calm him down.

"Okay. I believe you."

And just like that, the wolf stood up and began to elongate. Reagan's breath hitched in his throat, but before he could utter the squeal that rose, Grayson was back, and pulling on his clothes.

Which he should. Megan was present!

"Good. I don't lie."

His knees gave way as though he'd faint at any moment.

"I've gotta sit down." He lurched for the kitchen stool he'd been sitting on minutes before and collapsed onto it, a hysterical laugh rising in his throat. "That's some crazy shit."

Grayson shrugged.

"It's what we're born with. No different than anything else about me."

Reagan choked on a laugh. "Well, your world is much more complicated than mine."

Grayson finished doing up his shoes and stared straight at him.

"This is your world too, Reagan. I'm not sure why, but you and I are destined to be together."

Reagan glanced at Megan, heat flushing his cheeks with embarrassment. When Megan didn't flinch, Reagan tried to shake off the feeling.

"You know that's a pretty intense thing to say to me when we barely know each other."

"But you're mated now, can't you feel the connection? The bond to Grayson?"

"What do you mean, mated? Because we fucked? That didn't do anything... Did it? "

Fear rose in his chest, tightening his throat like a hand wrapped around his windpipe. "Grayson?"

"Not just fucked, I came in you! You got my genetics inside you. And it might have started the process, yes. There's a possibility that we may have effectively mated this morning without meaning to. It doesn't usually happen as quickly as that, but our connection is a lot stronger than normal."

"Okay...but you still aren't telling me what that actually means. Are we linked, or something? Married? Not that that's even possible...but, what is it exactly?"

Megan moved away, pouring water, and boiling the kettle in an apparent attempt to distract herself. Grayson looked like he wished he could do the same.

"If you'd been born into the pack, I wouldn't need to have this conversation at all."

Reagan glared at Grayson. "That's not fair and not my fault, so please explain."

Grayson heaved a huge sigh. "All right. It's like being married, but a lot deeper than that. There will be no one for me but you, from now on. My wolf and I will never want anybody else. If you leave us...I... don't know what will happen. Just going to see Dad this morning startled my wolf to the point we practically ran back here."

"You what? Shit, that's intense!"

Grayson ran his hand through his hair in a frustrated gesture, his mouth quirking up at the sides as though it were a horrible joke. "I hate it. I feel weak, open to attack. I've never really known this feeling before."

The admission startled Reagan. Not because of the words said, but how they were said. With strength and anger, rather than the mushy smoothness you expect such poetic words to accompany.

"Ah...okay. I have no idea what that means either, but it's

obvious a whole lot is going on around here that I don't understand." He ran a hand over his face. How had his life changed so much in only a few days?

His head should be spinning, but instead, he wanted to stay and learn more. The rest of the world didn't even know wolf shifters existed and he was getting a first-hand invitation to learn all about them.

Did he need to go back to Melbourne today? Yeah, he had studies, but if he had access to the internet, he could probably do a bit from here.

"You know, if I could get access to a computer today, I could do some studying and maybe stay another night. Just until I understand this a little better."

As someone who'd lost his whole world in one night, ten years ago, in one tragic accident, Reagan certainly didn't believe in fate. But there was something otherworldly and very special about how he felt in Grayson's presence; and to just walk away now seemed insane too.

He looked down and flexed his arms. Strength, and hard muscle rippled beneath his skin. And whatever that was, was addictively beautiful.

He felt invincible.

"Okay, so where do I get a computer?"

Grayson made sure Reagan had use of his new laptop, then went out to spend a few hours at work. He had many overseer jobs in the pack, mostly having to do with the money coming in and out. He balanced accounts, checked on the builders and the farmers, dropped by to pick up another few pairs of jeans and tops for Reagan—a size bigger—then returned to his home.

He forced his twitching legs to slow down as he stood on his doorstep. His wolf gnashed his teeth, wanting to go inside more than he wanted his next breath. How was it possible to need someone so much?

Shaking his head, he pushed open the door, only to slam it hard behind him again.

Reagan was shirtless and draped over the dining table. Well not exactly draped, he was working, but the effect the sight had on Grayson's cock was as immediate as an opoid injection straight into the vein.

His wolf rumbled a growl through his chest, and Reagan turned and stood. His mate was even bigger than this morning, his body ripped with lean muscle. The sexy line of his abs dipped down beneath his denim waistband.

Grayson had never even looked at another man with this much desire, but with Reagan, it was all too natural. His world had completely changed. And his wolf was throwing so many old concepts and expectations completely out the window. What he saw now as beautiful was defined by his mate's face... and body. And everything inside him was howling with lust for a mate who he'd been waiting for all his life.

"Hey. What's up?"

Grayson charged forward and grabbed Reagan up by the hips, twirling him around and pulling his jeans straight down his legs.

"Whoa... missed me, huh?"

"Badly," Grayson told his mate, barely able to speak through the lock his wolf had on his jaw.

"Good."

"Get on your back."

Reagan kicked off his jeans and lay back on the dining room table, his perfect body set out for Grayson's enjoyment.

Grayson grabbed Reagan's cock and pumped the flesh.

"Oh fuck... Oh damn..."

Reagan's shaft thickened and grew in his hand, the head turning a deep purple beneath his ministrations.

When Reagan gasped loudly, Grayson let go of his cock and stood back. He opened his zipper, his cock bouncing out with painful relief. He was as hard as a tree trunk and as horny as a boy with his first erection.

Damn, Reagan got him so hot!

He couldn't wait a moment longer. Slicking himself up with as much saliva as possible, he flexed his hips and pressed his cock head up against Reagan's arse.

His mate moaned and bucked backwards, swallowing him up.

"Reagan... Damn, that's incredible."

He clenched his stomach hard, willing his cock not to come immediately, as it wanted to. He took a deep breath and began sliding in and out, luxuriating in the heat of his mate. The way Reagan bucked, and pushed back, and even struggled to get up as he moaned and gasped made Grayson's lust spike higher and higher.

"Ah... Oh... I'm."

"I know. Come on, squeeze my cock."

He could feel Reagan's orgasm tingling inside him. He didn't know how that was possible, but their communication seemed to have reached a new level.

Reagan cried out, planting both palms on the table and throwing his head back.

Hot tingles spread through Grayson's belly and flowed outward, like ripples in a pond. Reagan's body convulsed, milking Grayson in the most erotic way possible.

His orgasm burst through him, making him howl in pleasure as he squirted inside his mate, spreading his scent and his seed all in one.

Grayson collapsed on top of Reagan, pulling out quickly for his mate's comfort, then lay panting on him once again. They stayed that way for several minutes, Grayson's mind flicking in and out of consciousness in a dream-like way.

"Let's get you upstairs."

They needed somewhere warm and safe to enjoy the aftermath of their lovemaking, if you could call it that.

He pulled away and Reagan sagged against the table.

Grayson grinned, loving the satisfied look on his mate's face. "Come on, you sexy animal." He picked up his mate and threw him over his shoulder in a fireman's carry so he could race him up the stairs. Reagan's laugh was as beautiful a sight as the full moon and sunset combined.

His heart ached with the knowledge that his long-waited -for mate, was here. His gender may not have been as expected but everything about him signaled "home" to Grayson. The way he moved his mouth, his smile, everything was right. Every curve of his face, the taste of his mouth was exquisite.

The texture, flavor and scent of his skin literally flooded his bloodstream with erotic hormones every time he tasted Reagan. And along with that came a feeling of security and warmth in his brain. Telling him everything about this was just as it should be.

These were feelings he had been waiting for all his life. He didn't want to argue that it did not come from where he had expected. He was just thankful it was with him at last.

Life was often weird. Many of the things you expected as a child turn out differently as an adult. So, what was another twist to add to that list? He had found his mate and the world inside him finally seemed balanced and right.

They moved into his bedroom, and he settled them both into the mountain of pillows, the scent of sex and sweat enveloping them.

With his mind thoroughly blown and his wolf practically howling, Grayson drew Reagan to him and cuddled his mate close.

"You know if you were a woman I'd call you babe or something like it, but how 'bout I call you my mate, or mate?"

"Yeah sounds good. Simple."

Reagan looked up at him, his brown eyes warm and soft. "This feeling between us is pretty incredible. Isn't it?"

Grayson nodded and ran his hand up and down Reagan's back, the soft skin beneath his fingertips both soothing and arousing to his soul.

"It is, and if the legends are correct, it'll only get stronger with time."

Reagan kissed his shoulder and pushed up, stretching and groaning as he rolled out of bed and moved into the en suite. His gorgeous arse clenched and flexed as he walked and Grayson found himself staring after Reagan, totally taken by the artwork in front of him.

He pulled his gaze away with a struggle.

You've got it bad, mate. And another one bites the dust.

He grimaced as the old song played in his head. Although he'd always craved his mate and knew that the Fates would send him the right person when it was time, he never really believed the attraction would be this strong.

"Thanks for letting me use the computer today. It helped heaps. I checked the exams timetable, and I think as long as I'm home by Monday, I should be okay. I've got interviews for jobs and more placements, too."

Grayson sat up against the headboard and took a few breaths. Reagan had no idea how much it would rip them apart if they were to separate. Humans didn't experience the things wolves did, but if his body changes and the birthmark were any indications, then Reagan would not do well away from him, either.

"Yeah, no problem."

He wanted to yell, *you'll be working and living here with me*, but chose not to. He had to hope that if their connection was strong enough, Reagan wouldn't be able to survive without him.

Plus, there were advantages to Reagan returning home to finish his final exams. Having another qualified doctor for the pack would be a great contribution to their community. He'd done well with Fate's choice really... Even if his continued genetic line was going to be a problem.

"You ready to get some dinner? "

"Okay. But you're not going to run off again, are you?"

Reagan stepped back into the bedroom, scooping up his jeans. "These are so tight, I can't believe it. "

"I bought you some new ones. They're downstairs."

Reagan stared at him for a minute, his eyes wide and fragile. Then he glanced away. "Thanks. I appreciate that. You didn't have to."

"The way you're changing, you'll soon be bigger than me."

Reagan chuckled. "I never thought sperm had magical powers before, but yours certainly seems to."

Grayson grinned, his cock stirring at the mention of sex. If his sperm was the reason his mate was building muscle like a steroid junkie, he'd happily give him as much as he wanted. He wasn't sure his sperm was the reason Reagan was bulking up so quickly but he'd take the credit and give his mate as much as he wanted.

"Yeah, well, unless you want another dose, I suggest we get dressed and get down to the hall. I'm starving."

Although another session would be good...

"Well, you would've worked up an appetite." Reagan winked

at him and gave him a cheeky grin, the mood between them playful and relaxed.

Just as it should be.

They dressed and got out of the house in mere minutes, another advantage to having a male mate. No waiting around for hair and makeup.

"So what happened last night with the Rogues?"

Grayson grabbed Reagan's arm as they moved down the road. "How did you... Oh, Megan."

Reagan grinned again. "Well, someone has to tell me what's going on around here. You certainly don't."

He shrugged and opened the door to the dining hall. "I'll let you know if something's important."

Reagan rolled his eyes, playing the girl. "Classic man."

Grayson laughed, the unexpected comment surprising him. Reagan wasn't too serious, which was a bonus.

Grayson knew he could be a little too serious sometimes, with the stress of his job and leadership within the pack. It made sense that his mate would be able to bring levity into the relationship.

"Grayson! I heard you found your mate! Congrats." Aaron stepped up, Tony's son, one of the Alphas of his generation. And one of the unmated ones.

"You know I'm totally jealous. How come you get to find yours already and I haven't? You're ten years younger than me!" Aaron winked at Reagan and shook Grayson's hand.

Grayson pulled Reagan into his side with his free arm, his wolf rumbling inside him.

Aaron was a great guy and Tony's son. But he was also another unmated Alpha and Grayson's wolf was protective.

Aaron laughed, his usually profound and rumbly chortle sounding hollow. "Relax, buddy I'm still waiting on mine, remember. And it's been a bloody long wait."

Aaron lifted his shirt to display a huge birthmark covering half of his left pec and curling down to his hip. It wasn't a distinctive shape like Grayson's, but it was huge.

Grayson relaxed his arm, not wanting to offend his friend. "I know, Aaron. Sorry I'm a bit new at this. Good onya'. Anyway, did you speak to some of the farmers today? Anything new to report?"

"No, it's all quiet today. Although some of the farmer's wives have seen wolf tracks out in the forest. People are getting spooked."

That wasn't good. He'd always hoped the Rogues would find another pack, or just assimilate into the human community. But they were selfish, vengeful men. They wouldn't leave Greensborough alone.

"Damn. Thanks, Aaron."

They wove around the hordes of people until they reached the Alpha table. Most of the families had already started eating.

Everyone greeted them with a wave or smile, and Grayson grabbed Reagan by the elbow, tugging him to the buffet tables. "Come on. I'm starving."

Reagan picked up a plate and began piling food on. Chicken. Steak. Hamburgers.

Grayson stared at him, unable to believe the difference from last night. "Bit hungry, are you?"

Reagan froze and looked down at his plate, a strange wave of guilt flowing over his face. "Oh, I'm sorry. I shouldn't have taken so much. I…"

Grayson laughed and began piling up his own plate with more than Reagan had. "Don't be an idiot. Eat as much as you can. I'm glad you're hungry."

Reagan's posture relaxed, and he turned to go back to the table. Grayson followed, sitting down next to his mate as quickly as possible. He nodded at his parents, who were both staring at him, and he laid into his lamb chops, the flavour of the charred fat and marinated meat making him groan.

"What the hell happened to your mark?"

Marcus's voice hit him in the chest like a staple gun. Maybe he should have worn a long-sleeved shirt? Or bought one maybe, since he didn't own one.

He wiped his mouth with the back of his hand. "It's gone. Why?"

"What do you mean, why? That's impossible!"

The whole table had gone quiet, and the Alphas looked amongst themselves with questioning glances. Old Tony broke the silence.

"When did this happen, Grayson?" Tony asked him, his smooth voice floating over the table and calming the group.

"This morning, I think."

"After you mated?" Tony asked again.

He nodded once, his eyes shifting to his father, who remained silent. Watching and waiting.

"Yeah, and the weirdest thing happened. Look!"

Reagan pulled his t-shirt up to expose his newly morphed birthmark.

A general gasp and hiss went around the group, then deathly silence.

Marcus began to laugh. "That'd be right. You give a guy your cock and he steals your wolf." He laughed again, that horrible, grating noise that Grayson had loathed since they were kids.

Grayson considered Marcus the worst sort of Alpha. Pompous, arrogant, and selfish. How his genetics got into their elite pool, he had no idea.

And worse still, he'd already begun to breed more like him.

"Back off, Marcus."

"Why should I? You know that's wrong. An Alpha should not

be mated with a male. How are you meant to continue the line now?"

Grayson looked towards his father, who gave one shake of his head. Obviously, his dad didn't want him sharing the knowledge of what it could mean, nor the history of their pack.

He agreed that he didn't want to start a panic, nor change the way people saw their legends, but still. Marcus' attitude towards his mate was insufferable.

Grayson clenched his teeth and snorted in agreement. His father's will was law.

How to turn this around without throwing Marcus through a wall?

CHAPTER
EIGHT

Reagan looked back and forth between Grayson and the stupid big guy to their left. He dropped the sleeve he still held and wrapped his palm around the wolf with glowing blue eyes. He loved the new addition to his birthmark.

Scientifically, it wasn't possible. But since seeing Grayson shift into a wolf and feeling his body grow bigger and stronger in only a few short days, he was beginning to think anything was possible in this world.

But what was with the gay hate speech?

"What's he talking about, Grayson? Megan told me you guys don't care about gay and straight."

Grayson nodded once. "We don't."

Marcus, the slimy blond, sneered at him. "Grayson is the only son of his father's line. And you're his mate. Do you know what that means, little human? It means his line is done. Gone. And all because of you."

Reagan let his mouth hang open in shock. Was this guy fucking kidding?

When Grayson didn't respond with much more than a shrug, Reagan poked him in the ribs. "Aren't you going to say anything?"

Grayson shrugged again, his massive shoulders going up and down. "What can I say? He's right."

Ice tickled along Reagan's spine. He couldn't have been so wrong about Grayson, could he? What sort of person would agree with that blond dipshit?

"He's right about what? That I've destroyed your blood line?"

He turned in his chair to face Grayson better. His supposed mate better have a good reason for saying such a thing. What happened to them being fated, and all that shit?

"No, don't be stupid."

Now he was stupid? Oh, how he wanted to throw something! "Excuse me. I think I'll go sit somewhere else."

He grabbed his plate and stood up. Grayson's hand came down on his arm, hard. A shackle.

Reagan felt the vibration in his throat and released it with a growl. "Grrr.... Back off."

Their eyes locked for an eternity, then Grayson let go, looking away.

Reagan stomped over to a table in a corner where three young men about his age sat. "Can I join you?"

He didn't wait for them to nod, but they finally did, as he sat and began eating his food. Bloody hell! He swallowed some more beef and looked around the table. Damn, he'd piled on more than the three of them had together.

Screw it. Just eat.

He picked up a chicken leg and took a big bite. "I'm Reagan. How you doin'?"

The three men stared at him, then looked at each other with loud, wide, speaking eyes. Reagan waited. Finally, the guy to his right spoke.

"I'm Elliot... I'm okay. How are you?"

These guys must be Omegas. They were small in stature and build, not to mention timid. They resembled mice, where the Alphas resembled lions. He couldn't imagine them shifting into the powerful wolf that Grayson had become.

"Great...except for those jackasses over there."

He nodded his head towards the Alpha table, and the Omegas around him trembled.

"You shouldn't speak like that about the Alphas."

"I'll do whatever I want. I'm mated to Grayson now. Whatever the fuck that means!"

He grunted and shook his head. What a bloody mistake that was. Not that he'd known what was going to happen when they had sex, but still. Something had changed inside him.

"You're what...?" Elliot crept closer, his hand sneaking out across the table as though to touch him.

"I'm mated to Grayson. Not that I meant to, of course. I didn't know that fucking him would make it happen."

As the men around him gasped, Reagan rolled his eyes. Seriously? If all three of these men weren't gay, he'd bite his arse.

"What's your problem? Don't like the fact one of the Alphas is gay?"

He tore off some more chicken, washing it down with a nearby beer. Why did he feel so pissed off? Sweat practically rolled down his nose.

Elliot shook his head. "Of course, not, I'm...gay, as you humans label it. That's not a problem here, it has never been."

"Well, Marcus sure thinks it is! He just made it very clear that I've destroyed any chance Grayson had of having a family." His voice choked on the last words, and he cleared it with a rough cough.

He had ruined Grayson's chance for children. Dammit... What

in the hell could he do to fix that, though? Grayson himself had said their bond was irreversible.

Maybe if I leave...

Another one of the men groaned, the sound stronger than Reagan had expected. "Reagan, I'm Jordan. Marcus is a cruel and selfish Alpha. That's not why we're so shocked. There hasn't been an all-male Alpha pairing in generations."

The third man leant forward. "There are whispers within the Omegas that the original leaders of our pack were paired males, but no one knows for sure."

"Really?"

Now, that was interesting and would explain why Grayson was destined for a mate like him.

"Do you know if any of the other men are male paired too?"

Jordan looked away, staring at his hands. "Ah no."

There were strange emotions flicking over Jordan's face. Guilt and anger, even desire. He couldn't read it all at once.

"What's with that?" Reagan poked at Jordan with his free hand, eating some of the beef stew with onions with the other. His stomach growled with happiness.

"Jordan's got a secret."

"Shut up, Travis." Jordan snapped at the third guy, who hadn't been introduced yet, and for the first time, Reagan heard the growl in his voice. The command. Surely that was unusual for am Omega?

"Shut up about what? What's going on?"

"Show him, Jordan," Elliot said.

"No," Jordan barked at his friends, then started to get up and leave.

Reagan had the strangest urge to pull up the Omega's shirt. Did all these wolves have incredible bodies and weird birthmarks?

Time to find out.

"Hey, come here for a sec." Reagan reached over and grabbed the smaller man. Without thinking about why he was doing it, he pulled Jordan over to him and yanked up the hem of his grey t-shirt. The large mating mark was instantly visible.

And Reagan knew where the matching pair of it was.

"What the..."

"Hey! Leave me alone!" Jordan slammed a surprisingly strong fist into Reagan's shoulder.

"Ow!"

He let go, and Jordan ran from the room. Reagan swung back to the other Omegas. "How does no one else know about that? Doesn't he realise who that matches?"

The guy Jordan had called Travis nodded. "Yeah, he does, and he doesn't know what to do about it. Jordan was born without a mating mark, and everyone assumed it was because he wasn't meant to mate, or being gay, he didn't need one. But when he turned twenty-one a few years ago, like the females born to us, he developed it. Which is weird—and he's been hiding it ever since."

"But why? If everything Grayson has told me is true, Aaron will never be happy without Jordan, and Jordan will be struggling to stay sane, too."

He glared at the men in front of him, and they dropped their eyes and stared at their meals.

"Don't you get it? "

They continued to ignore him, and he groaned. He couldn't see any marks on them, so was it possible that they weren't meant to find a mate? That they didn't ache the way he assumed Aaron did?

What in the hell should he do now?

He couldn't let Aaron yearn for a mate who was within his reach. He seemed like such a nice guy.

Reagan ate the last scraps of pasta salad on his plate and stood up. He had no idea what this mating shit was, but it was bloody powerful, as was the magic of these people and everything that went on around here. He had to do something.

When he turned and walked back to the table, that idiot, Marcus, had gone, and Grayson was sitting with Aaron and a few of the fathers.

As he stepped up to the table, Grayson grabbed him and tugged him down into the chair.

"Don't you dare do that to me again."

A sliver of guilt wove through Reagan at his overreaction to Marcus' words, but they had a few things to sort out before he'd apologise.

"You and I can talk about that later. I found out something, and I think Aaron needs to know."

That got his attention. Grayson's frown disappeared, and he sat up straighter. Aaron leant in closer.

"What is it, Reagan?"

"Can I have a look at your mark again? The one on your chest?"

Grayson growled a little beside him. "Why?"

Reagan rolled his eyes at Grayson's ridiculous reaction. "Because I think Aaron's hot and want to perv at him. What do you think, you jealous idiot?"

Grayson and Aaron shared a look for a moment that showed they clearly didn't understand. Then Aaron shrugged and stood up, pulling his shirt up as he went.

"Just as I thought." Identical to Jordan's, the mark stretched over his chest and down his belly in a big black swirly, powerful mess.

He did have a pretty hot bod too.

The thought made heat sear his face, and he grabbed for a drink, trying to cool himself down before Grayson saw. The deep rumble in his ear from Grayson meant he apparently hadn't succeeded in disguising his blush.

“What do you mean, just as you thought?”

Aaron sat back down, his face creased with worry.

“Are you still looking for your mate, Aaron?”

Aaron grimaced. “Have been for almost twenty years—even longer than your mate there. We’re born with our marks, so although I kept a look out while I grew up, I didn't seriously start looking until after I turned about twenty-five. I’ll be forty-five in a few weeks.”

“Wow. You don’t look a day over thirty-five!”

And he didn’t. His hair was still a dirty blond, his face a little creased, but overall his skin looked better than most of the men Reagan knew his age.

Aaron chuckled. E.................... “Thanks. The wolf genes keep us pretty fit, but I certainly feel it. I’m exhausted, and I bloody ache for her, whoever she is. It’s gotten worse the past few years, as though she’s nearby and I can’t see her. But no one could hide a mark like mine, even if they wanted to.”

That’s what he thought.

Aaron chuckled and smiled as though it were a joke, but Reagan wanted to grab him and shake him.

“But that’s because they are nearby, you’re just not looking at the right table. “

“What?” Aaron’s face grew dark like a storm cloud. “Are you serious? You know who my mate is? Where is she? Tell me!” Aaron grabbed him by the arms and shook him.

Grayson pushed at Aaron and pulled on Reagan until they were roughly separated. Grayson then turned and pushed Aaron halfway across the room, where he banged into a nearby table, knocking some drinks to the floor. Grayson pulled Reagan behind him, snarling and on all fours, his arms bristling with black fur.

"I'm sorry Gray... Sorry..." Aaron was mumbling, his huge body visibly shaking. "It's just...you know how it feels. The needing. You only saw Reagan the first time a few days ago. You have no idea how this feels."

Grayson reeled his wolf in with all his might. Aaron didn't deserve this reaction. He wouldn't hurt Reagan. Clenching his teeth and gripping his animal tight, he stood up straight and shook out his arms.

"What the fuck Aaron..." He garbled out the words, the last of his wolf receding inside him as it recognised his mate was safe.

Aaron tapped both of his palms against his chest, his tone pleading. "Gray...you can't know how much this hurts. Please, make him tell me who it is."

Reagan was tugging at Grayson's shirt, trying to get free and come around him. Grayson released his mate and Reagan stepped up.

Grayson's stomach clenched tight. Whoever Aaron's mate was, he had the feeling it was going to be another bombshell.

"First, it's not a woman. Your mate is a male."

Aaron's mouth dropped open, and Grayson struggled to keep his lips straight. Laughter tugged at him in a hysterical kind of way.

"That's exactly how I felt the moment I realised who Reagan was."

"Um... Okay. I hadn't thought about that possibility."

"Is that a problem?" Reagan crossed his arms and glared at Aaron, his tone affronted and pissy.

Grayson did chuckle this time. Oh yeah, don't piss him off.

"No, no, of course not! I'm just not... Ah, I didn't think I'd... For fuck's sake Grayson, a little help!"

Aaron had been his friend for too long for him to enjoy seeing the guy suffer too much.

"Reagan, help him out. He's practically dying at the moment."

"His name's Jordan. He's an Omega."

"Are you sure?" Grayson grabbed Reagan's arm and twisted him around. "That would be very odd."

Most Alphas paired with other Alpha-born children or a human. But then again, Reagan was such a surprise, why shouldn't some of the other Alphas have male mates, too?

"Where is he?" Aaron was looking around the room, stepping closer to them again. "Can you point him out for me, Reagan... and, are you sure about this?"

Reagan rolled his eyes like a diva. "He ran out of the room when I pulled up his top and exposed his mark. There was something different about him. He's gorgeous, in a funky sort of way. Black hair, bright green eyes. But he's strong. He doesn't act like an Omega."

"But how do you know he's my mate?" Aaron asked again.

Reagan groaned and threw up his hands. "Because he has an identical mark on his belly and chest. Exactly the same. You can't miss it."

Aaron's eyes grew wide and round. "How is that possible? Someone would have noticed."

So true. How'd they miss that one? Damn...

Reagan shrugged. "His friends said he wasn't born with one, that it developed at twenty-one and then he hid it from everyone."

Aaron gulped and stared directly at him. Grayson understood that look too well. What if the other non-paired Alpha, Brad, was the same? Was it possible that they'd been waiting for a mate that was right beneath their noses?

"Go get him, Aaron. We'll talk to Brad later."

Aaron sprinted off, and Grayson could suddenly breathe better, as though a huge weight had been lifted off his shoulders. He could now be entirely free to express how he felt about Reagan. With Aaron in a similar situation, his unexpected pairing made sense. Plus, it meant there would be another all-male Alpha pair. This was a concept the pack had to get accustomed to, Marcus included.

But what were the long-term effects of so many pairings be? There would be fewer Alpha babies born now, but was it also an indication that the need for more strength at the top of their pack was needed?

He'd have to speak to his father about that... and soon.

Grayson grabbed his mate, pulling him tight into his body until their cocks lined up and their lips were a breath apart.

"I need you."

Reagan glared at him, and the room around them quieted.

He groaned and pulled away as he felt the eyes of everyone on him. He wasn't ready for a public declaration, despite the fact there was no going back now. "Let's go." He took Reagan's hand and dragged him out of the hall, Reagan shaking him off as soon as they stepped outside.

"I can't believe you let that pompous ass, Marcus, say those things. Do you believe I've stuffed up your whole life?"

Grayson wanted to slap Fate upside the head. He'd assumed getting a male mate would include mostly logical conversation. But here he was, and it was obvious he wasn't missing out on all the whiney wife bullshit.

"Reagan, shut up and listen. You're my mate. Fate chose you for me. There will be no one else. I'm done."

Reagan crossed his now beefy forearms over his chest.

Damn, he's getting ripped.

"Then why didn't you stop him when he was saying all that crap to me? Is your line going to die? Was he right about that?"

Grayson could see the fear and pity in Reagan's brown eyes and had to look away. Despite his acceptance of his Fate and Reagan as his mate, deep inside he still hadn't come to terms with the loss of his future family. "I don't know... I mean, my sister will have kids, so my dad's line will continue, probably. But I won't have any children now. Obviously, I'm not meant to."

There was the option of siring children on an unmated female, but he valued his balls too much to mention that to his mate right now. He forced himself to look back at Reagan and tried a smile. Fate had chosen him a male. Children were not in his future.

"It's okay." Sourness spread across his tongue.

It truly was a tough pill to swallow.

"So, you do feel like I've wrecked your future... Fuck me." Reagan's arms and shoulders dropped as though the weight of the world landed on top of him.

"Don't be stupid. I..."

He reached for his mate and Reagan swung out, connecting with his arm, knocking it away.

Pain ricocheted through his muscles and up his shoulder.

Whoa, he's strong now.

"Just don't touch me. This is way too much to cope with right now." Reagan began to pace and tear at his hair.

"I shouldn't even be here! And why the hell is my skin all itchy?"

He held out his arms as though he expected them to show raised marks and bumps.

Grayson turned his eyes towards the sky.

Full moon tonight.

"Because it's time to change. As animal shifters, we can turn whenever we want to, but on the full moon, we have no choice. I've been feeling the pull of the moon all day, but I'm not sure why you would be. Unless our mating has made you more aware of such things."

Another thing to talk to Dad about. As far as he knew, the women didn't feel that way around the full moon.

Reagan's eyes sprung wide, and his mouth dropped open. "I better not turn into one of those things you do! I'll die."

Grayson rolled his eyes. That was a slight exaggeration, although it did fucking hurt the first time he shifted.

"Don't worry. No one has ever turned into a wolf from mating with one. It's something you're born with. We're not contagious, like in all the stupid movies." Bloody ridiculous, they were.

"So, what does that mean? Are you going to take me home, or am I sticking around to see the spectacle?"

You're never fucking leaving me. Grayson blew out a long, hard breath. "I'd like you to stay and watch. You're part of our community now, whether you like it or not. I'm sure you can feel that?"

He waited, and Reagan finally nodded, the stubborn set of his chin relaxing a little.

"Good. Well, the guys will be gathering in about an hour, when the sun goes down. Do you want to go back and relax for a bit?"

"I need a shower."

Uh-huh. I'm sure we both do.

"Sure, let's go."

They walked back to the house, and Grayson pinned his mate to the kitchen bench and fucked him into the next room. Reagan bit him, scratched him, and blew all over him.

And amidst it all, Grayson knew one thing for sure.

If his mate left him... He'd never know such passion again.

CHAPTER NINE

"Tell me what's going to happen tonight. "

Reagan could barely walk straight as they made their way through town. Grayson had screwed him in every way possible. On his knees, on his back, standing, sitting, and at one point he was pretty sure he was upside down.

But either way, his arse was bloody sore!

"Us, wolves, will go into the clearing near the forest and stand beneath the moon. When the shift starts to happen, we rip off our clothes and turn into the wolves you saw me turn into the other night."

Reagan swallowed hard, fear streaking through his veins. That had been a pretty incredible experience, but it still scary. Not something he wanted to repeat.

"And where will I be standing?"

Grayson gave him a cheeky grin.

"With the women."

Reagan gave him a shove. Was he trying to be insulting? "I'm not a girl. "

"Oh, boy, do I know that." Grayson pulled him in close, snuffling in his neck and licking at the skin there.

New desire curled in his balls. Fuck.

How am I not sick of him yet?

"Get off me!"

Grayson released him, chuckling loudly.

"You'll be safe, don't worry. The Omegas don't shift either, so there will be lots of people around. With the Rogues as a constant threat, I do worry about your safety, but they'll be shifting too, they don't have a choice. And hopefully they'll be off running somewhere far away from here."

Reagan nodded, a deep pain in his gut warning him of something about to come. "You'll be careful though, yeah?"

Grayson laughed again as they entered an alley.

Reagan could hear people talking now. They were apparently getting close to the shifting site.

"Don't tell me you're starting to care about me."

He wanted to say *I'm starting to love you.* But Reagan forced the words to stay in his head. That idea, like most things about this place, made no logical sense. How could you love someone after only a few days? Especially someone who was so gruff, and rude, and just so.... bloody awesome.

"Reagan!" Megan ran up to him as they stepped out of the lane, the buzz and hum of a huge group of people assailing his ears like a nearby beehive.

"Megan, hi."

"You staying with me tonight while these guys go off and run in the woods like a pack of mutts?" Megan winked at Grayson and gave her brother a shove.

"You're just jealous, Megan."

"Too right I am."

Grayson turned to leave, then froze.

What was he waiting for?

Grayson hesitated then twisted back around and pressed his lips against Reagan's. Tough and fast, then he was gone again. "Take care of him, Megan!"

"Yeah, yeah."

She waved Grayson off and came over to link arms with Reagan. He welcomed her familiarity and closeness.

"It's not fair, Reagan. Why do they get to have all the fun?"

Reagan shrugged. He wasn't sure turning into a snarling beast would be that much fun. But what did he know?

He stood in awe and watched as a huge group of men congregated in the grassy meadow. It had been cleared, obviously for this purpose, as only twenty meters away lay a dense, thick forest.

"Do you always come and watch?"

Megan nodded. "Yeah, there's not much else to do when half the community is here shifting, and the other half wants to watch."

Reagan stared up at the sky, and a cloud moved to expose the white brightness of the full moon. A tingle of sensation, not unlike the feeling of Grayson touching his skin, moved over his body.

Light filled the arena, and the men started to change, writhe and contort. Hair of all colours—brown, gray, and black—sprouted from their bodies.

Shit, that was freaky.

Reagan took a step back, his heart pounding and his legs quivering with the need to run. They were animals, wild animals! This couldn't be safe!

Megan stepped back to him and grabbed his hand, squeezing tight. "They're totally safe. I've been watching this event since I was a baby and nothing bad has ever happened."

Reagan only nodded and concentrated on his breathing. In and out. Megan cooed to him, and although he could barely hear her actual words, her tone was soothing, lulling him to relax despite the anxiety swimming in his blood.

Grayson's human body had now completely transformed, and his wolf turned to stare at him, the bright blue eyes blazing a path of fire into his very soul. Reagan's heart leapt in recognition and love flowed through him like fiery rain.

"Wow. They're...incredible."

"I know... right?"

There was a collective howl from the huge wolves standing in the opening. It ripped through the night like the crack of a whip.

Then the pack of shifters turned and bounced off through the woods, chasing each other playfully, like pups.

"They just love that," Megan said next to him, and Reagan choked out a laugh.

His racing heart was beginning to slow down, but he could sense something else had changed in him, and he wasn't sure it was reversible.

What was happening? This was all so strange.

"Yeah, I think I'd enjoy it too, if I got to be that powerful."

Megan grinned at him and nodded her head towards the town. "Let's head back. They won't return for hours."

Hours? He wasn't expecting that. "Hours? What should we do, then?"

And what should the rest of the town do? If this happened every month, they should organise some sort of full moon party for everyone left behind.

"Well, most people just head to bed. Did you want to stay up and do something?"

It was tempting, so very tempting. "I'd love to, but my exams are like, seven days away, and I have to study for them. I'd love to spend more time with you. Sorry... do you mind if I go back to Grayson's house and get some work done?"

He so wanted to spend some more time with Megan. But he'd be able to do that after his exams, he was sure of it.

"Not at all. It's kind of cool you're going to be a doctor."

He grinned at her. "Thanks. I'll see you tomorrow, maybe?"

"Yeah, absolutely."

Reagan headed off home with a smile on his face.

Megan was great. He was so glad Grayson had a lovely family. His past boyfriends' families had often been negative and unaccepting of their sons' sexuality and hadn't liked him because of what he represented.

Having missed his parents like a severed limb for most of the past decade, the appeal of a family was huge. If Grayson's parents and his sister were willing to accept him, love him maybe that could swing the argument for where he moved after graduation.

Not that he was going to tell Grayson that yet! He didn't really know him well enough yet to fully commit.

Reagan got back to Grayson's house and planted himself in front of the computer.

When the door opened an hour later, he jumped. Grayson ran into the room, straight to him.

"What's wrong?"

"We picked up the scent of the Rogue wolves around the town. We don't know where they are."

Grayson's hands hurt his skin as they patted him down.

"Hey, stop." He pushed him off, grateful for the new strength he had. Without it, he would never survive as Grayson's mate.

Grayson stepped away, his eyes downcast and his lips pulled tight in a frown. "I just wanted to check you were okay. If you want me off you, I'll go."

Reagan jumped up out of his seat. Talk about an overreaction! "That's not fair. I was studying, and you surprised me! Then you were groping me and hurting me. You don't know your own strength."

Grayson lifted his hands and stared down at them. "Obviously not. All the other wolves seem to do fine with their mates. I don't know what your problem is."

Reagan bit his tongue, hard.

When Grayson continued to glare at him as though he were in the wrong, he knew Grayson wanted a fight, that was for damn sure. "You were being too rough. That's not on me. Just because I complain, doesn't make me wrong."

"Maybe if you'd grown up with our pack you'd fit in better," Grayson mumbled, as though talking to someone else.

"Huh? What do you mean fit in better? Did someone say something?"

When Grayson's mouth twitched, Reagan knew he'd touched on a nerve.

Grayson looked away, stepping around him and back towards the kitchen. "mmmhhrr. Sort of. A few of the elders have expressed concerns about your ties to the town. You wanting to go back so much. They don't think it's a good idea, not now that you've seen what we are."

Reagan straightened to his full height and thrust back his shoulders. They thought what? "Excuse me? What has my wanting to finish my six-year degree have to do with them? I'm going to be a doctor, for fuck's sake. I thought they wanted me because of that!"

"The mates of the Alphas don't usually work. They help the community and do other things..." Grayson's voice trailed off as a growl rolled through Reagan's vocal chords.

He barked out at the man in front of him. "I'm not a fucking woman, Grayson! I'm not going to sit at home and play house-hubby while you go off and save the world every second day."

Their door flew open again. "Grayson, we've found some of the Rogues, off Mason's Point. Come now." Aaron raced off, a trail of fire burning behind him.

"I've gotta go. Don't move, don't leave—just stay."

What am I now? Grayson's pet?

"Fuck off. You're the dog, not me."

Grayson glared at him, blue eyes blazing like twin full moons in the night.

Grayson marched over to the front door and pulled open a compartment that Reagan had assumed was a flaw in the plastering.

There was a huge red button on it that looked like a fire alarm.

"The whole town's in lockdown. This will seal all the exits, including the windows. I'll be back by morning."

Grayson slammed his fist into the red button and locks clicked and whirled around Reagan.

"No way."

"Get some sleep," Grayson said, as he marched through the front door and pulled it closed behind him.

Reagan raced forward and tried the door.

It was fucking locked!

And there wasn't any way for him to open it.

"You bloody control freak!" he yelled and raced to a window, where he tried to push up the sash, only to find it locked.

Seriously, what was with this town?

Why did Grayson refuse to see him as anything more than a fragile human who needed to be taken care of? Worse... he treated him like a child, who couldn't think for himself. There had been no conversation, no discussion. Grayson had just locked the door and thrown away the key.

For fuck's sake! He'd been an orphan for years now. He'd been looking after himself for all this time, and although he recognised that this was a different and dangerous world, a little respectful communication would have been the least he thought he deserved.

Obviously being someone's "mate," had a hell of a lot of submissive strings attached.

Reagan's heart raced with anger as he stared out the window and watched as fur started to spring from Grayson's pores and before his very eyes, Grayson became a huge black wolf once again.

Reagan's heart thumped against his ribs, but he didn't move. He let his arms fall to his sides and clenched his fists, glaring down at the massive animal.

Then the black wolf turned and fled into the night.

Reagan stomped back to the kitchen. *Seriously? Who did these people think they were?*

What was he on? House arrest? For what?

For being mated to the big, dumb idiot? Seriously.

He was getting out of here as soon as those doors opened again in the morning.

He'd worked too long and far too hard to throw it all away now. Especially for someone who treated him like some sort of helpless pet.

"Gah! Fuck you," he yelled at the perfectly pristine walls.

He glanced back at the computer that held his class notes, then at the comfortable guest bedroom. It was past midnight, no point trying to escape now, even if he wanted to.

He trudged off to his room and packed his clothes into a backpack he found in the wardrobe. He'd get some sleep and wake up at dawn. The wolf had better be back by that point, or there'd be hell to pay.

It was time to go home and finish the quest he'd started a decade ago.

Then he'd work out what to do about the wolf.

GRAYSON JOINED the pack on the outskirts of town and led the party as they ran out towards Mason's Point.

What did the Rogues want? Their plan still didn't make sense to Grayson. Did they want back in? Did they want the alphas dead so that they could take over?

What was it?

They ran through the thicket, Aaron to his left and Marcus to his right.

A legion of Betas on their heels.

The scent of the foreign wolves was strong. They'd really gone rogue. There was something truly feral in their scent now.

Something dirty, and evil.

Grayson checked for the presence of his father but found none. The older Alphas must be keeping the women and children safe in the tunnels.

Oh, fuck! He hadn't told Reagan about the escape tunnels.

When the alarm went to lock down the houses, most of the women and children would escape into the old tunnels that led out into the forest.

They'd been built in the hope they'd never need to be used, but if there was any sight of the Rogues in town, everyone would flee

The Omegas though... what would happen to them?

All the new homes had the safety features for the lockdown, but only the prime families had access to the tunnels.

That needed to change.

This couldn't happen again.

They rounded a group of trees and the scent became furiously strong.

There.

Their pack split into three groups and approached the edge of the cliffs with caution.

Grayson stopped suddenly, dropping his focus from the hunt.

Something was wrong. Very wrong. With Reagan. He had a dreadful feeling in his gut and the picture in his head was ringing bells on his mate.

He began to walk backwards, and although he saw the looks of concern on the Beta's faces, he couldn't follow them.

They continued on and he turned to flee.

There was wriggling anxiety filling his gut like a rising tide. Reagan was in trouble... maybe even hurt.

He began to run and had just gotten free of the thicket when he heard the staccato cracks of a machine gun going off behind him. Back where he'd left his pack.

No! It can't be!

He turned around again. The loyalties to both his pack and his mate warring against one another.

He searched his connection to Reagan and it was still there, stronger than ever.

His mate wasn't dead, but the premonition of death was upon him.

He needed to go back to Aaron and the Betas and find out if this feeling in his gut had anything to do with them.

He snuck back carefully, listening for anything that would let him know what was going on.

There was the rumbling of men's voices and growling of wolves, so he snuck closer.

Then anger struck him across the chest as he saw them, on the edge of the cliff.

His pack.

Held at gunpoint.

They'd obviously been ambushed by those fucking stupid Rogue wolves.

Five of them. Against dozens of Grayson's pack. But they held machine guns and his pack didn't.

And what a disturbing strategy these Rogues had. They had obviously stayed human so that they could carry weaponry, whereas his pack had hunted in their shifter form. As a powerful wolf, their teeth were usually enough to fight off any attacker.

"For the safety of your families, get down and stay down. We've got the women and the children trapped in the tunnels and we'll kill every one of them if you don't surrender now."

Aaron shifted back to human form instantly and got to his knees, putting his hands on his head.

No Alpha would stay standing while the threat of death was on his people.

"You won't kill everyone, Tollie. Who would run the town for you? Who would you breed with?" Aaron spat back at them.

Tollie sneered. "We'll just grab some of the humans from the city. As if we care. We can re-populate once the town is ours."

Aaron grimaced and glanced down at the ground.

Tollie grabbed his phone and spoke into it while aiming his gun at Aaron.

Grayson's stomach churned and tightened as he surveyed the scene before him.

Aaron's face was cut and bleeding, and the rest of the pack were slowly turning back to human.

These stupid Rogues had changed the game by bringing in machine guns. They were totally illegal in Australia, and Grayson had no idea where they'd got them.

Aaron and the rest of Grayson's pack were naked and defenseless now and it made Grayson clench his fists into tight balls at his side.

He coiled his energy, ready to attack. He may not get them all, but he'd put up a good enough fight.

Maybe Aaron would shift and kill the others. The Betas would surely avenge him if something happened.

Then Tollie's phone rang. "Yeah, we've got the hunting party, they're ready to give up. There's a few missing, including Grayson, but he'll be around somewhere."

Huh? They were looking for him specifically? Why?

"Your end is blocked? Great! Well done. I'm still waiting on my brothers to say they've secured their end... Ha, yeah, mental ain't the word for it. If I was going to let that cunt Grayson live, I'd mince what's left of the human and label the can 'Mate-Meat: Breakfast of Champions' and then feed him until he chokes."

"Hey, and well done on finding out about his stupid mate. That was bloody good work. Good ol' up-himself Grayson created the weak link himself. The irony is beautiful."

"Yeah, yeah... Hey, let's clear the line, I want my brothers to be able to get through. Just keep an eye on that end and make sure the women don't manage to dig themselves out or something. Talk to you soon."

Oh, holy God.

Grayson turned and started running back to Greensborough. He'd kill anyone who touched Reagan.

They had the tunnels blocked off. Why?

Had they hurt his father? The other Alphas that were down there? Why were the Rogues trying to hunt them all down? And why did they think going through his human mate would be the way to go?

Grayson ran faster than he'd ever run.

He leapt over logs and crashed through the trees. His heart

raced, sweat ran into his eyes, but he didn't stop until his paws were pounding the pavement down Main Street.

It was eerily quiet.

Everyone had retreated, it seemed. They had followed the escape protocol perfectly.

Unfortunately, that meant that the weakest of their community had put themselves into a strongly vulnerable position.

They council had never considered that the invaders would be people who knew them and their escape route. The assumption had always been that humans would be the threat.

But they'd been wrong. So wrong.

Grayson moved with stealthy speed. The main homes had been evacuated, that was clear. He couldn't sense anyone around.

The women and everyone else would have moved into the tunnels, to meet at the catacomb, the big room before the exit. Only... his mate didn't know the plan. Grayson had never explained it to him.

Could the Rogues be going through Reagan to access the tunnels after lockdown?

If they had the forest exit sealed off, and if they controlled the other end, everyone would be trapped, like fish in a barrel.

They had carefully hidden the forest exit from the humans. Satellite view couldn't even pick up where the exit was. But the pack knew. The Betas knew, and therefore the Rogues knew.

Grayson was approaching his house. A rental van was parked in front of his neighbour's home. Grayson crept up to it. No driver. It was full of gas cylinders and equipment.

Holy hell, they were going to gas them in the tunnels.

The Rogues really were willing to kill them all.

Grayson moved down the side of his house, checking the rooms through the windows.

He could see the back door, and it was open. What the fuck? How had they over-ridden the system?

His stomach clenched as he heard Reagan's voice coming from the kitchen.

"I told you to get out! How the hell did you get in here anyway?"

Grayson bolted towards the back door.

Grayson could hear Reagan's angry voice in the kitchen.

AL...................." "Come here, faggot, so I can gut you. If you ask me real nice, I'll make it quick and painless. Ned, get in here. Give me a hand to catch this mouse."

Grayson heard Ned on the stairs about to enter the kitchen, so he flew through the back door towards him, knocking him backwards. As Ned bounced off the door frame, Grayson's fist aimed for a weakness in the Beta, meeting Ned flush on the same nose that Grayson had broken less than 48 hours ago.

Then he grabbed the fading Ned by the back of his belt and collar.

Using Ned as a shield, Grayson went towards Alexander.

Alexander now dismissed his objective—Reagan—and focused on Grayson.

Reagan took the opportunity and began running around the bench to get behind Grayson.

The brothers had only knives, as they probably only expected to have to deal with a human. But Grayson was suspicious they could have guns so he moved as fast as he could, watching for Alexander's hand movements in case he went for something under his jacket.

Grayson threw Ned like a sack-of-potatoes at Alexander, so that he could grab Alexander by the wrist of his knife hand. Then swung the Beta around by his arm so that Grayson could get behind him.

Grayson whipped his other hand through the legs of the Rogue to grab him by the balls and lift him off the ground.

Alexander squealed as Grayson tilted him headfirst towards the bench.

The Beta managed to stabilize himself at virtual horizontal with two hands on the bench, still holding on to his knife.

With Grayson's force on his neck there was no way he could lift one hand without falling.

"Right Alexander, I could snap your back like a rabbit from this position, but all I want is some answers."

But when the Rogue raised the knife hand and attempted a swing that answered his question.

Grayson groaned and flicked the Rogue's other hand out from under him.

He slammed the Rogue's face into the marble bench.

If the Rogues jaw wasn't already in pieces from his previous encounter with Grayson, it sure was now.

"You guys are slow to learn, aren't you?"

The other brother, Ned, was attempting to rise so Grayson picked up Alexander and threw him on top of his younger brother. He placed one foot on his back, pinning them both down, just in case they became capable of moving.

"Grab me a roll of gaffer tape from that bottom drawer, will you, Reagan?"

Grayson taped Alexander's wrists behind his back and threw him to one side, face down.

Once Grayson had presented the Ned with his new gaffer cuffs, he threw the Rogue face down on top of his brother and sat on them.

Reagan grinned as he also wrapped their ankles with gaffer tape.

Grayson dragged the pair into the lounge and hung them over

the door handles. So with their hands behind their back, they were virtually resting on their faces.

Obviously, Reagan thought they hadn't had enough, so he grabbed another roll and gaffer-tapped their heads down to the carpet.

"Jesus, Reagan."

Reagan raised an eyebrow at him. "What? They can still breathe! I don't want them to get out."

Grayson couldn't help the smile that rose. "They won't get out of that. I'll be lucky to ever get that shit off the carpet. We'll be watching movies with these two guys' heads stuck to the floor. Oh, and by the way, this head is Ned and the other head is Alexander. I ran into them in Melbourne, just before I met you on the road. I had to give them a smack then, too. "

Reagan glared at him. "Well, so much for your bloody security system. It let in this garbage. But I couldn't get out to safety."

"There's obviously plenty fucked up in the security system. I'm so sorry, Reagan. I really am. But we'd never expected the threat to come from the inside."

He still had to get the group out of the tunnels. Then, barter with Tollie for the lives of the Alphas. At least now he had two prisoners as assets to open the trade.

Reagan collapsed onto one of the couches, his posture slumped.

"You stay here and keep an eye on these two. I'm going down the tunnels."

Reagan's eyes were glossed with swelling tears and Grayson stopped.

"What's wrong? " Grayson asked his mate.

CHAPTER TEN

"Thank God you came back." The adrenaline was draining away and his muscles had begun to shake.

"Mate, are you okay?" Grayson's hands were all over him, cupping his jaw and squeezing his arms, and for once Reagan welcomed the strange pain.

"Are you all right? Tell me! Please!"

"You...Locked... Me... In."

"I know! I'm so sorry! It's protocol when there's an attack. We had all the houses designed to withstand a siege. To protect our loved ones. Please forgive me."

Grayson's voice cut off with emotion. An Alpha begging for forgiveness. Who would have thought it?

"God, I love you." The words just fell out of Reagan's mouth and yet he'd never said anything so true.

Grayson stared at Reagan, his face now tender and soft. "I love you. Too much. I almost had a heart attack when I heard them saying they were going to the tunnels through you." Grayson's large hands cupped his shoulders, pulling him in for a rough kiss.

Reagan pushed him away. “What tunnels?”

“The escape tunnels I hadn’t told you about. Again—massive apologies. I never thought you’d need to know about them, because as far as I know, they’ve never been used for a real emergency.”

Reagan put one hand on his hip and stared at Grayson. He hadn’t answered the question.

“Oh, right. Come with me.”

They headed through the living area, opened the door to the laundry and then another door that Reagan had assumed was an extra toilet.

Only it wasn’t.

When Grayson opened the second door, Reagan was amazed at how thick it was.

“Does this have some sort of locking mechanism?”

The door had rods of steel through the center and strange markings on the edges.

“Yes. Once the alarms go off, everyone in town is meant to go down the tunnels, locking the doors behind them. That seals off this end and stops anyone from following them as they escape.”

“Very clever.”

Grayson grunted. “Yeah... anyway. When I was in the forest, I saw some Rogues grab the hunting pack and they were on a phone communicating with someone in town. They said they were going to hold the women and children ransom for the life of the Alphas, which of course we would surrender in a moment.”

Reagan gasped. “Is that what those assholes wanted? To get into the tunnel and hurt everyone down there?”

“Yes, I assume so, which is why I need to get down there and check on everyone. If they blocked off both exits and had people inside the tunnel as well, they’d have most of the town at their mercy.”

Reagan couldn't think of anything worse. To be stuck in a hole, waiting for someone to rescue you.

He shuddered.

"Let's go down and get them then. Come on."

Grayson grabbed his shoulder. "No. You can't go. They've probably got guns, not to mention they're fucking insane. The best thing you can do is wait here, keep the door open for anyone coming back this way."

A shiver coursed over Reagan's whole body.

"What are you going to do?"

Reagan knew he couldn't stop Grayson from doing his job, but a part of him didn't want to even think about the risks he was taking.

"First I've gotta get into the tunnels, and if everyone's okay bring them back up this way. Everyone's homes will be sealed off, and it's not safe to go out the other end. I'm sure Tollie has that end blocked off too. Then, I've gotta get Tollie to call off their attack, and I think I have the perfect ammunition. Those two dickheads are the brothers of the guy running the show. I'm going to swap them for the pack members they have out there in the forest."

"Okay... how?"

Grayson walked back to the dining room, grabbed a chair and shoved it into the doorway so that the tunnel entrance stayed open.

"First things first. Stay here and I'll be back."

Grayson stripped out of his clothes and lay them on the chair.

Reagan's stressed brain didn't even get to enjoy the beauty of his mate before Grayson was transforming into his massive black wolf and racing off down the tunnel.

Reagan sagged against the door frame.

What a night.

He closed his eyes, his mind going back to those moments when the Rogues were in the house and his heart had been hammering a hundred miles an hour.

When the Rogue had threatened to gut him, his first thought had been, *I'm going to die.*

Then flashes of his life had reeled across his brain like a torturous slide show of movies. His beautiful mum and dad, taken too soon.

Then Grayson, oh God, he could think of nothing but Grayson.

The love he'd found in that man's bed was heaven itself. Knowing pleasure like that, feeling protected and cared for, was beyond his wildest fantasies. And it was only the start. There was so much more to explore for them.

If he'd died, what would have happened? According to Grayson, there would be no other for him.

And the guilt of his death... Damn. That alone would be enough to kill Grayson.

Reagan walked to the kitchen and started pulling out bottles of water and whatever snacks he could find.

The people coming out of the tunnels may be hungry, thirsty, hurt, even.

Grayson and he had just met. They'd only begun their journey a few days ago and it would the cruelest twist of Fate if it all ended now.

Reagan walked back to the laundry and sat down on the chair propping the door open. He strained his ears for the sound of people walking up the darkened tunnel.

Please, God, don't let anything happen to Grayson.

Then there were the sounds of scuffling and running. Reagan jumped up and backed into the kitchen.

His throat tightened and his breath caught in his chest.

Should he have grabbed a knife in case an unfriendly came back into Grayson's place?

But then Grayson, in human form, was stepping back into the laundry.

Reagan exhaled the stress in his lungs as his mate, who was panting from exertion, pulled his clothes back on.

"What happened? Is everyone okay?"

Grayson nodded as he tugged on his shoes. "Yeah, everyone's fine from what I can tell. They are making their way up to the surface."

"So what happens now? Are they all coming up here?"

"Yeah, they have to. All the other doors have been locked from the inside. So if you could help them out when they come through, that would be great."

Suddenly a tinkling ring sounded in the other room and they ran to the lounge.

Reagan walked over to where the Rogues were struggling with their bindings and he pulled a small cell phone out of one of the guy's back pocket.

"Here."

Grayson answered the phone and put it on speaker.

"What the hell's going on over there, Ned? Is everything okay?"

"Nah, you seem to have a problem over here, Tollie."

"What? Who is this? Fucking Grayson. How'd you get my brother's phone?"

"The tables have turned."

"Turned, my arse. I've got your hunting party. Aaron and Marcus, and I'm going to kill them if you don't do exactly as I tell you."

Grayson laughed, the sound strangely evil.

"Tollie, I suggest you shut the fuck up and listen to me, you sick son of a bitch. I have your brothers, and I will let the elders kill them the old way——by skinning them alive. You were prepared to murder everyone in our pack, do you think your brothers should be shown any sympathy? Here's my deal, agree to return my pack unharmed or I will hunt you down to the ends of the earth. If you even touch one hair on their heads, you'll be sorry. I have been patient up until this point... I let you leave the pack with no repercussions. But you have taken it to a whole new level."

"Bullshit... you.... No way! We've got all the..."

Grayson growled down the phone and everything went strangely silent.

"Do the smart thing, Tollie. Run away. Live to fight another day."

There was a long silence and Reagan crossed his arms over his belly, the tension eating at him.

"Fuck you Grayson. Don't give my brothers to the elders."

"Smart move, Tollie."

"How're we going to do this?"

"Give me a minute."

Reagan bit onto his lip, hard. Grayson had to get this part right or the whole plan could go very south.

"You let Aaron and the pack go. When I know they're free and fine, I'll drop your brothers off somewhere and I'll give them their phones back. Then they can tell you where to pick them up. Now put Aaron on the line."

Grayson explained the trade to Aaron and told him to get to one of the outlying farms and call him back to confirm that their side of the deal had been kept.

Once they hung up, Grayson got his own cell out and turned to Reagan.

"A few of the elders have gun licenses for hunting purposes. The guards will need to carry them from tonight onwards."

Reagan groaned.

"Damn it. What did I miss?"

"The Rogues were planning to kill everyone, I saw the gas trucks parked outside. I need to make sure that doesn't happen."

"Okay, how can I help?"

"Just ensure the pack gets the help they need when they come up, then hang with my family. I've gotta sort this shit out before anyone else gets hurt."

Grayson's face twisted up and all at once Reagan realised that Grayson blamed himself for everything that had happened already. The locked house. The stupid Rogue wanting to use their home as a way into the tunnels.

The fact they attacked Greensborough at all.

And although Reagan still took great umbrage at being locked in the house, the intent was pure. It was the Rogues who were the real villains here and he'd deal with the so-called safety "protocol" later.

Reagan reached out and touched his lover's beautiful cheek, tracing his full bottom lip with his fingertip.

"This wasn't your fault, Grayson, and after all, you saved me. Go get the bad guys. I'm not going anywhere. "

Grayson's blue eyes widened, and a huge smile spread across his face. "Thanks, my mate. I love you."

Grayson gave him a quick, hard kiss and headed out to prepare his vehicle for transporting the two Rogues.

Reagan sagged against the door frame, the adrenaline finally leeching from his body.

"Hello, Grayson? Reagan?"

Reagan heard the call from inside the house and pulled himself up by the bootstraps.

He needed to focus on getting everyone back to their homes and doing his part in keeping everyone safe.

CHAPTER ELEVEN

After Grayson had left Reagan last night, the rest of his evening had been relatively uneventful.

Aaron and the rest of the pack had returned within ten minutes of his phone call to Tollie, so he'd delivered Ned and Alexander to an outback road, along with their phones.

By the time he'd gotten back to the Borough, everyone was out of the tunnels and settled back into their homes. Thanks, in lots of ways, to his helpful mate.

Grayson had a big council meeting organized for today to discuss everything he'd learnt, and to address the weaknesses in their security procedures.

He had the car running and breakfast packed for Reagan in the passenger seat by the time his human mate had woken. What he had to do today was going to be so much harder than anything he'd done with the Rogues last night.

He was taking Reagan home. Back to Melbourne.

He just had to hold it together long enough to get Reagan to safety. Away from him and the threat his world posed to his vulnerable human mate.

Reagan had almost died last night, and Grayson wasn't sure he'd survive if something like that happened again.

Reagan dead in the cemetery because of his mistakes? No—he couldn't live with that. He would just have to live without Reagan in his life.

Taking him back to Melbourne was by far the lesser of the two evils. And would be the only thing that guaranteed Reagan's safety.

After a final check with Doctor Sarah at the hospital, it was time.

Reagan stepped out of the entrance doors and walked towards him, his hair glinting with red in the morning sunshine.

Grayson's heart kicked out in recognition of his mate, sickening him and making his fingers tighten on the steering wheel.

"Hey. Thanks for waiting."

"No problem. Jump in."

Reagan slid in, and Grayson started the car. His throat was tight, too tight. As though he was the one on the ground with a foot at his larynx.

But as he swallowed down the pain, he focused on what he really needed to do. One step at a time.

"Here you go." Grayson handed his mate his coffee, his hands shaking as he put the car into gear and took off down the road.

He signaled to the two Betas he'd assigned to protect Reagan and they pulled onto the road behind him.

"Where are we off to?"

"I'm taking you home." Grayson injected a happy note into his voice that he wasn't feeling.

He hoped this wouldn't be as bad as he suspected.

Reagan had been trying to get back to Melbourne for days. Surely, he'd jump at the opportunity?

"What did you drive for? Your house is like, a block away. We could have walked. "

Reagan's assumption that home was Grayson's townhouse was like a sharp knife slicing into his ribs.

So much had changed in so little time.

"Ah, no. I mean, back to town. To your place."

Silence.

Deathly silence.

They cleared the outer streets of Greensborough and started heading down the mountain. It was going to be a long hour's drive if Reagan didn't want to go.

"That's what you wanted, right? To go back. You've been busting my balls for days about it."

But a lot had happened in those few days, he knew. His mate must be feeling the connection that they'd made together, and that would mean he'd ache like blazes at the idea of leaving.

Reagan cleared his throat. "Um...for my exams, you mean? "Cos that's great. I do need to knuckle down for this next week. There's three weeks of exams in total, and they are notoriously hard... But I would have liked to say goodbye to Megan and some of the others."

Grayson gripped the steering wheel and concentrated on the road, not the screaming in his heart. Why was Reagan making this so hard? Surely after the Rogues attacking him, and all the other shit he'd seen inside the pack's politics, his mate would want to go back to the safety of his old world and the overseas trip he had planned?

"Yeah, for your exams and your holiday. Didn't you have some three month European adventure planned after graduation?"

"Well, yeah... but I'd assumed you'd want me to change those plans."

Another kick to the guts delivered beautifully. Of course, his generous mate wanted to change his plans to fit in with Grayson and the life they should be building together.

But it wasn't to be, and he was thankful for the plans Reagan had made. It would get his precious mate away from any trouble the Rogues may still be brewing. They'd attack the town again, that was for sure.

He risked a glance at Reagan, who still looked pretty calm, considering he'd almost been gutted by a Beta last night.

Grayson shuddered at the memory.

He'd known something was wrong with Reagan. He'd have bet his life on it. And thank God, he had. Or none of their families would be alive today.

So why had the Alphas treated their mates like children? Their Omegas?

They'd almost killed their entire pack, and he was going to see that it never happened again. It was time for things to change.

"Grayson... Hello?"

He glanced to his mate again who was busily consuming the mountain of food Grayson had packed for him. "Oh, sorry. Still thinking about last night."

"Yeah, it was fucking scary, wasn't it?"

Grayson turned to him in surprise. When was he going to get the bake for last night? "You're not angry with me?"

"Yeah, I kinda am, and we need to talk about the whole 'you locked me up for my own good' thing. I'm not a bloody child, and after all, it didn't work. But I've had enough stress for this week, so at the moment I'd like to just focus on the fact that we're all alive and well."

Grayson grunted. It was because Reagan was alive that he was doing this. "Don't worry, things are going to change in the pack. I'll make sure of it."

"Great to hear. You didn't tell me how the drop off went with the Rogues. I assume they didn't like the fact they'd been beaten so soundly?"

"That was kind of fun. When they started abusing me, I told them I was taking them out to the woods to bury them. They sucked up after that."

Reagan chuckled. "Good one. They deserved it. Bastards."

Grayson reached out and flipped the switch on the radio. Music filled the cab of the truck as they drove down the hill. Grayson ignored the howling in his head and the pain in his belly. He'd done a lot of tough things in his life, but letting his mate go was going to be, by far, the most difficult.

"Stop. Stop! Is that my car?"

Grayson pulled over near the wreck of what had been Reagan's car. They still hadn't towed it away, and it was a black, crumbling mess.

"Yeah. That's it."

Grayson saw the Betas pull their car over as well, hopefully far enough back that Reagan wouldn't notice them straight away.

Reagan wrenched open the door and jumped out, circling his burnt car, throwing his hands up in the air and putting them on top of his head. "Oh shit! You really did save my life that night, didn't you?"

Grayson shrugged. He had no idea. Fate was a weird thing. If he hadn't stopped to pick up his new laptop, he would have been half way home before Reagan had finished his shift.

Perhaps they would have missed meeting each other altogether? And in some ways, that probably would have been a good thing. For both of them.

His mouth twisted. "Yeah, only to be nearly gutted in my kitchen a few days later."

"And then you saved me again."

Grayson turned back to the car. Were both times his fault? If he hadn't been on the road that night, would Reagan have been all right? Would he have still hit the tree?

He had no idea. And foresight he did not have.

"Let's go, Reagan."

"I found my phone! It's pretty toasted, though."

Reagan grimaced as he stared at something in his hand, then threw it back on the pile of twisted metal.

By the time he got back to the car, Grayson was practically shaking. Was he really going to send his mate back to the human world? Cut off all ties and live his life alone?

It was better than watching him die.

Grayson clenched down hard on his teeth and slid into the driver's side of his car. Reagan hopped in the passenger side, and they took off again.

"You need to turn right at the hospital, and I'll direct you from there."

Grayson could only nod as his wolf howled inside him. This was going to hurt like damnation.

"There's my place. The house with the white fence."

Reagan pointed to a house that surprised Grayson. It looked just like a normal family home, nothing like the student accommodations he'd expected.

"Nice house."

"It was my parent's place. Their insurance didn't pay it out fully, but I've managed to keep it. By the skin of my teeth sometimes, but it's still mine at the moment."

Grayson loved so much about Reagan. He had guts and determination. Strength and the ability to love, and he stood up for what was right. Qualities Grayson admired, that he thanked the fates for giving him in a mate.

But it wouldn't be enough in Grayson's world. Not with the power struggles, the old ways, and the Rogues still at large.

If he couldn't protect Reagan, he'd rather be without him.

At least he'd be safe.

"Well done."

He better get going.

"Are you going to come in?"

"Ah...no. I better get back. Got a lot of stuff to do with the Rogues still on the hunt. Good luck with your exams. I know you'll do brilliantly."

He waited for Reagan to get out of the car, but his mate just stared at him with wide eyes.

"And when are you coming back? Or am I driving back up in a couple of weeks once everything's done and dusted with University?"

Reagan's eyes were eager and bright, and far too beautiful. Grayson pushed his gaze back to the steering wheel. He couldn't stand looking at Reagan's happy face anymore.

Just as he couldn't stand the fact that he was about to push his mate out of his life forever.

His mate... Fuck. The mate he'd been waiting his whole life for.

My wolf's gonna kill me.

"No. I think it's best if you stay here. Go through with the next steps of your medical degree. Go on your trip. Stay a part of the human world. It's where you belong."

"What?"

Grayson turned back to Reagan with a groan, reaching for some anger in his belly. It was mostly at himself, but it would do to get through this conversation. "Reagan, get out of the car and go. Go back to your life. You'll be better off without me."

"Without you? You mean, you'll be better off without me, don't you?"

Grayson shrugged, not sure what to say to that one.

Reagan groaned as though he were in pain. "What the hell happened now? I thought you said we were mated, unable to be separated. Now you want to break up for good? What sort of bull-shit lies did you feed me in Greensborough?" Reagan was huffing and puffing now, his face turning red as he spoke.

Grayson grabbed on to the chance to provoke his mate. There was only one way he was getting out of this one, and that was to make Reagan walk away. "We aren't mated, Reagan. Not the way you think, or Megan would have told you. We didn't go through with the ceremony. We aren't married or anything binding like that. You're free to be with whoever you want."

He practically choked on his own tongue as he threw the words at Reagan.

Be with someone else? Reagan kissing someone else... Touching another... Fuck no!

"What are you talking about? You said—"

"Stop it, okay! I was wrong about us. I'm sorry. Just go!"

"You're sorry? You have to be kidding me. There's another reason, isn't there? "

"Of course there is, there's a hundred reasons. You're smart enough to figure them all out, I'm sure."

"Like what? I'm human, you're not? I'm sane... and you're not? I know it's all crazy, but we can work this out... I know we can."

Grayson chuckled without humor. "Oh, my God. You are worse than breaking up with a woman."

He rubbed his forehead, a strange side of his personality finding all of this weirdly funny.

"Grayson... seriously. Stop being so god damn insulting. What the hell are you talking about? We're meant to be together, you know we are. I know we are. Everyone knows!"

"But that's not a good enough reason to be together Reagan. Not anymore."

"Oh, come on! My birthmark changed—it changed! And yours disappeared! That has to mean something."

"Look... it's just not safe for you to be in my world. I think last night proved that. The Rogues have a vendetta going, against the pack and specifically against me. You need to be far away from that."

Reagan reached across the void and rubbed Grayson's thigh. "But you protected me from all that. You'll do it again."

"No! That almost killed me last night. Knowing you were in danger. No, I'm sorry. But this is the best way. Go, finish your degree, get on that plane and go to Europe. Be safe, somewhere else."

Reagan glared at him. "I think you've forgotten one, massive thing. You said you saw those Rogues in Melbourne a few days ago and gave them an ass-kicking. What's going to stop them from finding me? I'm not safer in Melbourne, I'm safer with you."

Grayson shook his head. He'd already sorted all of that out. "I know. That's why I've got a couple of the Betas to hang around for the next few weeks. They'll be your bodyguards and will ghost you night and day. But don't worry, you won't see them. They'll just watch out for anything dangerous. Then when you're done with your exams, you can go on your long, expensive holiday. Alone."

Reagan slumped, as though deflated by the logic. "You certainly have figured out my life for me, haven't you?"

Grayson rubbed his forehead with his thumb and index finger, pain exploding behind his temples.

"Why are you making this so hard? I don't want to be doing this with you. Have some pride, for fuck's sake."

"Pride? Oh... I get it. You're embarrassed about being gay, or whatever the hell you are. I knew you couldn't handle that part."

Grayson could work with that.

He glared at Reagan with all the anger he could muster. At his mate's strength, at his own weakness. At Fate's fucked up sense of humour.

"Yeah, okay. I admit it. I'm NOT gay. Never have been, never will be. I have no idea why you're even my mate. I've never wanted a guy before, and I hate that I'm the end of my dad's Alpha bloodline." He was the one panting for breath now as he watched his mate shrink beneath his words. He had to keep going, he could see the end in sight.

"How am I meant to have kids with you, huh? Unless you suddenly grow a pussy, what am I meant to even do with you?"

The words cut at him like glass in an open wound. Slicing him up and making him bleed. Was that really him speaking that horrible venom?

Reagan's eyes grew wide, his mouth dropping. Then his eyebrows drew low and tight, and he punched out at Grayson with his fist, the physical blow landing and knocking his jaw sideways, his head snapping back.

It didn't even put a dent in the screaming pain inside Grayson's head.

"Go to hell, Grayson." Reagan got out of the truck and slammed the door with enough force to rock the whole thing.

Reagan didn't bother to grab the bag full of clothes. He just stormed off towards the house.

Grayson just stared at the bag. He didn't want to get out to give it to him, just in case he couldn't get back in afterwards.

He watched as his mate scooped up a potted plant in the

garden, and seemingly found a key, because he marched straight to the red front door, opened it, and slammed it shut.

Not looking behind him once.

All the air went out of Grayson's body and he slumped over the wheel. He'd just destroyed his only hope of happiness. Well done.

He lay there for a long time before he realised he had to do something. Either go inside the house and apologise, or gather what strength he had left and get back to the pack.

Grayson pushed himself up off the steering wheel and turned the key once again. He forced his body into autopilot and maneuvered the truck back onto the road to Greensborough.

No looking back now.

Grayson crawled into bed when he got home, locked the door, and didn't come up for food, nor water for a whole day.

He couldn't get up and didn't want to. Every part of him hurt, and his dry lips bled.

He didn't care.

His mate was gone.

"Grayson! Hey, big brother! Are you in here?" Megan's voice echoed through the house, and he groaned.

She had a key. Why had he given her a key, again?

That's right.

For emergencies.

Her light footsteps tread up the stairs and into his room. Grayson kept his eyes closed as he felt his sister draw nearer. Cold air whooshed up his legs as the covers were pulled off him at speed.

"Argh... Go away, Megan." He rolled onto his side, unfazed by the fact he was naked. She'd seen him a thousand times before.

"What's wrong with you, and what have you done with Reagan?"

"I took him home."

"Oh, that's good. For his exams...but I would have liked to have said goodbye, you know."

Yeah, he knew. Reagan had slotted into his family so well. It would have been so easy having a life with him, not to mention how good his family would have been for Reagan.

His poor mate could have had parents again. People to care for him. But the Rogues had fucked everything up and now they could never be together.

"Can you go now? I'm alive. Reagan's gone. All is peachy."

Silence.

"Gone? What do you mean gone? And you're not okay. You look like shit. Get up and come get some dinner with us."

"No."

"What have you done, Grayson? " Megan's words were soft and spoken next to his face.

He groaned and rolled, sitting up while the stars danced around his head. He blinked a few times, clearing out the dust.

It probably was time to get back into his life. "Nothing. I'll come. Just wait a bit." He used every ounce of strength to stand and staggered to the shower, turning on the water and welcoming the blast of cold that hit him in the chest.

"Argh..." He danced around the tiles, both needing the cleansing rain and avoiding the icy cold. When he finally turned up the heat, he melted into the wall, his eyelids heavy, his stomach growling for food.

"Let's go, Grayson. I'm hungry."

He grabbed hold of his sister's voice as the depression tried to pull him down. "Okay, Megan." He forced his eyes open, and turned off the shower, drying himself and pulling on his clothes in a mechanical way.

"Still can't get used to seeing you without your mark. It's weird. "

Grayson just nodded. So, his mark hadn't come back despite him severing the connection to Reagan?

They walked out of his house. Grayson took some deep breaths, his body's aches lessening as his strength improved.

"Are you going to tell me what happened?"

He shook his head. Not on his life. "Everything's fine. Let's go."

Wisely, his sister just walked silently with him, helping him when he would have stumbled and directed him to the Alpha table. "I'll get you something to eat, "she whispered into his ear as she placed a hand on his shoulder.

He nodded. He wasn't sure he could get up again. His legs felt like toothpicks that wouldn't support his body weight.

Aaron sat opposite him, picking at his food like a bird. That was weird in itself. Let alone the slumped shoulders and look of pure defeat written all over the Alpha's face.

They'd saved everyone and had begun changes with the tunnel protocol within the council. Why was Aaron upset?

"What's up with you, Aaron?"

Aaron lifted his head. "Nothing. What's up with you?"

They shared a look.

Bloody mates. Ruined everything.

"You couldn't find him?"

Aaron shook his head. "No. A couple of the Omegas said he ran off before the lockdown even started, but I can't be sure about anything, except that he's gone."

"Yeah. Reagan's gone, too." He didn't mean to say it, but the words just fell out of his mouth.

"Gone? Where?"

"Home. Melbourne. He had to complete his medical degree, then go overseas for a while."

Aaron shrugged. "At least he'll be back, though. Right?"

Grayson didn't answer, just smiled at his sister when she dropped a plate of meat in front of him.

"Yeah, Grayson, when's your little boy coming home?" Marcus' snide voice made the hairs on his neck stand on end.

A growl began in his chest and spread up his throat. "That 'little boy' helped save your fucking life. So shut your bloody face, Marcus."

Marcus grinned, his spiteful look making a rocket of hatred shoot straight through him.

Grayson jumped across the table, grabbed Marcus' shirt and ploughed his fist straight through his jaw.

Marcus' eyes rolled back in his head, and Grayson threw him. He crumbled to the floor like a sack of shit.

Grayson sat back down and went back to eating, Marcus' wife crying out and attending to him where he lay on the floor.

Tony barked at him, "What in the hell is wrong with you, Grayson? Marcus is an Alpha, too. You need to show him respect. Show the pack that we are united. Strong. Not be fighting amongst yourselves like children"

Grayson shrugged, feeling the weight of the world lifting off his shoulders as he focused on the task he'd set himself. And one Reagan would be proud of him for.

"We are strong. And united. But Marcus is a narcissistic wanker and it's his lack of respect that earned him that. We should be shown more respect, being an Alpha male pair. Not less."

He could feel his father's gaze on him, and he ignored the subconscious warning.

"Do you know the legends, Tony? That Gray and Luc were a mated pair?"

There was a general gasp, and a hush fell over the pack.

"Grayson..." His father's warning went out. "Stop. Now. "

The command was unmistakable, and yet Grayson did not stop. Did not bend. "No, Dad, I will not."

The Alpha table stared at him, wide-eyed as he stood up and addressed their whole community.

"It's true! The original Alpha lines that we all stem from, come from a pair of male Alpha wolves. They bred with five different women, weaving the five strains of Alpha families, all their descendants. My mate is male, as is Aaron's. This is a good sign, and not one we should ignore. It is a sign of strength, of change, of legacy. Not only did we fail to protect you when we should have, from the Rogues, but we locked you in your homes, and then the tunnels for your own protection. Worst. Mistake. Ever."

There was a rumble from the crowd, people turning to each other and whispering.

"I believe we need to change policies to suit everyone in Greensborough. And we need to catch the Rogues and make them pay for what they've done."

A general cry went up, and he turned to see most of the Alpha table standing, their faces grim with determination.

Some weren't, and Grayson made a mental note of those who would oppose him.

Today marked a new day. He was going forth without Reagan, but with the strength his mate had given him.

Reagan would be safe now, in the human world. And he'd take what he'd learnt and move his pack into the future.

CHAPTER TWELVE

A month later.

Reagan's exams were finally done and he'd started packing for his trip and planning what he'd do when he returned. The Beta bodyguards still sat outside his house every night, but he'd come to feel comforted by their presence.

It meant Grayson still cared. Or so he liked to pretend.

Because the more he thought about it, the more he realized that Grayson had been right. Their relationship had been doomed from the very start, and they weren't meant to be together.

What had he been thinking a month ago, when he'd practically begged a wolf shifter to continue their weird relationship? It had to be the lowest point of many low points over the past month. It's amazing how fast you can get sucked in when you fall in love.

He scrubbed his temples with his fingertips and tried to push any thoughts of his mate from his mind.

His mate... fuck off.

Why couldn't he stop thinking that way?

"Hey... how are you, Reagan?"

Noah's voice made a smile lift his lips, the first in weeks. "Oh, hey, Noah. I'm good. How are you?"

Noah's blue eyes sparkled as he leant over Reagan's desk.

Noah had wanted Reagan for years now, but bent on finishing his course, Reagan had never submitted to Noah's request for a date. Too messy if everything went to hell.

"Great... great. Happy those exams are done. You got all your plans set for next year?"

"I'm off to Europe for a few months, but when I get back? I'm not sure, really. I still need to choose a specialty."

Noah chuckled. "Plastics for me... always."

"Yeah, I remember.'

The guy was vain and obsessed with wealth. Plastic surgery was the only specialty guys like him wanted to get into.

"Now that we're all done, are you finally ready to go on that date with me? I guarantee you a good time."

Noah's smile was sexy, his muscled arms huge as he crossed them over his chest.

"Oh, thank you but I can't. I have a... a..."

He choked on the words. Everything inside him denying the availability of his heart.

Noah's eyebrows quirked up. "You have a boyfriend? Since when?"

"Well, I don't exactly... I've been seeing someone but it hasn't worked out."

Noah relaxed his posture once again.

"Oh... his loss. My gain. Though I can't imagine anyone ever giving you up of their own free will."

"Oh, you give me far too much credit." Reagan stood up and leaned against the study booth.

Noah reached out and ran a long finger down his arm, "Not at all. You're hot."

Noah's gaze dropped to Reagan's arm. "Cool birthmark. Is that a wolf?"

Something angry shot along Reagan's bloodstream and he roughly pulled his arm away from Noah's touch.

"Yeah."

His hoodie was hanging over the back of his chair, and he grabbed it up and pulled it on over his bare arms.

"You don't need to be so precious. I was just looking."

His arm burned where Noah had touched him, the initial ache in his gut now turning into a true churning.

"I think you need to go, Noah. I'll see you at graduation."

Noah's lips twisted up into a snarl.

"No wonder your guy dumped you. You're a fucking drama queen."

Reagan clenched his teeth and let out the feral growl that had been building in his throat.

"Don't tempt me to smash your face in, Noah, because it would be a vast improvement if I did."

Noah's eyes went wide and his mouth opened and closed a few times before he strutted away.

"Bloody wanker."

The growls kept rolling through his chest and he had to sit down and breathe deeply to get them under control.

He was stupid to think he was going to get over Grayson quickly.

Even though their relationship was the very definition of a whirlwind courtship, and should have faded by now, it was anything but.

His nights were consumed with Grayson and his smile. Though rare, it was incredibly beautiful.

His laugh could bring Reagan out of the depths of despair.

And the sex.... Damn it, he got hard just thinking about it now. Grayson's hands, his mouth... damn it, his cock was magical. He took Reagan to places he'd never been to before.

And what tortured him the most, in both waking and sleeping moments, was all that could have happened.

And didn't.

All that they should have shared and would never have the chance to enjoy.

He groaned and threw his head back. What was it going to take to let him go? To move on?

Was that even what he wanted?

To let the big Alpha go? Could he do it with a permanent mark on his body, and Grayson's touch in his heart?

He'd thought a surgical fellowship would be best for him, but the more he looked into the future, the more he saw himself as a general practitioner.

In Greensborough.

"Oh, shut up. Stop it."

Why couldn't his brain understand that going back just wasn't an option?

Grayson didn't want him. End of story.

He should just put his head back down and forget about the love that he'd lost.

Because it was never coming back.

"Pardon me?" One of his professors stopped as he walked past and stared at Reagan with a confused frown.

He shouldn't even be in the University library, but he was putting off going home, where it was quiet, and he was alone all the time.

"Oh, sorry, Professor, I was talking to myself. "

Which he did all the time now. Despite his best effort, he was still having fights with himself about what to do about his life.

It had taken him about a week to get over all the hurtful, stupid things Grayson had said, and then he'd had to get through his exams with the only thing on his mind...that everything Grayson had said had been bullshit.

He didn't care about any of the gay crap, or anything else he'd sworn to. Grayson was protecting him, as a good Alpha did.

And that fucking pissed him off. Was he meant to just leave Grayson to rot in his own selfless act, or demand they both be given the chance to be happy?

It was too confusing.

"What's there to be upset about, Reagan? You did so well this year, graduating with honours!"

Reagan smiled at the kind-hearted man. The students hadn't received their actual certificates yet, but with his exam results, he'd get honours for sure.

His parents would have been so proud, and he spent many a night talking to his dad's photo, trying to sort out the problems of the world.

"I just... Um...it's nothing."

"No, please tell me."

Reagan hesitated. He shouldn't tell his teacher about his personal problems, but then again, who else did he have to talk to? He had no family, and his friends were limited to the few other medical students he kept in touch with around their hectic schedules and work.

"I...met someone, and they live in Greensborough."

"Greensborough... Greensborough... Is that the town in the hills, about an hour from here?"

Bit further, but, yeah, you get the drift.

"Yes, it is. Well, I met someone from there and kind of...fell in love with them, and we somehow didn't work out. But I'm still in so deep. Now I'm not sure what to do. Should I stay in Melbourne, take up a surgical residency, and bury myself for the next six years. Or..."

The professor laughed. "Or you could move to Greensborough and take up residency at their hospital and learn from Doctor Sarah Tomas, another former student of mine."

"You know Doctor Sarah?"

Small world.

"Of course. She was brilliant. You would do well learning from her, and although I'd have to check, the hospital she runs is accredited. We could organise for you to split your time between Melbourne hospitals and the Greensborough one. If you wanted to move there. If he's worth moving for, of course... "

Oh God, he is. He is so worth it.

But did he dare?

Yeah he probably did...because even with all the crap, the domineering attitude, and the lack of acceptance about him being a man, Reagan had felt safe, wanted, desired, and loved. Everything he'd ever needed in his life.

Grayson may have freaked out about the Rogue attack, and that was understandable. But he hadn't needed to call things off like he did.

Reagan could be killed at any point in time, which he'd practically proved last week. He could fall asleep at the wheel again and die in a car accident, Rogues weren't the only way to go down. And Grayson should have known that.

Reagan stretched out his hand and grabbed hold of the professor's arm.

"Do you really think that would work? I don't want to throw away my future...for..."

A guy who might not even want me.

His shoulder ached with the reminder of the wolf he carried every day. Mocking him. Those blue eyes burning with need. How was Grayson surviving without him?

The professor smiled kindly, his old face crinkling up like a newspaper. "Throw away a career for love? A family? You could do a lot worse, Reagan. But I don't think you need to choose between the two. If you want, I can make some phone calls today and find out for you. I wouldn't mind contacting Sarah, find out how she's been keeping."

Reagan's eyebrows rose high on his forehead.

"Would you really do that? I mean, I have a few other things to sort out too. My house. My overseas trip."

"Of course I don't mind calling her, and there are solutions to almost all of life's problems. Trips can be postponed, houses rented out. How can I get into contact with you?"

Reagan grabbed a piece of paper and jotted down his cell phone and email for the professor. "Here, Professor, and thank you. You're right. Call me anytime."

With a nod, the man walked away, and Reagan was left with a racing heart and butterflies fluttering in his belly.

Was it possible? The life he wanted?

Grayson. A home. His career, too?

There was only one way to find out, and he'd never been one to give up on his dreams. He hadn't before and he wasn't about to now.

"Did Doctor Sarah say what she needed, Megan?" Grayson spoke into his cell. His sister had called with the news he had to get down to the hospital right away and he had no idea what it was about.

"No, but she sounded pretty frazzled. Keep your wits about you, brother."

Grayson hung up and pushed his legs harder to reach the hospital quicker, several scenarios racing through his head.

What if something bad had happened? Had a Rogue been found? Had someone been injured? They still hadn't found the Rogues that attacked their town a month ago, although they'd searched high and low.

He scratched at his arm, the tingling pain of his lost birthmark still aching ever since Reagan had left.

It kept him awake in the dark hours, haunting him with what he'd lost. He barely slept and he'd lost weight. Everyone was noticing how terrible he looked, but he couldn't do anything about his health. His life-source—his heart—was missing.

He pushed through the front door of the hospital and looked left and right, sniffing the air for danger. Orange. Sweet...spicy... orange.

His cock stirred in his jeans. He started running.

No way. It couldn't be.

He burst into Doctor Sarah's office with his heart hammering in his chest and the gasp of anticipation in his throat.

"Reagan!"

His mate looked better than ever, dressed in a pair of blue jeans, white t-shirt, and a doctor's coat hanging open. Reagan smiled at him with carefree regard. "Hey, Grayson. What's up?"

His jaw dropped, he was lucky it didn't hit the floor. "Ah... what are you doing here?"

The heat was spreading through his body like a fever. Starting in his gut, it moved up his chest and into his arms. Sweat was beading on his face.

Grab him. Now.

His wolf howled inside him, and Grayson's knees gave out. He staggered to the closest chair and fell into it.

He hadn't sensed his wolf this whole month. Barely shifting long enough to fulfil the full moon ritual, he had withdrawn immediately afterwards.

"Doctor Sarah?" Reagan called out, and Sarah came into the room, clipboard in hand.

"Oh, Grayson, good, you're here. I'm glad you came so quickly. I know you're in charge of finances for the hospital and I wanted you to sign off on me hiring a new doctor. An intern, actually. I believe you've already met?"

She lifted a quizzical brow, her professional tone at odds with the massive smile on her face.

"Ah...yes. Whatever you think is in the best interest of the pack." Sarah was hiring Reagan to work at the hospital? Had he missed something?

She thrust the paperwork in front of him, and Grayson signed every dotted line she pointed to, his whole body vibrating with sensation.

His mate was back... His mate was back!

When it was finally done, Sarah bowed herself out of the room and the door shut behind her with a soft click that echoed in the quiet. Grayson reached out and grabbed Reagan's hand, a fission of energy pulsing through his body as he dragged his mate closer.

"You came back."

"Yeah."

Grayson tugged, and Reagan fell into his lap, his arms going around Grayson's neck. Grayson's heart soared with happiness. He knew he should be mad at this change in plans and push Reagan away again for his own good. But he couldn't. He couldn't be that selfless again. His loneliness was tearing him and his wolf apart.

"Are you back to stay? What about your trip?"

And how had the Betas who were meant to be minding Reagan not reported this to him?

Reagan sat up straighter, his eyes narrowing on Grayson like a laser. "The trip's been postponed for a while, and whether or not I'm staying depends on if you want me or not. I assume you haven't replaced me already?"

"Ha!" Grayson choked out a laugh. "I told you there would be no one else for me. I've missed you like a cut off limb."

It felt so incredibly right to have Reagan back in his arms. His stomach growled. Hungry. His appetite was back.

And for more than food.

"Are you over the whole, we can't have kids, thing?"

Grayson nodded vigorously. "Yes. I'm so sorry I picked a fight about that. We have a whole pack to protect and look after. We don't need children of our own."

Some of the rigid tension went out of Reagan's body.

"So, why'd you send me away then? Really?"

"I thought it was better if you were away from this world. The Rogues almost killed you, and I couldn't handle the idea of you dying while in my care. That would be just... I couldn't..."

He didn't finish the sentence, tears starting to tingle in his eyes. He coughed and cleared his throat as emotion threatened to fill him up. He stared deep into his mate's brown eyes. "I'm sorry I pushed you away. That was wrong. You belong here. With me."

Reagan pressed a gentle kiss to his lips. "I have to tell you though, if you lock me in that house again, you better not go to sleep... You'll wake up missing an appendage or two."

He laughed, his heart light. Who would have thought a threat like that would make him so happy? "It will never happen again. I promise."

Grayson cupped Reagan's face and pulled him in close, tasting his lips and running his hands all over his mate's hot, hard body.

Reagan pulled away. "You better not push me away again either. I'm strong, stronger than you think. And I want to be here, with you and your family. I want to be a part of that, a family again. You don't understand what that would mean to me."

Grayson groaned and stood up, keeping hold of Reagan's hand. "Well, let's go see our family and organise our mating, then. Time to make you part of the pack."

He pulled Reagan out of the room and along the corridor.

"Megan will have a field day with this."

Reagan's beautiful smile filled his vision as they wove through the town together.

If Reagan wanted a family...he'd give him one.

AARON'S MATE

THE BOROUGH BOYS SERIES
BOOK 2

PROLOGUE

Despite the hunger clawing at his gut, Jordan took another sip of water and forced himself to remain seated. He'd eaten everything on his plate, and as much more as he could get away with, without anyone noticing.

He was still starving.

How did the other Omegas eat so little? How did he used to be satisfied with practically nothing in his stomach?

"Can I join you?"

Jordan looked up and blinked at the man standing over them. It was the new comer to Greensborough, Reagan, standing next to their table. The one they all said was linked to Grayson in some way. He looked like a Beta in size but he certainly didn't act with any deference to the Alphas.

Human. Obviously.

Reagan didn't wait for them to reply, he just sat with an abruptness that indicated that he was angry and began eating his the firemountain of food. Meat and more meat. Pasta...

Damn, I wish I could eat that much!

Reagan picked up a juicy chicken leg and took a big bite. "I'm Reagan. How you doin'?"

Jordan stared at Reagan, comparing how he currently looked to how he'd been yesterday. He looked bigger than he had last night somehow. Taller, even. How was that possible?

He glanced over at Elliot and Travis. What were they meant to say to him?

Elliot cleared his throat, "I'm Elliot... I'm okay. How are you?"

"Great... except for those jackasses over there." He nodded his head towards the Alpha table, his face tight and angry.

Jordan frowned at the new comer and clenched his jaw. That was no way to talk about the men who kept them all safe.

Elliot trembled beside him and Jordan worked hard not to roll his eyes. Such a classic Omega. "You shouldn't speak like that about the Alphas."

Reagan grunted and shook his head. "I'll do whatever I want. I'm mated to Grayson now."

Oh my God, he's what?

"Excuse me...?" Elliot crept closer, his hand sneaking out across the table as though to touch Reagan.

"I'm mated to Grayson. Not that I meant to of course. I didn't know that fucking him would make *that* happen."

Jordan gasped at the language and the images Reagans words invoked. That would mean that Grayson was...

Reagan rolled his eyes and made a *pfft* style noise, his frustration obvious.

Jordan's head spun with the consequences of what this all meant. But surely it was impossible. Wasn't it? Reagan couldn't be mated to an Alpha. He was human, and a male! That wasn't how it was meant to be. How would the Alpha line continue?

Reagan glared at them all, angry lines appearing around his

deep set eyes. "What's your problem? Don't like the fact one of the Alphas is gay?"

Reagan tore off some more chicken with his teeth, washing it down with a nearby beer. He was awkward and big, moving as though he weren't used to his own limbs.

If only you knew. Silly human.

Elliot shook his head. "Of course not, I'm... gay. If that's what you humans, call it. That's not a problem here; it has never been."

Unless you're my mother. She beat that message into me every day. Being gay, being born without a birthmark was wrong. Wrong, wrong, wrong.

Reagan looked away for a moment, obviously struggling with something, before he turned back. Anger flared in his nostrils. "Well, Marcus sure thinks it is! He just made it very clear that I've destroyed any chance Grayson had of having a family." His voice choked on the last words, and he cleared it with a rough cough.

Poor guy. Marcus is a twat.

He had to speak up.

"Reagan, I'm Jordan. You're wrong about one thing. Marcus is a mean and selfish Alpha... that's not why we're so shocked. There hasn't been an all-male Alpha pairing in generations."

Travis leant forward. "There are whispers within the Omegas that the original leaders of our pack were all males, but no one knows for sure."

Jordan turned away as Travis explained their fairy tales. It was something the Omegas clung to. The hope that they weren't an aberration, weak or wrong. That they were an essential, and indeed strong, part of the pack. But it was a fantasy. One that his own friends bought into. The idea that a big strong Alpha might be able to love and protect them.

Not him. He didn't believe any of it.

Why would my mother hate me so much if those stories were really true?

Reagan's eyes went wide as he looked around their small circle. "Really? Do you know if any of the other guys are male paired too?"

Not in the Alphas. And if I have any control over my destiny, there won't be any more.

Jordan looked away and stared down at his hands. This was getting harder not to react to. "Ah no."

He couldn't look up. If only they knew that one of the other Alphas was destined to be mated to a male, too. How horrible the pack would think that was!

"What's with that?" Reagan poked him in the arm with his finger.

What?

He didn't respond outside, but inside his stomach churned and acid burned the back of his throat. What could he say to Reagan about this?

"Jordan's got a secret."

His head snapped up and he glared at his friend.

Traitor!

"Shut up, Travis."

Reagan looked between them both. "Shut up about what? What's going on?"

"Show him, Jordan," Elliot said, nudging him with his elbow.

"No," Jordan barked at his friends. How dare they betray him with the *one thing* he couldn't share? And when they promised they'd never tell.

He took a deep breath to steady himself. He didn't have to tell this stranger anything. Ridiculous notion. He pushed himself to his feet and prepared to leave and get away from a man who was mated to one of their Alphas.

It was far too upsetting. He'd tried so hard to hold back, despite the deep ache, the pain. Just so the man who was meant to be his mate could move on, find a suitable woman. He hadn't wanted to weaken the line, and yet here it was. Fate come to kick him in the arse again. Grayson was male mated, too!

"Hey, come here for a sec." Reagan reached over and grabbed him by the arm, the pressure hard and tight. Un-breakingly strong.

What the fuck...?

Jordan grabbed at Reagan's hand to push him off, but the bigger man just pulled him closer and yanked up the hem of his grey t-shirt.

No!

Reagan stared at Jordan's chest with wide, unblinking eye. Heat flamed in his cheeks. He was totally exposed. As was his secret. Maybe the human wouldn't know what it was?

"What the..."

Reagan's gaze flicked up to him and Jordan saw the dawning of understanding. The human recognised the mark? Oh shit!

"Hey! Leave me alone!" Jordan clenched his fingers tightly into a ball and slammed his fist into Reagan's shoulder as hard as he could.

"Ow."

The Alpha's mate let him go and he spun on the ball of his foot, sprinting through the Hall and out into the cool air.

His heart raced and his breathing was too fast. He was practically panting as his throat burned.

He'd known this day would come, and he hadn't planned for it.

What an idiot!

What on earth was he going to do?

Reagan had seen his mark. The huge, dark, sprawling mass that spread over his chest and abdomen.

It was still relatively new to him, too. He'd been born without a birthmark. Unusual, but not unheard of for a Omega, homosexual wolf.

Despite people saying it was still normal, his mother had not liked it. She had beat him regularly, reminding him of how unworthy he was of being a wolf. How she should have birthed a girl.

His mother had died when he was a teenager, and how ironic it had been that a few years after her death, on his twenty-first birthday, he had begun to develop his mark. Just as their females did.

How right his mother had been. He was wrong, oh so wrong.

But no one had seen it and luckily, unlike the women, no one had looked for it on him. He took every precaution to keep his mark covered, or bandaged. Anything to make sure no one recognised it for what it was.

Because if someone saw it and told the man who had the matching mark, he'd have to bond with him. And that couldn't happen. Fate had made a mistake. A HUGE mistake. He couldn't be fated to be mated to... him.

Jordan gulped down the fear that was threatening to strangle him and ran straight to his share house. He frantically searched the house, looking around for anything he might need.

Clothes! He begun stuffing his few pairs of jeans into a bag. A tank and a long sleeved top. The only one he had. Socks. He had one jumper. He grabbed it and pulled on over his head. He had to get out of here.

If the legends were true, and everyone in town believed them to be so, then he was the destined mate of Aaron Tanner. The oldest, most thoughtful and strong of the five Alphas in his generation.

Jordan zipped up the tote bag and let a long sigh release from his lips as he thought about the cruel situation he'd been put it.

He ached for Aaron. Like the earth needed the sun.

But it was not meant to be. Someone had seriously fucked up if they thought he had what it took to be an Alpha's mate.

Jordan grabbed his bag, all the money he had and the keys to an old car they shared. Hopefully the guys would forgive him for leaving like this.

He'd make it up to them somehow.

He stole into the night, got in his car and drove away as fast as he could.

Away from Greensborough. Away from his pack. And away from the mate that he'd never know.

CHAPTER
ONE

"Hey! Hey! I know you..."

Oh, damn it all to hell!

Jordan wanted to run. He could feel the adrenaline jolt along his veins and his knees shook with his anticipated escape.

But he couldn't move. Couldn't run.

He *needed* this job.

He forced himself to turn around from where he was making coffee, hot frothing milk over flowing from the jug he held. He put it down and lifted his gaze to the man in front of him.

He knew the voice... damn it.

It *was* him.

"It is you..." Reagan breathed out. His mouth half open in surprise and his big buff body barely contained in the singlet he wore.

"You're so big now." Jordan couldn't help saying, it was just so damn obvious.

Then his gaze dropped away. Heat flushing his cheeks like an open oven door.

Reagan chuckled. "I know..." He leaned closer and dropped his voice so that only Jordan could hear. "That Alpha sperm is full of steroids, I swear. A couple of doses and I'm ready for Mr. Australia."

Jordan coughed out a laugh, the images the playful human invoked too funny to contain. It was the first time he'd laughed in weeks.

If that was true, Jordan really should have stayed where he was and got a few doses himself. He was wasting away not being able to feed himself properly.

"What are you doin' here, Jordan?"

"What do you mean?"

He slid back into his place in front of the coffee machine. The money he'd had when he left the 'Borough hadn't even lasted him a few days. Luckily, he'd found this cafe after a week of searching and they'd given him a job and a couch to crash on at night. It certainly wasn't home, but it was out of the rain.

Reagan fixed him with a stare and then rolled his eyes dramatically. "Are you serious? What are you doing out of Greensborough?"

"What are *you* doing out of Greensborough?" He threw back at Reagan.

Why aren't you snuggled up with your big Alpha?

He focused on finishing the cappuccino and placed it on the bench. One of the waitresses came and took it to the appropriate table.

Reagan coughed as though embarrassed, his eyes sliding sideways as he clapped his hands together. "Um... well, Grayson and I had a bit of a falling out after the whole fire thing, but once I finish my exams I'll go back. Beat the dumb guy with his own fist if I have to."

A huge smile lifted his lips at the image. An Alpha being dominated like that? Oh, how he'd love to see that.

His manager walked up and Jordan jumped.

"Yes, Harry?"

"You're due a twenty-minute break if you want to take it now?"

Harry nodded towards Reagan and Jordan opened his mouth to say *no, I'll wait.*

"That'd be great. Thanks. We'll go get some lunch." Reagan said, cutting him off.

What could he say to that? He didn't want to go with Reagan.

"Let's go, Jordan."

Reagan tugged on his arm and Jordan shrugged him off, grabbing his wallet as he went. If he had to go, then he would. But seriously, the guy needed to back off.

"Would you stop doing that? You keep trying to manhandle me."

Reagan shrugged, opening the door to leave. "You need manhandling, it's as obvious as the day is long."

Jordan gaped at him but Reagan just ignored him as they strolled along the street, finding another small café.

"Let's stop here and eat. I'm starving."

Jordan nodded and followed Grayson's mate inside. Reagan had a very strong aura about him, and it was impossible to ignore him. Everything in Jordan's Omega brain wanted to obey.

They sat down in the café and he stared at the menu. He didn't have much money...

"My treat. You better eat. You look like a bag of bones."

"I couldn't do that..."

"Fine. I'll order."

Reagan called someone over and proceeded to order half the menu, times two.

"I can't eat all that!"

Reagan regarded him with shrewd eyes. "I think you can. Let's see."

As Reagan stared at him, the silence stretched. Jordan looked away and down at his hands, his belly tightening with fear as the moment ticked on. What was Reagan going to do? Would he tell Aaron he was here?

"Talk Jordan. Now."

The command in Reagan's voice made him look up. "What do you want me to say?"

"I want you to tell me what you're doing down here. I was under the impression you'd never even left the Borough before."

That was true, but...

A memory checked in and Jordan sat up straighter in his chair. "Did you say something about a fire before. What fire?"

"The Rogues drew the Alphas and Betas away from the town, and then set fire to the houses."

"They what?"

His heart began to pound, hitting his sternum with a sickening thud. Protocol would dictate that the Omegas and the women would be locked in their fail safe homes. Did that mean that the Rogues tried to kill everyone?

"The Alphas locked us all in and then the Rogues set fire to the houses. No one was seriously hurt, thank God, because Grayson turned everyone around and came back to the Borough, saving us all."

His mouth dropped open.

Dear God. What a tragedy that could have been.

"Oh. My. God." All his friends… they could have been killed. And he would have been down in Melbourne, and not even known.

Tears burned his throat and tingled in his eyes, guilt, a well-known emotion choking him.

"I'm still pretty pissed off at Grayson for locking us in, then breaking it off because he felt guilty about it." He growled, a deep disgruntled noise as he shook his head. "But I've got exams to concentrate on first. Then I'll deal with my mate."

Jordan swallowed hard, reaching for the water that had been placed in front of him. If he kept breathing, he wouldn't break down.

All those helpless people… the Alphas are there to protect us, yet that was used against them. How horrible…

Reagan stared straight at him again with those penetrating eyes and Jordan avoided his gaze, the weight of his judgement heavy on Jordan's shoulders.

"Speaking of mates, Jordan… are you planning on going back to Aaron at some point, or are you just going to let him suffer?"

Damn. He did read my mark correctly.

Part of him had hoped that Reagan hadn't seen Aaron's mark, so wouldn't know who his mark was matching to. What were the chances, that as a new arrival, and a human, that he'd seen Aaron half naked?

Obviously pretty good.

Their food arrived and the waitress had trouble placing everything down, filling the small square table with plates.

He couldn't possibly eat this food. There was so much.

"Reagan I can't…"

"Shut up and eat. I have money, so don't sweat it. I also have half an hour to beat some sense into you, so start talking."

Jordan dropped his gaze and reached for the nearest thing. A large, greasy beef burger.

He wrapped his hands around it and lifted the meat to his mouth, saliva dripping down from his lips. He sunk his teeth into the bun and groaned, the flavours flooding his mouth.

Oh, wow.

He swallowed hard and his stomach growled for more. He continued to eat, quickly, swallowing the whole lot too soon. The muscles in his gut stretched and ached.

He'd never eaten that much, that fast. But he was hungry.

He looked up at Reagan, who was staring at him, not having eaten a bite himself.

Reagan pointed to the chicken and salad wrap with a side of deep fried chips. "Keep going."

Jordan swallowed the lump in his throat. He looked around. He'd never eaten like this. A Omega didn't need so much food. His body was small and lean. He couldn't possibly.

Reagan leaned forward. "Jordan. I ate before. I just came to get a coffee from your shop so that I could keep going with my exam study. I know what you are, and as a true Alpha's mate, you need to eat." He sat back in his chair as though waiting for his words to sink in. "I know how I felt when I first met Grayson. The hunger, the need to eat, the muscle I put on. So get going, or I'll tie you down and make you."

Jordan stared at Reagan, his words hitting as hard as a cane across his back.

An Alpha's mate.

But he wasn't. He couldn't be.

But even as the thoughts hit and the shame enveloped his mind, his body followed Reagan's orders. He picked up the bowl of chips and began chomping on the fatty, salty goodness.

He tried to push the bowl away after a few handfuls but he couldn't, unable to stop eating now that he'd begun.

"I'm not an Alpha's mate Reagan. You're mistaken," he got out between bites.

Reagan laughed, really laughed. The rolling deep tones hitting Jordan deep in the stomach. He wasn't fooled by the levity. There was a hard glint in Reagan's eye he'd seen before. He wasn't to be messed with, that was obvious.

His hand hit ceramic and he looked down. The chips were gone.

No way.

"Drink the milkshake. I got vanilla and chocolate. Have both."

He eyed off the drinks. So much...

He picked up the chocolate one, hypnotised by Reagan's no-nonsense Alpha attitude.

Just stop when you feel full.

He put his lips around the straw and sucked. Creamy chocolate slid into his mouth, making him moan once again.

"Where are you staying, Jordan?"

Jordan slurped the drink as he finished the whole glass, a wave of bliss sweeping through his brain, wiping out all thoughts except how good he felt.

"At the coffee shop."

Reagan pulled out his wallet, grabbed something out of it, then slid a silver key across the table.

"You're staying with me from now on. I have a three-bedroom house about five minutes walk from here."

Reagan wanted him to stay at his house? Why?

"I couldn't do that."

"You are. No discussion. Here's the address."

Reagan jotted a few lines down on a napkin and pushed it over to him. With hesitant fingers, Jordan reached out for the paper and the key, his fingers clasping the cold metal and pulling it towards him.

If that was what his Alpha's mate wanted.

"Okay."

"Good. Now, I've got ten minutes until I have to get back to study, so if you don't mind... eat!"

CHAPTER TWO

Jordan couldn't stop the chuckle that rose as he dove back into the waiting sandwiches, pies and pastries. He kept going, eating more than half the food Reagan had ordered, before stopping, his stomach bulging beneath his shirt.

He put a hand to his belly, finally feeling full. Way, way, way too full.

"I have to stop. I'm going to be sick."

Reagan called a waitress over. "Can you wrap up the rest for take away, thanks so much."

The woman took the empty plates away and came back for the rest of the food.

"I don't cook much, so we'll eat some of that tonight. What time will you be home?"

Home. What an odd way to put it. "Ah... I finish at five."

"Good. See you after that."

Reagan picked up the bill and took it to the counter to pay.

Jordan fell back in his chair.

What had just happened?

Yesterday he was wondering how he would feed himself for the rest of the month, and whether he needed to start looking for a job that was less savoury... now, he had a house, a job, and a roommate.

Was Fate finally being kind to him?

Reagan walked back to him from the counter and smiled. "And don't even think about running away. I'll set the dogs on you."

Jordan frowned and stood up. "You wouldn't call them..."

"Of course I wouldn't, as long as you come stay with me. I want to know you're safe. So, you'll come straight home to my place tonight?"

"Yes."

He'd be crazy not to take the help that was being offered, not to mention that the threat of the Alphas chasing him down was enough to make him comply.

Reagan gave him a final smile and walked away.

Jordan struggled back to work, so full and bloated he could barely stand for the first hour.

But by five o'clock he was hungry again, and he felt stronger. His head was clear and his shoulders were straight again.

He asked for some directions and made his way over to Reagan's house, excitement rippling in his belly for the first time in three weeks.

He'd missed having a family, a pack. People to talk to, to count on. It had been bloody lonely living by himself.

The napkin he held the address Reagan had given him, and as he checked the letter box to confirm he had the right place, his jaw dropped open.

Now *this* was a home.

He stepped up to the red painted door and put the key in the lock, a little surprised when it clicked open and the door swung open with a push. Reagan hadn't been kidding. He really had invited him to stay in his house.

There was a long, wide hallway leading to a bright room at the back of the house.

He stepped inside, and looked around with awe. He'd grown up in a small shack with an abusive mother and no father, in the poorest area of the pack's land. This was a dream.

Photos adorned the walls. Reagan and two older people that must have been his parents.

Wow.

He crept along the hallway and stepped into the huge kitchen at the back of the house. Marble bench tops and shining steel flashed with grace and beauty.

He didn't have a kitchen in Greensborough, although he would have loved one.

As a Omega in a large pack, he ate in the Hall every day, so he didn't technically need one. He didn't make enough money to build his own home, although he would love to. He'd cook all day long.

"Jordan, that you?" Reagan's voice called out and made him jump towards the sound.

"Yes."

Reagan's voice was coming from somewhere off to the right, and a moment later, he stepped out into the kitchen.

"You came. Great. You want a drink? A tour? That all you got?"

He looked down at the tote bag that contained every possession he owned.

"Yeah."

"Cool. Follow me. Your room is down here. There's your bathroom. I have my own, so help yourself. You want a shower?"

Jordan's heart sang with happiness. He hadn't had a proper

shower in weeks, using the coffee shop's sink and basic bathroom to wash himself.

"You have no idea how amazing that would be."

Reagan grabbed a towel out of a cupboard and threw it at him. "Here you go. Take your time. I've got one more practise exam paper to go through and then I'll meet you in the kitchen for dinner."

Reagan smiled with casual ease and headed off down the corridor again, making everything easy.

Thank you.

His knees weak with gratitude, Jordan staggered into the shower and stood beneath the hot water. He closed his eyes and groaned at the sensations pulsing through his body. It was pure bliss. He never wanted to get out.

Finally though, he knew he had to. His body cleaned from head to toe and his hair washed three times, he stepped out of the shower, dried himself and brushed his hair.

I have a set of clean clothes in here somewhere...

He opened his bag and the bathroom door swung open.

"Hey. I'm kinda craving pizza. What do you want?" Reagan's gaze dropped, straight to the birthmark that had started all this craziness.

Jordan pulled his t-shirt on and grabbed his jeans. "Just cheese, please."

"Okay. Cool."

Reagan shut the door again and Jordan breathed out a sigh. When would this jumpiness end?

He was sick of feeling on edge all the time, and he knew it was more than just getting used to people again. He'd been like this for years now. And he knew why. He was denying his body all the basic needs it had.

Food. Sex. Even sleep sometimes.

He'd managed to play around with a few of the other Omegas before his twenty-first birthday. A few quick tumbles had fulfilled a basic need and desire. He'd never really got to that, *sex is the most amazing thing on Earth* space, but he'd assumed that would come with time.

But once his mark had developed, he couldn't allow anyone to see him naked.

He'd gone without sex, without touch, for so long.

It hurt like a blow to the gut, every day.

He made his way into the kitchen and found Reagan there, cutting up some fresh salad ingredients.

"Pizza's ordered. Should be here in twenty. Come have a beer with me."

There was a couple of drinks opened on the table. Really? Alcohol wasn't very common in the 'Borough. He grabbed one and stared at it.

Why not? When in Rome.

He swigged down the cool hops and smiled at his host, trying not to flinch at the unfamiliar flavours. "This tastes great."

"You guys don't drink much, do you?"

"No. Just not in the... culture, so to speak."

And it wasn't. They drank wine sometimes, but it wasn't readily available in the 'Borough. There was already too much testosterone in the pack, and alcohol only made it worse.

They sat still for a moment and then Reagan turned to him.

"I want you to stay here as long as you want. But I need you to know that I have to leave soon. If I get my way, I'll be heading back to the Borough next week after I get my final grade. I haven't worked it all out yet, but I can't leave things as they are."

Jordan swallowed some of his beer as his wolf rose to the surface, stretching, growling, aching to be heard.

I know you want to go back, but I don't!

He pushed him down with all his might.

"You going back for good?"

"No idea. The last time I saw Grayson he pretty much said that unless I was a woman, I was useless to him."

"That wanker!" He couldn't help it. What sort of Alpha said that to his mate?

"Yep."

Jordan snorted and shook his head. How stupid was that?

"You look a lot better since lunch, Jordan. Food helps, doesn't it?"

He nodded, seeing the understanding in Reagan's eyes. "Yeah, it does. I don't know how to thank you enough for helping me."

Reagan flicked his wrist in a dismissive way. "No stress. Now, you gotta tell me what's going on. Your friends filled me in a bit on why you won't go to Aaron and show him your birthmark, but it didn't make any sense to me. But maybe I'm missing something."

Hang on...

"My friends told you... wait... did you tell Aaron that you saw my mark?"

He couldn't have... oh no...

"Yeah... well, I had to."

Anger and betrayal boiled inside of him "No! You didn't!"

He slammed his fist into the table, rattling the wood and spilling both beers.

The anger drained away just as fast as it had come as he dove for the drinks and righted them. Reagan grabbed a cloth and started mopping up the spills.

"That's what I'm talking about Jordan. You're not a Omega. No Omega has your strength or your presence. Not to mention the fact that you have a mark on you that clearly screams Aaron's mate. How can you ignore that?"

Jordan looked away from Reagan's pleading face. How to explain the mindset his mother had given him to a man who obviously had a loving family?

"Reagan, it's not... I...." hmmm. "It's not that easy. You haven't lived in our pack, nor seen the pressure the hierarchy causes those who don't fit in. I was born a Omega, an unmarked Omega, no less. I'm on the bottom of the pile. The very, very bottom. I don't deserve, nor am I capable of, running the pack." He shuddered. The very idea gave him goose bumps.

"But what about your mark? Fate? All that stuff that Grayson believes in?"

He shrugged, finishing the last of his beer and enjoying the warmth it spread through his body. Despite the fact that he knew he should be grovelling at Reagan's feet in apology for acting out in anger, he wasn't.

He had assumed, of course, that the truth would come out, otherwise, he wouldn't have run away. But finding out the worst had actually happened was harder to deal with than he'd thought it would be.

"I know our legends, Reagan. But there's been a mistake. A massive mistake. And I won't let it go any further. If Aaron can't find me, he'll pair up with someone suitable. A woman probably. An Alpha born. They'll have children, continue the line, and everyone will be happy. Then everything will go back to how it was meant to be."

The doorbell rang and he went to get up. He had a few tips from today.

"Don't think about it. Save your money for when I'm not here."

He stopped. That may be a good point.

Reagan got up and headed off to the front door, returning moments later with four boxes.

"Order enough?" He joked. There was only two of them.

Reagan opened the first box and oily, cheesy pizza smells oozed out.

Jordan groaned with hunger and Reagan pushed the box towards him.

"I always order heaps. I told you, I don't cook much, and this way I can have it cold for lunch for a week."

Jordan began eating, consuming half the large pizza before stopping for breath.

"This is so yum."

Reagan nodded, eating the rest of his meat lovers pizza as Jordan picked up another slice.

"Ok... one more question."

Jordan grabbed his fifth piece and shot his new house mate a smile. He wasn't sure if it was the beer, or the relief to be in a comfortable home, but he was feeling intoxicated. Way too relaxed. "Shoot."

"Do you hurt as much as Aaron does?"

That sucked the breath from his lungs. He let the food drop back into the box.

"Aaron's hurting?"

He knew the legends of course, but he'd managed to ignore that side of the mating curse. His pain wasn't too bad, so he assumed with Aaron being so big and powerful, he wouldn't feel anything.

"You know he is. He practically ripped me apart to get the information about you. He's in pain, literal pain, and now that he knows that you're real, and that he hasn't been imagining it, he'll wait for you to return. If you think he'll pair up with someone else after waiting twenty years for you, you're delusional."

Maybe I am...

"But I'm a male, and I'm a Omega. It would never work."

Reagan pushed another beer towards him, and chuckled softly.

"If I've learnt anything since meeting you guys, it's this. You don't fuck with Fate, Jordan. You'd be an idiot to try."

CHAPTER THREE

Aaron struggled up the hill, his body tired and sore. His joints ached, his muscles pulled and tightened like he had the flu.

Walking away from the site of his new home always made it worse. He loved his new home, he'd been building for months, before finally finishing a couple of weeks ago. However, something inside him just wasn't sitting right. Was he too far away from the pack? The town?

No... That wasn't it. He was doing the pack a service being further out. It gave the farmers and some of the pack members who wanted more land an Alpha to look over them. Make them feel safe.

Then what was it...

Jordan...

A growl rumbled through his chest, vibrating through his vocal chords from deep within his body. His wolf hurt just as much as he did and in some ways, it was probably worse for him.

A wolf needed a pack, a family, and since his father had left town and left the Alpha responsibilities to him, he had no family at all.

A shudder coursed through him as he thought of the family he could have had, he should have had. He still couldn't believe that his mate had been here, within his grasp, for years. And he hadn't stepped forward.

Why? Was he so abhorrent? Too old? Too ugly?

Sure, he was twice Jordan's age, but was that enough to turn his mate away? To make him hide, and then run?

None of it made any sense.

After Reagan had told him about Jordan, he'd searched him out, finding an empty closet, in an empty room, and a car missing.

The pain that had cracked his heart that night had almost made him cry out.

Then after the panic of the attack the Rogues had launched on them had settled down, the true ache had set in.

And he couldn't get past it.

They had to re-build everything, and morale was low within their pack.

He might have been able to move on if he knew Jordan was safe, happy somewhere else, but he wouldn't be.

He couldn't be.

Number one. The mating bond made it impossible to be happy with another. And number two. The pack didn't train their Omegas to live in the real world. They had little money and didn't care for themselves on a daily basis, so how could Jordan survive?

He cringed at the thought. A gorgeous, young, gay man with no money and no connections. His mind conjured up horrendous images that had his wolf howling inside him.

Where would he have gone? What would he be doing? Where was he living?

Aaron wiped away the tears that filled his vision, and he pushed the sadness down.

He had to get through today, and tomorrow, and the next day. And he would. He had a pack to run and a mate to wait for.

There was no choice in the matter.

A WEEK LATER, Aaron was attending a Council meeting when Grayson stepped into the room, late. Which was unusual for the other Alpha.

What was more unusual, was the state of health Grayson exuded. He was practically glowing like a pregnant woman. With Reagan gone, and pack stress high after the Rogue attack, Grayson's smile made no sense.

What was up with that?

Grayson moved around to his side of the room, the smirk on his lips undeniable.

Aaron nodded at his old friend. "Well, don't you look like the cat who ate the canary."

Grayson grinned. "Regan's back. Didn't you hear?"

Aaron's heart stuttered in his chest as jealousy crippled his gut.

"What? He came back?"

"Yes. And we've sorted all our shit out, so he's staying."

That sounded far too simple.

"Woah, congrats."

He opened his arms and Grayson hugged him tight, the power and love between them flowing through. He missed this. Perhaps he shouldn't have moved so far away.

"Reagan asked me to find you though."

"Really, how come?"

Grayson shrugged as his gaze moved around the room to the

rest of the council. They would be getting ready soon. "He wanted you to help go get some of his stuff from his old house. Not sure why, but he wants you. Do you mind?"

Aaron frowned. That was odd. But he wasn't one to go against an Alpha's mate's wishes. "Sure. When?"

"Tomorrow if that's okay? I was going to go too, but Dad's given me another job for tomorrow with the re-build. And I know Reagan's safe if he's with you."

Aaron held a hand to his heart. "I'll guard him with my life." And despite the jovial tone he put into his voice, he was completely serious.

"Good man."

The meeting began and they both tuned into what Grayson's father and the other elders were saying. He wished his own father could be a part of the Council still, but he'd stepped down ten years ago. And after all his father had suffered, he understood his need for space.

Something nagged at the back of Aaron's mind. Reagan was the one who'd found Jordan. Maybe he had more information about where he'd gone off to?

He went to sleep that night with a little hope in his heart.

If he could get his mate back, then his life would be worth living again.

"THANKS so much for helping me with my stuff, Aaron. I'll probably have to come back to put the house on the market at some stage, but I can't stand the idea of selling my parent's home yet."

Aaron smiled at Grayson's new mate. He was a nice guy and had a great strength about him. And as a doctor and a leader, he'd be a great asset to the pack.

"You don't have to sell though, do you?"

"No... as long as I make enough money to pay the bills, I can keep it for a while. Turn left here."

They turned left and then right, pulling up in front of a gorgeous house with a red door and a white picket fence.

"Wow, what a great looking house."

"Thanks, I grew up here. Come in." Reagan checked his watch as they jumped out of the trucks cabin. "My housemate will be home soon, so let's get as much packed up as possible."

"Leaving them with no furniture huh?"

Reagan laughed. "Hardly. Wait till you see."

They stepped inside and Aaron looked around, admiring the old wooden furniture and brightly lit rooms. Something tugged in his chest and his heart ached. This was a real family home. Somewhere people had been very happy and loved. This was how he wanted his house to feel.

"You have a beautiful home, Reagan."

"Thanks. Can we start in my room? I want to grab some stuff from there first."

Aaron followed Reagan through the house, grabbing what knickknacks, clothes and furniture he wanted.

There wasn't much. Not worth bringing the truck for anyway.

"This it, Reagan?"

"I've got a bit more to get in the kitchen. You want a coffee while I pack?"

Why not?

Aaron shrugged. Why was he questioning Reagan's motives when he got a day out of the 'Borough and away from the ghosts that haunted him? "Sure. I'll just put this stuff away. Be back in a sec."

He jogged out to the truck. Packed the photos and bedding

away and headed back into the lovely warm kitchen, a familiar scent tugging at his nostrils.

"What's that?" He sniffed again.

"What's what?" Reagan asked, putting a huge coffee cup down in front of him.

"That smell... it's almost like..." It was getting stronger, sweeter. Like butterscotch. He'd only ever smelled that once before.

It was Jordan's scent.

He swung round and stared at Reagan. "Do you know where he is?"

Reagan's lips curled up too much at the sides and Aaron jumped out of his chair, grabbing Reagan by the arms.

"If you do, you have to tell me. You have to."

"Aaron. Take your hands off me." Reagan's mouth tightened into a grimace as he grabbed Aaron's arms and pushed back hard.

He wasn't any competition for Aaron's strength but he willed himself to let go of Grayson's mate. Reagan hadn't done any harm.

That responsibility lay solely on the man who smelled like butterscotch. A man who's face he didn't know.

The front door opened and they both turned towards the hallway.

That smell... Jordan's smell. Butterscotch.

Aaron's heart began to pound. Slowly. Powerfully. Filling every blood vessel in his body as he waited for his mate to step through the door.

A young man stepped into the room and Aaron was struck with how attractive he was. Just how Reagan had originally described him. Young, thin, and striking. Dark hair cut short on one side and blazing blue eyes.

"Hey Reagan. Thanks for the message you left with my boss. Sorry I'm late, work was crazy..."

Jordan's words cut off as he stepped through the doorway into the light filled kitchen.

Aaron's heart leapt in his chest as Jordan's blue eyes locked with his.

They all froze. Time slowed down. Aaron couldn't move. His body felt like it was encased in iced. Solid. Cold. Unmoving.

Then he saw it. The shift and twitch of Jordan's muscles as he readied himself to run.

No!

He broke free of whatever invisible bonds held him and leaped just as Jordan turned to leave. He wrapped his arms around his mate, dragging him backwards until he'd pulled them both into the lounge room once more.

"Get off me!"

Aaron flung his struggling mate away so Jordan didn't hurt himself, then stood in front of the door. Blocking the path to the exit. He was breathing hard but he didn't take his eyes off the man in front of him.

"You can't run again. And if you hide, I will find you."

Jordan squeaked, his lower lip trembling a little.

Aaron softened, letting his clenched fists relax and his shoulders slump.

Reagan moved around him and pulled Jordan closer. "You're scaring him, Aaron. Stop."

A growl rolled out of Aaron's vocal chords as blind anger tore through his head. "Take your hands off him."

Reagan let go and stepped away. Not too far, but enough to allow Aaron to calm down. Reagan was no threat to either of them, he realised.

His wolf was too close to the surface, he could feel it in the shimmer of his skin, the aggression racing through his blood.

Reagan raised his hands up. "How bout we all sit down and chat about this?"

Aaron glared at him. "You knew."

Reagan, the smart arse rolled his eyes. "Of course, I knew. Why do you think I dragged you down the mountain? And when you realise that I helped your mate get off the streets, and re-united you both, I expect a fucking apology for this ridiculous behaviour."

Jordan swiped out with a hand, whacking Reagan in the shoulder. "Not from me you won't. How could you betray me like this?"

What?

"Excuse me?" He shouted at his mate. "You run off on me. Breaking every code, law, and fucking... respect of our people, and you dare to say that to a person who helped you!"

Jordan had the good grace to bow his head but Aaron snorted and grunted some more. Fate had better not have given him some spoilt little shit as a mate.

I will not be impressed.

His mind was steam rolling over any good sense he had. Reagan was right, they should sit down and sort it all out calmly.

But fuck that!

"I haven't waited twenty-five years for my mate to have him run off on me! What? Am I too old, too ugly for you?"

Jordan's head snapped up and his eyes went wide, his beautiful lips parting in surprise. "No... no. What are you talking about?"

He is way too thin and fragile looking. Why would Fate give him a mate like this?

"Well, I have to assume I disgust you in some way. Why else would you run off in the middle of the night? Leaving the only home you've ever known..." And if he put all this together right, "and what, living on the streets? What sort of monster do you think I am that you'd settle for that instead of me?"

His throat constricted and he coughed out the emotion sitting on his chest. It felt as though an elephant had pressed his foot to Aaron's sternum, but seeing as there was only the three of them in the room, his imagination was obviously running over time.

Jordan took a few steps closer to him and the scent of butterscotch made his mouth water.

Woah, that's powerful.

No misunderstanding the mating scent on him. Why hadn't he ever smelled it at the Hall?

The Omegas sit so far away.

"No, no, you don't understand, I..." He stopped and held his hands up in placation, turning around as though asking Reagan for help.

"Don't look at me." Reagan said. "This is your beef. I'm a human with an Alpha werewolf mate. If I can work out my shit to be with Grayson, you'll do it easy. At least you understand and actually get all that..." Reagan waved his hand to encompass them and Aaron had to smile.

Reagan was right. They did have that at least. But then again, it made the betrayal even worse. Jordan knew what he was running away from. Reagan had not.

He took a deep breath and let it out very slowly. What to do? He could not, and would not, let his mate go. But how to make him stay?

"Jordan, I'll make you a deal. Stay one week with me. Explain to me why you want to go against our mating, and at the end of the week, if you want to go, I'll set you up somewhere you can be safe. A long way from here. At least then I'll have the chance to pick another mate and get on with my life."

It hurt to say and the look on Jordan's face was priceless, and complicated. There was joy and sadness, fear and excitement. The poor guy looked more mixed up than Aaron himself.

"Why?" Jordan's voice was small as he asked a question Aaron was not going to answer truthfully.

He was hoping that if Jordan got to know him, then he'd change his mind and stay. Because for whatever stupid reasons Jordan had, they were obviously strong enough to make him run from a safe place into an extremely dangerous one.

It was a gamble, but the only one he had.

Despite the fact that their mating looked doomed, he believed in his people. He trusted Fate. This was not a mistake.

When Jordan didn't respond, just stood there looking all sexy and rumpled and pulling on every nerve in Aaron's body, he let his eyebrows drop. "Because you owe that to me. And you know it."

He stared Jordan down and the Omega dropped his head.

Aaron didn't want to use his hierarchy and power to get what he needed, but dammit, if Jordan could run off in the middle of the night... he'd do it again.

"Swear to me you'll stay until this time next week. No running away. No sneaking off. No lying."

"Yes, Alpha."

Aaron's heart cracked a little at the sight of his mate being so submissive. There was a time and a place for obedience, but this was the last place he expected to see it.

Reluctantly given especially.

He looked towards Reagan who was staring at him with a hard look. Reagan gave him a nod that seemed to say, *Don't give up. This is best for both of you.*

"All right. Reagan, you ready to head back to Greensborough?"

"Yep. Might just clear out the fridge a bit since we won't be back for a while, but yeah. Let's go."

Within the hour they were back on the road. Reagan sat in the front with him and Jordan squashed himself into the small seat behind them.

He was taking his mate home. He should be elated. All his dreams had come true. But instead it felt so wrong. So very, very wrong.

~

THE DRIVE back to Greensborough was painful for Jordan for two reasons. One, because he'd stubbornly chosen to sit in an awkward position in half a chair behind the passenger seat. And two, because no one spoke, the entire time.

Jordan had rarely felt more uncomfortable and that was saying something considering the family like he'd grown up with.

"We're almost there! Awesome." Reagan was practically jiggling on the spot to get out of the truck and back to Grayson.

And I have to explain to everyone why I ran away. Fan-fucking-tastic.

"I'll drop you off, Reagan, then take Jordan home."

Aaron dropped Reagan off at Grayson's townhouse that was covered with tarps and scaffolding.

Woah. Look at all the damage.

He couldn't help gasping as he stared around at the houses. All of them had sustained injuries. Walls were gaping, roofs were missing. Thank goodness the weather was good or they'd all be camped in the Hall.

Aaron unloaded the few things Reagan had obviously collected from the house and walked him to the door.

Jordan waved goodbye and assessed his situation.

He had to move. And despite the fact that part of his stubborn personality wanted him to stay squashed behind the chair where no one could see him, his feet and arse were numb, and that would not bode well for when he needed to walk.

When Aaron got back into the truck, he had managed to climb into Reagan's vacant chair and stretch out his legs. The blood was slowly flowing back into this limbs, but the weird tingling pain was quite disconcerting!

Ouch.

"You ready to go home?" Aaron asked him, his amazing smell filling the cabin and making Jordan tremble.

He nodded and wrapped his arms around himself to stop his body from shaking.

How was he supposed to hold back from Aaron now that they were so close? His mate was obviously going to pursue him over the next week and try to change his mind about leaving.

They drove through the town and Jordan saw his old house. It looked undamaged by the attacks. Thank God.

He flinched as they got closer. Travis and Elliot were going to be pissed off about him leaving.

And you didn't bring the car back! Shit.

"My house is that one." He pointed to the old mud brick home they rented, expecting the truck to slow down.

Instead, Aaron's head stayed straight, and the truck continued along the road, leaving Greensborough.

"Where are we going?"

"Home."

And where is that?

He didn't have long to wait, a beautiful cottage surrounded by a wooden fence coming into view.

That can't be it.

It was so tiny, tranquil, and perfect.

Not at all what he'd expected for the big Alpha to choose to live in. It was new too, and rather picturesque.

Aaron pulled up outside the home and jumped out, coming around to Jordan's side of the truck and opening the door for him.

"This is my house. Come on. Jump out."

He held out both of his arms and Jordan fell into them, unable to dis-obey a direct command.

Heat swamped him and arousal curled up inside his body like a long lost friend. Aaron's breath caressed his lips and Jordan stretched up to meet them.

Aaron pulled away and took his hand. "Let's go."

Disappointment slammed into Jordan as he was tugged inside the house.

Don't sulk. You don't want him to kiss you, remember?

Yeah, right.

They stepped inside the little house and Jordan let out a sigh as beauty and warmth surrounded him in a tight cocoon.

"Wow."

"You like it?" Aaron's voice sounded uncertain as he circled Jordan.

Jordan could only nod as he took in each detail of the house. The country style kitchen, with its wooden bench tops and stainless steel appliances. It was like a magazine picture in its quaintness and perfection.

There was even an open fire place and a plush rug, just waiting for the right couple to crawl all over it, on a cold winter's night.

"You'll stay here with me while we sort all this out."

Jordan stared at the man destined to be his mate. "Where do I sleep?"

Aaron stomped across the floor boards and threw open a door with an aggravated flair.

"The spare rooms in here. Go for it."

He moved into the other bedroom and slammed the door shut.

Jordan trembled and let his body have its way. He slithered to the floor and wrapped his arms around his knees.

He didn't want to be here. He wanted to go home. But he didn't have a home anymore and with Reagan the traitor dobbing him in, he didn't have the friends he thought he did either.

He grimaced at the thought.

Why had he trusted a human like that?

He should have known better.

He glanced towards the front door and for a brief moment considered running. Again.

How far would you get?

He let a long sigh flow out of his body and he hugged his legs tighter. He couldn't do it. He'd practically promised he wouldn't, and how far would he get with no car anyway?

One of the bedroom doors opened and Jordan looked towards the kitchen. Aaron had stepped back into the room, his eyes narrowed. "It's late and I'm exhausted. There's food in the fridge if you're hungry. Otherwise, I'll see you in the morning."

Jordan nodded and bit his lip. Aaron sounded angry at him and it made him want to dig a hole in the front yard and bury himself in it.

Some Alpha's mate you make!

A groan rolled through the big Alpha with a tortured strength that echoed around the room.

"For God's sake, don't do that!"

"Don't do what?" Jordan wrapped his arms around himself and tried not to crawl into a ball and sob. An Alpha mad at him was bad enough, but his body recognised Aaron as his mate, and to hear his tones so harsh was as painful as a knife into his spine.

"Bite your lip, all sexy like that. I'll pick you up and put you straight into my bed if you keep tempting me like that."

The images Aaron's words invoked were pure bliss after the pain of his recent rejection. A moan slipped past Jordan's lips before he could stop it. It had been so long since anyone had touched him, and to feel Aaron against him would be the sweetest kind of torture.

Aaron froze, his nostrils flaring like a bull in heat and then he moved. Storming across the space and scooping Jordan up into his arms.

Jordan went willingly. Clinging to the huge man as Aaron carried him into his bedroom with a few fast strides.

"Get naked. Now."

Aaron dropped him down to the floor and Jordan couldn't comply fast enough. He knew that doing this would confuse him and make it so much harder to fight against their need for each other later. But as the blur of lust clouded his brain further, he let go of all resistance and flung himself into the path of danger.

Jordan ripped off his café uniform of black t-shirt and black pants, tripping over himself to get out of his shoes and socks.

He fell and landed on his knees, gasping in pain as his naked body bruised with the effort of doing what his Alpha told him to do.

Jordan looked up, and stopped moving. His mouth starting to water as he stared at the man mountain in front of him.

Aaron was magnificent.

His mouth fell open as heat spread through his core.

Aaron's body was huge and bulky, his muscles shining with good health and strength as he stood naked before him.

And between his legs...

Dear God in Heaven...

"Please..."

Jordan could see nothing but the flesh before him. He lifted his arms and beckoned Aaron closer with his hands. Aaron took the two steps that separated them and a flush of pure pleasure rushed over him.

Before him was the most beautiful cock he'd ever seen.

Thick, long, perfect. The veins bulging as the large head turned an even darker shade of red as Jordan stared at it.

And it was already hard and pointing straight at him.

Jordan wrapped a hand around the smooth shaft and glanced up at Aaron's face.

His eyes bypassed the huge birthmark that stretched across Aaron's chest and rested upon his green gaze.

Aaron didn't move, he was as still as a statue.

Time stretched and Jordan's limbs began to quiver as his own cock throbbed with need. He licked his lips and bent forward, taking the swollen, red head into his mouth.

Salty perfection slid across his tongue as Aaron's warm cock passed between his lips.

His eyes slid closed as he let pleasure flow through his whole body. He moaned at the perfection of the feeling and began to move back and forward, taking him in as far as he could and then popping back up again. He pulled off and Aaron groaned as though his heart had been ripped out, the big Alpha grabbing him by the hair and pulling him back on.

A smile pulled up his lips before he opened once again, loving the need and desire he could feel pouring off Aaron. He wanted this man to want him. He knew he shouldn't, that made him very selfish, but the compliment it paid him was too great not to cherish.

"Get up. Now." Aaron growled at him and Jordan gave the cock in his mouth a final long suck and then he pushed up to his feet, looking up into Aarons' eyes.

The green of his irises was almost black and as his mate's lips came crashing down on his, Jordan's knees buckled.

Heat seared his chest and pure sex poured into his mouth as Aaron's tongue delved inside his.

They fell, bouncing down onto the mattress.

Aaron pushed up and away, giving him a final quick kiss before descending.

"What are you...?"

Aaron's mouth went straight down onto his cock and bliss screamed through him. He cried out, grabbing hold of Aaron's blond hair.

"Oh fuck... Shit!"

Aaron bobbed up and down on him and heat fired down his legs. He was going to cum too soon.

Seeming to sense what was about to happen, Aaron came off him with a wet pop and pushed both of his legs up so that he was curled up, knees to chest, his arse in the air.

"Hmmm." Aaron hummed, making a happy noise as he dove back down between Jordan's thighs.

"Wow!" Jordan screamed as Aaron's tongue penetrated his arse, deep. His balls began to ache and tighten as Aaron licked him, stretching him.

He moved his tongue in and out, over and over again, until Jordan was out of his head with pleasure. He couldn't see straight as he screamed and grabbed at Aaron's head.

"Fuck me. Oh, please, fuck me!"

He was far past caring if he sounded needy, or pathetic. He needed to cum so badly!

Aaron stood up and grabbed Jordan's legs, pulling him to the edge of the bed.

His ankles were over Aaron's huge shoulders as Aaron pressed his cock head against Jordan's arse.

Jordan swallowed hard as Aaron thrust his hips gently, pressing and retreating.

His body opened and pain burned.

He gasped and Aaron frowned. "Grab your cock and pull it for me, gorgeous boy."

Jordan grabbed his cock and screamed as Aaron thrust deep, his thick cock forging a pathway deep inside his body.

He palmed his cock over and over again, squeezing his eyes shut as both pain and pleasure pulsed through his body.

"Open your eyes. I want to see you." Aaron grunted above him as he withdrew and then thrust back inside.

The pain had begun to subside and the pleasure was winning the race.

Jordan's toes were tingling as he forced his eyes to open, connecting once again with the huge man above him.

"Oh... fuck..."

He was gone.

Hot waves of ecstasy flowed down his spine and exploded inside his cock.

He arched his back and squeezed his cock hard with his hand as pulse after pulse of pleasure coursed through him.

Aaron cried out, over and over again as he pumped into Jordan's body, then finally thrust one more time, pouring his seed deep inside him.

They rolled and Aaron collapsed beside him, the only noise in the room now their ragged breathing.

CHAPTER
FOUR

Jordan's heart pounded like a bass drum inside his chest, loud enough to make his head throb and his blood thrum like a guitar in a rock concert.

"Fuck, that was..." Aaron's deep voice made Jordan groan, the fire that had just been quenched, roaring to life once again.

He had majorly underestimated the effect this mate bond would have on him. How was he ever going to convince Aaron they weren't right for each other, when the sex had been so unbelievably incredible?

"Yeah." He pulled himself up, his skin slick with sweat and his head spinning. "That was."

He swung his legs off the bed and pushed up. He needed some distance between then, and fast.

"Where do you think you're going?" Aaron asked, sitting up on the bed.

"Shower." He sure needed one.

He stumbled into the adjoining bathroom, throwing on the cold water and practically falling under it.

"Ah... oh..." shit...

The cold prickled his skin, waking him up and sending pain through his once buzzing body.

You shouldn't be here.

This is so wrong.

The word *wrong*, made him cringe and he pushed his head beneath the water flow. Tears stung his eyes, his mother's words buffeting his brain like a shit storm.

He was wrong. Had been born wrong. Too small, too skinny, no birthmark and gay to boot. His mother had been horrified, and had made sure he'd known every day how disappointed she was in him.

And she was right.

He didn't deserve Aaron. He was not Alpha mate material. What did he know about running the pack? He was a Omega, for pity's sake!

The room changed, the shift immediate and hot. Aaron's arm shot out and switched the water over, warming the temperature until Jordan stopped the shivering he hadn't realised he was doing.

"Come here."

Aaron pulled him closer, stepping into the shower himself. Jordan didn't fight him, but he couldn't bring himself to open his eyes. He wanted to pretend nothing had changed, but it had.

Aaron's hands were on him. Moving in wet, slow circles. His eye lids cracked open. Aaron's fingers were covered in white, foamy soap, moving over Jordan's body. His stomach, his abs. Along his arms.

"I still can't believe that I found you. After all this time." Aaron's soft voice made his knees weak. Aaron's hand slid over

Jordan's heart, tracing the borders of the large mark they both shared.

"Hmmm," Jordan hummed in response, unsure of what to say to that.

"Twenty-five years I've been looking."

"Longer than I've been alive." Jordan croaked out. That was so long.

A deep chuckle rolled out of Aaron's huge chest. "A lifetime... that's definitely how it's felt. More so in the past few years though. It was okay before that. I wrote it down one time. July, August, around then, two years ago. The ache became horrible, unbearable almost. That was when I organised with the council to buy this land, I had to get out of town."

Jordan swallowed, the lump in his throat making that almost impossible. The timing was unmistakeable.

"My twenty first birthday was July twentieth, two years ago."

"Okay..." Aaron's tone indicated that he didn't understand the relevance.

"That was when my mark developed, like it does on the women in the pack."

Aaron's hands stopped moving and Jordan looked up. Aaron's face had frozen, his mouth falling open. Then he shook himself and stepped out of the shower, towel drying himself quickly.

"Yeah, that makes sense."

Aaron's tone had turned frosty and his movements were sharp as he turned the water off and tossed Jordan a towel.

He shouldn't ask. He knew that.

Encourage his mood. He'll let you go home soon if he doesn't want you.

The words welled up and rolled off his tongue. "What's wrong?"

"Nothing." Aaron stormed back into his bedroom and began putting the covers back in order.

Jordan used the soft towel Aaron had given him and rubbed himself down quickly, sighing at the luxurious feeling of the cotton against his skin. Part of his mind unable to ignore how well Aaron lived. How beautiful all of his things were.

If you were his mate, you could live here forever.

A frustrated growl rolled out of his throat as he fought with the inner thought.

"What was that?" Aaron grumbled as he climbed into his large bed.

"What?" Jordan crept into the darkened bedroom and opened the door that would lead him back out to the living room.

"That growl. I've never heard a Omega make that noise before."

"Well... I've never been quite the normal Omega." He whispered, turning and moving part way through the door.

"No, you're an Alpha's mate. How can you not realise that?"

He stopped then turned around to watch Aaron roll away, turning his back on him.

Jordan bit his lip as the need to go back into the room and curl up next to his mate rose and burst through him like a lightning storm.

That was what was meant to happen after that sort of incredible sex and connection. Cuddling, petting, sleeping together.

If you accept him, you'll have to step up. Sit at the Alpha table. Rule over the people.

Jordan's chest tightened painfully and with a heavy heart, he sulked to the small bedroom off the kitchen. Sleeping in small bursts between a kaleidoscope of nightmares and hot dreams.

~

Aaron had one of the worse nights of his life. Even through sickness, injury, and fatigue he'd had better nights' sleep.

How could his mate ignore what they had? What they *could* have in the future. Their bond was indescribable, stronger than he'd ever believed possible, and that was after sharing only a couple of hours together. If they were together longer, who knew what could develop between them?

He rolled out of bed, his belly aching with a hunger that had been satisfied. Once. For one, brilliant hour, he'd had peace.

And he wanted it back.

He grabbed a pair of jeans and pulled them on, not bothering with a top, he strode out into the kitchen for his breakfast.

Jordan was already there. Sitting at the table in the dirty clothes he'd been wearing yesterday.

"Don't you have anything else to wear?"

Jordan jumped and twisted, his lean body and collar bones so thin you could snap them. The sight made Aaron clench his teeth together in anger.

Why was he so thin?

When Jordan didn't answer his question, Aaron walked around the bench and stared hard at his mate.

"Well?"

"I... um. No. I don't have any other clothes."

"Right. Then we get some today. Next, food. What are you eating? You're as thin as a grasshopper."

They both looked down at the glass of water in front of him. That wasn't breakfast for anyone.

"I ah..."

"Right. Do you want to go up to the Hall, or should I cook here?"

"I don't want to go to the Hall."

It wasn't the words, as much as the horror on Jordan's face that sealed the deal.

"Done. What do you want?"

"Toast, please."

"Ah, no."

He turned and went over to the fridge, pulling out what he'd normally have for breakfast, plus more for his mate.

He set the frying pan on the stove and threw in some oil and bacon, some sausages and tomatoes.

He turned around and saw his mate staring at him.

"Aren't you a cook? Do you want to help?"

Jordan bit his lip in that adorably sexy way that made Aaron want to fuck him. His cock began to lengthen and throb in jeans.

Damn it. Stop doing that.

"I... ah. Make coffees, do dishes."

"Ok, come here and learn. For at least this week, you're living here and I want your help. You all right with that?"

If Jordan wanted to be a Omega, he'd treat him like one.

"Oh, yes. Please. I want to help."

Jordan jumped up and practically ran around the island bench to stand so close to Aaron, his balls began to throb with need.

Damn it, that backfired.

Focus on your breakfast.

"Right, first you fry up the bacon, then mix up the eggs in a separate bowl."

He showed Jordan how to cook up a heart starter breakfast, set the table and even squeeze some fresh orange juice.

When they sat down, half on each plate, he could see the hunger in Jordan's eyes. The saliva on his lips as he wet them, over and over again with his tongue.

"I can't eat all this. You know a Omega doesn't eat that much."

Aaron grunted and picked up his knife and fork.

"I can see how big your hunger is. Just 'cause you don't feed yourself right doesn't mean you can't eat it. It's all yours, and if you don't finish it, I'll just throw it out."

The look of horror at that statement was akin to the one that he'd shown when Aaron had suggested going to the Hall to eat.

He looked down to hide his smile as he hoed into his meal.

Aaron had seen what had happened to Reagan's body and appetite when he'd mated with Grayson. He'd gone from being a nice, small Beta size, and turned himself into a man only slightly smaller than an Alpha. Aaron would say Reagan had put on at least thirty pounds of muscle in a few weeks.

Jordan and he may not be officially mated, but he'd bite his own arse if he was wrong about this. He was sure Jordan had the same ability to change and develop. He wanted his mate as strong as possible.

He glanced up to see Jordan hesitantly eating the scrambled eggs, his fork moving faster and faster, his head dropping lower as he ate more and more.

Aaron finished his plate, the greasy protein and fat sitting well in his belly. He sat back in his chair and picked up his orange juice as his scrawny mate continued to eat.

When the plate was half empty, Jordan stopped suddenly and sat back to assess his meal.

Looking up at Aaron, his eyes widened as though startled.

Aaron smiled. "It's okay. If you don't want it, I can chuck it."

No wolf, or member of their community, liked waste, and by the look of determination that crossed Jordan's face, it was obvious he felt the same.

He finished the whole plate, leaving only a rasher of bacon and half a tomato.

"I can't eat any more... I'm sorry. But that was amazing."

Jordan relaxed against the chair, his eyes gleaming with good health, his dark hair slicked back and pulled down on one side over his ear.

Fuck, he's gorgeous.

"Thank you for breakfast."

"Anytime." He had to get to work, or he'd fuck Jordan again. "I'm going up to town for the day. Gotta do some site checks and talk to some of the farmers. You want to come up and get some clothes, or should I just pick some up for you?"

"Umm." Jordan dropped his eyes as though he didn't want to answer.

Fine. You want me to be the Alpha, easy done.

"I'll get you some. Twenty-eight inch waist?"

"Yes." Jordan answered, his head still down.

Aaron looked around his house. His mate needed something to do all day and being a Omega, he probably would prefer a less physical task.

"Would you tidy up for me? I know this isn't your house but..."

"Yes! I'd love to." Jordan practically jumped up and Aaron stood up, picking up his plate and walking it over to the sink.

"I'll do that."

Jordan literally bumped him out of the way to take over the dishes and Aaron walked away with a laugh bubbling inside of him.

There was light at the end of the tunnel, he could feel it, see it.

His mate was in his home and it felt so right that he couldn't believe that Jordan didn't want to stay. In fact, he refused to even think about their deal. He was going to make life so good for his little mate, that Jordan wouldn't ever want to leave.

He glanced over his shoulder as he walked back to his bedroom and love flowed through his chest. Jordan looked so perfect in his house.

He moved into his bedroom, a ray of hope shining in his heart.

If he could just get his mate to admit what he was scared of, they could face it together, and get on with their lives.

He dressed quickly and headed out.

He called out to Jordan who was moving around the kitchen like a Tassie Devil. "See you later on."

"Okay." He called back.

Aaron left for work with a smile on his face for the first time in more years than he could remember.

JORDAN WORKED ALL DAY. Cleaning, then making some muffins. He'd learned to bake a little at the café in Melbourne and wanted to try out his skills.

Aaron's house was generally tidy, but the man needed someone to clean for him. And sort. His bookshelf was a mess.

Jordan couldn't believe the sense of calm that came over him from staying in Aaron's house. Even with a rift between them, he was at home. He hadn't had this sense of peace since he was a very young child. Before his father had left and his mother had taken out her anger and frustration on him.

He sighed, the memories of his childhood dampening his mood like a proper thundercloud.

He looked around the open plan living area. There wasn't much else to do. Perhaps he could rest? Aaron wouldn't be home for a while.

You could leave. Run away again.

He snorted at the ridiculous thought. Leave this brand new home where he was welcome, and fed, to live on the street again?

Ah. No.

He sat down on the couch gingerly. A strange sense of panic

filling his heart at the idea of being found slacking. Taking advantage of Aaron's hospitality.

He slid down lower, memories of last night's incredible sex flooding his mind.

"Yes... Hmmm..."

It had been amazing. The best sex of his life.

He closed his eyes and let his tired body slowly relax. Such a comfortable couch.

JORDAN WOKE up to a hand on his shoulder gently shaking him.

He jumped up off the couch and put his hands up to ward off any possible attacks, his heart hammering in his ears.

"Hey, it's okay. Sorry, I just thought you might wanna come out to dinner."

He shook his head emphatically. "No, I don't. Woah... you scared me."

He swallowed down the massive lump in his throat and let his arms drop, willing his racing heart rate to calm down.

To start with he'd been panicking from the sudden wakeup, but now his body was responding for a totally different reason.

What Aaron was proposing was not going to happen. He didn't want to deal with anyone, nor explain himself to people who would never understand.

Aaron crossed his arms over his chest and stared down at him.

Damn, he's huge.

"Jordan, you have two choices. Either come with me to the Hall and deal with everyone, or stay here and explain to me why you don't want to. And we're going to sort it out and then I'll make you go anyway. So are we talking now, or later?"

A growl rose and Jordan snorted out his nose. He had no intention of explaining anything.

"What was that?"

He didn't answer. Anger boiled in his belly like volcanic lava, spreading heat through his belly.

Aaron stepped closer, so close Jordan could feel Aaron's breath on his forehead.

"Jordan."

"Yes."

"Do I have to fuck the answer out of you?"

Jordan's belly tightened and jumped, his knees weakening as he imagined screaming out in the ecstasy of the moment.

Yes, please...

"You haven't asked a question."

Aaron took a step back, bent forward and put his shoulder into Jordan's belly.

He was lifted up and fell forward over Aaron's huge shoulders. The breath rushing out of his lungs.

"Oof. Put me down you big..."

"I would stop. Right there. If I were you." Aaron's voice was menacing, deep, and harsh. But so sexy Jordan relaxed against him.

Aaron walked forwards and then stopped suddenly. Jordan was thrown, falling flat on his back on the soft mattress where he was fucked so well last night.

Aaron knelt over the top of him, straddling his pelvis. Pinning him down as effectively as a steel rod across his body.

He glared up at the big Alpha, his heart racing and adrenaline pumping like a fight was around the corner.

"What's your problem? Get off me."

Aaron grinned, grabbed both of Jordan's wrists and leaned forward, pinning him down properly.

"No. You want to do this the hard way, then so be it."

Jordan tried tugging his arms down, only to find he was held fast. He arched his back and growled up at his mate in frustration.

Aaron's eyes shifted and he bared his sharp teeth. He opened his mouth and came down on Jordan's throat with his jaw open.

Jordan squealed and then lay silent as his mate gripped his airway, demanding submission.

He let himself go limp, fighting was futile. Impossible.

Why did you even try? You look foolish.

Aaron's teeth retracted and Jordan took a shuddering breath as relief came flooding in.

When Aaron finally pushed himself back up, he had a grin on his face that looked too happy to be smug.

Jordan couldn't even speak.

"I love how strong and fiery you are. I never thought a Omega mate would be so... hot."

Jordan rolled his eyes. How many times did he have to say this?

"I'm not exactly your regular Omega."

Aaron's green eyes, now returned to human, gleamed with lust. "Don't I know it."

Aaron sat up straighter so that he was still pinning Jordan down, but released his arms.

Jordan brought his aching limbs down instantly, enjoying the throb of blood flowing into his fingers.

"Are you going to get off me now?"

A gentle laugh rolled off his mate while his eyes sparkled with fun. "No. We're going to sort this out. Now."

Jordan huffed and turned his head away.

No way.

"First, you're going to explain why you didn't tell me, or anyone important, that your mark developed at twenty-one. Why would you hide that?"

Jordan kept his face averted.

"Second, you're going to explain why you ran away, and third, you're going to tell me why you won't accept me as your mate. Am I so very ugly and horrible to you?"

Jordan swung his face back to the centre.

"What are you talking about? You're gorgeous!"

Aaron stared at him with big soulful eyes and Jordan reached out to touch his mate's face. His strong jaw, fine lips.

Had Aaron really thought such a thing? How horrible. He knew what it felt like to be rejected by someone who was supposed to love you, and he didn't want that for his mate.

He'd have to tell him.

"Me running away, that wasn't on you. Me, not telling people about my mark, that wasn't about you, either."

"Didn't you know it was my mark? We don't have a lot to do with each other, so..."

He bit his lip, pained to admit the truth. "No, I knew it was like yours, I've watched you since I was a kid. I left because..." His throat tightened up and when Aaron made an encouraging noise he shook his head. He couldn't speak yet or he'd burst into tears.

It felt like someone had stuck a poker down his throat, hot and horrible. Aaron rolled off him and grabbed him at the same time, pulling him onto his lap while sitting on the edge of the bed.

"Tell me, please."

Tears gathered and stung his eyes, the memories of his childhood flooding back in.

"I can't... it hurts too much..." A sob escaped, the tears choking his throat. Mortification soon swept in, but he was too consumed with pain to be able to stop it all now. The sobs continued until they racked his frame.

"Shh... it's okay." Aaron rocked him and Jordan clung to his mate, the strength of Aaron transferring to him and settling him down.

The pain slowed, as did the tears.

"When you can speak, start talking. I think you've bottled things up too long as it is."

Jordan nodded again and let his eyes close, enjoying the gentle rock of his body on the wave that was Aaron.

Aaron was going to sort this shit out, no matter what it took or how long. His mate had experienced severe trauma, that was certain. But he was sure they could sort it out. Together.

"Tell me why you hid your mark for so long."

He had to know. And he swore to let his mate go if he had a good enough excuse.

"I... didn't want you to know that I had it."

"Because..." He led Jordan to continue.

Silence.

For fuck's sake, just say it.

He forced himself to breathe in and out, and not pound his fists to make his mate talk.

"Jordan..." He let his tone change, deepening. "I don't want to make you tell me, but I will, if you continue to refuse to speak."

There was another heartbeat of silence then Jordan coughed, as though clearing his throat.

"I... ah, ok. I don't really want you to Alpha me."

Aaron waited, holding onto his patience by his fingernails. He didn't want to dominate his mate every time he needed something. He wanted them to have a true partnership and that meant that both of them should have the choice of what to do.

"I didn't want to tell you, because you'd want to, you know, claim me as your mate."

And what's the problem with that?

Instead of screaming at his mate the way he wanted to, Aaron just made humming noises and nodded, encouraging him to keep talking. If he jumped in too early, he'd spook Jordan. And then he may as well say goodbye to any chance he had at a good relationship with him.

"It's not like I didn't want to be your mate. For goodness sake, you're the most beautiful Alpha in the pack."

Jordan gasped as though he hadn't meant to say so much, so Aaron pushed forward.

"Thank you, but that doesn't make sense. If you want to be my mate, then *be* my mate. You are my destiny. You know the rules. The legend. Your mark makes you mine, and I'm yours. I can't be happy with another, and neither will you be."

Jordan twisted in his arms and looked up so that Aaron now saw the passion and pain in his beautiful brown eyes.

"But don't you get it- there has to be a mistake. No male wolf is meant to develop a mark at twenty-one. I'm not a girl!"

Aaron groped his mate's muscular, sexy arse and gave him a cheeky grin.

"Oh... I know that."

"Oh, shut up. You know what I mean. Something's gone wrong. *I'm* wrong. You can't possibly be mated to me. I'm not good enough for you."

And there it was. The ridiculous reason he'd been waiting to jump on.

"Not good enough? For what? To love me? To fuck me? To spend each day in my home making me happy?"

"No... that's the easy stuff."

Aaron began to laugh. So hard he could feel the muscles in

his belly grip and tighten to a painful point. This was absolutely ridiculous. He'd missed out on all this time because his mate had thought he needed to live up to some ridiculous expectation?

"Aaron!" Jordan whacked him in the arm and jumped up off his lap, glaring down at him with as much rage as his beautiful little mate could probably muster.

So much for a little submissive Omega.

"Listen to me!"

At least he wasn't crying anymore.

Aaron let the last of the chuckles slow down and he grabbed Jordan's hands, pulling him down until his mate was kneeling in front of him.

He cupped Jordan's beautiful face and stared down at him.

"Jordan, stop. Listen to me this time, just listen, okay?"

Jordan nodded, but Aaron could see the tightness in his jaw. The rigidity in his mate's posture.

"No, I mean it. Sit down." He grabbed Jordan's hand and pulled him until he was sitting next to him.

"Jordan, I have spent, literally your whole life, alone. Sad. Aching for the mate the legends said would come my way and complete me. You don't think I've tried to fill the void? I've had women. Lots of them. Unmated, widowed, alone. Not one of them made me feel as happy as you do, just by simply being in my home. If you don't want to go back to the pack, then fine. I'll talk to Grayson, work out a way around it. But don't leave me. Stay with me. Love me. Make me happy by being in my bed every night. Please. It's all I needed. All I'll ever want."

Tears were beginning to swim into his vision and he blinked them away.

Jordan's face melted. "But, what if no one accepts me? Like with Reagan? But I'm not strong like him. I'm not an Alpha mate."

Aaron growled and nipped at his mate's neck as Jordan climbed into his lap.

"You *are* an Alpha mate. *My* Alpha mate. I told you, if you don't want to step up into the role, that's fine. I built this house for you. You never have to leave it, if you don't want to."

Jordan's eyes went wide, a smile slowly spreading across his incredulous face.

"Are you serious? I can really just stay here?"

Aaron nodded once, dropping his head to press a hard kiss against Jordan's mouth.

"Of course, you can. But I need you to know one thing. Fate gets nothing wrong. You were made for me. You are perfect in every way. And I don't want you to change a single thing."

A tear streaked its way down Jordan's face and Aaron licked it away, enjoying the salty taste on his tongue.

Jordan clung to him, moaning and kissing his neck. Aaron grabbed his mate and rolled him, pinning him to the bed.

"You'll be my mate then?"

"Of course, I will."

Then they needed to bond. Now.

"Strip then. I need you."

Jordan jumped up and pulled off his t-shirt and jeans, while Aaron stared at him.

"You're looking pretty fit, my mate."

Jordan's body had gotten bigger, his ribs no longer showed, his muscles had doubled in size.

Jordan looked down and held out his arms, staring at them as though he hadn't seen them before.

"I suppose with all the food."

Red flushed his face and Aaron pulled off his own clothes, puzzled by the odd expression on Jordan's face.

"Why do you look embarrassed all of a sudden?"

Jordan glanced away, a smile tugging at his full lips.

"Just... Reagan told me that your sperm would be like steroid injections, and we had sex last night and look at me today."

Aaron laughed again, loving the fact that Grayson's mate had shared such an essential part of the Alpha link story.

"Well, come here and I'll give you some more of those steroids."

Jordan walked right into his waiting arms and went up on his toes, offering his lips up. Aaron swooped down and kissed him, lifting Jordan's body up and carrying him to the bed.

He'd been looking forward to this moment for twenty years, and now that he was here, he couldn't take his time. He needed to be inside Jordan straight away. He put his mate down and turned him around, pushing his mate down onto all fours.

"Stay there."

He reached for the lube he had stashed in the cupboard and poured some into both hands.

He wrapped one fist around his cock and pressed the fingers on his other hand to his mate's arse.

"I can't wait to be back in this arse again."

Jordan groaned and thrashed his head against the mattress, pushing back against him with wanton need.

"Yes. Please."

Aaron's cock was already stiff and aching. He could feel his fangs drop down and press against his lower lip. The mating heat taking over his body like an invasion of lust. Hot waves flooded up his spine as he let his mind go, his body directed by something higher.

Without any prep, he lined up his cock with the tiny star of Jordan's arse and thrust forward.

Jordan screamed out and Aaron's hands locked down on his mate's hips. He bent forward as he felt his teeth sharpen and elongate. He opened wide, unable to stop himself as he latched onto Jordan's shoulder. His orgasm caught him up and hurtled through his body at an unprecedented speed.

He called out to Jordan who started shuddering and crying out.

Aaron's seed pumped into his mate, with long, hot streams. Then his legs began to shake, his whole body sliding into pure bliss and everything went black.

He must have passed out or fallen asleep, because Aaron woke up and he was lying on the mattress, curled around the sleeping form of Jordan.

Bloody Hell. What was that?

Jordan's eyes blinked a few times and he rolled his head from side to side a little before finally opening his eyes properly.

"What happened?"

Aaron pressed a soft kiss to his mate's pouty lips and lifted a hand to stroke the dark hair from Jordan's face.

"I'm not sure, to be honest. I haven't experienced anything like it before."

Jordan groaned and rolled closer, his palm sliding across Aaron's slick skin. "I haven't either, and may I just say that was the fastest orgasm, like, ever!"

Aaron began to laugh, the sound building and rolling through his belly. How his mate brought such fun and silliness into his life, he had no idea.

"It was. If we hadn't already had such an epic session yesterday, I'd be defending my lack of stamina."

Was that what the mating was meant to be like?

Whatever had happened, it had been amazing.

He sighed as he ran a hand down his mate's chest, which was getting bigger and more defined by the day.

"You are looking so much healthier."

Jordan arched his back and stretched, accentuating his abdominal muscles and sexy hip lines.

"I *feel* so much healthier."

Aaron let his fingertips follow around the dark edge of their mating mark. To think, it all came down to this...

"What's that?"

He stared down at Jordan's belly button, where an hour ago there'd been nothing. Now, there was more of the mark they shared.

"What's what?"

Jordan looked down at his own body and Aaron pointed at the addition to his mate's belly.

Jordan rolled out of bed and stood in front of the mirror on the other side of the room. He lifted a hand and traced it.

Aaron squinted. *Is that what I think it is?*

"It looks like a wolf. With green eyes."

Jordan twisted around to face him and his eyes bulged in his head while his mouth fell open.

"Your mark!"

"Yeah?" Aaron looked down and saw nothing. For the first time in his life he had a plain, tanned chest.

"What the hell? That's impossible."

Jordan came back to the bed and pressed his hand against Aaron's heart. "What is this?"

Aaron's heart was pounding but there was something niggling at his memory.

"Hang on..." He forced himself to slow his breathing. *Think properly.*

Don't freak out. Didn't this happen to Grayson?

"Ah! I think I know. I'm pretty sure this happened when Grayson and Reagan mated. I never really talked to him a lot about it, because it all happened around the time of the Rogue attacks, and then Reagan was gone. But I remember the Alpha's talking about the fact that Grayson's mark had disappeared."

He looked down at his body, marvelling at the smooth expanse.

"It's weird actually. I always wanted a plain chest. Thought I'd copped a bad run having such a large one all over, and yet, I'm not sure I like this now. Feels wrong."

Jordan shook his head. "I never thought that. Even as a teenager I'd watch you. You were always so beautiful. So strong."

Aaron grinned at his mate, feeling the bond between them tightening.

Jordan was sitting cross legged and as he leaned back on his hands, the wolf with green eyes popped back into view on his belly.

Aaron traced the new addition on his mate.

His wolf. Now part of Jordan.

He searched inside himself and yes, his wolf was still there. Sleeping and content.

"Hopefully he'll protect you." He grinned down at his mate. "Looks like we really are meant to be."

Aaron grabbed Jordan and rolled him beneath him on the bed once again. Happiness exploded inside his chest as he settled his mate under him.

"Yep. Maybe we are." Jordan grinned back and together they fell into a tangle of kisses and moans.

CHAPTER FIVE

Jordan reached under his t-shirt and pressed his palm to the wolf guarding his body now, or that was how it felt. Which, if he was honest, was pretty cool. He could have used that strength for the earlier years, but at least he had it now.

His own wolf seemed stronger inside of him, constantly pacing and growling. At what, he wasn't sure. Nothing was the matter at the moment.

Aaron stepped into the kitchen and called to him. "I'm going up to the Hall for dinner tonight. I need to speak to Grayson about some things, this mating mark thing in particular. Would you come with me?"

Jordan turned towards his mate, his gut tightening at the prospect of seeing his old friends. He wanted to speak to Grayson and Reagan too, but perhaps they could come here?

"You said I wouldn't have to go back into town."

"I know, and you don't have to. I was just asking if you would. For me. I don't really want to go without you."

Jordan put down the glass he'd been drying and stared at

Aaron. Had his mate thought that he'd change his mind so quickly?

Some things had changed, he supposed, but he was still feeling very apprehensive about the rest of the pack and how they'd respond to him.

"You know I don't want to see anyone."

Aaron seemed to get taller as he straightened to his full height.

"If you don't want to, it's fine. I just thought, or hoped... I suppose, that since we're mated now, you'd feel more comfortable. You do have my full support, after all." Aaron's eyes dropped and he turned away.

Jordan's heart reached out for his mate and he opened his mouth to say the only thing he could. "I'll come."

His chest tightened. Damn, he hadn't meant to say that.

Aaron spun back around. "Really?"

His face was so lit up, his eyes bright and happy. Jordan couldn't bring himself to tell his mate that he'd acted rashly. Spoke without thinking. That would make him a total and utter twat.

Oh fuck it, what's the worst thing that could happen?

"Yeah, sure. Why not? Can I just have a minute to change?"

"Of course. You happy with the stuff I got you?"

Heat prickled his skin as it flushed over his cheeks. He'd forgotten about the bag Aaron had brought home for him.

"I haven't checked them out yet, sorry. Thank you so much for thinking of me."

He turned away and scooped up the bag Aaron had left for him on the couch. No one had ever bought him clothes before. His own mother had stopped when he was a pre-teen. Taking old clothes of neighbours' kids for him.

Second hand is good enough for you.

He shuddered as he turned away, rifling through the bag and pulling out several pairs of jeans and t-shirts.

They were both a size too big.

Don't whine. They still have their tags on!

He stepped into the spare room and took off his old clothes, ripped off the tags and pulled on the new clothes.

The jeans were hard to get up his thighs and when he struggled to do up the button he realised that they were too tight. And beneath the t-shirt he could see muscle bulk and stretch the material over his chest.

That's impossible. I've always been a twenty-six, or a twenty-eight, and these are a thirty.

He pulled on some shoes, checked his hair in the mirror and walked back out to Aaron.

"I thought these clothes would be too big. But look."

He gestured down to his body and ran a hand over his bulging thigh muscles. "How did this happen?"

Aaron chuckled. "You noticed, huh? I bought the size up because I heard Grayson and Reagan talking about it one day. They said that once they mated, Reagan started to grow. Huge and muscled. And I thought... maybe, it would happen to you, too."

Jordan stretched his arms out in front of him, marvelling at the corded strength he could see before him. Maybe there really was steroids in the Alpha's sperm.

"This is pretty cool."

He was still grinning as Aaron guided him outside and into the sunshine. He blinked a few times and got into the car.

Was it really possible that he was meant to be with Aaron? It was all adding up and falling into place. It might *not* be a mistake.

The mark. The mating. The smell. The change in Aaron's birthmark and his own.

And now him, growing stronger and bigger by the minute.

Was he really meant to be an Alpha mate?

"What are you thinking?"

Aaron's question caught him off guard and he swivelled around to stare at his mate.

"Sorry?"

"I can't keep up with all the different emotions flickering across your face. Whatcha thinking?"

"Oh... ah..." How to explain it all?

"Please, tell me. I like it when you open up and I can get to know you better."

Wow. No one had ever said anything like that to him before. Did Aaron really want to know him that well? He wanted the same thing. To know Aaron, to have a strong connection.

That was, if he was staying. Although the chances of him leaving were shrinking by the minute. He'd never survive away from his mate now that they had completed the actual mating.

With that thought, he waited for the panic to come, the sickness that should accompany the future he'd just boxed himself into.

And there was nothing but peace.

"I... am starting to believe, I think, that this isn't a mistake."

He braced himself for a barrage of abuse from Aaron, only to have him laugh heartily.

"Of course, it's not. Fate doesn't make mistakes."

Jordan grinned and sat back in the car seat. He should have more faith in Aaron's character and responses. After all, they were mated now. Aaron wasn't going anywhere.

They pulled up outside the Hall and parked.

Butterflies took wing inside his chest and his arms began to course with nervous energy. He'd managed to forget his fear on the way over, but now that he was actually here...

"Ah... I..."

"You… are going to be totally fine. I won't leave your side. I promise. Okay?"

Jordan nodded, a lump lodged in his throat. He couldn't speak even if he wanted to.

They got out of the car and Aaron took his hand, leading him into the Hall. He could do this, surely. After surviving the rest of his life, a dinner wouldn't be that bad.

The noise as they opened the door was massive, filling Jordan's head up like a buzzing bee hive.

He stepped so close to Aaron he could feel his mate's thudding heart beat through his own chest and whispered in his ear. "I'm not sure I can do this."

His heart raced like a galloping horse. Making his mind jump and leap so much he needed to run. *Run away.*

Aaron took his hand and squeezed tight, pulling him in so close, Jordan could feel the heat of Aaron's body sear his own.

"You are safe. I adore you."

And there, where they stood at the entrance to the Hall, Aaron made a loud whistling noise that made Jordan want to sink to his knees.

Everyone quieted. The whole hall went silent.

And looked straight at them.

Hell no.

Jordan twisted in his mate's arms and pressed his head against Aaron's beating heart.

I'm not here. I'm not here.

He squeezed his eyes shut and let Aaron's strong arms wrap around him like a vice.

I can't believe he's doing this. Not after everything I've told him.

"I would like everyone to welcome my mate back to the Hall. Jordan Macky. If he is upset by anyone, and I do mean anyone, they will answer to me."

The growl in his mate's voice was unbelievably strong and the tension in Jordan's body drained away like someone had pulled the plug on him.

Who was he to run and hide when Aaron would take on any man in the room for him? And he believed that he would, one hundred per cent.

Jordan stood up straighter and lifted his head to stare at Aaron.

Had he really just done that?

For him?

Aaron dropped his head and kissed Jordan hard, spearing his tongue into Jordan's mouth and cradling the back of his head when Jordan would have fallen back.

There was a loud wolf whistle and lots of clapping.

When Aaron finally pulled away, he gave Jordan a wolf like grin, a wink, then he was pulled into the melee of smiling people.

Oh my god.

He could see some of his friends at the back tables. Elliot was standing on one of the chairs to get a better view it seemed.

He really did need to go apologise to them.

But that was later.

Aaron pulled him to the Alpha table and pulled out two seats. Jordan began to shake as ten people turned towards him. Aaron dropped into one of the chairs and dragged Jordan with him.

"Everyone, this is Jordan. Jordan, I suppose you know everyone?"

He nodded his head. Of course, he did. There were a hundred Omegas, but only five Alphas. The empty space next to him was suddenly filled by Reagan. "It's great to see you."

Reagan wrapped his arms around him and Jordan couldn't move for a moment. This type of affection was very odd from another's mate.

But the longer Reagan held him, the safer he began to feel, until finally, he relaxed against him.

"Yeah, you too."

He closed his eyes, and then felt Aaron's hand on his back.

"Reagan, can I have my mate back please?"

Jordan pulled himself away and smiled at his old roommate.

"How are you doing, being back here?"

Reagan grinned, that happy-go-lucky look familiar and settling. "I'm great actually. We're rebuilding Grayson's house and I've settled into the hospital pretty well. Dr. Sarah's pretty amazing and she's pushing me a lot. But that's the best way to learn, I suppose."

Jordan nodded. What could he say? Reagan was a perfect match for Alpha Grayson— smart, confident, a productive member of the pack.

Aaron leaned around him and got Reagan's attention.

"Hey Reagan, we wanted to ask you guys a question actually. What happened to your birth mark after you and Grayson mated?" Aaron asked.

Jordan wanted to know the same thing. It would really seal the deal for him if what they assumed to be the case, was actually the truth. It would mean he really was Aaron's mate.

"Oh, haven't you seen it?" Reagan stood up, lifting his sleeve for everyone to see.

He had a wolf standing next to his birthmark, too. With blue eyes. Just like Grayson.

"Wow." Even though he'd half expected to see it, the presence of the image was still strangely shocking.

Jordan lifted his hand and traced the wolf like black shape on Reagan's arm. It looked just like his.

"Why do you ask?" Grayson asked, standing behind Reagan now.

The other Alpha made him nervous and Jordan pressed back into Aaron.

Aaron pushed back his chair and stood up, grabbing Jordan's arms and pulling him to stand, also.

"And Grayson's mark is gone, right?" Aaron asked.

Grayson nodded, pulling up the sleeve on his right arm to expose the bicep.

There was just plain skin where once there was a gnarly looking tree. He'd seen it many times, especially on the full moons when all the Betas and Alphas shifted in the light of the clearing.

He looked up at Aaron, who was grinning like someone who'd won the lottery. And in lots of ways, they probably had. This meant they weren't a mistake, they weren't wrong. Or if they were, then Grayson and Reagan were, too.

And it was pretty obvious that the two men in front of him were meant to be together.

A wave of happiness rolled through him so strong his head swam with stars. He stumbled a little and turned to rest against one of the chair backs.

This was amazing.

Aaron, his Cheshire cat style smile still firmly in place, lifted up his own shirt, exposing wash board hard abs and muscular pecs. Jordan's mouth began to water as he stared at the beauty of his mate.

"Your mark's gone, too!" Reagan said, grinning widely.

There was suddenly a deafening silence from the table behind him and they all turned to look at the members of the Alpha table staring at them.

Aaron pulled down his shirt and gathered his mate to his side to calm himself down. He couldn't believe how upset his wolf was inside his mind.

His mate was uncomfortable and jumpy, and his wolf wanted to drag him out of the Hall like a caveman.

But he wouldn't do it.

He needed to settle Jordan into their life as quickly as possible.

He let his gaze roam over the Alpha table and he could see Marcus smirking away.

God, I hate that guy.

Marcus' father and Grayson's father had worried expressions on their faces, and probably rightly so. There was a massive change sweeping the pack, and they couldn't control it.

If Grayson was right. Then the dawning of the all-male Alphas was back.

They probably should contact Brad. The only other unmated Alpha was off travelling the world. Why, Aaron had no idea. He liked having roots, people to protect. A pack.

Brad did not.

"What's wrong, Jack? Charlie?"

He missed his own father's presence. Ever since Aaron had stepped up in his responsibilities, his dad had stepped further away. Building a home much further out of town and enjoying a quieter life with his second wife. Aaron's own mother had died giving birth to a second child. Neither of them had survived.

Jack looked towards his own son and Aaron followed his eyes. Grayson's gaze was hard as he stared back at his father.

Charlie, Marcus' father stood up. "We accept your mate, Aaron, as we must. However, this is most unusual. You will be another Alpha that does not produce any children and we, and the pack, are concerned about that."

Grayson stepped up to face the elders.

"You all know there are lots of other options. Reagan and I have been talking about some, and I don't believe this will be the end of my Alpha line. If anything, this means we will be strong going into the future."

Marcus made a snorting noise that grated on Aaron's nerves and he stared at the other Alpha, who sat with his arm wrapped around his pregnant mate.

"What's your problem, Marcus?"

He grinned. "At this rate, I'll be the only one to birth any new Alphas, which is just fine by me. I'm happy to take up the slack and make up for all you guys that are letting the pack down. Obviously Fate wants your genes out of the pack, and I think it's bloody hilarious."

Anger boiled in Aaron's blood at the arrogant comments. Marcus had always thought he was better than everyone else, but he was usually smart enough to keep his opinions to himself.

"I don't give a fuck who births the new generation Marcus, but I can guarantee you won't be the only one. If a Omega can be an Alpha's mate, then all the rules have changed. I suggest you get your head out of your arse and..."

Jordan tugged on his shirt and he unlocked his gaze from Marcus', looking down into his own mate's worried eyes.

"What's up, Jordan?"

His mate went up on his toes and whispered in his ear. "I'm really hungry. Will you come with me to get some food?"

His anger dissipated in one moment and he nodded. "Of course."

He looked back at the group of men. "Excuse me. I'm going to focus on my mate, since I've finally found him after almost THREE decades of looking."

He stared hard into the faces of each of the men, until the tugging on his arm started and he walked away. The elders should understand what he was going through at least. He thought most of them had at least some empathy.

Why couldn't they just be happy that one of their Alphas had finally found his destiny?

"I told you they wouldn't like me." Jordan whispered at him as they picked up their plates and began gathering food.

Hmmm... The chicken curry looks nice.

"It's not you, Jordan. You missed the speech Grayson gave everyone after you left and after the Rogue attacks. He told the whole pack that the original Alphas of our pack Luc and Gray, were a mated pair. They bred with five women, and that's where the original families come from."

Jordan gasped and turned to him. "So the stories were real? Oh my God, the Omegas must be flipping out!"

Why would the Omegas care about that?

"What do you mean? And keep going! I know you need to eat more than that."

Jordan had put about three pieces of chicken on his plate and Aaron knew he could and should eat a lot more than that.

Jordan gave him a lopsided smile and began grabbing carbs. Bread and a creamy pasta bake that would load up his calories for the day.

"Good boy. Now explain what you meant."

"Half the Omega wolves are gay, right? And most of them are unmated, or unmarked. Well, there's always been whispers. That being an all-male pairing was not a bad thing, but instead, a sign of strength, and indeed, a normal part of a pack."

Well, that made sense.

"So you guys have known this all along?"

That would be a twist of Fate. The Alphas felt that the Omegas were stupid and simple. And here they were, the only ones who actually had an inkling about the real origins of the 'Borough.

“Well, we always thought that Gray and Luc were men, I mean, who was the female? Gray? They’re both pretty masculine names.”

Aaron thought about it for a minute, and then laughed aloud. He’d never even thought about it. He’d just taken it as law.

“You’re pretty clever, aren’t you? My little mate?” He nuzzled into Jordan’s sweet smelling hair as they headed back to the table and began to eat, the hole in his belly filling with each mouthful.

“So, did I miss anything else while I was away?” Jordan asked him quietly.

Aaron caught Grayson’s eyes. “Hey Grayson, Jordan wants to know what else he missed in the past few weeks. You wanna fill him in?”

Grayson nodded, pushing his empty plate away.

“Well, I’m sure you know about the Rogue attacks, biggest and worst thing that’s ever happened here. I still shudder to think what could have happened. I’m in the middle of re-writing a lot of our protocols actually, to make sure that sort of thing doesn’t happen again. I made a promise to the pack, and I’m going to fulfil it. I promised to catch those responsible, and to keep our pack strong. There’s only one way to do that, and that’s to work together.”

Jordan was nodding beside him. “Yes. I agree.” His mate said quietly.

Grayson continued. “One new development however, and one I haven’t shared with the group yet, is that one of the Betas caught a Rogue the other night. One who was stealing through the perimeter to do reconnaissance.”

This was news to Aaron.

“Really? Did you question him?”

Grayson nodded, his eyes gleaming with the remembered

scene. "Yes, and we found out more about their set up, which was a lucky break."

"It seems that the men running the group are mostly Cody and Allen, two of the Betas that caused the most problems here last year. The wolf we tortured, I mean... questioned, was actually from a northern pack who'd been sucked in by Cody. They all speak of equality, but what they really want is to be the Alphas. But with no responsibility, only the power that comes with it. They have no fricken' idea what it takes to run a pack."

"But they don't want to take care of their people- look what they did to us!" Aaron ground out between clenched teeth.

He still couldn't fathom the fact that some of their own Betas had tried to kill the women and children of a pack they had once belonged to.

"I know. It's totally upside down logic. They want an equal society, but that means getting rid of our pack. Not sure how it works, but they believe we're all wrong with the way we run everything. Maybe that was why they went after the women and children, so we'd have no one left? Perhaps they hoped we'd all die due to loneliness, or something."

Aaron didn't want to think about how terrible that could have been. He'd seen his own father teeter on the brink of life after his mother's passing. A wolf rarely got over their mate's death.

They'd all counted their blessings when Alison, another widowed Beta's wife, had offered his father comfort in exchange for a home. She couldn't have children and was of no use to anyone else.

That had been perfect for his own father- who would never have wanted to put another woman through the trauma and possible tragedy of birth.

"Didn't they know we'd avenge our families?"

Grayson shrugged. "According to the wolf we have, that was

what they wanted. They want a fight, and they expect to win. They'll get our lands, the houses. The women, if they'll comply, which would be horrendous for them all. The Rogues look like they'll do whatever they can to keep us as weak and provoked as possible."

Aaron growled, his wolf vibrating with anger in his chest. He finally had Jordan, he wasn't losing him now.

"Bring it on. We're ready for them."

Jordan's hand slid over his forearm, and his body immediately calmed.

"Do you mind if I go and speak to my friends, Aaron?"

"Of course not. Go for it."

He looked down and saw that his mate had cleaned up his whole plate.

Jordan blew out a long breath and seemed to gather himself together, then smiled and got up to leave. Aaron watched him walk away and head towards the Omega tables.

He let the tension release from his chest through a long sigh.

This was a really good sign. Hopefully, Jordan could find his place again, but this time, at his side.

Jordan's arms were trembling as he forced his legs to move, one foot in front of another. Why was he doing this? He'd barely been in the Hall for an hour and he was already going over to his friends?

What had gotten into him?

As he stepped closer he could see Elliot and Travis sitting at the furthest table. Loners, they never socialized with anyone else.

They both turned to look at him, as did almost everyone he

walked past. His knees went weak as he walked and he could hear the pounding of his own heart in his ears.

Why are you doing this? Screamed a voice in his head that told him that running away was by far his best option. But as he stepped closer and recognised the anger and hurt on his friends' faces, he knew he was doing the right thing.

"Can I sit down?" He asked.

"Don't you belong at the Alpha table?" Elliot bit back.

He waited and didn't respond, then eventually Travis pushed out a chair to him.

"Sit then."

He collapsed onto the chair and decided to bite the bullet straight away.

"I'm sorry I left without telling you guys."

"And with the car. Where is it by the way?" Elliot asked.

He grimaced. "I left it parked at Reagan's place, but I can go get it tomorrow. Sorry about that, too. I was just too scared the night I left. I didn't think."

"Scared of what? Of going to your mate? I always said you were stupid for that." Travis hissed at him, then looked away, anger clear in the set of his jaw.

He sighed and let his shoulders drop from where they were being held too tightly. There was only one way to deal with this, and that was with brutal honesty. Rip the band aid off quickly.

"I know. You guys were right. I should have gone to Aaron two years ago when my mark first developed."

That made both of his friends turn back to him, their faces more accepting now.

"You both knew my mother... what she was like." They nodded, sympathy written in their eyes. They knew all right.

"Well, that just haunted me. I didn't think I could do this, and

I still don't. I can't be an Alpha Mate and help with the running of the pack, I don't want to."

"What does Aaron say about it?" Travis asked.

"Aaron says I can just stay at home if I want. I don't have to help."

And there it was, the solution he wanted. It was so obvious, and now that he said it aloud, he sounded like a coward. And a stupid one at that.

"You could help us, you know." Elliot said, his hands coming together in a clasp on the table.

"Yeah, you could. You know the Omegas, how we're treated. Grayson said he wanted to help the pack, fix things, well, you could, too. You're in a position of power now."

Jordan found himself nodding along with what his friends said. It was all true. For the first time in his life he was in a rare position of power with knowledge that none of the Alphas had.

"But how can I do anything?"

He couldn't even bring himself to speak at the Alpha table, let alone draw attention to a part of pack life that needed changing.

"Aaron will listen to you, Reagan, too. Come on, Jordan, if you want to make it up to us, try and get us enough money to build our own homes, or the ability to change jobs if we want to."

Jordan shuddered in remembrance at that one. The Omegas stayed in the same job, their whole lives. It drove some of them insane.

"Okay. I will. I'll talk to Aaron tonight."

"Great." Elliot said, a huge grin lighting up his face. "And even though we still miss you at our place, we're glad you're back in the pack."

Jordan smiled at his lifelong friends and got into the latest gossip of everything that had happened while he was away. He'd missed this part of being in the pack, the closeness, the comradery.

Maybe hiding in Aaron's house forever wasn't such a good idea?

CHAPTER SIX

Jordan looked over at his mate while they were dressing for the day. He'd been working up the courage all night to speak to him about the issues Elliot and Travis had mentioned last night.

"Um... Aaron, would you mind if I took your car back to Reagan's house today?" He glanced down at his new jeans. They were really tight now, he could barely do the button up. Yet, he certainly wasn't getting fat. His stomach looked like an ice tray, each individual square muscle standing out.

"Are you leaving me?"

Aaron's voice sounded so wounded and shocked that it struck pain straight through Jordan's chest.

He reached out for his huge mate, grabbing hold of his bare arms.

"No, no, don't be ridiculous."

Oh shit, I haven't told him yet.

"I'm never leaving you. Don't you know that by now?"

He'd forgotten about the one week deal that Aaron had

proposed initially to get him back here. The poor guy probably thought it still held.

Aaron's shoulders relaxed and his lips curved up into a smile.

"I suppose I do... then you believe me when I say we're meant to be together? You're not going to run off on me again?

He shook his head. "No. I promise. No matter what." And that was a big thing for him to admit. "As long as you let me hide in our house whenever I need to."

Aaron drew him close, pressing his lips to Jordan's with painstaking slowness.

"This is your home, too." He whispered over Jordan's mouth.

Sexual hunger roared to life in his belly and he opened his mouth to welcome Aaron's tongue, but his mate pulled away and grabbed one of his work shirts.

Cold anger replaced the heat in his gut.

Damn!

Even after being fucked well into the night, he would have loved a little more.

"What do you need the car for, then?"

What was the reason again? Oh yeah!

"Ah, I need to get my own car back. Well, actually, it's one of the cars the Omegas share. It's parked at Reagan's and I promised my friends that I'd go get it. I thought Reagan, or one of my friends, could come with me, and we could drive both the cars back again."

"Sure. No problem. I'm sorry I can't go with you, but Grayson called earlier to say there were problems on one of the outer farms, and we need to go check it out."

The Rogues were at it again.

Jordan supressed the shiver that rode him.

"Okay. Well, can I drop you somewhere, or...?"

"Yeah, that would be great, actually. If you could take me to the farm, then I'll get a lift back later. Or you could come get me. You'll only be a few hours and I'll be there all day probably."

Melbourne was almost two hours each way, but he'd be back early afternoon, so that was do-able.

"Sounds perfect. Let's go."

He walked out of the bedroom awkwardly, the jeans tugging on his hips and making moving hard.

I'm getting too big for these.

Aaron's chuckle as he opened the door was beautiful, a sound that shined through Jordan like the sun.

"What's so funny?"

Not that he didn't know. He must look like the tin-man.

"I need to get you some new clothes. You grew out of them before you'd put them on practically."

They got into the car and the mention of clothes and money made him think of what Travis and Elliot had been saying.

"I was wanting to speak to you about something like that too, actually. Is that okay?" He twisted his fingers together, pain flicking through the joints.

"You can talk to me about anything. We've got about ten minutes until we get to the farm."

Aaron turned the car to the left, heading even further out of the 'Borough.

"Well, I was speaking to my friends last night at the Hall and they were hoping I'd talk to you about some of the Omega stuff."

He swallowed hard, saliva pooling in his mouth as nervous energy wriggled through his body.

"Like what?" Aaron asked, glancing over at him, and then back to the road.

There wasn't any house around for kilometres out here. It was very beautiful though. All green hills and cleared farming land.

"Jordan?" Aaron repeated.

He must have been thinking too long.

"Oh, sorry. Well... some of the Omegas, not all mind you, would like the chance to train in other areas, change job perhaps."

"What do you mean change jobs? Don't they let you move around?"

Jordan shook his head. "No. I've worked in the same café since I turned sixteen. Same job."

"You're kidding me? That's ridiculous." Aaron scowled.

He shrugged. He'd assumed everyone knew what their lives were like. Why wouldn't he?

"It's just how it's always been according to some of the older guys. The Alphas or whoever originally organised the rules must have thought we were too stupid to learn more than one thing, but I can tell you, it can be a major brain drain."

"What else?" Aaron asked, and he actually sounded interested.

"Well... there's the houses and the money side of things, too."

He stalled, suddenly embarrassed to admit how little money they made. Did they have the right to complain when the pack provided all their food? Maybe they were asking too much?

"What do you mean?"

"Well... the wages are pretty basic, as you can imagine. We work sixty hour weeks, which is fine. Of course. And we make enough money for rent, maybe a little more. But that's it. We could never afford to save to build a house, or get nicer clothes. I know that sounds materialistic... but..."

Heat flushed up his face as he began to stammer. How would Aaron understand? He was an Alpha. He was limited by nothing.

"That's terrible, Jordan. Seriously, I had no idea it was so bad for you guys and I'm.. sorry I never noticed. That does not reflect well on me, either." He cleared his throat roughly and Jordan stared at his mate, once again amazed at how deeply he felt things around him. *This* was a true Alpha.

"I'll get Grayson to look at the pay and rent structure tonight, okay? Promise."

Jordan stared at his mate.

Wow. He sounds like he really means it.

"That would be really great, Aaron. Thank you."

Aaron pointed ahead and Jordan turned to look out the front window of the car.

"Here's the farm. I can't see anything out of the ordinary. Stay in the car while I check it out."

Jordan nodded, watching his mate jump out of the car, lock the doors and prowl towards the house.

His heart leapt into his throat as he watched and waited, sliding into the driver's seat just in case he needed to start the engine quickly.

Ha. As if you'd be any use in a dangerous situation.

He scowled into the mirror as the negative thought charged through his mind. He really needed to stop that self-deprecating voice kicking him all the time.

Aaron stepped back out of the house, a smile on his face as he jogged back to the car.

Jordan wound down the window and looked towards his mate.

"It's all good. But by the feeling I'm getting from Martin, I think I'll be here for the day. Poor guy is rattled by something and I can definitely smell the Rogues around the house. You all right to pick me up when you come back? You remember the way?"

He should be fine. He'd take more note driving back now.

Aaron nodded back towards the top of the hill. "It's pretty much straight, if you head back, there's just one turn, and you follow the signs back to Greensborough."

"I'm sure I'll be okay. Thanks for letting me do this. I'll see you in a few hours."

Aaron grinned and tapped the window edge before heading back to the house.

Jordan reversed the car up the drive and headed back to the 'Borough. He'd pick up one of the boys and drive back to Melbourne, make it a bit of a day trip. It was Saturday, so Elliot should have the day off.

Either way, the sun was shining and it was going to be a lovely day.

AARON WATCHED his mate drive away and he headed back into the house, a nagging ache tugging at his chest. Damn, he hated that feeling when Jordan left him. He should be used to it now, but after being alone so long, he much preferred Jordan close.

He stepped back in through the front door and looked towards the Beta whose face was pale, his smell stinking of fear.

"So, what's happened Martin? What has you so spooked?"

Martin's face crumpled, the stoic farmer's eyes shimmering with unshed tears.

Aaron frowned and took a step closer. This wasn't like the Beta wolf at all. "What's going on? I thought you said everything was fine."

Martin shook his head and one of the doors off the lounge room opened. Out stepped a man Aaron recognised.

A dimple in his chin and a gun in his right hand.

"Coby."

The bastard that set fire to the 'Borough.

The Beta wolf grinned at him, the smile as evil as any he'd

seen on a man. Aaron was sure he could see the insanity gleaming in Coby's dull blue eyes.

"Aaron the Alpha. As I live and breathe. What are *you* doing here?"

Aaron's brain was going ten to the dozen. Why were they here? How many of them were there? Where was Martin's wife? His kids?

Forget about the fire. And the gun. Something's going on here you don't understand and you need to get to the bottom of it.

And try not to die.

Despite the fact that his wolf was clamouring for a fight inside of him, he decided he better stay calm and just answer the question in front of him.

"Grayson called me last night. He said to come and see Martin this morning about some Rogue activity."

That was the truth.

A strange gargled chuckle rolled out of Coby. "The Rogues? Is that what you guys call us? How cute. And apt. Hmm.."

He seemed to lose himself for a moment, then his eyes struck back on Aaron's like lasers on target.

"Ah yes. I asked Martin to lure one of the Alphas here. I didn't expect you, to be honest. Not sure why..." Cody's mouth twisted.

Who had he wanted? Have I thrown a spanner in the works for his plan? Good!

"Who did you expect?" He asked, trying to keep his tone light, but the craziness in Coby's eyes was not boding well for Aaron's health today.

"Oh... someone with family. I suppose. You see, I intend to hold you for ransom. For my pack. We need some money and supplies to set up our new town, and Greensborough has too much of everything."

That's because we work hard, and Grayson manages our money very well.

"But no matter... Marcus would have been better, even Grayson. Their father's would have paid handsomely for their safe return. You... well... Could I convince you to call Grayson and get him down here?"

Aaron crossed his arms over his chest and stared at the man who held a gun pointed at him.

Not on your life, or mine, for that matter.

"I didn't think so. What if I told you I'd kill Martin if you didn't call?"

He grabbed Martin by the shirt and pulled him to the ground, pressing the gun into the man's temple.

Martin began to shake, closing his eyes as though he knew his life was over. But he didn't make a sound.

Aaron exhaled sharply. Martin had four kids, and a lovely wife. But if they weren't here in this room, where were they? Already safe? Or being held somewhere else, still in danger?

Either way, Aaron had to think about the pack. Not an individual, and that included himself.

"Nope, sorry. I'm not giving you another Alpha to barter, you'll have to deal with little orphan me. But if you kill Martin, then I'll shift and attack you."

Cody sneered at him. "I'll shoot you before you can pounce."

"Then you'll have two dead men and no money."

His heart was pounding in his chest now and his wolf howled in anguish.

Poor Jordan. He will be so lost if I die.

He had to stay cool. If all they wanted was money, then no one should get hurt.

Cody lowered the weapon and kicked Martin in the back, flattening him. Martin grunted and stayed down.

Martin's submissive response surprised Aaron, he was a strong man. A good Beta. He would not usually be so ready to comply to another Beta, no matter the circumstance.

Then the truth hit him like a gut punch. Martin's family were not safe. No wolf, no matter what ranking, would submit unless forced to.

"Looks like I'm going to have to just deal with you then."

Coby walked towards him, twisted the pistol in his grip and swung, knocking Aaron sideways with the metal to his temple.

Pain exploded in his brain, triggering his wolf to react. A vicious growl ripped through him and the shift began.

"Get down." Cody bellowed, lowering his gun and pulling the trigger.

Fire exploded through his thigh as hot blood ran down his leg.

His wolf cowered inside him and his half morphed body shrunk back to human. He grabbed for a nearby chair, sinking down into it.

He didn't dare look away from Coby's gaze, but instead clenched his teeth and focused on the madman in the room.

He didn't want to die, but he wouldn't get anyone else killed either.

"Okay, Aaron. Here's the deal. I'm going to give you a phone and you're going to call Grayson, or his dad. Whoever you think has more power with the money. You are going to explain that I want five million dollars transferred into my account, a reasonable sum, I think. Or I will start killing people. Starting with little baby Molly."

Shock made Aaron pause. Cody had the family? All of them? That changed everything.

Damn it!

"The pack doesn't have that sort of money, you know that.

Especially after the attack you guys launched. We're rebuilding everything."

A strange angry frown crossed Cody's face. "Yes. That should have worked perfectly, but instead Grayson came back too quick."

Aaron nodded, letting Cody talk, his skin crawling with sweat.

He squeezed his leg tight. He needed to wrap that or he'd bleed out.

"All right. I can call the pack and tell them of your demands."

Cody grinned and swung the gun around like he was having a great time.

"Here's the phone."

THE TRIP to Melbourne with Elliot was brilliant. They caught up on all their news and Jordan even got to talk about his fears for his relationship with Aaron.

Elliot was supportive and kind, but also straightforward. Exactly what he needed.

They loaded both cars with some things Reagan had asked for, and headed back towards the 'Borough. Elliot driving their old car, and Jordan driving Aaron's new car.

He still couldn't believe he had a mate, let alone an Alpha.

Surreal didn't even begin to cover it.

As they headed back up the mountain, he checked the time and grinned. They hadn't taken long, he'd be home with Aaron before he knew it.

As they drove into Greensborough there was a strange feeling in the town. Nothing looked out of the ordinary, but he knew something wasn't quite right.

He waved goodbye to Elliot as his friend took the old car back to their old share house and he kept driving forward.

As he drove out of the other side of town, his stomach began to wriggle with happiness. He'd see Aaron soon, and maybe they could go home for an afternoon delight before Aaron went back to work.

It was Saturday after all.

He headed along the road, then turned left towards the farm. He wouldn't mind working further out of town. Now that he had more muscles, maybe they'd let him do some labouring or building perhaps?

Aren't you getting a little ahead of yourself?

He frowned at the negative thought and pushed it away. Those voices, both real and imagined, had ruled his life for too long and he was sick of it.

He waited for the negativity to pop up again, but it stayed quiet.

Wow. Cool.

He grinned as he saw the house ahead of him, slowing down on the dirt road.

Fear prickled along his skin, out of nowhere.

He slammed his foot on the brake and pulled over onto the grass. What was that feeling that just moved over him? So strange.

He couldn't breathe right.

He lifted his gaze to the house ahead of him and saw two men walking out of the front door onto the porch.

They looked his way and he dove down, pressing himself into the seat.

What should he do? There was something majorly fishy going on here.

He didn't know those men's faces, and he knew everyone in the pack. Were they strangers visiting? And if so, where was Aaron? Or Martin?

He simply couldn't shake the idea that something was very wrong. And hadn't Aaron said he was coming out here today to investigate some Rogue activity?

But wouldn't Aaron have taken care of them if they were a threat to the pack? He was a strong Alpha.

Jordan didn't dare turn the car back on, in case it got their attention. So he grabbed the keys and slid up slowly, looking towards the house once again.

Nothing.

Relief flooded his hyperactive nervous system. He didn't want to stay where he was. Maybe he could sneak up and take a look inside the house?

Since when do you have courage?

He frowned at the bad voice and took a deep breath.

Since my mate could be in trouble.

He opened the car door and then softly shut it, his heart hammering in his chest so loud he was terrified they'd be able to hear it from the house.

Wolves had increased senses of hearing and smell.

But he was still a bit away and there was a lot of distracting noises and scents in the Australian bush.

A Kookaburra sung from a tree nearby, his loud cackle a sound that on any other day, Jordan would have loved hearing.

Case in point.

He crouched low to the ground and raced over to the nearest tree, hiding behind it, and peering off towards the house again.

What do I do? What do I do?

He could go back to the 'Borough. Get help. Or at least Reagan to come with him to investigate.

Something deep inside him told him to stay. Not to leave.

He crept around another tree, and then sprinted to the next one. His lungs heaved as he dragged in as much air as he could.

Cracking branches and men's voices caught his attention and he turned side on, hiding behind the thick gum tree in front of him.

He gasped, then held his breath, trying so hard not to be seen.

The men who were walking towards his car held guns, and both of them looked like they hadn't showered in a month.

Which, as a person who had only recently been taken in off the streets, he knew what that looked like.

They peered into Aaron's car, then drew back an extended arm and smashed in one of the side windows with the butt of the gun.

The man with the red tinged hair put his arm in and unlocked the door, pulling it open to rifle through it.

There wasn't anything in there except a water bottle, and oh damn... some of Reagan's books were in the boot. And some of his clothes.

The men didn't seem too interested in what they found, instead sauntering back to the house as though they didn't have a care in the world.

So, what did he have?

Unknown men. A home his mate was probably still in, and a smashed window on his car.

At least he could still drive it.

If he had to.

Fuckkkk.

He let his head fall back against the hard trunk of the tree. His wolf practically quivering inside of him.

He was terrified and he had no idea what to do.

A gun shot rang out and a growl ripped through his throat.

Okay. Get serious. There's no time to go get help.

You're it. So pull it together and think only of Aaron.

If he's safe, and okay, you can fall apart then.

He nodded once, inhaling deeply through his nose.

Now that he'd pulled himself together somewhat, it was time for action. He twisted around and looked towards the house, and then over the terrain between the house and him.

It wasn't too far, but he'd need to be careful.

He hunkered down and pushed his feet into the ground, springing off and sprinting to a tree about a hundred metres away.

His heart hammered in his chest as he reached for the tree, ducking behind the huge oak, then blowing out the breath he'd been unconsciously holding.

He could hear them now. Men talking, their gruff, raised voices making the hairs on his arms stand up.

Jordan breathed in, breathed out, looked across the wrap around veranda and darted across the open lawn, ducking in behind the nice little country home.

His body shook suddenly and he could sense pain, and fear. And it wasn't his.

Oh, no. Aaron.

How many of them are there?

Oh shit! What am I doing? I should have gone back to the 'Borough for help. How am I going to go up against those two men, let alone anyone else?

Tears stung his eyes and he closed them, willing his panic away.

He was only going to check what the scenario was for now.

Jordan crept along the floorboards, and bent down beneath one of the open windows.

The voice he heard sent real shivers down his spine.

"Well, it looks like you and every one of those brats is dead, Aaron. Your pack won't save you. The men you trusted, they don't give a shit about you."

That's not true.

Jordan held his breath and listened more.

"What did Grayson say this time?" A weak voice asked.

That was Aaron! And shit, he sounded terrible.

Jordan pushed up from his feet and slowly looked over the wooden window ledge.

Aaron was in a chair, bleeding from the leg and holding his belly with his hands. Three men stood up and walked around him.

Jordan's stomach dropped and a snarl ripped through his mind.

He swallowed it down before it emerged, but marvelled at the strength of his wolf.

He'd never known that sort of power before.

"That they don't have it and they won't go to the bank for it. Which means, they don't believe me when I say I'm going to kill people. Perhaps we need to start with the children, what do you think?"

"No. Me. Start with me." Aaron's voice said and the anger that ripped through Jordan's head was the worst he'd ever felt.

What the hell is he doing? Sacrificing himself?

Well. I'll fix that.

Where's the back door to this place?

He raced around the back and found the old wooden door unlocked.

He couldn't take on a room full of Beta crazy wolves, but he could help take away some of their power. Maybe.

He was risking himself now.

And what's the point of living if Aaron's dead?

He paused for a long moment then shook himself.

Seems like the mating's complete then. I'm not living without that man.

He opened the door with agile fingers and snuck inside. He

couldn't hear anyone speaking, but there was a baby making soft crying sounds in the next room.

He pushed the door open, praying that there wouldn't be another wolf in there guarding them.

The room was empty, save for a woman and several children clutching her long skirt.

Their eyes were wide, the woman's face red and streaked with tears.

He put a finger to his lips to indicate they needed to be quiet.

"Let's get you guys out of here." He whispered and the woman shook her head.

"They said they'll kill my husband if I try and escape."

"Well, they're in the front room threatening to kill your baby, so I suggest you get the hell out of here."

The woman looked down at the infant in her arms and nodded, standing up and grabbing hold of one of the kids' hands.

"Stay close, Billie." She said to the older child who was clinging to her.

"You need to run and hide in the trees." He opened the door to the hallway, made sure the coast was clear, and then held open the backdoor.

It creaked and his heart leapt into his chest.

They were made.

He ushered everyone out the door, but no one came.

Thank God. They were probably enjoying what was going on in the front room too much.

Jordan grabbed hold of the two children's hands that could walk and looked straight at the mother.

"Don't stop. No matter what."

He looked towards the front of the house, but when he saw nothing he grabbed the kids and whispered. "Run."

They ran for the edge of the woods, one of the children tripping and falling, but Jordan scooped him up and somehow they made it.

"What are you going to do?" The woman asked, her voice high pitched and scared.

"I don't really know. But you can help. Just up over the rise, I left my car. Here are the keys. Go get help. Tell Grayson, or Marcus, to come here now."

He handed her the keys out of his pocket, amazed at how steady his hands were.

"And they smashed a window, so there will be some glass, so be careful."

She took the keys and patted the baby in her arms.

"I will. Good luck, and thank you."

"Go. Please. Quickly."

The woman grabbed her children and began hiking up the hill.

Lovely calm woman, he hadn't met many of those.

He twisted back around towards the house and closed his eyes, focusing on the sounds coming from the front room.

There was a grunt and a thump.

Aaron. They're hurting him.

His blood began to boil, his belly ripping apart his gut from the inside. The shift started to take him over and he let go of his humanity.

He dropped to the ground and watched in awe as his hands became paws and his back prickled with fur.

Take them down.

He ran for the front of the house, a growl ripping through his chest.

He jumped in through a side open window and went straight for the man holding the gun.

His teeth latched onto the man's throat as he screamed and Jordan clenched tight. Until the screaming stopped.

The room erupted in growls and screams.

He dropped the man to the floor and turned around.

Aaron had shifted and his big black wolf had flattened one of the other men.

Martin had shifted too, his smaller brown wolf going face to face with two other wolves. Already shifted Rogues.

Jordan launched forward, going shoulder to shoulder with Martin, snapping and growling at the other two wolves.

The Rogues took a step back, and seemed to hesitate. Jordan snapped his jaws and bent low as though he was going to attack them.

One of them made a whining noise and they both turned tail and fled.

Jordan ran after them, jumping off the balcony and following them into the bush.

They were fast and he stopped, unable to follow them.

He turned back and ran to his mate.

Aaron had returned to human form, his naked, bloody body a real mess now.

"Well done, Jordan. I knew you had it in you."

Really? I didn't.

Jordan let his wolf go, a creature he'd only inhabited a handful of times in his life.

The Omega wolves did not shift often, unable to feel the pull of the full moon like the Alpha and Beta wolves did.

Something had changed inside him.

And it was all to do with the man in front of him.

Martin shifted back to his human self too and ran off down the hall.

"They're gone! They're gone!" Martin bolted back into the front room, screaming in terror.

"No. It's fine. I got your wife and children out. They're safe."

The expression of pure gratitude and relief on the other man's face was indescribable as he fell to his knees and dropped his head.

Jordan turned his attention back to his mate. He didn't look good.

"Let's get you home again, Aaron. I think Reagan might need to take a look at those wounds."

Aaron nodded weakly and Jordan ducked down, pulling his mate's arm across his shoulder.

"Martin. Do you have a car we could use?"

The man on the floor jumped up, his harried hair standing up on end.

"Ah yeah, yeah I do." He left the room and returned in a moment.

"You'll be okay." Jordan reassured his mate, who was leaning on him a little too heavily. Jordan panted as he struggled to hold Aaron up.

"Can you help me with him?"

Martin stared for a moment and then ducked forward. "Oh yeah, sorry."

The poor guy's head was probably in three places at once.

"I feel so terrible, Aaron. I'm so sorry. They shot him twice, I think. Maybe three times."

Jordan's heart stuttered in his chest.

"They what?"

He looked down Aaron's naked body, the bruising and blood making more sense. It was everywhere. His gut, his thigh, his legs.

He ignored the fear catapulting through his body. Aaron was an Alpha.

"He'll be fine."

They got to the mini-van and wrestled a semi-conscious Aaron into the car.

Jordan jumped into the back with him, where he lay across some of the seats, and just as he was about to pull closed the door, a huge black wolf bounded down the hill.

Jordan pulled the door shut and bared his teeth, only to hear Martin's whoop of happiness.

"Looks like the cavalry's arrived." He wound down his window to talk to the weres that had arrived. "There's a couple of dead wolves inside and the other two ran off down the hill towards Rosedale."

The black wolf that must have been Grayson headed off and Martin started the car.

"Ten minutes and we'll be there. Just hang on."

They took off up the hill and Jordan wrapped his arms around his mate.

Aaron moaned and nuzzled into his shoulder.

His breathing became ragged and as Jordan pressed his fingers to Aaron's wrist he noticed his mate's pulse get fainter and fainter.

Oh no!

"Hurry Martin! Hurry! He's dying!"

The car groaned as it accelerated fast up the road and Jordan held on for dear life, praying to all that was holy and everything in between that his mate would survive this wretched day.

CHAPTER SEVEN

Jordan turned to Elliot who sat beside him in the hospital's quiet waiting room.

"What if he dies? What am I going to do?"

Now that the shock had worn off, he was shuddering like a leaf in a thunderstorm. His skin was so cold he couldn't feel it properly. Such an odd feeling.

Elliot frowned at him. "You need some clothes, or a blanket, or something."

Jordan looked down at himself and couldn't find the energy to care. Somewhere deep inside his mind he was shocked at the sight of his ripped body covered in blood, naked and shaking.

But Aaron was going to die.

And nothing else mattered.

Elliot squeezed him leg. "Wait here. Don't move."

Jordan nodded and wrapped his arms around his body as his teeth clattered together.

What was he going to do?

Elliot came back and wrapped a scratchy blanket around his shoulders.

"Here." Elliot handed him a cardboard cup, with a lid on it. "It's a hot chocolate. You need it. Drink."

Jordan put the cup to his lips without much thought, going on autopilot, he followed his friend's instructions.

He almost dropped the cup, his hands were shaking so much.

Elliot sat down beside him and helped him bring the drink to his lips, the creamy chocolate sliding down his throat and warming a cold, gaping hole in his gut.

A soft moan escaped his throat and he relaxed into the chair, shifting his weight so that the blanket covered more of him.

He could tell the difference between the hot and the cold parts of his body now. That was a good sign.

They sat in silence and Jordan drank, trying not to think about what they were doing to Aaron in the other room. When they'd arrived, Reagan had been on duty and he'd called for Dr. Sarah and they'd taken him straight into surgery.

Not a room they used very much in Greensborough. Wolves healed so well generally, so few of them ever needed operations.

"They'll fix him up. You know that. Dr. Sarah and Reagan... well, they're awesome."

The calm words soothed him a little. It was true. They were both doctors, and Dr. Sarah was especially trained in werewolf physiology.

Surely Aaron would be okay?

He was an Alpha for pity's sake. They should heal twice as fast as everybody else.

What was taking so long?

The white door at the end of the corridor swung open and Jordan jumped up, dropping the blanket to the floor.

Cold air rushed around him, making him shake once again. Elliot scooped up the blanket and wrapped it around Jordan. He gave his friend a grateful smile and dropped the empty cup in the bin.

Dr. Sarah wore green hospital scrubs and was covered in more blood than Jordan, if that was possible.

"He's alive."

Jordan's knees gave out and he sunk into the waiting chair behind him.

"Can I see him?"

Worry creased itself along Dr. Sarah's face. "Ah. You can, but not for too long. He's in a coma, and I'm not sure how long he's going to be in it for. You need to go home and get some sleep, you're going to need your rest, I fear."

The cold arm of death wrapped itself around Jordan and he struggled not to succumb to its icy embrace.

The door banged open this time and Reagan joined them.

"Jordan. Come see him with me. As his mate, I'm sure you'll be able to do something miraculous that we can't."

Maybe... What can I do?

When he didn't move, Reagan reached out and grabbed his hand, pulling him along the sterile corridor until Jordan was somewhere he'd never been before. Inside a hospital room, staring down at his pale mate.

"He looks like death." Jordan whispered, reaching out a hand to touch Aaron's forehead.

He was clammy to the touch, but also feverish. An unhealthy and weird combination.

"We removed the bullets. Stopped the bleeding. But he's lost a lot of blood and he's not healing how Sarah says he should as a wolf."

"What could it be then?" Jordan asked, running his fingers over Aaron's beloved face.

He didn't look like Aaron. The warm, passionate man he'd grown to love.

It was very strange.

"It's only a suspicion, but I think they may have poisoned him somehow. Soaked the bullets in something maybe, I'm not sure. But we need to keep an eye on him."

Jordan glanced around the white room. "I'll sleep here and watch him."

"Oh, no. There's no space for you."

Jordan turned around and eyed the only man in Greensborough that should understand how he felt.

"Reagan, if you don't get me a bed, I'll sleep on the floor next to him. I. Do. Not. Care."

A ghost of a smile tipped up the other Alpha mate's lips.

"I'll talk to Sarah. I'm sure we can organise something."

He inclined his head and sat down on the bed.

The door opened and closed, and he stared at his mate, a strange panic and sadness swimming through him. As though he could feel Aaron drifting away. Down a long, cold, river.

"No!" He clenched his fists hard and glared down at Aaron's comatose body. "Listen here, Aaron. I did not face up to all of my fears, shift into a wolf, and save you, for nothing. You got that? So you are going to wake up, and be proud of me, and go back to work. You have things to do, a pack to run. This place has a lot of fixing up to do and you're the only one who can do it."

His throat closed up as the tears threatened his ability to talk.

The anger had gone out of him now, but the strength in his heart was still there. The conviction that he was correct.

There was one other thing too.

"Plus, I love you. I always have. And I haven't got to tell you that yet, so you better wake up so I can."

The door opened again and Reagan stepped back in, panting a little as he dragged in new furniture.

"I have you a mattress and all that stuff. Where do you want it?"

~

Aaron could hear his mate talking and he tried responding, and yet nothing came out of his mouth.

He listened harder. Yeah. There he was again.

Why can't I get to him?

What's wrong with my body?

He couldn't speak, couldn't even open his eyes. Something was very wrong, and he didn't know what to do.

He was quiet for a long moment, just listening and feeling. His body was sick, but he'd get better.

There was something finally worth fighting for.

Someone worth living for.

There was Jordan.

~

Two days of living at the hospital eventually wore Jordan down. He finally relented to Grayson, who asked him to go for a walk, have a shower and come back in an hour.

He took the car and practically flew home and had the shortest shower he could when he had to scrub every inch of his body, and dress in his clothes that were still too tight.

He hadn't grown much more, thank goodness, or he wouldn't fit into anything.

No sex, and very little food, had his body starving once again.

It was like before, but so much worse.

He knew what it was to be weak, and hungry. But now that he'd known what it felt like to be full, to be satisfied, to be happy? This new limbo was purgatory.

Why know the warmth of the sun, only to be thrust back into the darkness?

He parked further away from the hospital and got out to walk. Grayson was right, he probably needed some fresh air.

The smell of cooking meat with garlic caught his nose as it drifted from the Hall on the air.

His stomach growled and tightened so badly he had to stop and swallow hard, scared he'd retch what little contents he had in his stomach.

He glanced longingly towards the Hall. He could just go in and get some food and bring it with him to the hospital.

Aaron would hate that he wasn't eating.

That decided it for him.

He dragged his tired body in the opposite direction from the hospital, confident that Aaron was in good hands with Grayson and of course Reagan hanging around.

He pushed open the door and the smell of the oily, flagrant food assailed his nostrils.

Oh... yum.

The muscles in his legs quivered as he moved around the people already seated and eating, then found himself standing at the huge tables laden with food.

His mouth began to water and he grabbed up a plate, piling food onto it. He didn't care what anybody else thought about him eating so much.

He needed it.

A soft, white roll found its way into his hand and he brought it to his mouth, ripping it apart with his teeth and downing the whole lot before he even turned around.

"Hey Jordan, come here a sec."

He turned towards the deep voice calling his name and saw Marcus, the Alpha twat, his hand gesturing that Jordan should come sit with them.

He didn't want to be rude, but there was no way he was sitting at the Alpha table without Aaron.

His feet moved of their own volition and he went as bidden.

They probably wanted to know how Aaron was. He got to the table and held tight to the plate in his hands.

"Yes?"

He was dying to eat the rest of the food on his plate, but he really should get back to the hospital.

"How's Aaron doing? I'm sure the whole council would like to know."

Well, they could ask.

He turned towards the older men at the end of the table who were looking at him expectantly.

"Aaron's still in a coma and they don't know when he'll come out of it. But Doctor Sarah and Reagan are looking after him."

"Thank you, Jordan." Grayson's mother said, smiling kindly at him.

He returned the smile, a small amount of joy returning to his heart.

"I better get back to him."

He began to turn away but was ripped back, Marcus's strong hand holding tight to his arm.

"Where are you going, Omega? You haven't been dismissed."

The rest of the table went suddenly quiet, and Jordan felt the same stirring of his wolf that he'd sensed just before he shifted.

He took a deep breath to try and calm himself. This was not the same situation.

You're not in danger and neither is Aaron. So try to behave.

He cleared his throat. “Excuse me, but I need to get back to the hospital.”

Marcus didn't let go and the rest of the table didn't speak up for him.

His wolf flickered inside of him, gaining strength as his anger grew.

Who did this guy think he was?

Marcus glared up at him, beady brown eyes that turned his stomach.

“I told you to stay, now stay.” Marcus pulled hard, dragging him to his knees on the floor like a dog.

Like a Omega.

A growl ripped through his throat like a knife and he snatched his arm back, partially shifted and swung a clawed paw at Marcus, jumping to his feet in one move.

Marcus's head snapped sideways and then he too got to his feet, Jordan's claw marks drawing blood from his cheek.

Jordan glared up at the big Alpha, for the first time in his whole life, uncaring of what would happen to him if he stood up for himself.

“I am not a Omega wolf anymore, and even if I was. You. Do. Not. Treat. Us. That. Way.”

A nasty, venomous growl rolled out of Marcus as his eyes shifted to yellow and his arms bunched with muscles at his sides.

“I'll treat you however I Goddamn like. I'm an Alpha of this pack and you are nothing.”

He began to shift and Jordan heard the commotion as everyone behind him got to their feet, the cacophony of movement like an elephant stampede.

There was heat on his spine and he sensed the men at his back. He glanced behind him. Every Omega in the place was standing, their faces determined, their small fists clenched.

They were going to fight.

And they were going to fight for him.

His own wolf charged forth within him and he faced back at the half shifted Alpha Marcus. A man unworthy of the title.

"I am an Alpha Mate! Chosen by Fate herself. And YOU are nothing but a lazy, selfish arsehole who doesn't deserve to be Alpha!"

He watched the fear appear in Marcus' eyes as his shift slowed down, the human understanding dawning.

Jordan let his animal take over and his clothes tore apart as he shifted fully, his wolf now taller, bigger, and grey, like Aaron's.

He planted his feet and snarled into Marcus' face.

The Alpha fell backwards, as did most of the other men at the table, drawing their own mates behind them.

Except for one man.

A man Jordan had never seen before. He stepped forward and spoke, his tone soft and placating.

"Jordan. Calm down, it's fine. Shift back and we'll talk."

The voice was familiar in a strange way, and his eyes.... This was Aaron's father.

He let go of his wolf and he shrunk back down into his human flesh, the buzz of the noise around him calming down until almost no one was moving, or speaking.

The man in front of him smiled softly, his eyes straying down Jordan's body to rest on his chest.

He was much older than Jordan, his lined face creasing even more as he studied Jordan's birthmark.

"Then it is true." The man whispered, his hand moving out slowly to run his finger-tips over the new addition to Jordan's birthmark.

Jordan forced himself to stay perfectly still, the warm hands of the other man feeling cool compared to Jordan's own overheated flesh.

His breath still shuddered in and out of his lungs and his chest rose and fell with too much speed.

He swallowed and tried to slow his racing heart.

"Who are you?"

Although, I'm pretty sure I already know.

The man's green eyes lifted up and met his. Aaron's eyes.

"I'm Aaron's father. Tobias. It's so, so good to meet you finally. My son has waited an eternity to meet you."

"Look! I told you." Marcus' whingey, horrible voice interjected into their warm family bubble. "He is a freak! What the hell is happening to this pack? We're being overrun by gay fucks."

Jordan turned to deal with the Alpha arsehole but instead watched with glee as Grayson's dad ploughed his fist straight through the other Alpha's jaw, effectively knocking him out.

For a moment anyway.

As Marcus began to stir, Jack gestured to one of the other Alphas. "Get your son out of here, Ron. Before the Omega's show him just how powerful they really are." Jack said, stepping forward to join them.

"Good to see you, Tobias." Jack patted Aaron's father on the back. "Looks like we have more in common than we thought. Two sons who are all-male Alpha pairings, incredible isn't it?"

Tobias nodded, his eyes straying once again to the wolf on Jordan's chest.

"Jordan, here you go." A young woman, married to one of the Betas, walked up close to him and gently handed him some clothes, a black pair of jeans and a grey tank.

"Oh, thank you so much."

Being the only person naked in the whole Hall was intimidating to say the least.

The Omegas hadn't moved from their protective stance. They were still standing behind him. He needed to say something.

He turned so that he could address both the Omegas and the Alpha table.

"I need to say thank you to everyone who rose up to help me today. Especially after everything I've gone through lately, I appreciate it more than you know."

He turned more towards the Alpha table. "Before Aaron got hurt a few days ago, I spoke to him about changing some of the laws. A lot of you don't realise that many of the Omegas would like a choice in what sort of job they have, and perhaps even to make enough money to be able to save, or build new housing. Our lives are extremely limited, and although not everyone wants that, the options need to change."

There was a heavy murmur within the Omegas, and many of them, including Elliot, who stood nearby, gave him a huge smile and a nod.

"My son wanted to help you change these things?" Tobias asked.

"He wanted the pack to be stronger, better. And yes, he said he would speak to the council and Grayson as soon as possible. Unfortunately, Fate got in the way."

Sadness swept over him and his stomach pulled tight. He was still starving.

"I know my son wants this pack to be stronger, better." Jack said, his thoughts obviously drifting to Grayson who was at the hospital still.

"Then I will help, too." Tobias agreed.

There was a great silence, and then Jordan's stomach made a loud growling noise and a laughing twitter went through the crowd.

He couldn't help but smile and put a hand over his stomach.

"I really need to get back to the hospital, so please, keep eating. I'll let you know if anything changes with Aaron."

"I'll come with you." Tobias said and everyone else began to disperse. "You better get some more food though."

Jordan looked at the mess on the floor that Marcus had created and sighed. What a waste.

"Yes. I think I will."

He scooped up the broken plate and as much of the spilled food as he could, before dumping it in the bin.

Most of the room was still heavily buzzing with conversation, but Jordan just wanted to get some food now and get out of there.

His shoulders were aching with the stress.

He made another plate, this time not so high a pile, then turned to leave, Tobias sticking to his side like a web that was attached to him.

"Tobias, why haven't I seen you around before? Aren't you one of the Alphas?"

He'd known that there was always five born in each generation, but for some reason had never questioned that there was only four sitting at the table.

And speaking of which...

"Also, why is there only four of Aaron's generation? There's Aaron, Grayson, Marcus, and Tom."

Tom and Marcus were both married to women and with babies on the way. Where was the fifth?

"Oh well, that's two questions. But to answer the easy one, Brad is the fifth. He's Charlie's son. He's a bit of a lone wolf, so to speak. A wanderer. Not one for a pack."

"That's odd." He didn't really know how else to express it.

"It is... but it happens. He wasn't a bad kid, just unusual. Not into pressure, or expectation."

Jordan nodded, waiting for the answer to his other question.

He picked up another bread roll, this one filled with butter and garlic and chomped into it.

Ecstasy flowed over his tastebuds and he groaned as he ate the whole thing.

"You are hungry."

He shrugged as he picked up some chicken. "It's been days of hospital vending machine soda. And... I am growing into my Alpha Mate body, I think."

He was slowly getting more comfortable with that idea.

Tobias smiled brightly. "I really am so glad to have met you."

Jordan stopped walking. They'd arrived at the hospital. "Are you going to answer the other question?"

The older man ran his hand over his head, an uncomfortable expression crossing over his still handsome features.

"My wife, Aaron's mother, died when he was younger. Giving birth to his brother."

"Oh, I'm so sorry."

How terrible.

"Yes, well, I was not in a good way after that, and it was only really when my second wife approached me for a mating, that I began to pull myself out of my grief. Once I saw Aaron grow to be the strong young man that he is now, I left the pack. Moved out of town for some stress free living."

Oh, poor Aaron. A dead mother, an absent father, and then a non-existent mate.

The pain of his own betrayal struck deep. Oh God. What had he done? Poor Aaron must have thought he was practically un-loveable.

"Ah, thank you for telling me that. It makes more sense why Aaron was so happy to find me."

Tobias chuckled. "He always wanted a traditional family. A home. Someone to be close to."

"You're not disappointed that I'm not... well, a girl?"

Tobias's earthy laugh shook around him. "Me? No, not at all. Sure, I'd still like to see Aaron produce a son for the next generation of Alphas, but that's still possible. According to legends, the original wolves that founded this pack were an all-male mating. They fathered the five lines of Alphas and all the generations since. We don't need the numbers now, but anything's possible."

Horror struck Jordan square in the guts. Could Aaron do that? Have sex with another woman while mated to him? He certainly couldn't.

He shuddered at the thought and Tobias patted him on the back.

"It's not necessary- I was just saying that Fate never makes mistakes. So I would never second guess you, or your birth mark."

"Thank you."

A moment passed where there seemed to be a true understanding between them, and together they walked into the hospital.

Aaron's head was throbbing like the fiery pit of hell, and he desperately wanted to wake up from whatever nightmare he was in.

Who was that? He could hear an unusual voice, one he knew.

There was someone else in the room, Jordan.

A soothing coolness flowed over his whole body, relieving the ache.

They were chatting, touching him. And he so very much wanted to wake up.

He forced his sleeping wolf out of its coma with mental force.

Come on. You can do it. Just open your eyes.

It was like dragging nails through his eye balls and hammers to his temples.

But he pushed through with all of his might and the sun cracked through, his eyes opening slowly. Painfully.

“Aaron?... Aaron?” Jordan’s voice echoed loudly in his head. Whereas before the voices sounded like he was under water, far away.

Now they were boomingly loud.

The white light pierced his eyes as he stared up at Jordan’s beloved face, his dark hair, wet and slicked down on one side of his face.

“Hmmm...” He tried to speak but not much came out, his throat too dry, his tongue too thick in his mouth.

Jordan turned away and then came back with a glass of water, holding it up to Aaron’s lips.

He let his mate tip the water into his mouth and he swallowed the knife that slid down with the liquid.

“How do you feel? Should I get the doctor?”

Aaron shook his head, reaching out and grabbing his mate’s hand.

He didn’t want Jordan going anywhere. Somewhere, in that dark black nightmare, he’d been terrified he’d never see his mate again.

He was in Heaven now.

“You look like crap, son.” His dad stepped up behind Jordan and gave him a half smile, a shimmer in his eyes looking suspiciously like tears.

“Dad. Hi.” He croaked out and pushed himself to sit up.

He needed to get moving. This sickness was stagnant in his body and he felt like death. He couldn’t handle it anymore.

“Help me up.”

He pushed off his blanket and struggled to swing his legs off the bed. His limbs didn't work. Feeling instead like they were injected with lead.

"What are you talking about?" Jordan yelled, grabbing for the buzzer and pressing it.

"I need to get up."

Reagan came hurtling through the door, breathing hard. "You're awake! What are you doing?"

"Gotta get up."

"No. Please. Lie down."

Aaron growled, a healthy, aggravated noise that made every man in the room stand back.

He grunted as he pushed himself to his feet. "I need to shift. Run."

He knew he'd heal better in wolf form.

Reagan seemed to take pause and the nodded. "Go for it then."

"I'll go with you." Jordan said, stripping his tank and jeans off in a couple of quick movements.

"Ah, sorry?"

Omegas didn't shift. They could, sometimes, with the full moon.

A vague memory assailed him. A small grey wolf saving him, flying through a window.

He shook his head to clear the broken images.

His memory would come back with time. He was sure.

"Let's go, Aaron."

His mate walked ahead of him, gloriously naked. His perfect arse clenching and tightening with each step.

Heat stirred in his loins and he grinned.

Even half dead, he can get me aroused.

They stepped outside into the sunlight and Jordan dropped to all fours. His fur sprung through his skin, transforming him into a beautiful grey wolf.

Wow.

Another advantage to having a male mate, they could shift together. Run together. He'd never even thought about it. None of their women shifted, only the males did. So, this is something he'd never thought would happen.

He called forth his wolf and pain ripped up his insides, forcing his humanity deep inside.

He would have screamed if he could, but the sound echoed in his mind.

Once he had fully shifted, he head butted his mate and together they ran through the city streets and headed for the border.

He wanted to know what had happened, how long it had been since he'd been injured. But right this moment, it didn't matter.

He bolted for the trees, watching his mate, obviously new to shifting, stumble and fall as he wove around the bushes.

God, he's beautiful.

Together they ran, played and rolled in the grass. A perfect day. And with each moment that passed and Aaron ran, his head cleared and the pain dwindled away like a stream.

He focused on his connection to Jordan, their fated love, and everything in his life finally felt worthwhile.

CHAPTER EIGHT

"My dad said that I could father a child on some random woman?" Aaron asked Jordan while they lay in their bed, him fully healed and catching up on everything he'd missed.

And he seemed to have missed a lot.

"Well, he didn't say a total random. He just pointed out that if you wanted to father a child, the next Alpha, then you could. Like Luc and Gray did."

He frowned at the thought. He supposed it was possible... but not really in his plans. "Well, to be honest, I'm not sure I can. I had... relationships with several different women over time and none of them have even had a scare. No pregnancy's, even with... you know..." Not ever trying to prevent it.

Jordan looked away. "Yeah. I understand the biology. Well... then we don't have to worry about it at the moment anyway. But, you know, are you desperate to have a child of your own?"

Aaron went to answer the question instantly, but instead

thought better. It wasn't an easy topic and he shouldn't be glib about it.

"Hmmmm, well, to be honest, I'm not sure. My own mother died in childbirth, so... that's not a legacy I want to repeat."

Jordan grinned and rubbed his flat, muscular belly. "Don't think that's going to happen to me. And I'm your mate, so..."

"So... What? If we chose another woman who wasn't my mate, it would be okay?"

Jordan shrugged. "Not sure."

He cocked his head at Jordan's unusual postures. "I would never do anything that you didn't want."

"Oh, I know. It's just, I never even thought I'd have a mate, let alone, a, what would they be? A stepchild."

A laugh rolled through him as he readjusted the blankets around them.

A baby. A child. God. What would they do with one of them?

"Tell me more about how it all went down with Marcus. I still love the idea of Jack flattening him."

Jordan laughed, then laughed again. The sound light, happy, musical. "It was great."

"And you told them all about your plans for the Omegas?"

"I did."

He sighed and tried to imagine just how good that would have been. To see his mate standing up for what he knew to be right. In front of the whole pack. And he'd missed it! "I wish I'd seen it."

"Yeah? Well, you should have seen the way the Omegas all stood up to protect me. They would have all gone after Marcus if they needed to. I could feel it. There is so much more strength in the Omegas, Aaron. More than I even thought there was."

Jordan was just gorgeous to watch. His stomach rippled with his laughter, his smile lighting up his face like sunshine.

"Come here."

He grabbed for Jordan's arm and twisted, pulling him underneath him. Their bodies pressed together and a moan was dragged from both of their mouths.

It had been too long since he'd been inside his mate. An hour at least.

Their lips met and his cock began to harden as he pressed against this mate. Ready to join them in the life they were forging together.

EPILOGUE

A month later.

"Your dad's here."

Aaron turned towards the door, Jordan's announcement making a smile rise onto his face.

He loved that his father came up to the house so often now. To chat, talk about the pack. Enjoy Jordan's cooking. Everything.

Life was pretty sweet.

Aaron stepped out of their bedroom into the open lounge and went to greet his father with a smile, but his dad's expression made his freeze.

"Dad. What's wrong?"

His dad shut the door behind him and rushed inside.

"There's something brewing, and it's bad. I've heard rumours from some friends in a pack to the north, that they were attacked by the Rogues. They killed a lot of people, but the Alphas managed to drive them out. But only just. They're wanting help. Guidance."

"Damn it! I was hoping that with Coby and that other one dead, that it would be done."

His father shook his head. "No. It seems not. We need to be as strong as possible, they're calling a Victorian Alpha meeting and at least half of us need to go."

He didn't like the sound of that.

"That will leave our pack vulnerable, it'll leave all of the packs vulnerable. Where are we meeting?"

This wasn't a good idea. And there was no way he was leaving his mate behind.

"We're meeting up near Red Cliffs. All ten packs are sending their best. I know it's not safe for everyone to be without their Alphas, but we need to get a cohesive unit together to hunt them down. Or at least come up with a system to neutralise them. This is getting ridiculous."

He agreed.

"All right. Well, I'll stay here. I want to be with the pack."

His father smiled, despite the graveness of the situation.

"And with your mate, of course."

He shrugged. Yeah. And?

His father grinned. "Grayson wants to stay too, so we'll take Marcus and Tom. But I was hoping we could get one more to stay here, and then us elders could all go to Red Cliffs."

"Like who?"

"I think we need to get Brad back here. Do you know how to contact him?"

"Oooh. The missing Alpha. I don't remember him at all." Jordan chimed in, stepping up next to Aaron and running a hand over his back.

"Yeah, he's been travelling for years. On and off for over a decade. I wouldn't even know where to start. Does he still have a cell phone? An email we use to contact him on?"

"I'll check with his dad, but we need him, I think."

Jordan leaned against him and Aaron moved his arm to wrap around his young mate. The pup loved affection and Aaron couldn't get enough of him.

"Is it possible that Brad has a male mate, too? Or would that just be too weird having three out of five Alphas be all male paired?"

Aaron and his dad stared at each other for a moment, the same thought passing through their head.

Finally, his dad spoke. "It is actually. Very likely. Brad's always preferred males, but he is also a loner. I'm not sure how we'd ever get him to mate."

"What does his mating mark look like? I might have seen it."

Aaron stared down at his mate, amazed at the doors he'd opened up for them.

"You are a real asset to us, you know that, Jordan?"

His mate elbowed him in the side and turned a beet red. "Don't be silly. Reagan is an asset to the pack, I'm nothing..."

His dad jumped in on that one before he could. "Don't be ridiculous. You mating with Aaron alone was enough of a service to the pack. You took a lonely, unhealthy Alpha, and have made him whole, as strong as can be."

Aaron felt, more than saw, the happiness flow through his mate and he gave his dad a grateful smile.

"That's true, but it's more than that, Jordan. By knowing the Omegas, their lives, what they need, you will help us truly make this pack a better place for everyone."

Jordan turned his face up, like a flower opening up to the sun.

Aaron couldn't turn down the invitation, and dropped a kiss on his mate's succulent lips. Swearing to himself to finish what he started as soon as his dad left.

When he drew back, he could see the confusion on his dad's face.

"What's wrong dad?"

"I can't remember what birth mark Brad had. Was it on his leg or something?"

An image appeared in Aaron's mind and he began to describe it. "I remember it being big, like mine. Stretched over his hip on the left and going down his thigh."

"All the way to his calf and then twisting around his ankle?" Jordan asked, his eyes wide and unblinking.

"How did you know?" Aaron asked. He thought Jordan had never met Brad.

Jordan swallowed hard. "Because I've seen it. On a Omega, well, he used to be anyway. He challenged the pack last year and has taken on some Beta jobs."

"Oh, is that him? I remember that guy. Good kid, a bit head-strong. But a team player."

A strange hysterical smile danced on Jordan's face.

"What's so funny?"

"Stephen's a wild card and as straight as they come. Brad's going to have a hell of a time getting him to mate."

Aaron grinned and drew his own mate into his side. Let Brad deal with his destiny, Aaron had already found his.

BRAD'S MATE

THE BOROUGH BOYS SERIES BOOK 3

CHAPTER ONE

The heat of the Queensland sun beat down on Brad's face. The waves at Maroochydore were notoriously huge, but today it was flat. Especially this early in the day.

He glanced around at the soft swell, the sun sparkling off the bluey-black ocean in white, glistening light.

It was a beautiful day and thanks to the lack of surf, the beach was deserted save for a couple of grommets who weren't at school yet.

It should be a perfect day for him.

And yet, as he sat on his board letting his fingers drift in the chilly water around him, his chest ached.

What the hell was going on with him lately?

Something wasn't right, and no amount of surfing, eating, or fucking random hot guys was sorting him out.

There had to be something else, and unfortunately, a part of him knew that the 'it' that was wrong had to do with the 'Borough.

Nothing else made sense. He was a werewolf. He didn't get sick and yet he *felt* unwell. Not to mention the fact that he was also an Alpha, the biggest and strongest of his kind.

There were legends though, that told of this ache. A pain that would tug him back to his roots.

A place he didn't want to be.

His accelerated hearing picked up on a decent wave headed his way and he fell forward onto his board, putting the power into his shoulders. He coasted along until the roar of the wave opened up and he popped to his feet as the majestic water picked him up.

The wave coasted and took him along, the usual thrill that pumped along his veins annoyingly missing.

As the wave fell flat he purposely fell from his board with a roll of his eyes, loving the icy coldness that wrapped around his heated body and cleared his head.

The surfboard attached to his ankle pulled along behind him and he grabbed it up as he made his way into shallower water. He shook his long hair out of his eyes, trotting along the cool sand to where his duffle bag sat.

A sharp twang pulled at his heart and he groaned, rubbing the spot over his left pec.

What the hell is that?

A growl rolled through his throat as he pulled the wrap-around from his ankle, grabbed his bag and headed up the sand dunes to his jeep.

He'd been pretty slack with contacting anyone back in Greensborough, he hadn't checked his email in months. It was probably time to do that.

He turned on his car and headed into town, mulling over the past couple of years.

He hadn't been back to the 'Borough since his thirtieth birthday three years ago. It had been a bit of fun to travel back after being gone for so long. The boys had put on a great party and he'd loved feeling the strength and comradery of the pack around him.

But that happiness had been short lived. Within a week or two those same unsettled feelings had stirred in his gut. So, he'd packed and left.

The Alphas had not been happy. The entire council had given him a dressing down. But he didn't really give a shit what they thought about him and his life choices.

Sure. He was born an Alpha. That didn't mean he was tied to Greensborough for his whole life.

Bloody ridiculous to be tied down because of some freak accident of birth.

He spotted the small internet café ahead of him. He pulled into a spare car park on the side of the road and turned the car off.

If the pack did need him. Could he go back again?

He frowned as he groped for his wallet.

Yeah, he probably could. For a little bit, anyway. Catch up with his dad. His sister. He kinda missed her, and he was sure she'd be mated up by now. Have a kid maybe, too.

That stupid uncomfortable ache surfaced at the thought and he shuddered.

To think, they were all paired up by the supposed wondrous Fate.

What a crock of shit.

Sure, he had a massive big birthmark stretching down one side of his leg, but that didn't mean he had to tie himself to some random stranger.

Especially if they turned out to be a woman! What the hell would he do with one of those?

Fate could be cruel like that.

He pulled on a tank top and headed into the small shop, instantly spotting the hot young guy behind the counter.

He swaggered over and gave the guy an easy smile.

When the blond's eyes widened and roamed over Brad's body in a hungry, lustful way, he knew he had a date for the night.

Brad nodded at the guy in front of him. "Hey."

"Uh, Hi. Can I help you?"

"Yeah. I just need to check some emails and stuff."

"Oh, yeah, sure. For how long?"

Brad perused the laminated list of prices that were shoved at him and pointed to the smallest one.

"Only need it for half an hour." He pushed a five dollar note at the guy and he stumbled to show Brad to a computer.

As desire flourished in his gut, making his cock ache in the right way, he smiled to himself. These were the times he thanked his forefathers for his genes.

At six foot five and weighing a good one hundred and twenty kilos, he was most bottoms' wet dream.

"Thanks."

He clicked a few times on the old-fashioned mouse, staring at the screen until what he needed popped up.

His stomach dropped low in his gut, burning with disappointment.

"Damn it."

There was an email from Grayson. Sent only yesterday.

He snorted at himself and his ability to feel things from so far away.

Why do I still have such a link to them?

He'd assumed after being away so long he'd no longer be linked into the web of the Alphas. Obviously, he'd been wrong.

. . .

Hey Brad,

I hope you're enjoying gallivanting around the country, or the world. Not even sure where you are at the moment. But I'll keep this brief.

I need you to come home for a few weeks, like... yesterday. I wouldn't ask unless it was urgent.

Call 0438 7896 0125 if you wanna talk, otherwise, I'll check ya soon.

Grayson.

Brad didn't need anything else. He knew Grayson as well as he knew himself. The man was the Alphas' perfect boy, but he was also a good friend, and not someone to pull Brad's strings. If Grayson needed him. He was going back.

He punched in a quick reply.

I'm getting on a plane. Be back tonight, tomorrow morning at the latest.

He could drive all night if he had to, but flying was preferable. Quicker, in theory. If he could get a flight out tonight but last minute could be tricky.

Brad calculated the time to drive versus the flights that would be possible to Melbourne tonight. He tapped on the computer, pulling up the flight schedules for today and frowning at the lack of choice, not to mention the outrageous prices.

Hmm... driving might be the way to go.

Maroochydore was out of the way and he'd need two flights to get to Melbourne. Then he'd need to drive to Greensborough, which was another two and half hours from the airport.

He sighed with regret as he waved at the hot guy behind the counter. That blond would have been so much fun. Heading outside to his trusty jeep he jumped in and turned on the car.

It would be eighteen straight hours driving to Greensborough, but he could do it. And he'd probably get there quicker than waiting for the planes and then driving a rental car up.

A strange shiver crawled up his back as he considered what could be wrong back there. Was someone threatening them? Had something happened to his parents? The other Alphas?

The more he thought about it, the more his gut churned and the more worried he got. He headed straight to the petrol station to fill up. He'd been camping and living out of his car for months. He didn't need to pack anything up. He could leave right now. Like a turtle, he carried everything he needed with him.

That same shiver made his body shake once again. Grayson would never call him home unless something was very wrong. No one in the pack had ever done it before and he'd been travelling for over ten years now.

He pulled over and filled the car up with gas.

He was going home. And hopefully it was still standing when he got there.

"Hey Stephen. Aaron and Grayson wanna see you at the Hall."

Stephen looked up. His focus still on the nails he held in his hand. "Ah. Okay. How come?"

He was enjoying his work as a Beta. Rebuilding some of the damaged homes was a great way to stretch his overly energetic body. He had energy to burn, all the time, and he'd almost gone insane in the small Omega position he'd had up until last year.

"Don't know." Craig shrugged, one of the other Betas working on the site. "But you better go."

Stephen blew out a long sigh. He hated dealing with the council. It had been hard enough when he'd challenged his ranking last year. They'd all talked about him behind his back and stared at him for months after he'd won the right to work as a Beta. It was just starting to settle down. What did they want now?

He slid his hammer into his work belt and grabbed a short-sleeved shirt he'd hung on a nail nearby. It got too hot to wear a top while working in summer and he'd had quite a few of the unmated women looking at him while topless.

The attention was great. The muscles he'd built in the last year were definitely handy for more than lugging wood around.

He walked the five minutes to the Hall, looking at each of the building sites as he moved past. Anger churned in his gut like a hot melting pot. The Rogues had done so much damage to their town and for no good reason.

He still marvelled at their ridiculous notions. Thinking they should be the Alphas of the group. Sure, he hadn't been happy with his lot in life. He hadn't wanted to be a Omega either. But he would never, EVER, have hurt anyone to go up the rungs like the Rogue were trying to do.

He'd gone through the appropriate channels and was being treated well. Why hadn't they done the same things?

Because they're lunatics, that's what.

CHAPTER TWO

Stephen walked into the Hall where they all gathered to eat and searched for the two Alphas that had called on him.

He saw the two huge men and took a breath as fear quivered in his belly. Unfortunately, despite now being a Beta in the pack, he still found the Alphas intimidating, but he did his best not to let them see it.

He stepped closer and they both turned to him.

"Thanks for coming, Stephen." Grayson said, giving him a welcome smile.

Where was the rest of the council?

"No problem. Can I help you guys at all?" He flipped his head to get his hair out of his eyes and leaned all his weight on one leg.

Aaron's eye brows rose and those shrewd green eyes took his measure.

Stephen stared straight back at him, unable to look away without a direct command. He didn't let anyone push him around and despite his initial hesitations, he knew that being casually confident was the way to go with these men.

"Yep. You're perfect for the job it seems."

"Pardon me?"

What job?

Neither of the Alphas stood, but they didn't have to. He was a good eight inches shorter than them, so even with them seated, he wasn't that much taller.

Aaron and Grayson both twisted right around so that they were facing him while sitting at the Alpha table. "We have a favour to ask of you. Can we trust you not to tell anyone if we share some information with you Stephen?"

Oh, he liked the sound of this.

"Of course. What's up?"

"The other Alphas all left this morning to go to an Alpha gathering near Mildura."

"Really? I didn't realise that those sorts of things even existed."

He couldn't remember a time when all the Alphas weren't always here.

"There isn't, usually." Grayson replied. "But with the threat of the Rogues, another pack north of us have called a meeting and they had to go."

He looked at the two recently mated Alphas. They'd be the last two who'd offer to leave their mates. It was still a little odd having all male pairings in the Alpha group- but hopefully it meant a hell of a lot of strength and stability for the pack. That was what the legends inferred anyway.

"And you two stayed to protect us?"

They both nodded. "Yes. Someone had to stay, and we've called Brad home, too."

"Brad?"

Never heard of him.

"Brad's the fifth Alpha of our generation. You haven't met him before?" Grayson asked, his eyes strangely interested, as was his tone.

Obviously, the favour they were going to ask had to do with this guy.

"Ah no, I haven't."

"He's the missing Alpha, haven't you ever wondered why there's only the four of us? He's been travelling for a good decade."

"Oh, okay. Well, I only reached maturity last year, so I don't think I've ever met him."

He had a vague memory or a dark-haired man and a huge party a few years ago, but unable to drink, and stuck in the Omega's quarters, he hadn't had much to do with it.

Grayson and Aaron shared a strange look and then Aaron addressed him again.

"Well. We need someone who knows all three tiers of the pack. You know all the Omegas well, I assume, and you now know all of the Betas now, too."

He nodded. "Yeah. And...?"

"We need to know that everyone's happy and feels safe. With Brad coming home, he's going to need a little time to adjust, so we'd appreciate it if you could be an intermediary between all three levels. Especially between Brad and the Omegas if necessary once he's back."

A smile stretched across Stephen's face. "So, Brad won't know his arse from his head and you want me to make sure he slots back in okay? Why?"

Grayson grinned at him. "Because he's only really here for a couple of weeks. We called him back because we're afraid that the Rogues will take the opportunity to attack once again when the pack is at its weakest. You know everyone. So, if you see anything fishy. Please. Let us know."

Stephen crossed his arms over his chest and stared at the two Alphas. This was probably something they could do on their own. Especially with Reagan and Jordan on their side.

"The only fishy thing I'm seeing is you guys. You're acting very odd."

A brief flutter of panic went through his heart as the two Alphas glanced at each other.

Then suddenly they burst out laughing and the tension between Stephen's shoulder blades relaxed.

"Ah, yeah. We kinda are, I suppose. We're not used to having to look after the whole pack without any back up."

He could only imagine how stressful that would be.

"Well, you can count on me. As far as I know, everyone's pretty happy, especially with the prospect for different vocation choices for the Omegas- you've done a really good thing there, Aaron."

Aaron smiled at him and nodded his head once. "Thanks. I hope it helps everyone."

He waited, and although there seemed to be another burgeoning question, the Alphas weren't talking.

"Okay. Well then, I better get back to work."

"Ah, Stephen. We were just wondering if you were mated."

Stephen frowned, not sure he understood the tone Grayson was using. He sounded hopeful, almost.

"Ah, nope. Haven't been lucky enough to find my girl yet."

Aaron smiled, but the light didn't reach his eyes.

"And your mark. Where is it?"

"Why?"

"Um... well, to be honest." Grayson began, his gaze darting away for a moment. "No one really knew what yours looked like and I'm still searching for my sister's mate. She's pretty lonely and she's about your age."

Stephen sucked in a breath at the compliment being paid him. Sure, he wanted his mate to come along, but he'd only been searching the Omega females.

He would never have even looked at an Alpha born.

"Oh. Well, I doubt it would be me in any case. But my mark's here." Stephen pulled his left belt line down a fraction to show them the top of his huge birthmark on his hip.

"Oh yeah? Megan's is on her leg, too. How far does it go down?"

That startled him. No way was he an Alpha mate. That would be bloody ridiculous.

Not if you look at Jordan and see where he mated.

"Ah. Do you mind if I strip to show you fully? It's impossible in jeans."

"No, of course not."

As men who stripped bare in front of the whole pack regularly to shift beneath the full moon, Stephen wasn't surprised when they agreed.

He pushed off his shoes and pulled his jeans down his now lean and muscled thighs.

He was still half the size of the men in front of him, of course, but he was twice the size he had been, and he was proud of it.

"There you go."

He turned side on and stood for them to look at the huge mark he now possessed.

He'd been born with a smudge of a birthmark over his left butt check but since coming into maturity it had spread down his leg. Which he didn't quite understand, but assumed it had something to do with him challenging the Alphas for a Beta role.

"Ah, no. That's not Megan's. Sorry. But thanks for showing us."

He glanced over to the Alphas and saw excitement and awe in their faces.

He pulled up his jeans and stuck his feet back in his shoes.

"Is there something wrong with the mark? Have you seen it before?"

"Have you always had that Stephen? I would have assumed something like that would be hard to hide." Aaron asked, ignoring his question.

Aaron had once had a huge mark, all over his chest, but if the gossips were right, it was gone now.

"No. I had a partial one, but it got bigger last year. I think it was because of me changing to a Beta."

He stared at Aaron and Grayson for a moment, his curiosity getting the better of him.

"Is it true that you guys have lost your birth marks?"

Grayson grinned. "Not lost exactly, more like our mates took them."

"Huh?" That made no sense when their mates had identical marks. That was how you knew which mate was yours.

The males in their pack were the only werewolf shifters. The females couldn't shift with the moon and were essentially human.

The way the fated mates legend worked was, the boy children were born with a birth mark, and generally at twenty one, a female developed their mark and it would match one of the males, therefore calling to their perfect mate to claim them. Fate was kinda amazing in that way, and Stephen trusted their legends.

"Well, after we both mated, Aaron and I, we woke up with our birthmarks gone and Reagan and Jordan had new ones."

"New ones?"

"Yes. They both have black marks in the shape of a wolf on them."

Stephen could feel his eyebrows climbing his forehead and he tried to stay calm. His heart was racing now as though he'd run a race, galloping in his chest. That was just so very odd.

"Oh. That is unusual."

Grayson burst out laughing, the deep tones rolling around the Hall in a soothing way. "Yes, it is. But then again, so is an all-male Alpha pairing, so we just kinda go with the flow. After all, I got a human."

"And I got a Omega." Aaron added.

"I wonder who Brad's mate will be then?" Stephen mused. Would he also have an unusual pairing? "Maybe he'll have a Omega female! Do you know what his mark looks like, I could tell you if I've seen it."

"Oh, well... ah..." Aaron stammered and he looked to Grayson.

"Ah...no. Brad was always pretty cagey about his mark."

That was odd, but he took them at their word.

"All right. Well, I'll head back to my job. Thanks for asking for help in this way, I appreciate the compliment being paid."

"So, you'll help then?"

He nodded, there was no question about that. "With the Rogues and Brad? Yes, of course."

CHAPTER THREE

Brad glanced ahead of himself and the long stretch of road, his tired eyes pulling at his subconscious to sleep.

The sun was finally rising, casting beautiful yellows and pink across the horizon. But instead of watching it rise over the blue ocean as he had yesterday morning, Brad was seeing it from the viewpoint just above Greensborough.

He could see some of the houses at the edge of town, and the thick foliage made him itch to shift just looking at it.

How much had he loved running through the forest when he was younger?

A shiver coursed down his spine as he stared at the home of his forefathers. It had never felt quite like home to him when he was younger, but he was older and wiser now, so hopefully coming back to visit wouldn't be too painful.

He pressed his foot to the accelerator and drove his jeep down into the valley.

A house ahead of him was having the roof replaced which was a little odd.

The hairs on his neck stiffened as he noticed another house, burnt windows and broken glass decorating the otherwise pristine home.

What the hell?

More and more houses appeared fire damaged as he drove through town, his belly tightening with fear and trepidation as he pulled up outside the Hall.

What had he missed?

He pushed open the door and practically fell out of the car, his stiff legs and numb feet struggling to stand as he shuffled along the pavement. Yeah, far too long in the car that time.

He checked his watch.

Yeah, eight hours straight is a bit much for the blood flow.

He stretched his arms over his head and leaned back, enjoying the pop and release of over-stiff joints.

Oh yeah. That's better.

Heat began to flow along his limbs once again, his nervous system back on full function as the beautiful clean air around him soaked into his lungs.

A smile rose, unbidden.

Yep. He was back. Nothing like this feeling.

He stepped forward and moved up to the Hall.

If he was lucky, they would have breakfast already served and ready for some of the pack that worked early shifts.

His mouth began to water as he pushed open the door and the smell of frying bacon and fresh baked bread curled inside his nostrils.

Oh yeah. That's the stuff.

He glanced around the room, which was mostly empty. With only a few tables of Betas, a table or two full of Omegas, and the Alpha table empty, it was the quietest he'd ever seen the 'Borough Hall.

His belly ached and grumbled at him as he stood like a dummy in the doorway.

Hurry up and eat before you pass out.

He stormed forward and snatched up a plate, his eyes devouring the feast before he could even pick up a spoon. He'd missed this. The unending food that warmed you and filled you up after a long day.

Unlike all the other Alphas, he'd never gone to University. Wasn't interested in running anything. He liked using his hands. Building houses and ploughing fields.

Put him on a farm any day over the business of the town.

Which went against the grain as far as the pack was concerned. Alphas were meant to be the figure heads, the smartest. Betas worked hard with their bodies, built their homes.

Maybe he was meant to be born a Beta.

He reached down and grabbed a serving spoon, then begun shovelling food onto his plate. Grilled fish and poached eggs. Crispy bacon and buttered rolls.

Yummmm.

He picked up some cutlery and poured himself a coffee, walking over to the large round table he knew to be the Alpha table.

He sat down alone and began eating. It was all so good, and just as delicious as he remembered. He finished it in no time and sat back in his chair, enjoying the slightly uncomfortable feeling that came with being overly full.

"Excuse me." A man's voice over his shoulder made Brad turn around and the heat that flowed through his body at the sight of the Beta made him groan and push himself to his feet.

He now towered over the guy in front of him, so the Beta took a step back, tilted his head and looked up so that their eyes met.

What an amazing shade of blue...

"Are you Brad by any chance?"

Brad could only nod, the pulsing pleasure rippling over his skin and moving through his chest making it impossible to talk.

He assumed the guy was a Beta, if his size was any indication. Five foot nine, wiry muscles. Blue eyes that bordered on a light grey.

But it wasn't his youth and his handsome face that was making Brad's heart pound and his cock harden in his pants.

There was something else. Brad had to drag in a heavy breath and clench his fists to stop himself from grabbing the man in front of him and pulling him in close.

"Well, I'm Stephen. Grayson and Aaron asked me to liaise with you when you came into town."

The man before him didn't seem to be affected by him at all. And by the way Stephen's eyes kept sliding away and sideways, he obviously wasn't gay.

"Great." Brad managed to croak out, then he banged on his chest with his fist to clear his throat. "Sorry. I drove eighteen hours straight to get here. I'd appreciate it if you caught me up. Where are the other Alphas?"

Stephen stepped a little closer, dropping his voice so that no one would hear him. Stephen's scent was like caramel and bronzed sugar and made Brad's mouth water.

Brad inhaled sharply and held his breath, this man's smell intoxicating in the extreme.

His cock throbbed against his tight jeans.

Thank God for black denim.

"Grayson and Aaron are probably best to catch you up with everything. But what I do know is that all the other Alphas had to go to a big meeting near Mildura, so that left us vulnerable."

Cold dread tickled along Brad's spine. He'd never heard of such a thing happening before. Why would they have done that?

He risked breathing again, and regretted it. The thrum of a near orgasm knocking him sideways as Stephen's scent filled him up.

He stumbled and fell back into his chair, staring up at the stranger who was affecting him like no one ever had before.

"Who *are* you?"

Stephen frowned at the question and took a step back, the relief of the loss of caramel sweetness making Brad relax against the chair.

"I'm Stephen. Why? What do you mean?"

The Beta crossed his arms over his chest and his lips twisted into a strange pout.

"I just. You smell... amazing to me. And I don't get it."

"Yeah? So what? You smell good to me, too."

Brad shot to his feet as adrenaline coursed along his veins.

Oh, hell no.

"I do?"

"Yeah. Why?"

He didn't want to deal with this.

No!

"No matter. Sorry. Just been too long since I came home. Where can I find the other two Alphas?"

"They'll both be at home still, I'd say. Grayson's in a town house a few blocks away and Aaron built a house near the farms. They'll both be in here for breakfast in a few hours. Maybe you want to rest somewhere?"

Brad groaned as images of the hot young Beta writhing beneath him filled his mind.

"Ah, yeah. That would be great. I've got my tent in the car."

"You can sleep in one of the rooms next door. We've set up emergency bedding for everyone affected by the Rogue attacks."

Oh, a real bed would be amazing.

"Attacks? What attacks?"

Stephen inclined his head and made a 'follow me' motion with his hand.

Brad followed, walking through the Hall and stepping into a large room full of several empty single beds.

"The Rogues, a band of Betas that were unhappy with their posts in life, broke away from the pack a few years ago. But I think whatever sense they had once has left them, because they've gone feral. They set fire to the houses after leading the Alphas away, and shot Aaron three times a few weeks ago. It's been pretty rough around here."

Brad's heart cracked like an ice sculpture hit with a hammer, pain splintering through his chest.

I've been gone far too long.

"Get some sleep Brad and I'll come wake you when the other Alphas arrive."

Stephen gave him a soft smile and turned to leave.

Brad pulled off his tank and shuffled out of his shoes, calling out to Stephen as he left the room.

"Hey, how'd you know it was me?"

Stephen turned back around. "Well, you were sitting at the Alpha table, no one does that. And Grayson told me you were coming."

"Is that all?"

He sat down on the bed, fatigue rolling through him like a steam train, obliterating any strength he'd once had.

"Well... yeah." Stephen looked confused, his brow furrowed in an odd way.

"Ok. Cool. Thanks."

Brad lay down on his back, still wearing his tight black jeans, and pulled a blanket over him. His mind was whirling with all the implications that Stephen was throwing at him.

For the pack, and for them.

But his body was so tired, his mind overwhelmed and his heart crying out for more things that he'd ever wanted before.

CHAPTER
FOUR

What seemed like a moment later, a hand was shaking him awake and Brad pushed himself up to sitting, his head spinning with the grogginess of sleep.

"They're here."

Brad's sugary, caramel smell made him moan, lust hitting him in the gut like a punch to the abs.

"Yeah, thanks."

He blinked open his eyes slowly and was grateful that Stephen had left the room by the time he'd pulled himself together.

"Argh..." He stretched his back and ran his hands through his shoulder length hair, the tangles and knots catching his fingers. They were half dreaded already. Stupid things. "Okay. Let's go." It was a struggle to push himself up, but the urgency of the day made his muscles work.

He pushed open the door, blinking as the pain of white light hit his sleepy eyes.

"Brad!" A familiar voice called out and he moved towards the noise.

His eyes adjusted just as Grayson's huge figure cut in front of him, giving him a huge hug and knocking the wind out of him.

"Glad you came." Grayson said into his ear and Brad hugged him back. His best mate since before they could both speak.

"Me, too."

Grayson released him and they moved over to the Alpha table where three other men sat, including Aaron.

"Aaron!"

The oldest of their generation of Alphas looked amazing, his bright green eyes sparking with good health.

He grabbed Aaron up in a big, hard hug and Aaron chuckled in his ear.

"Good to see you."

He released Aaron and stepped back. "Yeah, you too. You look ten years younger than last time I saw you. What happened?"

Aaron stepped further back and put his hand down on the shoulder of the young man sitting at the table still. He was very pretty, his non-symmetrical haircut quite spunky.

"I found my mate. Brad, this is Jordan."

Jordan smiled up at him, his fashionable hair style screamed *gay* to Brad, but how was that possible?

"Huh? I thought I was the only gay Alpha in the pack?"

They all chuckled and he turned to see a blond human standing beside Grayson.

"Then you'll find this even funnier. Brad, this is my mate, Doctor Reagan Forster."

Reagan, a large Beta size man, extended his hand and Brad shook it, admiring the beauty and the strength of Grayson's mate.

"Woah. Now this is bloody incredible. I leave for what? Three years? And you both get shacked up with beautiful men."

"I got a human." Grayson added.

"And I got a Omega." Aaron grabbed up his mate and for the first time, Brad noticed how small he was.

"Wow." That had never happened in the pack before, not in their recorded history. "Well, you all looked remarkedly happy considering you're bonded for life." He grimaced at the idea.

"I see you haven't changed your mind about that, then?" Grayson asked.

"About being shackled to one person for the rest of my life being the worst thing on the planet? Ah, nope."

He forced out a laugh as the men around him cuddled into contented pairs.

It was an odd feeling to feel uncomfortable and slightly envious of the mates around him.

He loved his carefree life and had never wanted the responsibilities of one person, let alone a whole pack, but that had been easier when the other two Alphas had been single as well.

As the only one left standing, he was now truly alone.

"So, tell me why you pulled me off my surfboard and back to this backward town?"

Grayson growled at him and he laughed at his old friend. "Oh, shut up, I don't have to love the 'Borough as much as you do. I'm definitely a coastal guy. Put me near water and I'm happy. You know that. So, tell me, what's going on?"

"Sit down and we'll fill you in."

The five of them sat and Grayson filled him in on the Rogues trying to kill their families in the tunnels, the kidnapping and shooting of Aaron to get money, and now the Alpha meeting that left them all vulnerable.

"Fucking hell. That's a hell of a few months you guys have had."

They all nodded, Aaron's mate Jordan's eyes so intense it made Brad look away for a minute. This was all very strange.

"We have something else to tell you, too." Aaron started, glancing at his intense Omega mate.

A Omega mate... for an Alpha. He would have said it was impossible if he hadn't seen it himself. There was no questioning the perfection of the two couples in front of him.

"Oh yeah, what?"

Jordan stared at him, his nervous swallow obvious in the working of his slender throat.

"Ah..."

Jordan glanced up at Aaron and the Alpha nodded, turning back to Brad.

"We've found your mate."

Ice slid down Brad's throat, making him gasp and grab for some water on the table.

No. No. No. No. No. No!

"Ah. Are you sure?"

Aaron nodded.

Bloody hell. He still had options. He could leave, not ever find out.

But that damn ache was back, stronger than ever. Wrapping around his heart and squeezing hard.

"Who is it?"

Why did he even ask? He already knew.

The instant attraction. That smell.

Aaron opened his mouth and Brad held up his hand. "It's okay. Don't tell me... it's Stephen, isn't it?"

Aaron's eyes widened as he snapped shut his mouth.

Jordan sat up straighter, leaning forward as though he had a vested interest in this.

"How did you know?"

He shrugged and chugged back the rest of the water. He'd ignored it when he'd seen all the signs before. Part of his brain refusing to register the fact that he had just met the one Fate had destined for him.

Damn it.

"Well. I could smell him."

Aaron groaned and grinned at him. "Oh yeah. Damn, those first few times smelling Jordan... I was practically on my knees."

Jordan tilted his head and let it rest on Aaron's shoulder, the love between them as obvious as the nose on Aaron's happy face.

"Well. What are you going to do about it, Brad?" Jordan asked, staring up at him from the safety of Aaron's embrace.

He shrugged and shifted in his chair. He had no plans to do anything about it. Yeah, so Fate had their plans. Didn't mean he had to follow along with them.

He'd bucked every other tradition so far. Why not this one, too?

"No idea. But that's the last thing I should be thinking about at the moment. With everything you've told me, the pack and the safety of everyone, especially the Omegas, should be our number one priority."

Thankfully, they went on to discuss what they'd need to do to put in better surveillance for the four days the Alphas were away. But through the whole conversation Brad could feel Jordan's heavy gaze on him.

Somehow, he didn't think he was going to be back on the road by the weekend, as had been his plan.

STEPHEN LIFTED his juice glass to his lips, his arm shaking with the nervous energy pumping through his body.

He could literally feel Brad from across the room.

How was that possible?

A flash of red tank top caught his eye and he turned towards the woman who'd sauntered into his gaze.

"Hey, Stephen. How are you?"

"Great Teags. How are you?"

Teagan rested her hip against the table, flirted, and pouted. Doing everything Stephen knew to be the signs she gave off when she was horny and wanted him in her bed again.

Which was generally a couple of times a month.

He waited for the normal reaction to overtake him, the clench in his gut, the throbbing in his cock. A feeling he'd experienced a hundred times before.

And always when Teagan put out her call. A classic unmated Beta woman, she knew what she wanted and how often she needed it.

Must be a full moon.

"Ah. I have to finish up with work, but you wanna come over tonight?" He asked her, deciding he may as well jump straight to the end of the conversation.

She grinned, winked at him and headed off to another group of young Beta females.

His friends around the table gave him a knowing smile and a few of them smirked at him. He tried his best to reciprocate the look and appear excited by what had just been offered to him.

He was straight, or that was what the humans called it anyway. He'd always felt that way. Even though most people in the pack believed sexuality was fluid and should not be labelled, it made sense to him.

Men were for working next to, friendship, conversation.

Women were for companionship, affection, and sex.

And never the twain should meet.

His gaze slid sideways, pulled unerringly by that intense attraction he'd felt for Brad since he'd first seen him this morning.

Sitting alone at the Alpha table, gorging himself on the food as though he hadn't eaten in days. Stephen had been unable to sit by without going over and speaking to him. He hadn't *had* to, he could have waited for the other Alphas to arrive. But he hadn't been able to stay away.

That burn in his body that was usually reserved for the hot women in the Omega and Beta packs, now ached for a huge man sitting at the Alpha table.

How the fuck was that possible?

Reagan, Grayson's mate, was walking towards him, eyes pinned on him.

He swallowed hard, the blond doctor's casual confidence a trait that he himself wished he had.

"Hey, Stephen. How are you?"

"Pretty good. And you?"

"Good. Thanks. Hey, I was wondering if you could come to a meeting tonight? Grayson said you might be able to help us with something."

His smile and his eyes seemed to indicate that Stephen should know what he was talking about.

And he did. Kind of. "Ah. Yeah. Sure. After dinner?"

"Yes, please. Back here, if that's okay? Does that work for you?"

He'd have to put Teagan off for a bit, but that shouldn't be difficult. She'd wait for him.

"Yeah. Of course."

Reagan walked off and some of the guys around him looked at him with curiosity. He couldn't answer their questions, so he just shrugged and went back to eating his meal.

CHAPTER FIVE

Brad's body was restless and full of energy. He went looking for Stephen after lunch, unable to stay away from him for along length of time.

Despite the fact that he knew that he would be leaving soon, and that this man was not going to be his mate, he was also curious about the man that Fate had picked out for him.

He kept walking, following an odd sense of direction as he moved further out of town.

He should have asked one of the other guys for directions, or even just where Stephen worked, but he hadn't. Stubborn arse that he was.

Ahead of him was a lovely homestead and as his gut tightened in recognition, his gaze settled on a gorgeous young man hammering away.

His back glistened with sweat, his muscular arms getting bigger with a proper day's work, not in the gyms so popular with the human men he met.

He cleared his throat as he stepped closer.

Damn, he's hot.

"Hey. Need some help?"

Stephen turned around, his eyes narrowing. "Not really."

Brad chuckled as he pulled his own tank top off and Stephen's eyes roamed down his chest.

"I think you do. And I could use the work out, to be honest."

Stephen slid the hammer into his tool belt at his waist, slung low over his sexy, lean hips. "Don't you Alphas go to University and sit in an office all day?"

He laughed loudly at that one. "Shit. Don't tell me that's what Grayson and Aaron do all day?"

"Well... yeah. I think."

Brad grabbed the saw that was lying on the ground next to Stephen and picked it up.

"Well, unlike all the other Alphas, I never went to Uni. Much prefer to work with my hands, make something tangible."

He looked around at the house Stephen was building. "You need me to make some frames? Or I can just follow you around."

Stephen cocked his head to the side. "You really want to work with the Betas?"

"What do you take me for? Some stuffy prick whose head is up his arse?"

When Stephen's eyes goggled, Brad laughed. "Why do you think I left the pack? I really don't like the hierarchy, the pressure, and crap. I like working with my hands, it's what I do on the road."

"On the road? Where have you been?"

"Where haven't I been? I've worked everywhere from the stinking hot marble bar, to freezing cold fisheries in Tasmania. Any where I could get work, doing anything my body could handle. Building houses is a dream compared to a lot of other jobs I've done,"

"Okay then..." Stephen indicated he should follow and they put up a frame together, working the nail gun to get it into place.

"So, why travel so much then?"

Brad shrugged, enjoying the fact that Stephen wanted to know more about him, his interest was obvious and palpable.

"I don't feel settled in any one place, I get restless. It'll probably settle down as I get older, but for now, I want to keep moving. See as much of Australia as I can."

"Sounds like you've seen most of it already."

Brad grinned and reached for a hammer. "Yeah, probably have."

They worked together, putting up the whole first floor frames as they chatted. Brad's body felt as strong as an ox. There was no restlessness, no pain. No need to take a deep breath as his lungs got squeezed by his ribs.

For the first time in a long time, he was relaxed, and that had everything to do with the man in front of him.

Almost eight hours later Stephen had finished his last job, thanks to the ever strong and energetic Alpha Brad, eaten dinner, gotten word to Teagan that he'd be a bit late and he was back in the Hall again.

He still couldn't believe he'd spent most of the day with Brad, chatting about travel and life. It had been lovely. Strange, but one of the most relaxed work days he'd ever had.

The guys body was monstrous too, so his strength had helped a lot.

He looked around the streets as he stepped up to the Hall door. There weren't too many people around, most gone home for the night.

The full moon rose tomorrow night, so they'd all meet in the clearing and go for a run.

But tonight, it seemed, he had to deal with the Alphas. Not that he had anything new to tell them.

His breath caught in his throat as he walked across to the Alpha table, full of the five men who wanted a meeting with him.

They all shifted in their chairs as he stepped closer so that all five were facing him.

"Hi. You wanted to see me?"

He focused his gaze on Grayson and Reagan, and yet the skin on one side of his body was burning. The side that was close to Brad.

Grayson addressed him. "Yes. We wanted to ask you about the pack from your side of the fence. We're going to be putting in a round the clock guard of the perimeters for the next three days. This is the list of the men we think can handle it."

They handed him a list of about twenty names and he frowned as he studied them. Some good choices, but they'd left a lot of good men off it.

"Something wrong?" Reagan asked.

"Not exactly." He handed the list back and his gaze moved to Brad.

Brad was staring at him with barely restrained hunger, the heat in his gaze causing an involuntary tightening of Stephen's groin.

What the fuck is that?

"What do you mean, Stephen?"

"I mean. The list is okay, but you've left off a lot of good Betas. Even some of the Omegas could do this for you. Especially if they were in pairs."

Brad scoffed and Stephen finally had an excuse to look at the new man to the pack.

He raised an eyebrow at Brad in question. Who the hell did he think he was? Casting aspersions on the very men who looked after this town?

Brad looked around the group, obviously for support, but when no one spoke, he turned on Stephen. His dark-brown eyes narrowed.

"The Omegas can't help with security."

"Why not?"

"Because they're small. And weak." Brad glanced over at Jordan who was glaring at them. "No offense."

Stephen didn't let Jordan respond, fireworks of anger exploding in his belly. "Well, it's offensive actually, so I suggest you take it back. The Omega men are faithful, and loyal to a fault. They'd die for their families, and their friends. Their pack. Unlike you."

He looked down his nose at the Alpha in front of him. Sure, Brad made it sound cool and interesting that he travelled all the time, but what did it really mean? He was a deserter, a lone wolf.

What sort of man, what sort of Alpha, ran off from his pack for over a decade?

His brain hadn't pulled it all together before, but now that he thought about it, he was beginning to detest Brad and what he stood for. It was everything that Stephen himself was against.

Brad jumped off his seat and glared down at him.

"Excuse me?"

There may have been eight inches of height and thirty odd kilos of muscle difference between them, but Stephen wasn't scared of this over-grown kid.

"You know exactly what I mean, Brad. If you got guilted into coming back for a few days, then fine. But don't go around insulting the people who make this place a home. A family. We are all capable of pulling our weight. Are you?"

He let his gaze slide down the huge bulk of the man in front of him and then flicked back up to his face.

Brad's eyes had darkened and the muscle in his jaw was ticking away with anger.

"This is bullshit." Brad threw up his hands and stormed away. The opening and closing of the large door the only echo in the room.

Stephen took a few steadying breaths, his heart pounding in his chest like a steam train on the tracks.

Once a little calmer, he turned back to the other men, who were all smirking in a strange way.

"What's so funny?"

Grayson grinned. "Sorry, yeah... I enjoyed that far too much. Brad's been gone too long and he doesn't realise how many things have changed."

"He's a bloody baby, and a coward at that. What sort of Alpha deserts his pack?"

He turned and glared at the now shut door.

What a prick.

A giggle behind him made him turn and Jordan was smiling brightly.

He lifted his chin at Jordan. "What's up with you?"

He'd known Jordan for years, and had always suspected there was more to the guy than the Omega skin he wore.

Stephen had assumed it meant he was meant to be a Beta like himself, not an Alpha's mate. That had been a pretty big shock for everyone.

"You have no idea who he is, do you?"

"What are you talking about? I met him for the first time this morning."

Jordan stared at him as though his eyes could communicate the message. "Have you seen his birthmark?"

"No. Why would I?"

He checked his memory of what he'd already seen of the Alpha's body. Bare chest... arms... there had been nothing.

"Then I suggest you check it out. Full moon tomorrow, yeah?" Jordan glanced over to his mate and Aaron nodded.

He couldn't mean...

The pieces of the puzzle began to fall into place with the pain and precision of a shattering glass.

No....

The smell... the instant attraction... it couldn't be.

"Jordan, you better not be saying what I think you're saying... I like women!"

He couldn't be the final Alpha's mate! And to a man who they all termed as a lone wolf, not a pack man.

Stephen was the very definition of a pack man.

"I don't believe you." He glared at Jordan. The young Omega who was only a few years younger than him.

Jordan stood up and met his gaze. Stephen struggled not to flinch.

Jordan was now several inches taller than him, and the breadth and strength of his shoulders was impressive indeed.

When had that happened?

"Could you write down a few names of the people you think could help us also?" Aaron asked him quietly.

But Stephen couldn't think straight. He needed to find out if this was possible.

"Ah... I'll just assemble a group if you want. Bring 'em here in an hour. Um... Jordan, you're not serious, are you?"

Jordan tilted his head. "Do you trust me, Stephen?"

"Yes."

He didn't even hesitate in his answer. Even as a Omega wolf

Jordan had integrity, grit, and strength. His mother's abuse had bent him, but he'd never broken.

"Then go find Brad and force him to show you his birthmark. You need to see it."

The strange meeting he'd had with Aaron and Grayson the other day floated into his conscious mind and he rounded on the two Alphas.

"Is this why you guys wanted to see my mark?"

Aaron shrugged and Grayson nodded. "Yeah."

He spun on his heel and headed for the door.

This was fucking impossible. There had to be a mistake. Maybe Brad's mark was similar? And his *had* changed quite a bit in the past year or two, just like their females did when developing their marks...

Shit!

He pushed opened the door and took several inhalations of air before gathering his courage and storming off down the path.

He wasn't sure where the big dumb Alpha was, but he needed to sort out this nonsense now.

He was *not* an Alpha Mate.

He was *not* the mate of a male.

And he was certainly not being forever linked to a man who had no roots and no integrity. He wanted more than that.

CHAPTER
SIX

Brad yanked off his tank top as he stepped into the clearing, the anger and fear inside his gut rolling and fighting for supremacy.

He hated being back here. Hated knowing that he let everyone down just being who he was.

That being himself, a wandering wolf, was not enough.

Grrrr...

His black wolf rose inside him like the sea at high tide, strong and swift.

It had been too long since he'd shifted and run under the moon, his wolf was hesitant and angry.

He should wait until tomorrow night, but the power of the 'Borough called to him and he needed it now. Which was not good, or healthy.

He shoved off his shoes and ripped down his jeans. He was safe here near the 'Borough and if he stuck to their borders, there should be no hunters or anything to fight.

"Brad!" A now familiar voice called out to him and he turned, now naked, towards the man entering the clearing.

Stephen's eyes went wide and his mouth opened like a fish.

Brad's cock stirred, lifting and lengthening in anticipation of the man before him falling to his knees and sucking him.

As he should.

"What the hell do you want?" He growled at Stephen, his supposed mate.

What a joke!

"I... oh... fuck!" Stephen was staring at his leg as though it were about to jump up and bite him.

"What?"

He clenched his teeth and waited for his mate's rejection. Fate may have got it right for Aaron and Grayson, but he definitely hadn't got it right for him.

"You're... that's my..."

"Your mark? Yeah. Or so they say." He rolled his eyes and flexed his shoulders, readying himself for his shift. "I'm gonna run. See you later on."

He waited a heartbeat, a small part of him hoping that Stephen would say something amazing. Change everything somehow.

Or strip and shift with him. That would be kinda cool. To have someone to run with, play in the night. He didn't want a mate, not in the traditional sense that the pack talked about, but Stephen was simply gorgeous. Brad was sure they could work out something that suited them both.

But Stephen didn't say anything. Quite the opposite.

He began backing away, the horror in his expression too easy to read.

Fucking hell.

Brad turned and let loose, his wolf ripping through his body as he fell to all fours and began to run.

Pain rippled through his muscles as he transformed like it was the first time he'd ever shifted.

He bit back the howl that echoed in his mind.

It had been far too long. He shouldn't have stopped his shifts each month as he had been.

And he wouldn't do it again, he promised his wolf.

He ran through the Greensborough forest, his eyes catching glimpses of the houses on the farms around him. The delicious smell of the world around him filled him up and saturated his senses from every angle.

He'd forgotten how beautiful the woods were. How natural. How clean.

He skidded to a halt and twisted left. That was an unusual smell.

He followed it, unable to ignore the danger it spoke of. The foul, dank scent of death rising and meeting him until he stopped in front of the body of a dead man.

Not someone he recognised, but how would he know who lived here now?

Especially if he were a Omega.

Brad inspected the body properly, circling the odd angles and twisted limbs.

The man was small, a Omega probably. And he was ripped apart. Some of his arm was missing, and blood still pooled on the ground around him.

This was fresh. In the past day or so.

This is not good.

Although he was hesitant of the pain it caused him, Brad took another big sniff. He needed to know more about what had happened here. He closed his eyes and focused.

He could smell other wolves on this Omega man, and he could see the claw marks, the bites to his face.

Other wolves had done this. Rogues probably.

He took off at a running speed and made a large circle around the body. Checking behind trees, sniffing out further areas. Finding nothing else.

He shifted back to human, his lungs heaving with the strain.

I have to carry him back.

With a heavy heart, Brad carefully lifted the mangled man onto his shoulder, the smell causing a retching in his throat as his gut convulsed.

He swallowed hard and focused on his feet.

One foot in front of the other.

He began running. Dodging trees and brush. His lungs burned with the strain and his arms ached. His heart hammered in his chest and he could barely breathe, but he kept moving.

Damn. This is a lot harder in human form.

He ran and walked, retching a few times along the way, before finally making it back to the clearing.

He dropped the body as carefully as possible onto the grass and staggered away.

Fuck, I'm unfit.

He shook his head to clear his fragmented thoughts and grabbed his clothes, pulling them on over his sweaty and trembling body.

He may be surfer fit, but when it came to shifting, his body was out of practice. He'd forgotten just how much energy it took.

"Hey! Is there anyone out there?" he called out, unwilling to leave the body unattended.

There was a rustling of the trees that protected the cleared area and two young women came through the clearing.

"Oh, my God..." As they stepped closer, one of them cried out in a grief-stricken wail, falling backwards onto her back.

"Can you go get the other Alphas? Tell them to come here now."

The girl who wasn't crying grabbed the other girl and they ran out of the space.

Brad coughed and gagged, spitting onto the grass and moving a few more feet away from the body.

He let his body have its way and he too fell onto the lush grass, bending his knees and resting his arms on his legs.

Was this what he'd come home for?

To see people murdered before his eyes?

A great growl rolled through the clearing. Aaron and Grayson jumped onto the grass, half shifted, their clothes shredding as they ran.

They reached him as two great black wolves, then slowed down, sniffing and circling both him and the body.

He let them interrogate his scent without a fight. A wolf's senses were so much keener than a human's. If he'd been able to carry the body in wolf form, he would have, but dragging it with his teeth would have taken forever, and caused too much damage to the man's already massacred body.

There was a scream and several cries as a group of Omegas rushed towards the body, pushing past the Alphas and surrounding the dead man.

Aaron and Grayson backed away and shifted back, their faces solemn as they stared at the group.

Brad watched with fascination as the women wailed and cried, one blonde woman in particular holding the man's head in her lap.

The tears streaming down her face spoke of her heartbreak.

"Kate was his mate. They have a baby." Aaron said into his ear, as the two Alphas dragged him further away, leaving the Omegas to deal with the body.

There was twenty of them at least and as he was dragged away, Brad marvelled at the strength in numbers the group had.

Hmmm....

"What the hell happened, Brad? Where'd you find him?"

"Do you know who he is?"

Grayson nodded. "His name is Ray. He was a worker at the Hall. He's a Omega, so I don't know a lot. We'll have to ask his mate why he was out there. Where'd you find him?"

"I shifted and went for a run to clear my head after the whole, you know, Stephen thing. I found him about a click from here. Covered in wolf smell. I'd say fresh. Last day or so. I can show you where I found him. I had to come back on foot."

They nodded in understanding, the anger settling in.

Brad's gut churned. "What the hell has been going on while I've been gone?"

Aaron answered. "Nothing up until a few months ago. Those Betas rose up and wanted to challenge us a year or so ago. They wanted an Alpha's status and power, which of course we couldn't give them. We beat them in the challenges, of course, and they left. We hear nothing for twelve months and the next thing we know, we have a group of power hungry Rogues to deal with."

Grayson growled and wiped his hand across his brow, his frustration clear. "They're here. That's obvious. We need to get everyone to safety, now. But where and how? The Hall maybe? And I'll call Dad and tell him they need to come back."

Brad wasn't sure that was a good idea. "They could just be passing through, or trying to distract us from their real target. The Alphas will be home in three days. We can wait until then. Especially if we get full pack support."

"We will."

They walked back to the group of people and begun to ask questions about what had happened and why. Ray's mate Kate had thought Ray had gone to visit a farming friend and when he hadn't come back, she'd assumed he'd stayed the night to help. A true pack man.

The sadness that soaked into Brad's soul at that moment was life changing.

CHAPTER SEVEN

No matter how hard Stephen concentrated on Teagan's hot mouth wrapped around his cock, nor the delicious pussy that he knew was waiting for him, he could not get hard.

"What's wrong with you tonight?" She threw at him, still on her knees and staring daggers at him.

Oh yeah, like that was going to help.

He pulled away from her and grabbed his jeans.

"It's not full moon. Wait until tomorrow night."

He pulled on his jeans, tucked his flaccid cock away and zipped himself up.

How fucking embarrassing.

She pouted, crossing her arms over her perky little breasts. "You've never worried about that before."

"Yeah, well. I am this month. Okay? Just come back tomorrow."

He threw her tank top and knickers at her, and watched with a strange detachment as she got dressed.

The door to his room burst open and Brad stuck his head in.

Teagan jumped, squealing as the Alpha came into the room.

Stephen pushed himself to his feet going nose to nose with the man whose birthmark was identical to his.

"What's your problem?"

Brad took a deep whiff through his nose, his nostrils flaring. He could probably smell Teagan, she gave off a strong heat smell.

"You've gotta come now. One of the Omegas has been killed."

All his anger fell away like he'd thrown it off a cliff.

"Oh, my God. What happened?"

A strange growl came out of Brad's mouth as he looked over Stephen's shoulder at Teagan.

Stephen clenched his fingers into a tight fist and slammed his hand into Brad's shoulder.

"Leave her alone. As if you haven't had lovers before."

Brad took a step back and shook his head as though clearing the fog.

"Come on."

He turned and left and Stephen followed, not bothering to throw his once favourite bed companion a second glance.

He caught up with Brad as he charged along the street.

Had Brad come just for him?

"What's happened? What can I do?"

"I found the body of a dead Omega in the bush. I carried him back but he's covered in wolf bites. It's pretty gruesome."

Oh fuck. They're here.

"Was it the Rogues?"

"Yeah, I think it was. There's wolf stink all over him that isn't his. We need to get everyone into the Hall. Maybe for the next few days. How do you think that will work?"

They slowed down as they stepped up next to the Hall and Brad opened the door.

Stephen frowned at the Alpha. "You're asking me?"

"Of course, I'm asking you. As you so delicately pointed out, I'm not even a part of this pack anymore. I have no idea what would be the best place to hide everyone, let alone what this pack is capable of."

Brad was panting as though he'd run a marathon and Stephen's heart went out to him.

The Alpha must struggle with his place in life a lot. He was born to be an Alpha, only one of five in his generation. Yet he was obviously uncomfortable, unhappy.

Why was he fighting the man he was born to be?

"Is everyone in here?"

"They've grabbed most people I think."

He didn't think to question that, he just pushed into the Hall, where he saw several groups of people milling around and some were even crying.

There had already been one death. Was it the first of many to come?

"Oh fuck. This is going to get worse, isn't it?" He whispered at Brad as they moved over to Grayson and Reagan.

"It could. According to Aaron, the Rogues want to rule the 'Borough. If that means they have to wipe us out first, then they'll probably try."

Reagan grabbed him by the arm and squeezed in a strange, reassuring way.

"Glad you're okay. We couldn't find you."

"He was fine. He was fucking some slut in his room."

This time when he punched Brad, he aimed for the gut and put all his weight behind it.

Brad doubled over and stumbled backwards.

"I wasn't fucking her, thanks to you! I couldn't even get hard!"

As Brad straightened up and pure relief flooded his face, shame burned into Stephen.

The room had gone strangely quiet and Stephen trembled with the need to run and hide.

He'd just hit an Alpha. By anyone's standards, that was a pure challenge. Which, by wolf law, meant Brad had to accept it, and put him in his place. Physically.

And yet Brad seemed happier now, his shoulders relaxed and down. A smile firmly on his face.

What a mess.

Reagan's hand came out to him again, squeezing his forearm hard. "Yep, that's the curse of being mated to him. You won't want anyone else now that you know who you're meant to be with."

"I'm not meant to be with him, okay!" Stephen yanked his arm back from the human's hold. "This is seriously fucked up."

There was silence for a moment and Stephen took the chance to get his head on straight. He had to focus on the pack, not on himself.

"Look, I'm sorry. Ignore all that. Tell me what's happened? How can I help?"

Grayson stepped closer. "Aaron and Jordan are rounding up the rest of the pack and bringing them here. Do you think that's a good idea? Is there a better alternative to keep everyone safe?"

The fact that another Alpha was asking him such an important question blew his mind and for a moment, he couldn't think.

"Ah... well, putting everyone together has the advantage of knowing where everyone is..." Except if they know that. "But what if that's their plan? Get everyone under the same roof and then burn us alive?"

Reagan looked at Grayson, his eyes wide with fear. "Is that possible here? What sort of protection does this building have?"

Grayson grimaced. "Very little, actually. It's mostly just wood and metal. Normal glass, not the unbreakable stuff we all have on our houses."

"Shit." Brad bit out.

Yep. My thoughts exactly.

"It could still work, but you'd have to have patrols going around the Hall constantly so none of the Rogues could get close enough to set the fire."

The Alphas all nodded and the doors burst open, the room flooding with the rest of the pack. There had to be two hundred people in the room.

"Where's everyone going to sleep?" Reagan mused.

They were wolves, they'd sleep where they fell.

"Don't worry, Reagan. As a pack, we sleep together just fine." Grayson reassured his mate.

"Who's doing the first shift?" Brad asked and the play on words made Stephen's lips pull up. Because despite the anger rolling through him and the twist of Fate that had brought them together, Brad's presence still gave him a giddy, hysterical feeling.

"Are you going to shift for your shift?"

Brad stared at him, a light in his brown eyes that made Stephen's heart flip over.

How was it possible that this was the person Fate had deigned right for him?

You could just wait and see...

He shook himself and began to pull his own t-shirt off.

"I'll patrol with you for the first couple of hours. You guys right to put together a roster? Talk to Jordan. He'll help."

For some reason, he didn't want to leave Brad now that he knew what sort of danger was nearby. Even though Brad was a bit of a dick, he was also an Alpha. Therefore, he was the hardest to kill, but he was also a major target. And that didn't sit well with him.

"Okay." Brad agreed and they both moved towards the door at the quieter end of the Hall.

"You going to show me your mark, too?" Brad asked, a strange type of weakness creeping into his voice.

Stephen shrugged. How could he stop Brad from seeing something that big?

He stripped to his briefs, turning slightly so that Brad could see that huge dark mark that ran the length of his leg.

"Woah."

"Yeah. Let's go."

Stephen stacked his clothes neatly and pushed open the door, shifting easily into his wolf.

After upgrading from Omega to Beta status, he'd found he could shift at will. And he'd been practicing.

A strange groan behind him made him turn and he watched the huge black wolf that was Brad stalk forward.

They began to run. Around the Hall and further out. They all needed to work together if they were going to fend off this attack, and Stephen's greatest concern was that he had no idea if he could trust his mate.

And even worse, if they'd even both be standing in the morning.

CHAPTER EIGHT

Brad shifted back to human form, the pain slightly better than last time, and stepped back into the Hall. He didn't want Stephen to see how aroused he was, so he grabbed his black jeans and pulled them on, ignoring the fire in his loins and the throbbing of his balls.

You're meant to mate him. Go! Go get him now!

He grabbed hold of his own hair and tugged hard, enjoying the shooting pain that emerged from the movement.

In wolf form, it was so much harder not to grab Stephen and fuck him.

His wolf knew who his mate was, and it was that gorgeous little grey wolf who'd been following him for the past hour.

What a tease that had been. To have Stephen yapping at his heels.

Damn. How much he'd wanted to turn and grab him, slide his cock straight into that waiting arse...

The door opened and Stephen stepped in, his hands covering his privates.

Was he as hard as Brad himself?

Stephen glared at him as he moved towards his clothes, but Brad refused to look away.

Stephen turned his back and grabbed his clothes, pulling them on in jerky movements.

Spoil sport.

When Stephen turned back around his eyes were thunderous.

What's wrong, pretty boy? Can't handle the fact that I want you so bad?

"What are you looking at?"

Brad wasn't copping that attitude. He stepped forward and pressed into the man meant to be his mate.

Due to the difference in their heights, his cock pressed into Stephen's belly and against his thigh he could feel the rock-hard length of his mate's cock.

He stared down at his mate, Stephen's bluey grey eyes going wide just before his pupils began to dilate with lust.

"I'm looking at you. Is that all right?"

Stephen didn't respond and Brad forced himself to step away, but his heart was pounding as he did.

He wouldn't force Stephen into anything he didn't want, and if that meant walking away from him and never returning, then that is what he would do.

Grayson stepped up next to them.

"Aaron and I are going to go next. You right here?"

"Yep. No problem. We didn't see anything."

Aaron sauntered over and grabbed Grayson.

Brad's belly rumbled and he tilted his head towards the food tables. "Wanna eat?"

Stephen nodded and followed, grabbing a plate and piling the food onto it.

Brad didn't say a thing, but was a little surprised that a Beta needed so much food.

"Come sit with me."

"No. I'll go sit with my friends. Thanks."

Stephen walked away and Brad watched him go. What else could he do?

His heart ached, but he didn't call out.

It was obvious Stephen was used to women. A male lover at all, let alone a dominate male like Brad himself, must scare the shit out of someone like Stephen.

Brad walked over to the Alpha table, the large round table looking surprisingly huge with only Jordan sitting there, eating his own large meal.

"I don't mean to sound rude, but ah..." How did he ask such a weird question?

"Ask me anything." Jordan replied, forking some beef and eating it.

He indicated to the plate that was now half empty in front of Jordan, although it had obviously been quite full before he'd started eating.

"Do you Omegas and Betas always eat so much. I mean... I didn't think you did."

It was a simple formula. You ate as much as you needed to maintain your body size. And since the Alphas were by far the biggest, it made sense that they ate a lot more than the Betas, and more than twice what the Omegas ate.

Both Stephen and now Jordan appeared to be eating an Alpha sized meal.

Hadn't Jordan said he was a Omega?

Jordan laughed, the sound almost musical.

"Yes, well... when we become Alpha mates, we grow. A lot. Well, Reagan and I have. I don't know if it's for protection, or what, but as soon as I developed my mark, I became sooo hungry, but I was scared to show people how much I wanted to eat." He forked some potatoes and ate them with a huge smile. "It is such a relief not to have to hide it anymore."

"You developed your mark? When?"

"At twenty-one."

That was odd for a male.

When he didn't respond, Jordan chuckled again. "I know, it's strange. I don't know why exactly, but that's how it worked for me. Reagan's human, so he was born with his. Mine developed at twenty-one, but being twenty-two years younger than Aaron, I don't know what the reason was other than to keep us apart until I matured."

Woah, that's even weirder.

His mind went to Stephen. "Did Stephen always have my mark? It's pretty hard to miss."

Surely someone would have spotted it when he was younger.

"No. I think he had a small hip birthmark which changed and grew last year when he turned twenty-one."

An arrow hit Brad square in the chest, robbing him of his breath and reminding him of all those months he'd ached for something he couldn't fill. No man, whiskey, or food had made him feel better.

"When was his birthday?"

Jordan grinned. "You've been feeling odd since last year, haven't you? A painful feeling around here?"

Jordan circled his hand around the region of his heart and Brad rolled his eyes, grabbing his own knife and fork.

"Is that normal, too?"

"For the unmated, yep I think so. I kept my mark a secret for two years, so poor Aaron was hurting for ages and didn't know why. I felt so bad when I found out."

"You kept it from him, why?"

Wouldn't any Omega want to find their mate? Especially if that mate were one of the most powerful wolves in the pack?

Jordan shrugged. "Long story, but the main point was, I didn't want to be an Alpha Mate. I didn't think I had it in me. You know all the responsibility… and crap."

Brad cackled, the strange barky laugh erupting from his throat. Of all the people he'd hoped would understand his feelings, a Omega Alpha Mate was the last person he'd expected.

"Yep, I know that feeling. All that crap is right."

"Is that why you stay away? The pack responsibilities?"

Brad went to answer right away but instead thought on it for a minute, scooping some of the chicken stew into his mouth and enjoying the warmth and the full flavours.

"Hmmm…. Pretty much. It's not like I couldn't cope, necessarily…" *Not that I tried…* "I just feel restless all the time when I'm back here. Like I should be somewhere else."

Jordan nodded and they both continued eating, while Brad stewed on everything that had happened so far since coming home.

He'd found that the pack was in mortal danger, his own father and some of the other Alphas were missing from their posts. His mate was a Beta wolf who didn't want to give him the time of day.

Yep, everything was going just peachy.

"What are you going to do about Stephen?"

I have no fucking idea.

Brad forced a shrug. "No idea."

"You can't leave again without him, you know that, yeah?" Jordan said.

Bullshit I can't.

"Of course, I can. Look, I know the legends, but so long as we don't complete the mating, which there is no chance in hell of happening, then we'll both be fine. He can move on with the little skank I saw him with before, and I'll go back to the beach."

"Which skank?"

Brad shrugged and glanced back towards where Stephen sat, unsurprised to find the same girl loitering around.

"That one. With the red top and tiny shorts."

Jordan twisted around then turned back. "Oh, she'd just the Betas' bike. Don't worry about it."

A snarl ripped through him and he turned away. He hated the idea of his mate fucking anyone else. Especially a woman like that.

She oozed bitch.

"I won't."

He finished his meal and a wave of fatigue flowed over him like a hot wave. Which he wasn't surprised by. He'd had two hours sleep in the past thirty-six.

"I might check that everything's okay, then crash for a bit."

"Sure. You know where the beds are?"

Brad nodded and pushed himself to his feet.

He couldn't walk past Stephen without speaking to him, the compulsion was just incredible.

He tapped him on the shoulder as he walked past. "I'm just going to get some sleep. Can you come wake me if they need me?"

Stephen twisted to look at him, and nodded, something in his eyes tugging on Brad's heart strings. But instead of grabbing his mate up in his arms like he wanted to do, he trudged forward and fell onto one of the beds in the large room off the Hall.

A strange anger filled up his gut, making him toss and turn on the mattress. He was leaving as soon as the Alphas were home.

It was time to get back to his life and leave the pack alone.

CHAPTER NINE

Stephen glanced towards the bedroom door where he knew Brad slept.

He tried to pull his mind back to the conversation at hand, but there was nothing he could do to fight the need clawing at him.

Teagan was pissing him off, and the crappy gossip his friends were dishing up was starting to annoy him, too.

When had his life become so tiresome?

He glared towards the door again.

Since Brad came into your life.

A growl cut through his throat and he shook his brain free of the thought. Once Brad left again, everything would go back to normal.

Hopefully.

He wasn't sure how he was going to cope knowing that his mate was never going to show up now. None of the cute little Omega females were suddenly going to develop his mark.

That dream was gone, crushed. Under the giant foot of Brad Talon.

"Hey, Stephen. Do you think we should offer to do the next watch?"

Two of his Beta friends, Cal and Will came up to him.

That would be a great idea.

"Yeah, sure. You right, or you want me to grab Aaron for you?"

The men glanced between themselves and Stephen waited. Some of the Betas still saw him as a Omega, so the fact that they asked him for advice at all was a great sign they were beginning to accept him.

"Come. You know. If you want. You seem to have the Alphas' ear at the moment."

A grin rose onto his face as he pushed up.

He would so love this role. To be able to join the three rankings of wolf so that they were one cohesive unit.

This is what I was born to do.

He frowned at the unusual thought as he walked over to where Grayson and Aaron were shrugging to get their clothes on.

Was that really true? That he was born to be an Alpha mate? He could do so much good if he was.

Pity the Alpha they chose for you is a wandering idiot.

"Hey Aaron. Grayson." He called out and the Alphas walked over, their huge bodies packed with muscle.

Stephen waited for the wave of lust that he assumed would accompany the sight of the two Alphas beautiful bodies, and yet, there was nothing. Just like there had always been.

I'm so not gay.

Then what the fuck's with Brad then?

"Grayson. Will and Cal have offered to do the next run. They're both very capable. Is there any instructions you want to give them?"

Grayson sighed. "That would be great, actually. We didn't sense anything on our run, but if you see, or smell, anything unusual, come back straight away. Howl if you don't think you'll make it."

"Fine by us." Cal grinned, pulling at his clothes in preparation for the run.

It was about time that they all worked together like this.

"Actually. Let me just grab another person, Cal."

He twisted and walked over to the Omega area. As he stepped up to the tables, everyone went quiet and looked to him with wide, searching eyes.

"Hey. We're all taking turns doing perimeter runs. Cal and Will are going now and need a third. Does anyone here feel comfortable shifting and going with them?"

He looked pointedly towards two of his old friends, both of which he knew could shift easily. Dean and Tom.

No one spoke.

"Oh, okay, I'll go ask the Betas then."

Dean pushed himself to his feet. He was proud and strong. "I'll go."

Atta boy.

"Great. Come."

Dean followed him back to where the Betas stood, ready to shift.

"Guys, this is Dean. He'll be your third if that's okay? His wolf is very strong, so if you need a hand, don't hesitate to ask."

The Betas looked at Grayson, their faces hesitant. The Alpha however grinned widely.

"Nice to meet you properly, Dean." Grayson held out his hand and Dean stepped forward, shaking the Alpha's outstretched palm. "Thanks for the help."

"No problem. This is my family too. We've gotta work together." Dean managed to get out, though his voice shook.

"Three sounds better than two. Let's go." Cal said and the three of them headed off.

Stephen watched them go and Grayson patted him on the back. "You did good there. Do you think many of the other Omegas will join in? I didn't think they could shift very easily."

"Tomorrow's the full moon, so that will help. There's probably a dozen or so that I know of. So, yeah. I think we'll be fine for the next few days."

Grayson winked and patted him once more. "You're a great asset to the pack, you know that? I hope Brad pulls his finger out and gets you guys right."

Stephen tilted on his heels, rocking backwards, but he tried not to take a step back from the Alpha. Grayson's words however, shocked him.

"You want Brad and I to be together?"

"Of course. You're destined to be. Fated mates."

Stephen looked away and struggled not to roll his eyes.

Grayson continued. "Look... I know you've probably been waiting for some girl to turn up with your mark."

Yep.

"I was, too. So was Aaron. Brad was the only Alpha who preferred male lovers to female. I never thought I'd ever have sex with a male, but you know... that's a twice daily occurrence now and I'll never go back."

Stephen glanced back at the Alpha. "Twice a day?"

He was lucky to get it twice a month.

Grayson grinned, his white teeth flashing brightly.

"One of the many benefits of having a male mate. No moon cycles, no drop in hormones. Constantly high sex drive."

A shiver ran down his spine and Grayson must have noticed, because he laughed.

"Yep. So, don't knock it till you try it, and since I know Brad will be high tailing it out of here as soon as our dads get back, I'd be jumping at the chance to be with your mate."

Great. As if I have any idea about being a lover to Brad.

"Yeah. Thanks."

Grayson shrugged and gave him a half smile, then stepped away.

Stephen turned around and stared at the room that housed the man Fate said should be his mate.

Should he get close to him and see how things went?

A heat bloomed over his face at the images the mere thought provoked. Brad was an Alpha which meant that he, the Beta, would have to take it.

His arse tightened on its own accord and he took deep breaths to calm the huge butterflies flapping in his belly. It couldn't be that bad, could it? Reagan did it, so did Jordan.

He ran a hand through his hair and tried not to focus on the actual physicalities. He never thought he'd even be considering such a thing, but here he was, following his instincts that screamed at him to go to his mate.

He glanced at his watch.

Eight thirty.

Everyone would be up for another few hours before they crashed. No one had to get up and work in the morning, so no one was rushing to sleep. That meant he had a little bit of time, maybe.

His gut flipped and his breath caught in his throat as he reassessed his plan. Should he really do this?

His legs began to move of their own accord, until he'd stepped into the darkened room and looked around.

Eight beds were set up and they were all empty. Save for the one where Brad was.

Please let there be a lock.

Brad checked the door and there was a sturdy lock, newly installed maybe? He didn't know and he didn't care.

He turned the knob and the lock clicked into place with a metallic chink.

Brad sat bolt upright, "What's happening? Do they need me?"

"Ah. No. It's just me."

"Oh." Brad's posture relaxed and Stephen's eyes began to adjust to the dim light. Stephen saw Brad's bare chest, his handsome face, and lust stirred deep in his gut.

"I've never been with a man before."

Why did you start it like that?

He wanted to slap himself in the face.

What an idiot.

"And you want to try it?" Brad asked, his voice croaky with sleep. Or something darker.

"I... don't have any idea what I want."

And that was the god's honest truth. He was so bloody confused.

"Then why did you come in here?"

"Because you're my mate, whether we both like it or not, and I..." He didn't want to finish the sentence.

Did he really want to see what it would feel like to be fucked by the magnificent man before him?

He let out a long sigh. He didn't want to think anymore.

"Come here." The deep rumble of Brad's voice was hypnotic and a shudder coursed through his body.

He took a few steps closer, his heart racing in his chest.

"Strip." Brad's second command.

Stephen reached for his t-shirt with trembling hands and pulled it over his head.

"Slowly. I want to remember this."

When I'm gone... seemed to hang in the air, but Stephen pushed away whatever pain came from such an idea and opened his jeans with slow movements.

The zip hissed in the room and the whoosh of the material as they fell around his ankles seemed exaggerated by the silence.

He swallowed hard.

"Now the shorts."

Stephen hooked his thumbs into the waistband of his underwear, his blood throbbing south and extending his cock.

He bent forward and pulled them down, enjoying the bounce of his dick against his belly.

He'd never been so hard, so fast.

Maybe you've been fooling around with the wrong sex.

He stared at Brad, who'd thrown back the cover, opened his own jeans and was stroking his cock with long pulls.

The look Brad gave him punched him straight in the gut, causing orgasmic tingles to pulse along his skin.

No. Never felt anything like this before.

He put his own hand on his cock and watched as Brad grew bigger and harder before his eyes.

"Come and suck me."

I have no idea how to do that.

He moved over to his mate on legs that trembled and knelt. Brad's hand came up to cup his skull.

"Please, Stephen. I need you."

He stared at the throbbing, red head and bent forward, pressing a kiss to the soft skin before opening his lips and enveloping the flesh.

CHAPTER TEN

A moan caught in his throat as his mate's flavour burst forward.

He took more of him into his mouth, and began bobbing up and down as he knew felt good. His own body throbbed with the anticipation of what would come next.

"Argh..." Brad grabbed him by the hair and pulled Stephen off with a loud groan. "You are too fucking good at that."

Brad swung his legs off the bed and pulled Stephen to a stand.

Brad stared down at him, their eyes locking, the animal magnetism between them pulsing like a live wire. Pure electricity and molten lava.

"Kiss me."

Stephen went up on his toes and Brad came down on his, crushing him as their mouths met. Connected.

Brad pressed his lips open and devoured him, his intense flavour absolutely wiping Stephen's memory of every kiss that came before him.

Stephen wrapped his arms around Brad's neck and squeezed

tight, pressing their bodies together and returning the kiss as much as he could. Brad's body was hard, his skin hot and slick with sweat.

When the kiss became so passionate Stephen could barely breathe, Brad pulled away, panting.

"Lean over the bed. I have to have you now."

Brad shucked off his jeans and Stephen went down on all fours on the bed, fear tickling along his spine as he waited for what would happen next. Was this going to hurt like hell?

He felt Brad move, and then a wet tongue was probing him from behind.

"Oh fuck!"

Pleasure exploded in his mind that rivaled every orgasm he'd had before tonight.

Brad worked his flesh with his talented tongue. Moving it in and out, around and around. Stephen knew he should have been ashamed to be enjoying such a thing, but those sensitive tissues were lighting up from the attention.

Wow.

His eyes fluttered shut as wave upon wave of pleasure buffeted his system.

Brad pressed a final kiss to his arse and stood up.

Stephen could feel Brad's cock at his now wet arsehole and he pushed back, feeling the feral need to be fully connected to his mate.

He rocked back and Brad's hands held his hips.

"Hell. I need you so much." Brad grunted at him a moment before he thrust forward, hard.

Stephen screamed out, his body exploding with need and lust. Love and pleasure. All in one brilliant, earth shattering moment.

His cock hardened to an almost painful point, then he began to cum.

He cried out again, gripping the sheets beneath his hands hard as Brad made a feral groaning noise and his heat squirted inside of him.

Stephen's seed pulsed out of him in hot, overwhelming waves. Fireworks exploded in his head as hot fire scalded his back and he passed out.

Knock, knock, knock.

"Hey! You guys! Open up!"

Stephen came awake again to the loud sounds of someone trying to enter their room.

He jumped up, the unfamiliar ache in his arse making him twinge.

"What happened?" Brad asked, moaning as though he too had been hit with a lump of wood.

"I don't know." He turned towards the door. "We're coming!"

He began pulling on his clothes and he could hear Brad chuckling. "No, we already came. Woah. I've never felt anything like it."

A wave of relief washed over him and Stephen smiled at his lover. "Good. I thought it was just me."

He stumbled over to the door and unlocked the door as Brad pulled himself to his feet too.

Reagan was on the other side. "You guys okay? Everyone wants to get some sleep and we're organising the beds."

"Already?"

"Already? It's close to midnight."

Fuck me...

He turned back towards Brad, who was pulling on his jeans. "Really? Woah."

Reagan narrowed his eyes and flicked on the light.

Stephen blinked rapidly as white sparks flicked across his eyes.

"How did you not know that close to four hours had passed?"

"I have no idea. We must have fallen asleep..."

Reagan's smile turned upside down. "Did you guys just... how's your birthmark Brad?"

Oh no... we couldn't have...

He turned back around and Brad was pulling on his shoes. "What do you mean?"

"Check for me, would you?"

There were people clamouring behind Reagan, but he didn't seem worried.

Brad frowned, obviously not understanding why Reagan was asking or what it would mean if something had changed. Stephen knew though... and his heart began to pick up pace inside his tight ribcage, waiting for the inevitable crash.

Brad pulled down the left side of his black jeans and there was nothing but bare, gorgeous flesh.

Stephen's stomach dropped to the floor and he fell against the door frame.

They'd completed the mating ritual without knowing it.

If they'd truly mated, they couldn't be apart. Ever.

"What the?"

Brad pulled off his jeans and stared down at his bare leg, the skin now free from the huge birthmark he'd had his whole life.

His head snapped up and he glared straight at Stephen. His heart trembled at the sight of his mate's anger and he bit his lip as he waited for the backlash.

"What the hell have you done?

~

Brad stared at his bare leg, unable to believe the skin belonged to him.

"Where's it gone?"

Reagan was grinning like a lunatic and Stephen looked like he was about to vomit. What was going on?

"You guys come out and let these people in to sleep." Reagan beckoned to them and Stephen went, his head down.

Brad frowned, but did as he was requested.

The hairs on Brad's body were standing up in freakish outrage. His mark was gone.

It was GONE!

What the fuck did that mean?

He followed Reagan, zombie like, over to the Alpha table, relieved to see that most of the pack were settling to sleep in groups on the floor, or going into the two makeshift bedrooms.

Reagan practically skipped up to Grayson. "Guess what! Brad's mark's gone!" He said it with such glee, Brad's hands fisted into uncontrollable balls.

"Stop. Fucking. Saying. That."

Grayson turned and sent out a low warning growl, pushing his mate behind him.

"Get your shit together, Brad. Look."

Grayson pulled up the left sleeve on his short-sleeved shirt and Brad's world fell away.

He stumbled onto the chair.

Aaron chuckled. "Me, too. Check this out."

He lifted his own black top and revealed smooth washboard abs. "Do you remember how big it was?"

He sure did. He'd spent his childhood growing up with Grayson, ten years behind Aaron. They played together, shifted together, and bonded together as the Alphas always did. He knew both of their birthmarks well.

"What's happening around here?"

His folks had always talked of the magic and power of the wolves, of the energy that swirled in the trees around Greensborough. But he'd never believed it was possible for such a thing to happen.

"Where did they go?"

Jordan stood up and lifted his top, revealing the same birthmark he knew to be Aaron's.

"So? Aren't you meant to have the identical one to Aaron?" He asked, totally and utterly confused.

Beside him, Stephen began to strip. His shoes, and then his pants. What was he doing now?

Jordan grinned wide. "Check it out. See if there's a wolf on his leg. See, here's mine." Jordan pointed to a black wolf like shape close to his belly button.

Brad couldn't remember if Aaron's birthmark had that same pattern or not. What were they trying to say?

"Oh fuck. They're right." Stephen said, his voice sounding shocked.

Brad dragged his eyes down to his mate's mark- still there in vivid black.

His gaze travelled further down and there it was. An addition to the mark. A large, black wolf stood proudly beneath the winding tendrils of the original mark.

Anger pooled in his gut like the rising sea, hot and turbulent.

"Oh, my fucking God. Are you telling me..." He whirled on his friends. "That these guys STEAL our birthmarks."

Grayson began to laugh, and Aaron smirked at him. "Don't know what you're complaining about. You look normal now. It's Stephen that should be complaining. He has to carry your wolf around with him as a constant reminder of YOU!"

Brad closed his eyes and searched, finding his wolf inside his mind, rested and calm now that he was properly mated.

What?!

His eyes sprung open and he took a step back, glaring at the group of Alphas.

"Is this what I think it is?"

Reagan crossed his arms over his chest and sent him a hard look. "It means you guys completed the mating. You should feel a lot more settled now."

His world spun around him.

That meant he would never be able to be without Stephen, or the pack, again. Gone were the days of travelling, living in a tent and coasting through the outback.

Oh fuck.

"Yeah, he looks rapt, doesn't he?"

He heard Stephen's disappointed voice and he struggled to come up with a reply. He let the anger drain away as he realised his mate hadn't wanted this either.

He opened his mouth to say something, but nothing coherent came out. He didn't know how to respond.

"Ah... Um..."

Everyone was silent around him and the awkwardness only grew.

Another wave of resentment flooded in. He'd just been trapped, good and proper. Stephen couldn't have done a better job if he'd got pregnant.

Fuck it.

"I might do the next shift. I doubt I'll get much sleep."

He lifted his gaze to Grayson, ignoring the man who was now his mate, who stood a few metres away.

"I'll get a couple of the Betas to go with you." Jordan said and moved away, speaking to a few guys and returning with two older, harder looking men.

"Tony, Lee, have you met Brad yet?"

Tony and Lee nodded at him. "I remember you from that massive party we had a few years ago. Your thirtieth, wasn't it?"

"Yeah. It was. Great. Let's go."

He didn't want to stay here any longer, and for once, it wasn't his wolf who wanted to shift to escape the human world. It was him.

He headed to the door without a backward glance, that strange ache that he'd carried with him for almost a year, totally vanished.

Oh. Damn it all to hell.

CHAPTER ELEVEN

Reagan stepped closer to Stephen and leaned heavily against him. Considering the guy was a human, he had great instincts for comforting a wolf.

"Don't worry about him, Stephen. Some of these Alphas need their arses handed to them before they realise what they've got."

"Yeah, I suppose."

He stared after the man that was now his mate and did his jeans up again. He now had an addition to his massive birthmark, and he didn't know how he felt about it.

Numb was probably the best way to describe it.

"So, I really am an Alpha Mate."

Reagan clapped him on the back, hard. "Yep. Welcome to the club."

His heart fell. He didn't want to be part of the club.

Reagan must have seen his face because he went on to say, "Just think about how much good you can do for the pack. It's a great advantage."

True… and that did fit into his pack man mentality perfectly.

"Yeah, I suppose. But that's only if Brad sticks around. What if he leaves again when all the Alphas come home?"

"You're still an Alpha Mate." Grayson chimed in, "And we'll treat you as such. I promise. I won't let anyone take that away from you. If Brad wants to leave, let him. He'll be miserable without you, trust me. If Reagan hadn't come back to me after a couple of weeks apart, I think I would have crawled to Melbourne and begged him to come home."

Stephen managed a laugh at that one. The idea of an Alpha begging for anything seemed so odd. Worse than odd, impossible, actually.

"Yeah, well. I doubt that'll be Brad."

He couldn't imagine the biggest, grumpiest, and most loner of all five Alphas begging him to come back to him. Not after making it very clear he'd never wanted a mate in the first place.

Grayson shook his head. "Brad doesn't understand how strong the mating is, and neither do you, Stephen. He literally won't be able to live without you, and you won't survive well without him, I'm sorry to say."

Stephen straightened his shoulders and tossed his head back so he could look at Grayson properly.

"I'll be fine. I have my friends. The pack. I don't need anything else."

"Spoken like a true Alpha." Grayson grinned.

The compliment winged through Stephen's heart, settling a lot of the pain left there.

He hadn't meant to mate with Brad. Not at all. But now that it had happened, he knew that it was what was meant to be.

He trusted Fate and the destiny laid out for him. Even if he didn't understand it, he had faith.

"I suppose. Thanks, Grayson. I better settle into some sleep, too."

He excused himself and went to a corner where Johnno and Tim were sleeping. There were pillows everywhere and a few extra blankets.

He settled onto the cold floor and wrapped the blanket around himself.

For the first time in his life, he didn't wish for the sweet body of a willing female to help him sleep. He wanted Brad. The big, muscular frame that had just taken him and blown apart his mind.

That was what sex was meant to be like. Explosive. All consuming.

Maybe next time it'll be longer though.

Don't fool yourself into thinking there will be a next time.

He squeezed his eyes shut and curled into a ball, once again feeling like a helpless Omega.

He'd worked so hard to become stronger, fitter, bigger. To excel, to stretch out from the confines of the box he'd been born into.

And now, with a few words from his mate and a rejection for the record books, he was worse off than he'd ever been.

Unwanted and unloved by the one person who was meant to need him.

THEY ALL GOT through the night still alive and with no sign of the Rogues. Brad was counting the hours until he could go home.

Grayson had received an email from his father saying the meeting was going well and they would soon have a plan of attack. Then it was a day's drive home for them all. So, if all went well, they'd be back by tomorrow night.

Despite the fact that he was still physically exhausted, Brad slept terribly. His mind kept going to his mate, sleeping at the other end of the Hall.

Stephen was meant to be next to him. Brad knew that. His wolf was furious and pacing inside him at the lack of his warm body.

But Brad also knew that maintaining a safe distance from his mate was the best thing he could do for them both.

He didn't want to stay, and Stephen was the quintessential pack man.

Although he'd originally behaved badly, the shock of the mating news had now worn off and he could see it wasn't Stephen's fault. Stephen hadn't been the one to make it happen. They both did something to set it off. And he doubted that Stephen even wanted to be mated to him.

It was going to painful for both of them to go back to the worlds they'd come from.

Now mated. And yet alone.

But he could do it, he was sure he could. He'd achieved harder things before.

He groaned as he rolled onto his back, stretching his arms above his head and rolling up into a seated position.

The smell of frying bacon and the undeniably yummy scent of cooking bread made his gut churn and scream for food.

Breakfast time.

He got up off the floor, wishing he'd been able to sleep outside on the grass. It would have been a hell of a lot more comfortable.

His thighs ached from a lack of blood and he shuffled over to the tables laden with food, lifting his heels and stretching out his quads.

A whole day in the car yesterday probably didn't help either.

"How are you this morning?" Grayson's voice made its way into his ears.

"Yeah. Not bad."

He concentrated on his food, ladling the plate with as many eggs and rashers of bacon as would fit.

"Hopefully the other Alphas will be back tomorrow night and you can disappear into the distance again, huh?"

A prickle on his neck warned of something coming.

"Grayson. Back off."

His friend chuckled and walked away and a vision of Brad's sister came into his mind's eye.

"Tabitha."

He turned around and marched over to where the others sat, eating and chatting.

"Hey, Grayson. Where's Tabby? I haven't seen her yet."

With all the news about his parents being gone, then meeting Stephen, he hadn't even thought about his kid sister.

Grayson's eyebrows drew together. "I haven't seen her either."

A trickle of dread coursed down Brad's spine, the memory of that Omega's body lying dead in the bush assaulting him.

"I'll grab Megan and we'll find out."

Grayson left and Brad sat down with a thump. Hadn't they done a proper check that they had everyone? Where was his sister anyway?

Grayson came back with a gorgeous young woman, her bright blue eyes identical to her brother's. He pushed to his feet, noticing the good height on her. Alpha born females were always tall.

"Megan. Is that really you?"

Last time he'd noticed Grayson's little sister, she'd been wearing pig tails and a school uniform.

"Brad. Welcome home." She stepped up and gave him a brief hug, then took a step back, her brow furrowed just like her brother's.

"Tabby lives with a group of Beta girls at the end of town. I haven't seen her and I don't know where they'd be if they're not here. We searched almost every house."

Just like last night, the hit of new information slammed into his chest and his world fell away.

He turned to Grayson. "I need to find her. Now."

Something was wrong. He knew it.

"We'll go together. Megan, go check if anyone else is missing. Ask around, do a role check of sorts if you can."

"I'll try."

Megan turned and headed off and Brad left his meal on the table and charged for the door. "Let's go."

Stephen came out of nowhere, grabbing his arm. "What's wrong? What's happened?"

Warmth poured through him, calming his fear, as Stephen's characteristically caramel smell surrounded him.

"My sister's missing. We're going to find her."

"I'll go with you."

"No. Stay." *I don't want to have to worry about you, too.*

Stephen fell back, obviously hurt by the rejection, but Brad didn't have the time to explain it all to him.

"You can help by finding out if we're missing anyone else. Go ask the Betas, the Omegas. We can't lose anyone else."

Stephen nodded and hurried back to the pack.

How had this happened? Why had no-one noticed that they were missing people?

Grayson pushed open the door to the outside and together they walked out.

"Megan says she lives this way. Let's go."

"Should we shift?"

He wasn't sure he could handle seeing his sister dead from his human eyes.

"Not sure. I want to be as inconspicuous as possible, so maybe stay human unless we see something odd. Then shift."

Brad nodded and followed his friend along the street, keeping up with his strong, long stride.

He was definitely emotionally compromised and he wasn't sure he could trust his own instincts in this case.

"Is she mated?" He assumed not if she was living with other girls and her mate hadn't noticed she was missing.

"No. She isn't. She developed a mark around her twenty first birthday but it didn't match any of the Betas. We didn't check with the Omegas of course... although, the way we're matching up with people now, we probably should have."

Brad frowned at the idea, and yet he knew he was being narrow minded.

Aaron's mate was a Omega wolf and he seemed to be a great companion.

"Where's her house?"

"It's just down this road."

They turned left and continued down the sidewalk, when he caught a scent on the breeze. Something ugly.

He grabbed Grayson's arm, halting him.

"I can smell something bad. Like the death in the forest."

Grayson began to pull his clothes off to shift, but Brad knew in his gut they were too late.

He waited to see what would happen and his heart clenched tight, seizing his breath. A man walked out of the house ahead of them, holding his sister by her beautiful red hair that shone in the sunlight like fire.

She was twisted up and there was blood on her shirt and over her lovely face.

You would fight them, wouldn't you, Tabby?

"Grayson, stop. Look."

He pointed ahead and began walking towards his sister.

The man, an ugly Beta sized male, held a black handled knife to her throat.

"Brad the Alpha. I knew you'd come looking for this bitch."

He spat on the ground and Brad noticed the blood trickling from the man's mouth.

Yep, Tabby could land a punch on practically anyone.

"I have. Now what do you want to do with me?"

He held up his hands as though he were giving up, which he was.

He'd do anything to save his sister.

"Get inside. Both of you. Now."

CHAPTER TWELVE

He pulled Tabby down hard, making her cry out.

"You too, Grayson." The guy yelled.

Oh fuck. This wasn't good.

His friend was at his back. "What do you want?" Grayson called out.

"I want you to go inside. Now!"

"Okay, okay. Be cool."

They walked down the small path and opened the door on the lovely house his sister was renting.

The stink of death hit him like a heat wave and he stopped breathing as his belly heaved.

They walked further into the house and there was a scream and a door slamming shut.

Brad twisted around and saw Tabby lying on the floor.

He pushed past Grayson to pick her up.

"Tabby... I'm so sorry. Are you hurt?"

She let out a strangled sob. "No. It's not me. They killed Katie."

He didn't know who Katie was, but he thanked God it wasn't his sister.

"All right, it's all right." He cradled his sister in his arms, feeling a wave of relief wash over him.

"Where is he? How many are there?" Grayson asked.

She lifted her head and looked out the window.

"I don't know. He shoved me in here, then locked the door. I've seen three or four different guys come through here, but there's more. I could hear them outside. I'm so sorry..."

Her lip trembled and he flinched to see the blackening around her eyes, along her jaw.

"Sorry? For what?"

"They used me to lure you here. And I couldn't stop them..."

"No, you couldn't. But we're going to get out of here. Don't you worry! Grayson!"

The other Alpha stepped back into the lounge where they stood and gave a report.

"There's two other girls, dead, in the other room."

"Two... oh no. Not Millie, too."

Tabitha began to crumple and Brad held her tight to him, offering her whatever type of support he could.

"It's okay." He stroked her hair and let her cry into his shoulder. This was just horrible.

"What do we do?" He asked Grayson.

"Well, we have Tabitha and they've killed the others, so I say we try to sneak out."

"Or fight our way out." Brad growled. He couldn't believe he was locked in a house by some lunatic Betas.

Grayson snuck up to the front door and Brad put Tabitha down onto the couch, the furthest from the window.

Grayson looked out the window and then tried the door.

"It's locked."

"Let's break a window then."

"You can't. They're all impenetrable. We built all the new houses like fortresses to keep everyone safe."

Oh. for fuck's sake!

Brad rolled his eyes and yelled out in frustration. "Well, find a fucking way Grayson. Because my mate is back at the Hall and you know that's where they're going to attack!"

Grayson glared back at him. "Mine too, you selfish wanker!"

"Mate? What mate?" Tabby jumped up and came over to him, her eyes now clear, though her face was still blotchy and tear stained.

Brad glanced at his sister, his heart pounding in his chest. Stephen was back at the Hall and that wolf was going to them. Aaron was the only Alpha standing in their way.

"Yeah. His name is Stephen."

His sister's smile was just beautiful as she sighed, such a contrast to the situation they were in. To see her be so happy for him was a balm to his otherwise tattered soul.

"I was so hoping you'd find your mate... hang on. Stephen. Is he the Omega that challenged the Alphas last year to be a Beta?"

"He what?"

Why hadn't anyone told him that? That meant his mate had done something that barely a man did every decade. He was strong, and proud. Successful, too. No wonder the Fates chose him to be an Alpha Mate.

Yeah, pity they picked me to be an Alpha, too!

"We need to get out of here."

There had to be a way.

"Let's go into each room and find a way out."

Grayson ran off and Brad followed, searching each room for something to break down the door.

There was a crackle and snap, and smoke teased his nostrils.

No way. You fucking pricks.

Brad ran back into the front room to see the front of the house was on fire.

Adrenaline coursed through his veins as he saw his way out of the house. Those stupid wolves hadn't thought about what the fire would do to the integrity of the house.

Perfect.

"Grayson. Let's go!"

Tabby ran back into the room. "What are we going to do?"

She'd begun to panic, she couldn't shift like they could.

"We'll shift and jump through the fire. You get on my back, and hold on tight."

His wolf ripped through him as he heard Grayson growl with aggression.

He dropped to all fours and let the shift take him over.

The fire was ravaging the roof now. Red and orange flames licking at the wood, making the paint curl and fall onto the carpet. Smoke billowed into the room like black sails.

He pressed his body into Tabby and she cried out as she climbed onto his back, grabbing tight to his fur.

Grayson stalked towards the wall, waiting, as Brad was, for the right moment.

The roof crackled and burned, the window shattering in the blackness and falling with a theatrical crash to the ground.

Let's go.

Grayson leapt through the opening and Brad stepped forward, the fire licking at his fur.

Hold on, sister.

He leapt through the opening and heard Tabby scream.

Heat engulfed them, and then they were free, and she was still clinging to his back.

He bent down so that she could get off.

Tabby gripped on tighter. "No. Let's get back to the Hall. I'm coming with you."

He would have loved to stay and fight out the point with her, but it was a waste of time.

Brad took off at a run, trailing behind the fleeing figure of Grayson.

Hold on, Stephen. I'm coming.

CHAPTER THIRTEEN

A few of the Betas on patrol had seen a large pack of wolves coming through the woods. They'd come back quickly and alerted everyone. Aaron had locked all the doors and there was utter chaos ensuing.

Stephen yelled out to some of the women. "Quick! In here. Lock the door and don't come out unless I specifically tell you to."

The women in the pack were unable to fight. They couldn't shift and their fear paralysed most of the men.

The women scrambled into the room, pushing at each other to get into the bedroom. Some carrying children, screaming and worried.

There were so many helpless people, and anger boiled inside of his belly that some wolves that used to be part of their own pack could do this to them.

He shut the door and motioned to some of the others to do the same thing.

The Rogues were here and they were in a hell of a lot of trouble.

People were running everywhere. They had no weapons, save the wolf inside of them.

He saw Aaron and Jordan in the centre of the room and charged forward, grabbing hold of the Alpha's arm.

"Most of the Omegas are safe. Hopefully. What happens if they light this place on fire?"

"Then we all run. This place will go up like a box of matches."

"Yeah, but at least we aren't locked in!" Reagan yelled to get above the noise.

"Aaron, where's Grayson and Brad?" They couldn't fight with just one Alpha.

"They're not back yet. They went to find his sister."

Dear God in Heaven.

"Oh fuck."

"Oh yeah."

Aaron was looking lost without the power of the council behind him, but he was still the Alpha.

"Aaron, you need to calm everyone down. Use your Alpha thing."

Aaron grinned at him. "Okay. Let's do it."

Aaron extended to his full height and partially shifted, his skin darkening as his eyes flashed to his wolf.

His great Alpha growl broke through the room, silencing everyone's panic and making some of the men stop running. Everyone turned towards them.

"On your knees. Silent. Now."

Everyone in the room fell to their knees.

Stephen did not.

And as he looked around at the room, he knew that his time had come to step up into the role of the Alpha Mate he was born to be.

"We need to work together." He implored the pack. "We are

many. They are few. Together, we can fight them and win. Come on 'Borough Boys! Betas! Omegas! Anyone who can shift. If you love your home as I do. You will fight to keep it safe and strong. With or without the Alphas- we are still a pack!"

There was a great roar as everyone jumped to their feet.

The tearing of clothes signalled that the real fight for the 'Borough had begun.

He turned to Aaron who was grinning fiercely, still half shifted.

"Well done." He growled through pointed teeth, the words barely recognisable.

Reagan couldn't shift so Stephen turned to the doctor. "You need to keep the women safe. They can't shift, and they can't fight a Beta wolf off alone. Some of the Omega males can't shift either."

Reagan nodded once, his jaw set and tight. "We'll get some weapons from the kitchen."

Reagan ran off and began grabbing Omega males, the men's faces changing from helpless to determined. They had a job, too. Protect their families, their women and children.

The room was now full of wolves. Small brown and grey wolves, with one black Alpha in the very centre.

This was going to be the end of the Rogues. He was sure of it.

He only hoped that they didn't lose too many of their own in the fight.

He ran to the window and gasped at the sight.

There were wolves everywhere. All grey. Betas. Snarling, snapping wolves that had come to kill them, take their land, their home. Well, it wasn't going to happen.

Aaron threw back his head and howled. Full moon.

He was the only one left human so he ran to the main door, and looked straight at Aaron.

The wolf seemed to nod and crouch down. Stephen attacked the locks, throwing open the doors.

Aaron charged forward and ran straight out the door and into the fray.

Stephen raced across the room and unlocked the door on the other side of the Hall, pulling that open and watching as the other wolves charged outside to meet the Rogues.

The moon called to him and he let his wolf emerge.

He transformed and as he looked down upon his paws he saw how big they were.

Had his mating changed something?

Probably.

He pushed the thought aside and ran outside.

The fight was really on.

There were wolves pouncing and biting, snarling and attacking, each other.

There were inhuman cries in the night and blood spilling on the ground.

The noise was incredibly loud and the air itself was cloying and hot with the anger and passion raining down upon them.

He saw a Beta Rogue pounce on a couple of Omegas, tearing at one of their throats.

Stephen bolted forward, baring his teeth and sinking it into the wolf's ear, ripping it off.

Blood spurted into his mouth and he spat out the ear, the Beta jumping at him in anger.

He swung his clawed paw, knocking the Beta sideways, then jumping onto his belly and ripping out his throat.

Fuck. He'd never felt this strong.

The Omega who had been hurt was still down, but he was alive, and Stephen pushed the empathy to the side.

There was more to do. They weren't losing but it didn't look like they were winning, either.

He ran through the pack, helping where he could. Biting and snarling, using his claws to rip a Rogue off another Beta. Then he saw Aaron. Surrounded by four Rogues and he was barely on his feet.

Blood poured from a wound in his side and Stephen could see Jordan beneath Aaron.

Aaron was guarding him and they'd both be dead soon

No!

He threw back his head and howled to the moon.

Brad! Where are you?

The wolves surrounding Aaron and Jordan were preparing to pounce and he attacked. Tearing at one of their necks as he charged into the circle, standing back to back with the Alpha.

The Betas relaxed their stance, seemingly unsure now.

Fucking cowards. A fair fight isn't what you want, is it?

He growled and snapped at them.

They howled back and began to get into formation again.

He didn't want to die, but if he did at this moment, he'd die doing the right thing for his pack.

Brad could hear the snarl of the wolves ahead and he kept on running.

Please let us not be too late.

Then he saw them.

The pack were fighting the Rogues! Without them.

He stopped and waited impatiently for his sister to get off as he saw Grayson take out a Rogue.

Tabby fell to the ground and he raced off.

Please get to safety little sister. This isn't a fight for you.

He ran into the fray and saw Aaron surrounded by a group of wolves. And who was at his back, but Brad's own mate!

Fucking hell! They're going to die!

The Rogues pounced and Brad knew he was too far away. He raced through the pack, jumping for the wolf attached to Grayson's neck.

He ripped him off and threw him away.

Stephen cried out and Brad charged, head butting the wolf who had flattened his mate.

He jumped on top of Stephen and he could smell blood. His mate's blood. He was hurt. Brad had failed to protect the one person he was meant to. Pain gnawed at his heart.

Oh shit. Focus. Focus.

The wolves were going down all around him. He could only see about five Rogues still fighting on top of the four surrounding them.

And the Rogues seemed to know they were losing too, because the two that still stood in front of them suddenly turned to flee.

Nope. Not this time.

Aaron and he bolted after them, leaving their mates.

He didn't want to leave Stephen, but he wasn't doing this again. These Rogues were going down.

Now.

He caught up to one smaller grey wolf and pounced on his back, pulling him to the ground and ripping out his throat with his teeth.

Aaron took down the other and he heard a howl ahead of him in the bush. Hopefully someone else had caught the remaining strays.

He left the Rogue on the ground, bleeding to death, and headed back to the pack, and his mate.

His mate. What the hell was he going to do with a mate when he left?

He could sense Aaron at his shoulder as together they made it back.

Stephen and Jordan had shifted back to their human forms, as had most of the pack. Dead wolves littered the outside of the Hall everywhere. Some of them pack members, the rest Rogues.

Brad let go of his wolf form and staggered over to his mate, dragging the kneeling Stephen into his arms.

"Oh, my God. Are you okay?" Stephen smelled of ammonia and stress. The air was clogged with the stench of death.

"Yeah, I'm fine. But Jordan's hurt."

Brad looked down and Aaron was lifting his mate into his arms. Jordan was barely conscious, massive chunks of flesh missing from his upper shoulder and flank.

"Reagan!!!" Aaron roared and the blond doctor came running.

Reagan took one look at him, then said, "Quick, the hospital."

Together, they ran, and Brad turned to his mate, inspecting his injuries. "You're hurt, too."

Stephen flinched away from him. "Nothing I can't cope with. Come on. We need to get the other injured to the hospital, as well."

Stephen staggered away, blood on his legs and down one side of his face.

He was tough. No one could say otherwise.

And a Omega born. Brad shook his head and stared after Stephen. He could not be more blown away by the intelligence, strength, and heart his mate had. For his pack, and everyone around him.

Imagine how he'd treat you if you let him.

Brad shook the thought away. He'd never craved the stability of a mate. His parents set a good example, he couldn't complain, but it just wasn't him. He wanted the wind in his hair, not shackles on his feet.

He turned away from his mate and began checking bodies. So many dead. It was such a horrible waste. Too many men.

He glanced around at all the fallen and he bent to pick up one of their dead Betas. Someone had to help the dead, and he could do that. Separate the bodies from the Rogues and put them somewhere safe at least, until their families claimed them.

The Rogues could stay out in the elements and rot.

"You okay?" Grayson grunted at him as he lifted a wounded Beta into his arms.

"Yeah. Reagan just went with Aaron to the hospital."

Grayson nodded his thanks and headed off.

Brad glanced around at the battlefield of bodies.

Damn. Where was the council when you needed them?

CHAPTER FOURTEEN

The night was long and hard, but the sun finally rose over the mountains, bringing with it a new day.

Stephen had gone inside as soon as he was sure it was safe, and opened the doors, bringing out the Omegas to help.

Husbands and sons were gone.

They lost almost twenty of their own.

But they had won the war. At a massive cost.

Grayson contacted the Alphas to let them know that a strategy was not needed any longer. They had killed all the Rogue wolves.

Twenty-eight in total.

No one had known they'd grown to such a number.

The Alphas were due home in a few hours, and the funerals would begin tomorrow.

To say he was physically and emotionally exhausted would be an understatement, but at least everyone could go home and feel safe now.

"What's the final count?" Brad asked as he sat down next to him.

Stephen put his head in hands, the pounding of a drum going off in his brain.

"Twenty-eight bodies on their side, twenty on ours, and a few touch and go at the hospital. Jordan included."

So many people, and to think he'd been one of the ones to encourage them all to fight. Did that mean their blood was on his hands?

No. It was all on the Rogues. He was lucky to still be here.

"Fuck. Is Jordan going to be okay?"

Stephen shrugged, his eyes drooping shut. He needed some sleep.

"I'm going to go lie down before the Alphas get back. I'll see you later, okay?"

"Can I come with you?"

Stephen turned to his mate, his heart aching for the closeness only Brad could provide. But that was the last thing he needed. To feel that beautiful connection another time, only to have Brad take it all away again.

"I don't think so."

He pushed up and stood, wavering on his feet.

Brad's arms came around him. "I'll take you back. Come on."

He didn't have the strength to push him off again. So, he let Brad accompany him home, mostly because Brad was keeping him standing.

They went straight to his house, a home he rented with two other Betas.

He unhooked his arm from Brad's body and opened the front door, walked inside and went straight to his bedroom.

He needed a shower, but that would have to wait. He couldn't stand a moment longer.

"Thanks for walking me home."

He began to strip, uncaring that the Alpha was still standing in the doorway and all the unresolved issues still lay between. Today was not for discussing such trivial things when his friends lay injured or dead.

Brad stepped closer. "I want to stay."

He fell onto his bed and crawled beneath the covers. He had a queen-sized bed, so he didn't really care if Brad wanted to crash with him.

"Fine. But I'm not having sex."

Brad closed the door slowly and undressed, sliding beneath the covers too. Brad's warmth and bulk was comforting even though he wasn't actually touching him.

Stephen closed his eyes, his body calling for the rest and healing only deep sleep could give him. But as he lay in the dark, images of the night-time war zone flashed before his eyes.

He cringed into the pillow, pulling the blanket tight around him.

"What's wrong?" Brad asked, rolling towards him and pressing his hot body against Stephen's spine.

"I can't get those pictures out of my head. All that death."

Brad's hand ran up and down his arm. "I was so scared for you. When I saw you facing off against that pack of wolves, my heart almost stopped."

Brad pressed a kiss to Stephen's shoulder and his traitorous body moaned in anticipation of the pleasure his mate could give him.

"Let me help you sleep."

Brad rolled him onto his back and moved down his body.

Stephen's exhausted muscles screamed at him. "No. Please. I can't."

"Shhh... let me just make you feel better. It'll clear your mind."

Brad was laying between his legs now and Stephen watched his mate's head descend.

He wasn't...

Brad's hot mouth sucked up the end of Stephen's cock and his hand wrapped around the soft base.

A moan vibrated through him as he closed his eyes and let the magic happen.

Brad stroked him softly, while licking and sucking on the sensitive head. Tingles of sensation tickled along Stephen's spine as Brad worked him over.

Blood began to throb south and he could feel himself begin to stiffen, despite his body's exhaustion.

He got harder and thicker, the pleasure spreading through his gut and along his thighs.

Brad hummed and moved faster, taking more of Stephen's length into his hot, wet mouth.

Stephen's orgasm began to build and he gasped, grabbing hold of Brad's long hair.

Brad gripped Stephen's cock harder with his hand and sucked on the end.

His balls tightened and he cried out as Brad stayed where he was, wrapped around Stephen's cock.

He began to cum. Pulsing white light filled his vision and he let the groans that burst from his throat fill the room.

As he slowly came down from cloud nine, he relaxed into the mattress and let his arms fall to the side. Exhausted and replete.

Brad licked him clean and then crawled back up the bed to lie down again with his head on the pillow.

"I can't move." Stephen managed to get out and Brad's deep chuckle filled the space between them.

What an incredible thing for his mate to do for him. He could barely think, and yet he knew that he'd just been given a beautiful gift.

"I think you're so incredible, Stephen. And I'm so proud of

you." Brad's words, so sweetly said into his ear, cracked his heart wide open.

Why did the man make it so hard to hate him?

"I ..." He couldn't form words. The sleepy tendrils of darkness reached up and wrapped around his ankles, pulling him slowly down.

"You're safe. Now sleep."

"There they are."

Brad pointed to the convoy of sedans he could see driving up the main drag of town.

Their parents were back.

"This is going to be fun." Grayson mumbled as he stepped forward to greet his father who was in the first car.

Brad hung back, watching the council emerge from the vehicles.

His parents were in the last car and they walked forward with grave looks on their faces.

"Brad." His father extended his hand and Brad shook it, a lovely warmth running through his body at seeing his family again.

"Brad. Oh, I wish we were seeing you under better circumstances." His mum stepped closer, hugging him tightly.

She was tall for a woman. As an Alpha born she was close to six feet and he didn't have to bend down to squeeze her.

She'll tower over Stephen.

The thought made him smile and as she pulled back, his mother noticed.

"What are you smiling for?"

"Oh, I have some good news on top of the horrendous news, but I can save that for later. Let's get you inside and briefed."

They all walked inside the Hall and sat down, the families filling the whole Alpha table with no room left for them.

Brad stood with Grayson, ready to address the Alphas that were meant to help the pack in times of need, but instead had been MIA.

"So, it seems you were right, dad. The Rogues did use the fact that you all left the 'Borough to attack." Grayson began, addressing Jack.

"And what happened?" Marcus asked, his surly tone catching Brad's attention.

"They got hold of Tabitha, which meant that Grayson and I went to look for her." Brad explained.

His mother bit her bottom lip and grabbed hold of his dad's arm for support.

"We found her alive, but two of her roommates had been killed and the Rogues were there, holding her at knife point."

There was complete silence in the room as they told the tale.

"They lit the house on fire, but we got out and ran back to find the Hall being attacked by the Rogues."

"How many were there? The reports we'd gotten said there weren't more than a dozen Betas. That shouldn't have been too hard to handle." Marcus's arrogant voice asked.

Brad gave him a hard glare. Who the fuck did Marcus think he was? Brad had always disliked the guy as a kid, and he was even worse as a grown adult.

"We killed twenty-eight Betas. They're all outside if you want to count them."

"No need to be sarcastic." Tony chimed in.

Brad turned his gaze on the older Alphas, his blood beginning to boil. He could feel the acid in his gut burning and he let it build. There was no holding back for him. He had nothing to lose.

"Listen here. You are bloody lucky to be coming home to a pack at all! Grayson and I were almost killed and that left Aaron and the Betas against twenty-eight savage wolves."

"Then how did you do it then? Kill all of them alone? With that number, you would have been very evenly matched." Tony asked.

More than matched, actually.

"The Omegas fought too."

There was silence around the table and a sneer lifted Marcus's lip.

"Yeah right."

There wasn't a word spoken against Marcus by anyone in the council. He couldn't bloody believe it. Brad looked over at Grayson, who's eyes had flashed to wolf in his anger.

Brad's fists curled tight and a coiled spring loaded in his gut. This guy was not only ignorant, he was a nasty piece of work.

"Listen here, oh all mighty council. This pack does not belong to you. It belongs to its people. The men who stood and fought to keep their home. Protect their women. Who died for you. We lost over a dozen shape shifting Omegas last night, but they were there. You were not. So, I suggest you pull your heads out of your arses and go and thank them for everything they sacrificed for you!"

He picked up the nearest chair and put all his frustration into throwing it as hard as he could across the room. It flew ten meters, crashing against the wall and then smashing into hundreds of pieces as it splintered on the floor.

He looked back at Marcus, his breathing laboured and fast. "Be glad that isn't your head, because if we could down grade someone, I can tell you, Omega would be too high a ranking for a man like you."

"Brad..." His dad said, the warning clear.

"I second that." Grayson said and there was a hiss around the table. "No longer will the term Alpha be used to describe someone's birth. You have to earn it, just as Stephen earned his Beta status last year. Step up, Marcus. I challenge you." Grayson pointed to the pathetic example of an Alpha who sat opposite them.

"You can't do that." Marcus whined, his tone so pathetic it set Brad's teeth on edge.

No. This man definitely does not deserve to be an Alpha.

"Then hand over your Alpha status and we'll appoint a new one. I'm sure some of the Betas who survived last night would love to step into your role."

The older Alphas surged to their feet, their anger obvious in their tightened fists and furious glares.

"That is not how it is done, Grayson."

Brad glared at them all. "Then that is how it will be for now on. This pack has to change. And we'll be starting at the top. As the three all male paired Alphas, we will be changing things. Just as Luc and Grey did all those years ago." He glared at his parents, and in turn each of the council members.

He knew the legends. His father had confided them to him when he'd been a teenager. Brad had been nervous about his sexual orientation and how the pack would take the news, but his father had told him that it could mean great things for the pack.

Well, he wasn't sure about that, but he knew that things had to change.

"This is the tide of change, and I suggest you embrace it, or you will be swept out with it."

"This is *our* pack!" Tony growled at them.

Grayson stepped up next to Brad, shoulder to shoulder. If they'd had Aaron next to them it would have been even better, but the poor guy was still at the hospital with his mate.

Grayson growled back. "No. It's our pack. We saved them, brought them together to fight and all while you were off playing bullshit games with the other Alphas."

Brad snarled at them. "None of you know what it took to get them to work together to save the pack last night. You keep them so segregated that none of the Betas even speak to the Omegas."

But they knew who'd pulled it all together.

Stephen.

Aaron had told them both how Brad's mate had rallied the whole pack to fight, then saved one of their own Alphas.

Brad's heart was literally bursting with pride and he couldn't even say it aloud at the moment.

"You'll regret this." Marcus spat at him.

Brad laughed. "I won't regret a thing. You, on the other hand, will. Grayson, Aaron, and I will draw up some new laws and we'll meet on Saturday night and explain it to the pack. We have a mass burial to attend tomorrow and I suggest you all get on the phone and tell your special group of old Alphas that we've taken care of their problem for them!"

Grayson and he turned around and walked away.

CHAPTER FIFTEEN

Brad's wolf was literally vibrating just beneath the surface and as he heard a movement behind him and metal scrape against the table, he twisted and saw Marcus picking up a kitchen knife. A look of pure evil on his face.

Hell no.

The wolf, one he hadn't sensed before, leapt forward to attack.

He shifted as he ran, his own flesh tearing and muscles lengthening in a new way. He jumped on Marcus with a strength he'd never known and knocked him flat. He sunk his teeth into the flesh of Marcus's shoulder. Hot blood flooded between his teeth and bone's cracked. Marcus screamed out in a high-pitched wail.

There was a huge commotion around him and Grayson was there, snapping and growling at the others. Protecting him.

Don't kill him.

Brad unlocked his jaws and stepped away slowly.

He looked over at Grayson and couldn't believe what he saw with his own eyes.

Flashes of silver ran through the blackness of Grayson's coat.

And he seemed bigger.

A lot bigger.

But it was hard to tell when Brad himself was looking down on his father's six foot four head from above, too.

The new wolf had a firm grip on him but he pushed hard, forcing the wolf to retreat and he slowly shrunk back into his human skin.

Grayson stayed a wolf a moment longer and Brad got to see the true magnificence of the new Alpha that they had become. Twice the size of any wolf he'd ever seen, Grayson was magnificent.

He faced the council, wiping the blood from his chin.

Grayson shrunk to human and walked over to him, his chest heaving with the stress and exertion.

Brad gestured to the man lying in his own blood on the floor. "Take him to the hospital if you like. It's full of all the other war wounds."

The council gaped at him, his own parents staring wide eyed.

He bumped Grayson with his elbow and they walked out the door, leaving a bloody mess behind them and uncaring of it.

As soon as they'd cleared the Hall's embrace, Grayson grabbed his arm. "Did you feel that? What the hell was it?"

So, the other Alpha had sensed the difference too? Good. It wasn't just him.

"You mean the new wolf? I've never sensed my shifter like that before, and you should have seen your coat!"

"What? Did I have the silver too? I saw you! And you were bloody huge!" Grayson's excitement was beginning to transfer to him, or perhaps it had always been there.

He grinned at his friend, feeling the bubbling excitement in his belly. "You were shining like the full moon. It was pretty incredible, actually."

Grayson grabbed his arm, stopping them from walking along the street.

"Let's go grab some clothes."

Brad chuckled and followed Grayson back to a two-story town house, the adrenaline still pumping through his system and causing a light heartedness.

"This your place?" He asked the other Alpha as he stared up at the new windows.

"Yep. Come on in."

They strolled into Grayson's house, naked. And yet it all seemed so normal. Acting like they had when they were kids. When they couldn't control their need to shift and they'd shred their clothes everywhere they went.

"Feel free to jump in the shower. The bathroom's there." Grayson pointed to a door on the bottom floor. "I'll go grab some clothes from upstairs. You're covered in Marcus' blood."

Brad glanced down at his chest and shrugged. He didn't really care about that. He'd had worse men's blood on his last night.

"I wonder what Marcus' family will do about that?" Grayson asked.

"I don't care. But to be honest, I doubt they'll do anything. If this new wolf thing is a sign that you, and I, and Aaron are meant to be the new wave of Alphas, then Marcus' line is defunct."

"You're probably right." Grayson said as he trotted up the stairs.

Brad stared after him then looked down on his body again.

A shower probably wasn't a bad idea. If he was seeing Stephen later, he shouldn't be smelling of Marcus's disgusting stench.

He headed off to Grayson's pristine modern bathroom and he enjoyed the longest shower he'd had in years.

"Great meeting guys. I'll be sure to take everything to the Alphas today." Stephen grinned at the Omegas around the table and they all smiled back.

Thanks to the war they'd fought and coming out as the victors, it was time for a change in the pack and he was going to be a big part of it.

The Omegas who wanted to change jobs, or build a house for themselves, he'd written on a list. With details, strategies, and ideas. New training. More affordable housing. Share housing that was much larger than the current average home.

With so many widows after last night, a lot of the women would need help surviving without their mates.

There were a lot of names of the list and his pages now numbered seventeen. But it was a start!

A hot, prickly, rather pleasant sensation rolled over his belly and he turned around. His mate must be here.

"Hey, Brad." He said, a pleasurable twitch hiking up his jeans.

The guy was so hot.

If he hadn't been so dead on his feet last night, he definitely would have gone a few rounds with his mate.

Brad stepped closer and Stephen was amazed to see that he didn't have to tilt his head right back to look at him, he passed his shoulder easily now.

"Stephen." Brad's tone oozed with sex and as he gathered him up, Stephen couldn't help but be swept away on the intense feelings that their mating gave him.

Brad kissed him and gripped his arse tight, pulling him into his huge frame.

Their tongues duelled and fire burst between them.

When Brad finally pulled back, Stephen's knees were unsteady and his head swam around in the clouds.

"Ah... hi."

Brad grinned, took his hand and led him to a table and chairs.

Stephen fell into the seat heavily.

He wasn't sure he'd ever get used to the impact Brad had on him.

"So. My parents are back. The whole council is."

I wonder how that went.

"Whoa. What did they say about everything that happened last night?"

"Well, they were... well, I should say, *Marcus* was pretty fucking rude about it all. I think they're mad they missed out on all the fun."

Stephen frowned at his mate's use of the word fun. "Seriously? We're fricken' dying out there, and they're jealous they weren't here?"

"Yeah. Classic Alpha bullshit. They want to be the heroes and I made it perfectly clear that the Omegas saved the day, and they didn't like it at all."

Had he really? Well, hadn't Brad learnt a thing or two about the pack?

"Really? You told them?"

"Of course, I did. I know I didn't know shit about the Omegas before I came back, and I missed a lot of your speech according to Aaron, but it was pretty obvious with the body count who was fighting hard."

Stephen looked down, heat filling his face. "Aaron told you?"

"That you rallied the troops to fight? Absolutely. You were amazing. Wish I'd been there to see it."

Stephen swallowed hard, the question he needed to ask

burning a hole in his heart. He lifted his head and gathered some of the courage he'd experienced last night.

With that in mind, he pushed forward. He had to ask a simple question. It shouldn't be this hard.

"So, does that mean you're staying?"

Brad glanced away, his jaw tightening in an obvious way. "Not sure if I'll actually have a choice or not after what I just did to Marcus."

His heart skipped a beat. "What did you just do to Marcus?"

"I bit him."

In wolf form? Oh, crap. That wasn't good. "You shifted?"

Brad shrugged, a muscle in his jaw throbbing like an angry dwarf jumping up and down. "He made me angry. So, I shifted, so did Grayson, and I bit his shoulder. He shouldn't even be an Alpha with his attitude."

"Ah... what?" This was sounding so un-like the man he thought Brad was. "If you didn't do anything wrong, then you need to stay. Our pack needs Alphas like you, Brad."

"I don't think so. I'm sure they'll just do fine without me."

There was a hard edge to Brad's face now. One that Stephen hadn't seen before, yet knew that fighting him would be an impossible task.

So, what was the solution here? Brad was obviously run by his emotions and hormones, so it looked like it fell to him to be the rational one.

"Okay, well, then. What do we do? Can we break our bond, or what? How am I going to survive with you gone? I don't know about you, but going insane is definitely not on my bucket list."

He tried to make his voice sound light, but instead his chest ached with a pain he hadn't felt before. Even in the year leading up to meeting Brad and he'd known something was desperately missing in his life.

This pain was worse. It was like someone was stepping on his heart, squeezing the life from him.

"No. Come with me. You'll love the road. We can see Australia together. The beaches, the bush. It's all amazing."

Stephen recoiled from Brad so fast that Brad's hand that was resting on his leg fell away.

"Leave? The 'Borough? Are you crazy?"

He jumped to his feet and watched as Brad dragged himself up, a horribly detached and bored expression falling onto his mate's face.

"I can't leave. It's my home."

He couldn't breathe right now, and he could feel the red cloud roll into his brain, blocking out any signs of logic

"It was my home too, and believe me, you can leave."

Brad said it as though what he had done was easy, what everyone should do. Well, that was not how he felt. He was never going to be like Brad.

"I don't want to leave. There are too many things to do still."

Brad bristled like an echidna, his spine straightening as he rolled his neck in a way that made the vertebrae pop.

"Fine. I'll go. I'm not staying here. Hemmed in like a fucking wild animal in a cage. You guys will be fine without me, and screw the prophecy bullshit."

Brad glared at him once more, his intense brown eyes angry as a thunderstorm, then turned and stomped off. Stephen was left staring after him, his gut trembling with fear and misunderstanding.

What prophecy bullshit?

CHAPTER SIXTEEN

Brad stormed off to the Hall, muttering to himself like a loon. He was getting out of here, and no one was going to stop him. Least of all his supposed mate who wouldn't even consider coming with him. Who did that?

He grabbed the few clothes that he had and stuffed them in his car.

"Hey. Where are you going?"

He didn't turn around to the now familiar voice.

"Home Reagan. I'm going home."

The words didn't ring true, and he grimaced at the truth screaming at him.

He didn't have a home. And that was who he was. He had to stop calling the road his home, he had none.

Reagan grabbed him and surprisingly spun him around to face him.

Nice muscle human.

"You can't leave! What about the all-male pairings ruling

Greensborough, and all that jazz? Not to mention the whole, we just had a massive crisis and you should stick around and help us put the pieces back together again."

Ha! Like that was his problem.

"No. I should not. There's nothing I can do now, Reagan. You're ten times more useful to them than me."

Reagan glared at him with all the heat of a true Alpha and Brad felt the tingle of fear at the back of his neck. "It's not a fucking competition, Brad! They need you."

"No, they don't." He shook his head and swung his keys around in his fingers.

"What is wrong with you? How are you and Stephen going to survive apart? Because I assume with your surly-arse mood that your mate isn't going with you?"

He didn't answer that ridiculous question because he couldn't. He just growled out his frustration and got in the car, slamming the door on his trusty jeep.

"Tell Grayson that I'll check my emails regular. If he needs me, he knows how to contact me."

"Fine."

Reagan turned and stomped off and Brad was pretty sure he heard the doctor muttering 'stupid, selfish, prick,' as he walked away.

Yeah. Well, maybe I am.

Brad threw his car into gear and hit the accelerator. He didn't bother to explain to his parents, or anyone else. They knew him too well by now.

When it was time to go, it was time to go.

No sad goodbyes. No bullshit.

He'd be back. Someday.

He hit the edge of town and turned left, back up the hill and headed towards the east coast. Maroochydore was a great place to start and it was only a day's drive. He might stop in Narooma on the way through. Do some swimming.

With his head full of the ocean and his heart screaming out to turn around and go back to the 'Borough, Brad and his angry wolf kept on driving.

~

He didn't make it to Maroochydore, he barely made it to Narooma.

By the time he'd made it to the sleepy little town with magnificent views of the ocean, he couldn't stand it anymore.

Pain, unlike anything he'd ever felt before, tore at his insides. He pulled over and fell out of his car, the hot needles threading through his muscles forcing him to his knees.

What the fuck is this?

But even as he knelt on the pavement, staring out at the sparkling blue ocean, he knew the answer to his ridiculous question.

"No. No. I am not falling for this trick. It's fucking... Impossible."

He pushed himself to his feet, one painful inch at a time while ice pricks pressed into the corners of his heart.

Inhale. Exhale.

He forced the cold air in through his nose and collapsed onto the park bench.

How on Earth was he going to go through his life feeling like this? And if his ancestors were right and the legends were true, then the pain would only get worse the further away he got from his mate.

"No. No."

That couldn't be! He had so many places he still wanted to see.

He took some more careful breaths and the pain dulled, his wolf calming as he timed his breathing with the rise and swell of the ocean.

This was him. This was where he needed to be. He'd stay sitting on the bench, staring out at the ocean. He could stay here for a while. Until he had the strength to continue up further north.

The pain was getting better and his stomach tightened with a loud gurgle. He was hungry, that was the problem.

He got back into his car, a slight euphoria filling his mind as the pain subsided. He drove through the small town, finding a trendy café and going in to order some lunch.

His chest had stopped squashing his heart and as he sat waiting for his burger and fries to arrive, hope sprung anew.

Maybe his family was wrong. Maybe it wouldn't get worse the longer they were apart.

Maybe it would get *better.*

As he began to eat and his body settled down even further he began to smile.

He could do this. He'd gone against every other law, rule, and regulation they had.

Why couldn't he beat this, too?

He managed to find somewhere cheap to stay, treating himself to a cabin at a local caravan park. He didn't want to deal with hard floors or sleeping in his car tonight, he was still reeling from being away from Stephen.

He grabbed some dinner and settled into his cabin.

His stomach hurt, his chest ached. Like someone had stuck a knife in between his ribs and twisted.

No. I can't stand this.

Shock treatment, that's what he needed.

Another man maybe?

His wolf howled so loud inside his mind that Brad had to cover his ears with his hands, the painful sound echoing in his head.

Okay. So, another lover was out.

A drink?

His head pounded just thinking about it.

Great, his two go-tos, fucking and drinking, were out.

This sucks.

He pushed himself to step back out into the fresh air, the call of the ocean tugging on him.

Yes. A Swim.

That would clear his head and make him feel more like himself.

He pulled on some boardies and stripped off the rest of his clothes.

He knew that was the point and the main problem. Ever since going back to the 'Borough and meeting Stephen, he didn't feel like himself anymore. The man he'd become over his years of travelling, the man who loved solitude and freedom, he seemed to be disappearing with the wind.

Brad closed the door on the unit and walked down the beach road. The ocean was before him, magnificent in its wide, sweeping beauty.

The wind had picked up and it whipped his hair around his face.

The water would be freezing but no matter, he was going in.

He charged across the cool, soft sand and started running, the freezing water embracing his feet as he took a few running leaps, then diving beneath the icy spray.

He pushed on, moving his arms in a circular movement, swimming out further and further, past the break, until the water was calm.

He treaded water, the ocean beneath him a writhing, beautiful creature.

It was quiet out here and finally he was completely alone with his thoughts.

And all he could see, all he could think about, was how much he missed Stephen.

His beautiful courage, his strong stare.

Everything about his beautiful mate.

Brad groaned aloud and began swimming back to shore.

His mate. He'd completed the mating, and now he was going to pay for it with utter loneliness.

A wave rose behind him and he paddled faster, catching it and body surfing closer to the shore.

There was no adrenaline spike, no deep happiness at being one with the ocean.

All the parts of him that he used to love, were gone.

Would they ever come back?

He shook his head as he stood up and began walking through the now waist deep water, back to the sand.

He cleared the water and fell to his knees, dropped his head and prayed.

Please God, or whoever you are up there. Give me back my life.

He waited for an answer to come and finally, when nothing came to him, he pushed up to a stand once more and trudged back up the hill.

As he stood beneath the streaming hot water the answer finally came to him.

Go home, Brad. Go home.

But where was that?

STEPHEN TRUDGED through his daily chores like an exhausted kid on a dairy farm. His legs ached, his arms stung. He could barely stay awake during the day, yet a decent sleep was stolen from him as he was haunted by weird dreams through the night.

Brad had been gone four days.

Four days!

He rolled his eyes at his pathetic self as he trudged up to the Hall and opened the door.

He'd never hurt like this. Not with his first shift, not after the battle that earned him Beta status. Not. Ever.

And it seemed utterly ridiculous that all these feelings were because his mate was in another state.

Brad and he hadn't severed their connection. The lone wolf had just gone wandering again.

Why did that hurt so much?

He knew the answer, of course. They were meant to be together, and no matter how hard he tried to put Brad out of his head, it wasn't working.

He'd thrown himself into pack business like never before, and yet, that didn't seem to be enough either.

"Stephen!" Reagan and some of the other Alphas were at the Alpha table and calling him over.

Well, the second of the two Alpha tables, because the council was now split.

The old and the new.

And guess which one he belonged to?

“Hey guys.” He dropped down onto the seat, a sigh leaving his throat in a huge gush. “What's up?”

Reagan and Grayson exchanged looks, then Reagan pinned him with a stare.

“You okay?”

He shrugged. *Hell no.* But what could he do about it?

“Yeah. Why?”

“Because you look like shit.” Reagan said.

Stephen coughed out an awkward laugh. “Thanks. Is that the medical term for it?”

“No. I think the medical term for it would be...”

“Heartbroken.” Grayson finished for him.

Stephen looked away from the knowing looks that made him want to cry, swallowing the uncomfortable lump that had risen in his throat.

“I'm going to go grab some food.”

He left them and headed for the tables, absently spooning food onto his plate, uncaring of what it was.

His appetite was ziltch and he was struggling to maintain his current weight.

“Stephen. How are you?”

He turned to the strangely familiar voice.

“Hi ... I'm all right. How are you?”

Brad's father. He'd been around, of course. But he sat at the old Alphas' table and since Brad had left, his father hadn't approached Stephen at all.

Marcus was still in the hospital and Dr. Sarah wasn't releasing him for a while yet she said.

“I'm fine thank you, but my wife and I are a bit worried about you.”

Stephen frowned. “Oh, have you heard something I should be aware of?”

He gripped his plate tightly. Those arseholes over at the other Alpha table better not be saying anything about him.

"No. No. We've only heard great things about what you're getting done with the pack. There's two new Betas I hear that passed the tests yesterday?"

He nodded. Yes. Two of the five Omegas who'd stepped up had passed. They now had a better job, more money for their families, and the respect of everyone in the pack.

"That's not what we mean. We're worried about you, because you look sad. All the time. I can only imagine how much you must be missing our son."

Stephen looked straight at the ground as his throat burned and his eyes tingled with impending tears.

"Yeah... well."

What could he say to that?

"I'm very sorry Brad hurt you by leaving. It took his mother a long time to get used to his wandering, but he always comes home."

Stephen lifted his head and held onto whatever pride he still had.

"Yeah, well. I don't think I'll ever get used to it. That's not what mates are meant to do. Live in separate states."

Brad's father's eyes were sad as they stared at him. "No, you're right. You're not. I don't know how Brad is surviving out there without you."

Well. I hope he's hurting twice as much as me.

"Thank you. I better get back."

He moved away from... and sat back down next to Grayson.

"Is Jordan coming home soon?" He asked Reagan, hopefully changing the conversation away from himself.

"Yes. He's healing nicely. As are several of the injured Omegas that were brought in."

They continued to talk about pack business and Stephen relaxed into the monotony of his every day existence. The excitement he'd once felt from being a part of the pack was somehow missing nowadays. Despite his status and everything good he was getting done for his friends and everyone he knew, something was drastically missing.

His heart.

CHAPTER SEVENTEEN

The next day Stephen woke up with a start. He bolted upright and saw a dark figure sitting on the chair beside his bed.

His heart thundered with the power of a thousand horse's hooves over his chest as adrenaline zinged through his veins.

"It's me. I'm sorry."

Brad's voice made him jump a little more and he swiped out his hand, whacking him in the leg.

"Don't do that to me! You scared me half to death!"

He lay back down, taking slow breaths to calm his racing heart.

He turned to his mate, who was still mostly in shadow. He didn't like that at all. Brad could probably see him just fine.

He rolled over and reached across to his bedside table, flicking on the lamp.

White light blinded his eyes for a moment before they adjusted, finally focusing in on the beloved face in front of him.

"What the hell are you doing here, Brad?"

Brad's brow furrowed as though he wasn't happy. With his question, or the answer, Stephen couldn't tell.

When he didn't answer, Stephen glared at him. "Well?"

"I can breathe here."

"Yeah. Well, so can I. All the trees around help. What's the problem? No air at the beach?"

As the words ripped through his throat, he realised how angry and bitter they sounded. He hadn't thought those feelings were so strong, but now that he had his mate in front of him, he could barely stand the amount of acid boiling in his gut.

He pushed himself to a sitting position and pressed himself back against the headboard so that he could look at Brad properly.

"I shouldn't have left."

"No. You shouldn't have." Stephen crossed his arms over his chest, afraid his heart may explode from his chest at any moment.

The pain in his arms and legs was gone. He could probably jump out of bed right now and run through the forest.

That was a very good idea. No point staying here and letting his anger have its way.

"Let's go."

He threw back the covers and stood up. Excitement coursing through his limbs and making his entire body tremble.

"Where are we going?" Brad asked from his seat. He still hadn't moved.

"I want to go for a run. Come shift with me."

Brad got to his feet and began to undress.

"Why should I?"

"Because I have something special to show you."

Stephen didn't want to watch his mate while he became naked. He wouldn't have the control to stop if Brad wanted him. Even after his mate had left him, and practically broken his heart with his rejection. God, how he yearned for the pleasure only Brad could give him.

And what was this thing that Brad wanted to show him? Surely it was something to do with their shifting?

He stepped out of his house and embraced the chilly night. The moon was waning and the freshness of the season made his skin prickle.

Brad stepped up behind him, his warm skin pressing against Stephen's back in an oddly reassuring way.

"Let's go."

"No, wait." Brad grabbed his arms and stopped him from shifting into wolf form.

"What?"

Brad turned him around and Stephen stared up at the man Fate had chosen for him.

Brad reached up and cupped his jaw, staring at him with a reverence that Stephen had never seen in his mate's face before.

"I missed you so much. I know we hardly know each other, but I can sense you, like I can hear my own heartbeat. I don't want to ever be away from you again."

Stephen pulled away, scared to hear all the words that he knew he needed to hear so that they could start their lives together. And yet, there was still so much pent up hurt, and he knew only a run through the forest was going to help with that.

"What did you want to show me?"

Brad grinned, his sharp white teeth flashing in the dark night.

"My new wolf. Have you seen Grayson or Aaron shift yet?"

Stephen frowned, confused. What new wolf?

"No. What are you talking about?"

Again, there was that brilliant smile. "Ah... I'm glad, because it's right that I tell you about it. There is a prophecy that has been lost, about all male Alphas ruling a pack. With the three of us having all male pairings, we knew something was up. Then the Rogues attacked and I thought that was why we needed you, to be strong for our pack, to survive, but its more than that. Because of you, I am an Alpha's Alpha. All three of us are. We are a new breed, something that will pass down through the generations and breed us a new line. We're starting again, just as Luc and Grey had to. Time to cut out the rotten, old blood, and throw in the new. Yours included, my beautiful, brave, Omega turned Alpha."

Stephen's heart began to thunder in his chest and a shiver coursed over his spine. What was Brad talking about? Something inside of him knew that this was a turning point, a major crossroads in his life and he needed to memorise it.

"I don't understand."

"Watch me shift and then turn with me. You'll see what we have created together, how I can't be the best of me without you."

Stephen waited and watched as Brad dropped to his hands and the shift began to overtake him.

Awesome vibrations of shock rippled through him as he watched a massive wolf emerge where Brad once was.

Twice the size of his old black Alpha wolf, this wolf had flecks of silver through his coat.

The wolf titled his head towards the woods and Stephen hurried to comply. He dropped to all fours and shifted form, his wolf ripping to the surface in record time.

He started running and he could feel Brad behind him. He turned right and headed for the forest. Chasing each other around the trees and jumping over the low brush, they played and enjoyed themselves as only wolves could.

This new wolf was still his mate, he could feel it as he had before. Their connection, the rightness in them being together.

If this was who Brad was meant to be, then Stephen was honoured to be a part of such an incredible legacy.

When Stephen was tired and he was slowing too much, he made his way back to the clearing and let go of his very contented wolf, sinking down into the soft grass in his human form.

Brad lay down beside him on his back, his chest heaving with exertion.

"Wow, that was fun."

Stephen nodded, but lay silent. That was exactly what he'd needed. To be able to run free and play with his mate. Every part of him was re-energised.

"I can't believe you've got a new wolf. He's incredible." Stephen said, glancing over at his mate.

"Yeah, pity he didn't come out in time to kill all those Rogues."

Yeah, that would have been a sight.

"True. But perhaps there's a bigger plan for you three."

Brad reached over to him and grabbed his arm. "And our mates. None of us would be able to be like this without you."

Stephen stared into his mate's eyes and felt his heart do a double kick. If there was any doubt that Brad was the one for him, then this feeling of utter perfection put them all to rest. His wolf was happy now, so it would make the talking part so much easier.

"Why'd you come back, Brad?"

Brad rolled onto his side and stared down at him. "Because I couldn't stand being away from you. It was killing me."

"Yeah, I know the feeling. So, what are we going to do?"

He hoped to hell Brad wasn't going to suggest severing the mating, he wasn't even sure if that was possible.

"I'll stay, if you'll have me. I have some money. We can buy a block of land out of town. Build a house maybe? Not too close to my parents, of course." He said it all with a cheeky grin, but Stephen could see the stress behind his eyes. How much was weighing on Stephen's answer.

He rolled to face his mate as well. "You're serious? You want to stay in the 'Borough? Settle down with me?"

Brad nodded. His eyes as serious as a heart attack. "I do. I must. I can't do without you and you're a pack man. I'm sure I can be one, too. For you."

The sadness that flowed over him at that moment shocked him. Brad was saying everything he'd hoped to hear. That his mate would do anything to be with him.

But now that the moment was here, he didn't want it. Brad sacrificing who he was to be with him, that made no sense.

"The pack needs you too, Brad. It hasn't been the same without you. Aaron and Grayson are a little lost, and they're at a disadvantage against the rest of the council. With you, they'd be strong."

Brad ran his fingers down Stephen's arms and a tingle of longing passed through him.

"I'll do anything for you, Stephen."

Including destroying your own self. No. I can't have that.

"But I don't want you to do that. There has to be a compromise we can both be happy with."

He'd never even left the 'Borough. Maybe a bit of travel wouldn't be a bad thing, as long as he was with Brad.

Now that Brad had shown how much he'd give up for him, Stephen could suddenly see options, whereas before, his way seemed the only way.

"I'll tell you what. How about we meet halfway? We spend six months in the 'Borough, and six months travelling. That way, we can have roots, and a pack, but you don't feel chained up and you can show me the world."

There was a moment of complete silence as Brad's eyes widened like the full moon and his mouth dropped open.

"You'd do that for me?"

"Of course! If you're willing to stay here for me, then I'm willing to go away with you. But we have to stay in contact with the pack. So, if they need us again, we come straight home."

Brad climbed on top of him, pressing him into the grass.

"What did I ever do to deserve you?"

Stephen grabbed hold of Brad's long hair and pulled him down for a kiss.

Their moans lit up the sky as they touched and kissed.

Brad aroused Stephen's body as his heart soared with happiness and together they soared to the stars. Their mating bond finally complete as they both wholeheartedly chose each other for their destiny.

EPILOGUE

"Really? That's awesome news, Aaron. We'll get on a plane today and we'll be home by tonight sometime."

Stephen hung up the phone and headed outside, searching for his mate who'd left only a few moments ago.

They'd been staying in this caravan park for a few weeks, and they were very comfortable. Doing odd jobs and handyman work for the owners in exchange for a free cabin worked well for everyone.

"Brad!"

Brad popped out of the cabin opposite them, a tool belt hanging low on his hips.

Stephen's groin ached at the site of his muscled body and sexy smile.

"What's up?"

"Grayson's son has arrived and I told them we'd jump on a plane today and go home."

They weren't far out of Brisbane, so a direct flight shouldn't be hard.

"A son, huh? That's pretty cool. All right. I'll let Bill know we're heading off. You sure you don't want to drive? What about the Jeep?"

Brad's beloved Jeep was always a consideration for him.

He grinned at his mate. He'd already thought of a plan

"We can just leave it at the airport in long stays, and pick it up when we come back in a few days."

Now the smile transformed Brad's face. They'd only been gone three weeks and they'd hoped to make this trip a longer stay. He knew Brad would be disappointed to go back this early.

Grayson's son was about three weeks premature. If they'd known he was going to come so early, they would have waited around in Greensborough.

"You want to come back straight away?"

"Yes. I love it here. And once we catch up with the family and I check in on the pack, I'd love to come back here for another month or so. That suit you?"

"Hell yeah." Brad charged forward to give him a hard kiss. "I'll go call Bill now and let him know what we're doing."

Within three hours they were on the way to the airport, on the plane and flying home again.

"I still can't believe they had a kid." Brad sat back in his tiny aeroplane seat and shook his head.

Stephen grinned at his mate. He'd thought long and hard about this and he had a few beliefs of his own. "Well, the Alpha line has to continue. Especially now with you three being so important to the pack. There needs to be a re-birth of the right blood. Why do you think fate gave Marcus a girl? I bet ya he doesn't have any boys at all. And Toby's mate still isn't pregnant after how long? Three years? You're it for the new Alpha line- I'm sure of it."

Brad's mouth fell open. "Are you sure about that... because I don't want to go fuck some random woman..."

Stephen laughed, the look of pure horror on his mate's face bloody hilarious. You'd think Stephen had suggested sticking needles into Brad's testicles.

"It wouldn't be that hard. Reagan told me about it when we were home last time. They went to Marianne one night together, had a threesome and Grayson came in her. Baby. Done. It wouldn't be that bad, Brad. Especially if you get a baby out of it."

He shut his mouth quickly as Brad's eyes zeroed in on him. He may have given away too much.

"You want a baby, Stephen?" Brad's words were soft but Stephen could hear all the emotion behind them. They hadn't talked about any of this stuff yet, and although he had feelings on the subject, he knew everything was fluid in his future.

Everything except Brad. He was the rock foundation of Stephen's world.

"I'd love a bigger family, kids and stuff. I always thought I would." *Back when I thought my mate would be a woman.* "But, with our travelling and stuff, it would be pretty hard, unless we found a woman who'd be okay on her own and didn't need us for support or anything."

He gulped down the emotions rising in his chest. Saying it all aloud made everything so much more real.

Brad sat back, his serious face on. His eyebrows were lowered, his lips pulled down on the sides. "Okay, let's talk about this. Would you be the one to impregnate her, coz I don't think I could do it."

That wouldn't work for the blood lines, nor the prophecy of the new Alphas.

"You're the Alpha Brad, not me."

Brad's lips curled up at the side into a gentle smile. "Honey, you're as big as me now as a wolf, unlike Reagan, and you're an Alpha Mate. Why wouldn't you be able to sire the next Alpha?"

Stephen's heart trembled in his chest. He'd never thought that was possible, or that Brad would want that with him.

"Okay... suppose I can and did, how would that affect us? Could you handle a baby for us being related to me, rather than you?"

Brad chuckled. "You're kidding me? I NEVER thought I'd have a child, so why would I suddenly get all macho about it being mine? If we decide to do this, it would be our kid. Our family. No questions asked on my side. I'd love to see you look as happy as you do right now."

He must have been grinning like a loon, his heart soaring in his chest. Could he really have everything he'd dreamed of?

"I would love a child. A son. But I still think he should be yours genetically. I'd love him just as much if he was yours."

Brad pulled him over for a quick kiss as the plane began to descend into Melbourne.

"I would too."

They landed and hired a little sports car, zipping through the bush and up to Greensborough in record time.

The sun was just setting as they entered the 'Borough, the burnt orange of the setting sun a beautiful welcome home.

"Where to? The hospital?"

"Hmm... Maybe just call them and ask?"

Greensborough had always had low technology, but since they'd left, the Alphas all carried cell phones for easy communication.

Brad dialled the number and spoke to Grayson briefly, hanging up fast.

"They're all at Grayson's place. The mum is living with them for a few weeks while she recovers."

And with Reagan being a live- in doctor, you didn't get much better care than that.

"Let's go."

Grayson's town house was just around the corner and as they stepped up to the door, a wave of familiarity washed over him. Although he loved being a bit of a hippy with his mate, his heart belonged in Greensborough.

Brad knocked and pushed open the door.

"Hey!"

They stepped into a huge room full of people and Stephen's wolf settled contentedly inside him.

"How are you all?"

They hugged everyone. Aaron and Jordan were there, Grayson and Reagan, and their now not pregnant female, Marianne.

"Congratulations." Stephen gushed, sitting down beside where Reagan sat, holding the new infant, wrapped in a pale blue blanket. "Oh, my God, he's beautiful. What's his name?"

"Luc."

There was a strange prickle at the back of his eyes as Stephen gazed down at the next Alpha of Greensborough. "Perfect."

"You wanna hold him?"

"Yes." He held out his arms and let Reagan place the little one in his arms, his heart melting into a big puddle on the floor as he ran the tip of his finger over the baby's perfect face.

"He looks so much like Grayson already."

He kept staring and there was a strange silence in the room.

He looked up and Grayson was grinning, elbowing Brad as they both stared at him.

"What?"

Grayson laughed. "It's so your turn next!"

Brad pushed Grayson in the side. "Shut up. I don't even know what I'd do with a baby!"

Stephen concentrated on the infant in his arms, its perfect face at peace while he slept.

"Looks like you wouldn't have to do anything. You just have to find a woman who suits you guys."

"I know someone." Marianne said, the woman who birthed Luc reaching out and touching her son gently with one hand.

"Who?" Reagan asked, never one to sit back while important matters were discussed.

Marianne turned towards Stephen and smiled gently at him as she sat back in her chair. She was quite pale but seemed otherwise well.

"Antoinette. She's a widow of the Rogue attack as well. She'd love nothing more than to have a baby to care for."

"Omega born?"

"No. Beta born, actually. But Antoinette's mother was Aaron's aunt, an Alpha born female. So as far as the blood lines go, I think she'd match up well."

Certainly sounded like it.

Stephen didn't want to say anything, so continued to hold the sleeping baby.

"Maybe we should meet her while we're home." Brad said quietly.

Stephen glanced up at his mate and nodded. "Sounds great."

He turned to Jordan. "How about you guys? Gonna sire the next line of Alphas?"

Aaron laughed. "Looks like we have to. Marcus and Toby aren't getting anywhere."

"See. Told ya." Stephen said, smirking at Brad.

"Told him what?" Aaron asked.

"I think you three are meant to birth the new generation of Alphas. Re-start the pack like the original Luc and Grey did. There has to be a reason for this anomaly, and your ultra-Alpha qualities."

"Glad you think that way, because we already have two on the way."

"What? Twins?"

Jordan looked sideways, glaring at his huge mate. "Not exactly."

Aaron smirked. "I didn't think it was a good idea to leave Jordan out of it. I mean, yes, he's Omega born, but he's an Alpha Mate. His genetics are meant to be in the line too. So, we found two Beta born women we connected with and we had a night with both of them."

"I never thought it would work." Jordan muttered, red staining his cheeks.

Stephen shot a quick look at Brad. If Jordan could have sex with a woman with his effeminate, Omega ways, Brad surely could.

"What worked?" Stephen asked.

Aaron grinned like a proud father. "They're both pregnant. And due around Christmas. So, our family's expanding too."

Woah. Now that was news! Why hadn't they said anything before?

"Where are they going to live? Next door, too?"

Aaron would have to build them a house since Jordan and he lived out on a small farm.

Aaron shook his head. "Nah. The girls wanted to stay in town. So, I organised for them to move into one of my parents' properties and we'll organise visits and custody as they get older. The first year they just need their mums really."

The baby had begun to wriggle and cry, making Stephen feel very inadequate. Marianne reached over and carefully took her baby back.

"Feeding time. Again."

She opened her shirt and put the baby to her full breast. The crying stopping instantly.

"Well, looks like we're falling behind then, Stephen." Brad grinned at him.

He got to his feet and elbowed Brad in the side. "It's not a competition, Brad."

He turned towards Grayson. "Tell me about the new pay structure for the Omegas we implemented a month ago, how's it going?"

Grayson began to talk about pack business. One of Stephen's favourite topics, but he could barely concentrate.

Coming home today had been the best decision possible, because now it seemed that he and Brad really would get the life they wanted.

A home. A family, and the freedom to travel as well.

The world had opened up and it was all thanks to the love of a man who Fate had chosen for him.

THE END.

MEGAN'S MATE

THE BOROUGH BOYS SERIES
BOOK 4

CHAPTER ONE

The Spring Festival was approaching too fast, and Megan couldn't get her head around the fact that soon, she might meet her mate.

Don't get ahead of yourself.

"How's it going, Terry?" She nodded at one of the Betas as he passed by, and he gave her a stiff smile.

A sigh wove through her vocal cords, and her shoulders drooped. So many of the wolves didn't know how to act around her, which was one of the main reasons she loved spending time with her family.

They didn't give her stiff replies and sideways glances. But of course, they were all Alphas or Alpha mates, and no one was above them in the hierarchy.

She turned left to walk along the path she'd been aiming for, and stepped up to Grayson and Reagan's new front door. She liked this one better than the first.

Her brother-in-law should be home, and she needed a level

head to talk to. She lifted her hand and knocked. Footsteps sounded, and the pretty new door swung open.

"Megan!"

"Reagan." Relief and happiness flowed over her as she stepped forward and gave him a hug. The young doctor, who had joined their pack last year, returned her embrace with vigour.

"How's Marie doing?" she asked, stepping inside the lovely little home.

"Great. Five months now, and the baby is doing really well."

She smiled as they stepped into the bright kitchen, the scent of muffins or bread filling the air and making her stomach growl. "I still can't believe I'm going to have a niece or nephew soon. Are you sure you don't know what it is?"

A smirk at the corner of Reagan's mouth gave him away, and she gaped at him. "You do know! Tell me!"

He grinned and put the coffee machine on.

She pointed at the machine. May as well have a drink while she chatted. "Hot chocolate for me, please."

He grabbed the milk from the fridge and put a chocolate pod into the machine.

Reagan continued to ignore her request, and she jiggled on the bar stool she sat upon.

"Come on, Reagan. Spill."

He chuckled. "It's not fair if I tell you. Marie and Grayson don't know."

"You know I can keep a secret! Please!"

Reagan heaved a huge sigh, heating the milk.

"Well... let's just say that there will definitely be a new Alpha for the next generation."

An excited squeal rose in her throat. "Really? Oh, my God. Mum and Dad are going to be so happy!"

She clapped her hands and jumped up and down. A boy! Her brother was having a boy!

"But remember..." Reagan's tone dropped to be serious.

She took the mug he offered and made a zipper motion over her mouth. "Lips are sealed. I promise. That is so exciting, though!"

Reagan made himself a coffee and sat at the table with her, dark smudges beneath his eyes the only indication that he was tired.

"Another long shift, huh?"

He nodded, taking a drink of his coffee. "Yeah. I don't think we really need to be manning the hospital 24/7, but the Alphas are still insisting on it."

Seven months ago, their pack had been attacked by a group of Betas gone Rogue. They had killed many of the Borough's men, Betas and Omegas. Ever since then, the medical staff had been patching people up, dealing with the widows and mates of the deceased, and waiting on tenterhooks for any possible threats.

"I know. It's strange. The Rogues are gone, so why do you have to do such stupid shifts?"

Reagan shrugged and stretched his back. "No idea. But I'll keep working them with Sarah until they tell me to stop."

"You're still coming to the Spring Festival though, aren't you, Reagan?"

He nodded, his eyes lighting up with mischief. "Of course. I wanna meet this mate of yours."

She waved her hand in dismissal.

"Oh, shut up. He may not even be a member of those northern packs."

Even as she shrugged off Reagan's assumption, her belly did a flip of anticipation.

"Yeah... but he could be. Or she."

"She? Shit, never thought of that."

Reagan chuckled and drank more of his coffee while Megan's head did a whirligig. A female mate? She'd never even considered that. She wanted a male. An Alpha, preferably, but then again. Had Grayson wanted a male mate? Hell, no. Was it the best thing for him? Absolutely.

Best to trust Fate to send her what she needed.

"How's Grayson dealing with this whole super-Alpha thing?" she asked Reagan. Her brother, Aaron, and Brad had all discovered they had some special quality after they fought the Rogues.

The whole pack knew that it had something to do with them being all male-mated, but they weren't sure exactly why it had happened. It was still hard to digest, but she loved that her brother was so powerful.

"Not sure, really. Grayson, Aaron, and Brad meet each day. They discuss pack business and train together. They believe that they have fulfilled some sort of legend, but that it also means that the pack may run into danger in the future, so they're being cautious. I think they want to stay here when we go to the Festival."

"What? They've never stayed behind before." She'd never travelled away without Grayson. She couldn't imagine leaving him here.

"I know. But like I said, they worry that there is another threat coming. But don't stress—I'll be there to keep you company."

Megan laughed, picking up a biscuit that Reagan offered her. "Yeah, I can imagine. You're almost as intimidating as my brother now."

"What? Me?" Reagan gestured down to his frame, slightly smaller than Grayson's. He was over six feet tall now, and so cut you could see the outline of each muscle through his t-shirt.

He may have been an average human size when she'd first met

him, but after a year of being mated to her brother, he was almost as strong as any Alpha wolf she'd met.

"Ah, yeah. You, Reagan."

She finished the hot, sweet drink he'd made her, and walked over to the dishwasher, cleaning up after herself.

"I'm... a little afraid of all this, Reagan," she finally admitted out loud, her back still to her brother-in-law. She wasn't sure she could face him for this conversation.

"Of what, Megan?"

It was hard to put it all into words. "Of what it will mean. Of the change..." *Of the sex.*

Reagan cleared his throat in an awkward way and Megan forced herself to turn around. She'd come here for a reason—to get help from her brother-in-law. No point being scared to face him now.

"Have you ever dated anyone, or... been with anyone, Megan?"

"Ah..." She looked down at the floor. The boys kept their house so shiny.

"I'll take that as a no?"

She nodded, forcing herself to lift her head again. "I'm only twenty-two, and my mark came up a year ago. I'm an Alpha-born, and well... me. So, my options aren't exactly many. Mum always said I should wait for my mate, so I have."

Not that she really had an option. No boy had even tried to kiss her, let alone do anything else with her.

She wasn't embarrassed or upset by the choices she'd made, but as she approached the day she might meet her mate, she was realising that she had little to offer.

"Do you think I should have? You know... tried it all out before now?"

"No. That's not what I meant, and as a gay male, I'm probably the wrong one to comment on this, but your virginity is special...

and to an Alpha, it will be a prize indeed. They're such jealous buggers. I think you've done the right thing, Megan. Definitely."

Megan's shoulders and chest relaxed. She hadn't even realised she'd been tense until the relief flooded in.

"Good. Well then, I suppose I'm ready."

She walked over to hug Reagan, and he squeezed her tightly. "Whoever he is, he is the luckiest guy on Earth to have you as his mate, Megan. You're awesome."

She squeezed Reagan back tighter, the warmth of his body pressing into hers. "So are you. My brother's very lucky."

"Yes. I am." Grayson's deep voice broke into their little hug, and Megan pulled away with a smile.

"Hey, big brother. Heard you aren't coming with us to the festival."

Grayson walked forward, pulling Reagan into him for a kiss that made Megan look away.

The heat that sizzled between those two was unbelievable.

She walked to the front door, pulled it open, and waited for them to stop snogging. She had to pack. They were leaving tomorrow.

Grayson finally broke away from sucking Reagan's face, holding his mate tight as he turned to speak to her. "Yeah. I want to stay. But Reagan wants to go, so against my better judgment, I'm letting him go with you."

Reagan elbowed his mate in the ribs and Grayson didn't flinch.

"Well, someone has to room with me." Megan winked at her brother and waved.

She walked back into the sunshine and took some deep breaths.

Something magical told her that this was it. That this next step she would take would bring her to her destiny.

She reached under her t-shirt and touched the mark that had shown itself the day she turned twenty-one. A crescent-moon shape that circled around her belly button.

A fearful, self-preserving part of her wanted her to stay calm. Not get excited. So she wouldn't be disappointed if she didn't meet her mate at this gathering.

Yet, the happiness was there inside of her, fluttering like a new butterfly. Frantic, new, and strong. Unfortunately, she knew she would be utterly devastated if she met the members of three more packs, and her mate wasn't among them.

THEY WERE ALL UP EARLY the next day, and Megan jumped in the car with Reagan and her parents. It was a five-hour drive to the Spring Festival, and they spent the time chatting about nothing in particular, listening to music along the way.

"We're here," her dad said, as the car began to slow down.

Megan looked up from her book and glanced out the window. Tents were going up everywhere, and the space already buzzed with dozens of wolves and their mates. "Wow. So many people are here already." There were cars and people everywhere. "Where are we staying, Dad?"

"As one of the Alpha families, we got a two-bedroom cabin. You and Reagan can stay in the other room."

"Great. Thanks." She grinned at her brother-in-law and took a short breath, then exhaled slowly. She could feel the weight of her mother's gaze, though she didn't say anything.

They'd both been looking forward to this weekend for a long time.

Her father turned off the car and stepped out into the fresh air. "Let's go, then."

They got out of the car, the buzz of the wolves around her making her lips lift in a smile. The energy wove through her, the excitement that she had been pushing down rising to the surface.

They grabbed their bags, unpacked in the small room they'd been given, then Reagan grabbed her hand. "You wanna go look around?"

"Definitely."

She wrinkled her nose as Reagan pressed closer. He had the oddest smell. She'd sensed something in the car, but the windows had been down and he'd been a couple of feet away from her. This close, he smelled funky.

"Do you need a shower, or is it just me?"

Reagan's handsome face turned crimson, like a brush fire spreading up his cheeks. "Ah. Maybe I should before we go out."

She waited. But he didn't move.

"What's going on?"

"Ah, Grayson made me promise not to wash for a day or so. He... ah... said the smell would keep all the other wolves away."

It didn't smell that bad. "Really? Well, it's just a little odd, nothing off-putting to me. Let's go, then. Don't want to upset big brother."

They walked out into the fray, hands linked.

"Our pack has most of this east accommodation, and food is being set up at the centre. If you want something to eat, we're going there now," her mum said with a relaxed smile.

She nodded. Why not? Breakfast had been a long time ago. "I could eat."

As though on cue, Reagan's stomach grumbled. "Me too. Definitely."

They made their way through the crowds of people. Old and young. Male and female. Such a good mix of the packs had been sent.

As they walked through the throngs, several of the bigger men turned towards Reagan and frowned as though he annoyed them in some way.

Megan gripped his hand tighter as they moved. What had Grayson done to him? Trust her brother to send his mate off to a Festival with a 'stay away, he's mine' sign stuck to his forehead.

When they made it into the centre of the tents, they saw dozens of tables set up and rows of barbeque grills. They'd arranged it so you could help yourselves, by the looks of things.

Her stomach rolled and grumbled. "I'm starving. Let's go."

They all walked over to the tables and grabbed plates, serving themselves as they would at home.

Megan glanced over at her parents who were similarly helping themselves to the meat and salads. "Is this okay, Mum? Who's paying for all this?"

"Each pack has provided money and food for the festival, so it's all taken care of."

Megan nodded and grabbed her plate, piled high with steak and salad. She so wanted to go to the dessert table straight away, but didn't want to look like a pig.

"Main meal first, Megan," her mother said, and she laughed.

Caught wanting to cheat again.

"Yeah, yeah. Where are we sitting?"

Her dad had settled into a small empty table, so they moved to his side, sat down, and dove into their lunch.

"This is really good. Who's been cooking it?"

Her dad shrugged. "They have a roster, and someone coordinating it, so all the Omegas should be organised."

Megan rolled her eyes and grabbed her plate. "I'm off for some dessert. You coming, Reagan?"

He sat back and patted his belly. "Not yet. Ate way too much already."

She winked at him. "There's always room for dessert." She headed off, putting her dinner plate where the dirty dishes went, and walking over to the dessert table.

She didn't like how little her father knew about the complexities of the pack.

That was why she was so proud to see the changes that the super-Alphas were making. Grayson, Aaron, and Brad were making their pack better.

"Excuse me." A young man pushed past her, causing her to stumble and trip. Her knees hit the ground, and she caught herself with her hands as pain thudded into her wrists.

"Ow."

"Shit. Are you okay?" The guy came back, or it sounded like the same guy—she could only hear his voice, not see him.

"Let me help you up."

He crouched beside her and offered her his hand.

Her brain was beginning to calm down as the pain receded into the back of her mind. She hadn't fallen over since she was a child, and she was surprised how much the shock affected her.

"No, I'm fine."

She got her balance back and pushed herself to her feet, her gaze suddenly caught by his silvery blue eyes. Her breath caught in her throat as his scent filled her nostrils.

Warm bread and butter. That was what he smelled like.

So, strange. Was he a baker?

"I... ah."

"I'm so sorry." He took a step back as he surveyed her height, his eyes flicking up and down her.

"It's okay."

His eyes were wide, looking almost frightened of her. "I didn't mean to trip you. Please accept my apologies."

"Where were you going?" She wanted to keep talking to him for some reason.

"Just to a festival meeting. I'm running the kitchen. I need to keep moving... ah..."

"Megan. I'm Megan."

He bobbed his head in a strange, submissive gesture. "An Alpha-born female. You must be from the Greensborough pack."

She nodded, disappointment flaring in her gut. She hated how she affected the Beta males in her own pack, and that effect obviously was widespread.

"And you must be a Beta, because you're backing away from me like I'm about to bite your head off."

She clenched her teeth and spun on her foot, marching over to the dessert table as anger poured through her like hot rain.

An unreasonable amount of anger, considering the small incident, but she couldn't seem to control her response.

She forced herself to take a deep breath, then exhaled very slowly. She'd been too hard on him, she knew that. It wasn't his fault that she was sick of the sort of treatment he had given her. The packs were taught to revere the Alphas, which unfortunately meant her also.

Her height alone gave her away as an Alpha-born, and she hated it. She was a woman, flesh and blood. Not a princess in a castle who should be ignored and bowed down to.

She wanted to be loved, not feared.

"Hey, look... I'm sorry..." She turned back around, but he was gone, and the coldness that crept into her gut surprised her with its intensity.

"Megan, you okay?" Reagan asked as he walked over to her, his keen gaze doing a once-over of her dirty knees.

"Yeah, I'm fine. Just got a bit of a shock."

She searched the crowd and Reagan tapped her on the arm. “Who are you looking for?”

“Oh, the guy who tripped me over. I kinda bitched at him, and I feel bad. Shouldn’t have done that.”

Reagan twisted around to peruse the desserts, though they had now lost their appeal to her. Which was strange as well.

“I think it’s him that should apologise, not the other way around,” Reagan said as he began scooping up desserts for his plate. “He knocked you over. We saw it from over there.”

She wasn’t sure what had happened exactly, but the whole experience of meeting the Beta had been very strange.

“Yeah… I suppose.”

She wandered over to the table and grabbed a bowl of chocolate mousse, dipping the spoon in and sucking the confection off the spoon. She waited for the normal buzz she’d usually experience with such a high-sugar treat to hit her. It was also missing.

“You okay?” Reagan asked again as they walked back to their table.

“Yeah. Thanks.”

But she wasn’t, and she couldn’t pinpoint what the problem was. Something had shifted inside of her, and she was uncomfortable, unsettled in a strange way.

Had the fall rattled her that much? Or had she somehow met her mate already? She’d heard that was what came with meeting your mate. An ache, a strange feeling that couldn’t be assuaged with food or other comforts.

She forced her attention back to the conversation with Reagan, and tried not to think about what was happening inside her.

CHAPTER TWO

Lucas rushed through the swirling crowd, his heart pounding like he'd just sprinted, ran a marathon, and then shifted. All at once

He'd never felt like this before. He could barely breathe.

"Lucas. The Borough Omegas are over there. Go give them their jobs."

Alpha Bill, one of his pack's Alphas, pointed towards a large group of fit-looking wolves.

"Thank you."

He made his way over to the group of small males and females.

Two of the men stepped forward, approaching him in a way that the Omegas in his pack wouldn't do. Their backs were straight, their heads high. Their faces showed a pride he didn't see in many of the Omega level.

He gave them a smile and introduced himself. "I'm Lucas. Beta of the Robinvale pack."

"Tommy." "John." The two men in front of him bobbed their heads as the others gathered around.

He handed them the printout he'd spent weeks organising. "Great. Nice to meet you. Here is your roster. All four packs have two meals to cater over the weekend. You do all cooking, serving, and cleaning up, then you have the rest of the time off. That work for you?" he asked, handing them the roster.

Terry grinned. "Of course. Thank you."

He pointed to the centre of the circle made by people's tents, tables, and chairs. "All the food is set up in there, so please help yourself. You're on for dinner tonight."

They smiled but didn't say anything else, and he said goodbye. He needed to see how the other packs were settling in. His job for the weekend was keeping the food going and coordinating the deliveries, the Omegas, and the wash stations.

Not an easy job, or a small one, but he was used to that. The Alphas always gave him more than anyone else.

As he moved through the crowd, his mind began to drift to the Alpha-born female he'd run into when rushing through the cafeteria area.

He could still feel the heat of her skin on his hands, the smell of her sweetness in his nose. Despite himself, a part of his wolf was screaming at him to go back and claim her. Which was... insane. He was a Beta. She was an Alpha-born. She was destined for an Alpha. No one else would be strong enough for a woman like her.

A woman like... *Megan.*

Her voice, her name. They kept going around and around his mind, making it impossible to focus on anything else.

"Lucas!"

A groan rolled through him as he turned around to face Kellie, one of the Alpha mates from his pack.

"What are you doing, standing around like this?" She put her hands on her hips and tapped her foot.

A bit ridiculous. She probably thought that her pointed shoes would actually make that annoying tapping noise here like they did back home.

Luckily, they didn't.

"I was just assessing the situation, Kellie. I've met with the Omegas from the Greensborough pack..."

"So you need something to do? Good. My mate needs help with some of the supplies. Go to the food storage and help him."

Translation. Her fat and lazy Alpha mate couldn't be bothered doing the work himself.

"Sure, Kellie. I'll go right now."

He turned and trudged off, wondering, not for the first time, why he had been saddled with such an odd pack.

The Alphas were not good leaders, nor were they kind or helpful. He'd heard rumours that some of the other packs had better Alphas, but his own pack kept him so busy at these festivals, he barely had a moment to talk to anyone else.

He took the long way to his destination, enjoying the chatter of the people around him: the wolves and their mates, the children they'd brought.

The point of the weekend was mostly socialising. Wolves, by nature, were social creatures, yet very few liked to travel. Staying close to home was more the norm.

He bumped into a solid wolf moving across the path.

"Oh, I'm sorry." He immediately apologised, dipping his head rather than looking up into the face of one of the other pack Alphas.

He was well over six foot tall.

"No problem. How you doing? I'm Reagan."

The tones weren't right and as Lucas lifted his gaze, sparkling blue eyes stared back at him.

He sniffed, a horrible scent wafting towards him.

The blond guy extended his hand and Lucas forced himself to shake the offered hand, although everything in him told him not to touch the guy in front of him.

He must have cringed, because Reagan was soon the one apologising.

"I'm sorry. I smell bad, don't I?"

Reagan crinkled his nose, and Lucas cocked his head. He couldn't smell it?

"Ah..."

Reagan grinned, his straight, white teeth speaking of a world outside of the one Lucas had known.

He's human. Wow.

Reagan went on. "It's okay, I know I do. Megan said I smelled bad, but I promised Grayson I wouldn't wash it off. Not yet anyway... I'll see how many people can't stand being near me first."

Lucas could only nod. He hadn't seen many humans before, and this one seemed strong and happy.

And covered in Alpha cum scent.

Reagan cocked his head. "What's wrong?"

"I... ah..." How could he put it? "You're human."

"Yep. And the mate of Grayson Nox, Alpha of the Greensborough pack. Nice to meet you....?"

"Um, Lucas. Lucas Noll. Beta wolf of the Robinvale pack."

Reagan leaned forward, a twinkle of mischief in his eyes. He actually wasn't over six foot; he was similar to Lucas's own height. He just *seemed* bigger.

"Tell me, Lucas. I was afraid to ask before. What do I smell like?"

Heat flushed up his neck, blooming all over his face. "Um... you smell like... an Alpha mate."

Reagan leaned back. "So you can smell his spunk, huh?"

A laugh simmered on Lucas's lips. This guy was nice. And confident. And happy. And an Alpha's mate. Amazing.

"Ah, yeah, I can. It's meant to warn any other wolf off you. But that's a good thing. Your mate must care for you a lot."

Reagan's smile changed, softened. "He does."

Then the penny dropped, like someone had smacked him in the head. "Did you say... hang on. There's an all-male Alpha pairing in Greensborough?"

"Haven't you heard of us? I'm surprised you haven't, since we killed all the Rogues and stuff. There's three now. Grayson, who's my mate, Aaron, and Brad."

His mouth must have been hanging open because Reagan leaned forward and tapped him on the chin.

Lucas shook himself. That went against what he'd heard. "Ah... no. We hadn't been told that. About any of it. The Rogues... we were told were just taken care of by the Alphas."

Reagan's laugh had a bitterness to it. "Of course. Stupid wankers take the credit for everything."

Part of Lucas wanted to high-five Reagan for saying such a thing; the other half was trembling. The beating he would have copped for saying such a thing...

"Yeah... well... it was nice to meet you, but I really must be going."

Lucas backed away and practically ran off. He had the feeling someone like Reagan would get him into trouble with his own pack. His wolf shifted inside of him, restless and pacing. There was change afoot, and that Reagan character had something to do with it.

"Alpha Raymond, I was asked to come over and help."

Raymond grunted at him, out of breath exerting himself for once. Lucas took over, moving boxes and organising people, just as he had been asked.

He spent his life in service to his pack, and although he could not imagine a better way to live, he noted the lack of appreciation and respect his Alphas handed out to the Betas and Omegas that served them.

Something told him things would be very different in Greensborough.

"Time for the meeting address, Megan."

Megan looked up from her book and nodded, stretching her arms above her head. "Okay. Time to get this show on the road, I guess."

Her belly was quivering with nerves. Tonight, she was going to socialise with the Alphas from the other three packs.

Then tomorrow, her parents were going to raise the issue of her mark, and see if any of them had identical matches. That was how she would know her mate. Fate gave each of their males a birthmark at birth. When their female mate turned twenty-one, she would develop the matching one so that they knew who they were destined to be with.

She had hers now, and since no one in her own pack had the matching mark, her parents had assumed it would belong to one of the unmated Alphas from another pack.

However, she wasn't sure exactly how she felt about it yet. Looking at her brother, and her parents, she knew that a great match would be possible. In fact, she had total faith that Fate would choose an amazing mate for her. But how would that change her life?

Would she have to move away from her parents? Her pack? Would she be able to keep working? She'd managed to finish her drafting degree, and she loved working with all the builders in the Borough.

"I'm a bit nervous, Mum," she confided as they walked outside.

"Me too!" her mother cried. "But everything will be fine. Have faith." She smiled and took Megan's arm, and they made their way through the crowds to where the makeshift stage had been built.

On stage was a man with a huge belly and a double chin.

She frowned. What wolf looked like that?

"Hello. I'm Raymond, Alpha of the Robinvale pack, and I want to welcome you all to our Spring Festival."

There was a round of applause and Megan leaned closer to her mum. "Who's that? He looks like he's going to drop dead of a heart attack."

"Don't be unkind, Megan," her mother snapped back.

Unkind? Wolves were strong, healthy beasts with such high metabolisms it was almost impossible for them to gain weight. They should not be, and were hardly ever, overweight or unfit. This man was both. And it made her wonder what sort of Alpha he was, not to be moving enough to keep his weight down.

Her gaze was tugged to the left of the stage as the Alpha on stage droned on.

Awareness flared inside of her.

There he was again. The man she'd run into at lunch, clipboard in hand.

His eyes were on the Alpha until he turned towards her, unerringly locking gazes with her as though he'd known she was staring at him.

Tendrils of heat curled inside her belly, awakening a lust

inside of her she hadn't known she possessed. The spot between her legs pulsed, and her nipples tightened beneath the lace of her bra.

"Has anyone caught your eye yet, Megan?"

With great difficulty, she tore her gaze away to look towards her mother.

"What do you mean, Mum?"

"I mean, you know. We think your mate will be here, right now. Have you felt an attraction towards anyone? I knew it the moment I saw your father who he was to me. That twist of my belly when he looked at me, not to mention the smell."

That got her attention, because she'd already been feeling something very similar for the clipboard Beta.

"Smell? What smell?"

Why hadn't she paid better attention in the past to these discussions?

"*The* smell. Your mate's scent is the most delicious thing you will ever smell. You'll know as soon as you meet him... or her."

Megan rolled her eyes. "Mum. You know it won't be a woman. I like men."

Her mother grinned. "Your brother thought he'd get a female mate, and look what happened to him."

She dismissed her mother's words. "Ah. Don't worry about it."

But her heart was pounding harder and she looked back towards the stage, searching for the young man who'd smelled so sweet to her.

He was gone.

A shiver coursed along her spine.

Who was he? Now that her mother had pretty much confirmed what she'd partly worked out herself, she'd have to find him.

"Enjoy the festivities, and let's make this Festival the best yet."

The Alpha on stage finished up his speech, and the crowd cheered and clapped.

Well, that Beta was the best lead she had, and since the main reason she'd come to the Spring Festival was to find out if she did have a mate in one of the other Victorian packs, then she may as well start the hunt.

"I think I'll go mingle, Mum. Anything else I should look for?"

Her mother shrugged. "You'll know with that first kiss, but since you already have your mating mark, you may as well just put a bikini top on and show off your belly, see if your mate comes to you."

"Mu...m!"

Why did her mother always joke about it in that way? She'd like *some* sort of introduction before she met the person she *had* to marry. Why couldn't she have both?

Megan stomped off into the fray, pushing past small Omegas and larger Betas. There were people everywhere.

Mostly strangers, although some of her pack were camped around the fire, chatting.

What did that guy say his name was?

Damn, she didn't think he had introduced himself at all.

What could she remember about him?

A sense of the man himself came into her mind. A strong, good person, and she didn't even know his name.

Fuck!

The Alphas were standing near the stage, and she took a breath, gathering her wits. Was it time to expose her mark and charge around asking who her mate was?

No. She wasn't quite ready for that yet. She'd rather know who he was first. Although she loved their legends and the idea that Fate would choose someone perfect for her, she wanted him to like her on her own merits. Not just because Fate said she was the right one.

Maybe she was being silly, but still. She wanted that for herself.

She moved closer and nudged her way into the circle.

"Hi, I'm Megan."

The Alphas turned towards her, and she gave them what her mother termed her super wattage smile.

The overweight Alpha nodded at her.

"You're from the Greensborough pack. Welcome."

"Thank you. It's great to be here. I was wondering if you could help me. I met someone earlier, and didn't grab his name. He was a Beta. Short brown hair, had a clipboard."

The Alpha began to nod. "That would be Lucas, a member of my pack. Why do you need him?"

The Alpha in front of her narrowed his eyes, and she had the feeling that if she said the wrong thing here, Lucas would be punished.

She straightened to her full height and stared him in the eye. "My dad has asked me to meet people from other packs, to learn from them. We can always take away new ways of strengthening our pack, and I'm sure Robinvale is a great place."

The man nodded, but didn't say anything.

"Is there a reason I can't speak to Lucas?"

"He's busy."

This was not appropriate behaviour for an Alpha. To be so cagey and rude. Despite the litany that sprung to her tongue, Megan bowed out, her parents' reputation foremost in her mind.

They'd only just arrived. She didn't want to cause trouble already.

"Thank you for your help. I'll go socialise with people who aren't busy, then."

She gave them a small smile, swivelled on her heel, and walked away.

What was with that Alpha, anyway? Just as she'd suspected, he was an arsehole.

She made her way through the crowd, spotted her parents and gave them a wave.

Where would Lucas be? He was obviously an organiser of sorts, so where were they?

She moved through the eating area and walked around the back to the storage areas and trucks.

There she found him, and she froze, staring as he hefted huge boxes of food, her heart pounding with the steadiness of a bongo drum.

Wow.

This was it.

She swallowed hard and continued to watch him.

He was a Beta, not what she had expected, but she pushed away any twang of disappointment. Aaron's mate was a Omega, and a more loyal, hardworking member of the pack you would never find.

He was her height, just.

Perfect for kissing.

She walked closer, her gaze running over the strength in his shoulders, the strong angle of his jaw.

As though sensing her, he turned, his brow furrowing as he straightened and twisted to face her.

"Megan. What are you doing here?"

He wiped his sweat-dotted forehead with the back of his hand.

His tone was strange, as though he weren't happy to see her. Which he should be, shouldn't he? If they were mates?

"I'm sorry, I felt really bad about our run-in before, and

needed to apologise properly, and introduce myself, too. I'm Megan Nox."

She stuck out her hand, and he stared at it without moving.

She waited, counting her heartbeats while she stood like an idiot in front of about twenty other men.

"Lucas Noll." He extended his hand and their skin connected, frissons of electricity pulsing into her arm.

His eyes widened, and he pulled his arm back so fast he knocked her off balance. She toppled forward, and he reached out to steady her. A delicious groan rumbled out of him as his hands touched her arms.

The sound vibrated in her mind, pulling at her core and making her melt.

"You need to go."

She shook her head. "No. Please. I need to know what this is."

"No. You don't. I have my job. I must do it. I'm a Beta, you're an Alpha-born. Go meet some other Alphas."

That wasn't fair. "But, Lucas."

"Go." His voice deepened, and the growl behind the words would not be denied. She bowed her head and backed away.

Not even her father had made her drop her eyes like that. Ever. What sort of secret Alpha power did he have lurking behind all that submissive talk?

She moved back into the crowd, her head spinning. She'd met her mate. She was sure of it. And he didn't want her. What was she going to do now?

CHAPTER THREE

Lucas's heart raced in his chest, and his wolf pounded at him with a fierceness Lucas had never experienced before. He wanted to shift, to run, to escape the feeling ripping through him like a hurricane.

She was his mate.

Damn it all to hell.

He couldn't have a mate. He'd convinced himself he couldn't. In fact, his Alpha had told him he so. His role in the pack made any family impossible. The Alphas kept him so busy, so exhausted, excluded from all pack gatherings, except to organise them from backstage.

They hated him, he knew it. But what he could never work out was *why*.

He could feel it in the way they looked at him. The tone of voice they used when commanding him. Not to mention what they'd done to his birthmark.

They wanted him to do all the work, of course... his status, or whatever they hated about him, never stopped them from asking him to do everything they didn't want to do.

Anger swelled in him like the tide, and he pushed it down and away, breathing evenly. Slowly.

"Who was that?" Tom, one of the other Betas, asked.

Lucas's eyes had clouded, and he could feel his wolf wanting to shift. He pushed and pulled and fought until his wolf receded.

His vision cleared and he managed to choke in precious air as he got his wolf under control.

Damn, that was a close one. He's getting stronger.

"One of the Alpha-born women from the Greensborough pack."

"What did she want?" Tom asked, his eyes narrowed with suspicion.

Tom answered to the Alphas, and it seemed to be his constant job to make sure that Lucas never had any space. Every small mistake was accounted for.

"Nothing I could help with. She needs to go talk to the Alphas."

"She does." He grunted, pointing to a box he expected Lucas to pick up. "Alphas should only associate with Alphas."

Tell him to go fuck himself.

Lucas shook his head as the errant thought ploughed through his head.

He was starting to worry about himself. Every now and again, his wolf bucked, and a strong voice in his head would show his distaste for the hierarchy in his pack.

He had to find a way to get his wolf under control.

"Of course." He agreed with Tom and bent to pick up the heavy box.

He continued until the job was done and then an apron was shoved at him.

"It's Greensborough's turn in the kitchen, and they need your help."

Tom smirked at him. *Little shit.*

But Lucas took it and tied it around his waist. He never minded helping out, and since meeting the Alpha Mate, Reagan, he was interested in learning more about the pack from Greensborough.

He picked up his clipboard and headed back to the food prep area, looking around, expecting to see utter chaos. But there wasn't any. Why had he been told they needed help?

One of the Omegas saw him, wiped her hands and came over.

"Can I help you?"

"I'm Lucas. I organise the festival for the Alphas of Robindale. I was told you guys needed some help."

The small woman laughed. "Oh, no. We're fine. You go enjoy yourself, Lucas. You look like you could use a night off."

A strange chuckle made its way out his throat. A night off? What was that?

Her unusual expression pulled a moment of honesty from him. "I... wouldn't know what to do with myself."

The woman gave him a quizzical look and turned to smile as an older woman came into the outdoor kitchen.

"Oh, here's someone who can help you. Katherine, this is Lucas. He runs the show, and he looks utterly worn out. Do you think you and the other Alphas could keep him company for a bit?"

The woman next to him had a beautiful face and was as tall as he was.

Had the Omega just told the Alpha mate what to do? What sort of alternative universe had he walked into?

"Oh, no. Thank you, but I couldn't join an Alpha group."

The Alpha mate next to him laughed. "You're kidding me?

That's not how we run our pack—not anymore, anyway. Thank you, Jeanie. I'll take this young man for a walk. What's your name, by the way, young Beta?"

She had a smile that reminded him of Megan's for some reason, but her colouring was completely different.

"It's Lucas, ma'am."

She whacked him in the arm in a playful way that made his mouth drop open. "Don't you ma'am me. It's Katherine. Now, let's go, I wanna know more about the festival and how it's all set up."

She grabbed his elbow like they'd known each other for years, and dragged him into the fray.

It was like being swept away by a current and nothing he managed to come up with for an excuse seemed good enough to say.

"Here. Come over and meet my husband." She dragged him to a group of chairs in a semi-circle near the huge open fire.

"Lucas, this is my husband, Jack. Jack, this is Lucas, one of Betas organising the festival."

The Alpha stood up, towering over them all, his piercing blue eyes looking unsettlingly like Megan's.

Oh, no...

"Nice to meet you." The Alpha said, extending his hand and shaking Lucas's with strong enthusiasm.

Lucas's stomach started to tighten, and his wolf howled inside of him.

"And, here she is. This is our daughter, Megan. Megan, Lucas. One of the organisers of this event."

The hairs on the back of his neck prickled as he turned and saw the woman he'd pushed away only an hour ago.

"I met Lucas earlier, Mum. Good to see you again. Sit with us."

She sat, as did her parents, expectant looks on their faces.

He couldn't do it.

"My Alphas will need me soon."

"Why? Do you have any jobs left for tonight?"

"Well, no. But they always find something for me to do..." His voice trailed off as he realised what he was revealing.

Megan's brows drew together, but her father just laughed that off.

"Don't worry. I'll sort 'em out if need be. Stay. Sit."

Lucas sat. The command in the Alpha's tone strong. Stronger than his own Alphas, by far, and he wasn't even trying.

"All right."

Jack slung his arm casually over the backs of both the chairs flanking him, his protection clear around his mate and his daughter.

A warmth unlike anything he'd ever felt filled Lucas's chest. Like someone had poured hot water into his lungs. But it wasn't unpleasant—quite the opposite.

"So, tell me about yourself, Lucas. It's strange. But I feel as though we have met before." Jack said, with a quizzical look.

"Perhaps at another festival, Alpha Jack. I've been running these events for years."

He knew for certain he'd never met the Alpha, but that didn't mean that Jack hadn't seen him.

"It's just Jack. We don't stand on ceremony in our pack."

"Really?" That was a surprise. Most Alphas he'd heard of, and certainly his own, loved hearing their rank a hundred times a day.

"Of course. So, tell us about your pack, Lucas."

"Ah." What could he say to that? "What would you like to know about?"

"Oh, everything." Katherine smiled. "We love learning about how other packs are run. Do all your Alphas have University degrees, for instance? Do your Betas? What do you think works well in your pack?"

Nothing...

"Ah. Well, the Alphas all go to school, and one of them has a degree in Accounting."

He barely passed, but who's counting?

"What about the others? The females?" Megan asked, her tone interested.

"Others? Our pack is mostly farmers. Our Alphas don't encourage anyone to go to school past about year ten."

Megan's look of horror was comical.

And then it clicked, and he leaned forward. "Are you telling me that you go to university?"

Megan snorted and mirrored his movements, her face only a few feet from his own. "Of course. I'm almost done with my degree. All our Alphas go to Uni. Well, Brad didn't, but he fought tooth and nail to get out of it. Half of our Betas do too, or at least a tech school, so they're all tradies, carpenters, etc."

"Wow." He couldn't believe it.

"So, you didn't finish school?" she asked quietly, and a hot flush crept up his neck and into his face. He shouldn't be embarrassed, yet knowing that the woman in front of him was so much better qualified in life than he... he was.

"I did. Not University, but I did year twelve. The Alphas saw that my brain for mathematics could be used better if I had more schooling."

Alpha Jack was frowning. "Why do you speak as though the Alphas in your pack use you for their own devices?"

Because they do.

He bowed his head under the scrutiny of the man in front of him. "I mean no disrespect to the Alphas. I only mean that I live to serve the pack."

Jack pushed himself to his feet and placed a hand on Lucas's shoulder, the weight heavy and warm.

He looked up to see the kind blue eyes staring at him. The setting sun slashed the sky with red and orange hues.

"I'm going for a walk. Stay and talk for a while. I'll be back."

Again, the tones were too strong for Lucas to get up and move away.

When he looked back to Katherine and Megan, concern was written all over their faces.

"Are you mated, Lucas?" Katherine asked suddenly.

And despite himself, his gaze slid over to Megan, then back to her mother's. "No, I'm not. There is no one in my pack that has my mark."

"Mum... don't be nosy." Megan butted in suddenly.

"Where is your mark, Lucas?" Katherine asked, ignoring her daughter's suggestion.

"Ah..." He didn't want to tell her, and most of it had been removed, anyway.

If Megan was his intended mate, then the last thing he needed was to let her parents know. They would force the mating, and then where would he be?

With a mate he didn't deserve, and pissed-off Alphas that wanted him to be their slave.

"He doesn't want to tell us, Mum. It's okay, Lucas. My mother's a matchmaker. She'd probably be able to find your mate in a few hours. So you don't have to tell her."

Megan gave him a strange, tight smile, and disappointment flooded his gut like icy water.

She didn't want to know, either. Of course she didn't. She would want an Alpha to mate her—who wouldn't?

"I think I better get back to my work. I appreciate you letting me sit with you."

"No. Stay. Please." Megan's voice was filled with heavy

emotion, but he ignored what it could mean. He shouldn't have gotten to know her at all.

Inside his mind, his wolf howled with longing. Lucas swallowed hard as he backed away, strange unseen ropes tying him to the place he'd been sitting.

"You'll be shifting tomorrow night, right?" Megan asked, walking forward, and he moved back.

"Ah, probably not. I don't shift much."

"Why not?" she asked.

He shrugged, gave Katherine a final smile and forced his way through the people gathering around the warm fires.

He'd forgotten that they'd organised a mass run for the wolves tomorrow night. He wouldn't be allowed to shift—the Alphas didn't allow it. They didn't like anyone except the Alphas shifting, and only when the full moon was out and some of the stronger Betas would start shifting involuntarily that they gave in and allowed a one-off change. And even then... they didn't allow it every month.

It kept them weak and disconnected from their wolves, and it wasn't healthy. He knew that. But if they shifted at random, they were punished. Severely.

He'd been locked in a cell under one of the Alpha's homes for a week for shifting for a run when it wasn't a full moon.

Hope filled his heart for a moment.

Tomorrow was a full moon—that was why they'd chosen this weekend to hold the festival. Maybe his Alphas would show some kindness towards their pack?

To the other Betas, they would. To him, it was unlikely. They detested him the most.

He trudged back to the kitchen area to help clean up.

It was what he did best.

Megan watched Lucas go, her heart in her throat. She was pretty sure that the man who'd just walked away from her was her mate.

A beautiful, kind, hard-working Beta. A mate she could be proud of, she was sure, if he could be the man he was meant to be.

"What's with all the submissive stuff, Mum? We have Omegas stronger than him." She spoke harsher than she meant to, but she wasn't happy. What sort of Beta wolf slunk around apologising for breathing?

"All the packs run very differently, Megan. We shouldn't judge."

She huffed in exasperation and turned to glare straight at her mother.

"You said that was what we were here for. To learn and grow as a community. What can we learn from a pack who obviously keep their people unhappy and suppressed?"

Her mother's lips twisted. "I don't know, but hopefully your father can tell us more."

"I can."

She turned around when she heard her dad's deep, booming voice. His forehead creased as he reached for his beer, chugging it down. The worry he was feeling settled over Megan.

"What happened, Dad?"

He grimaced and sat down. They followed suit, eyes pinned on him.

"The pack from Robinvale have only been running this festival for two years, so I've never looked at them closely. The pack from Mildura ran it for a decade before that, and they have an impeccable reputation."

He was vibrating a little, in anger, or something else, Megan wasn't sure.

"Yeah, so? What did you learn, Dad?"

He chugged a little more beer. Megan and her mother exchanged worried glances. No one in their pack drank much, her father included.

"What did you learn from Lucas?" he asked, and instead of pressuring him for an answer first, Megan was more than happy to oblige.

"Well, for one thing, they barely let any of the pack members graduate from school, let alone go to Tafe or university. And the way Lucas acts... it's just strange. Reminds me far too much of what the Omegas used to be like before Grayson and Reagan mated. He's scared, or something..." She didn't know the words to explain the strange vibes she got from Lucas.

What had they done to him?

"What did you find out, Jack?" her mum asked, settling a hand on her dad's thigh.

"I'm not one hundred percent sure what's going on with that pack, but I'm pretty sure everything's fucked up."

Megan's gaze darted to her mother's, whose shocked expression mirrored her own.

"Um... what do you mean, Dad?"

He ran a hand through his hair. "I mean, those Alphas that run Robinvale have some bloody strange ways of seeing things. And there is a creepy coldness that reminds me far too much of Marcus, but worse."

Marcus was one of their Alphas, and a selfish arsehole. Brad had torn him apart last year, and although he still held the rank, he didn't have much to do with the running of the pack anymore.

"And how they feel about Lucas... It's crazy."

"Pardon me?"

What did he mean by that? Her heart started to pump louder, harder.

"They are crazy possessive of him. I tried to give them a compliment. Told them what a good guy he was, and how we wanted to steal him to help us out at Greensborough. They practically bit my head off and started to threaten me."

"That's... Odd." And highly suspicious.

"It is, because when I first spoke about him, they rolled their eyes and were all fake smiles. So, I don't think they like him, but they want to keep him."

A dark anger grew in Megan's gut, making it a struggle to breathe.

"I don't like this, Dad."

He shook his head. "No. Me neither. And at the end of this weekend, I'll be calling an Alpha pack meeting to discuss Robinvale's policies."

Megan shivered as the hairs on her arms stood on end. The night was getting cooler.

Her father noticed at the same moment. "Time for bed."

She nodded, a strange ache filling her. Her mate was nearby, but she couldn't call him out yet. She had to wait for him to be ready for her, and she was not a patient person.

They retired to their room, Reagan finding her and chatting away about the people he'd met.

She fell into a fitful sleep, strange dark images chasing her through the night.

CHAPTER FOUR

Lucas stretched his shoulders and flexed his arm, pain shooting through his chest.

Alpha Bill had practically dislocated his shoulder last night after they'd all gone to bed.

His crime? The Alphas from Greensborough wanting to take him away.

He'd apologised and bitten his tongue, part of him grateful for the pain that still restricted his movements and made him want to groan aloud. Megan's parents had liked him! And not only that—it seemed they wanted him to go to their pack and stay there.

What a dream come true that would be. Not that it would ever happen. His Alphas would never let him go, but it was lovely to think he was wanted.

The day wore on, and he did his best to avoid Megan and her parents. Despite their best intentions, seeing them would only get him into further trouble and he still had two days left to survive this festival.

He raced around all day, coordinating people, food, trucks, and events.

The shifting would be tonight, and his Alpha had already declared that only a select few Betas would be permitted to shift with the group. Too dangerous, he'd said.

Yeah, right.

He, of course, was not one of the chosen few.

He tried to tell himself that he didn't mind too much. But inside, he did. His wolf ached to shift, run, and be what he truly was. A wild animal. Not allowing him to shift kept him weak, and they knew that.

Anger bubbled in his gut as he arranged some chairs in a circle. He didn't want to be weak.

"What's going on tonight? You running with the wolves?"

Megan's strong voice surrounded him, making a shiver of longing course down his spine.

"No."

He continued to pack away the chairs, flicking the metal rods to flatten the tables to make room for the wolf members.

"Why not?" She asked, her voice now closer.

"My Alphas wanted me to stay back and help set up for tomorrow, no big deal."

It was, but how could he tell her that?

"When did you last shift?"

Her question took him by surprise. Females in their communities couldn't shift. Only the males did, and only the Alphas and Betas. As far as he knew, Omega males couldn't shift either, although he'd heard rumours...

He turned around and his heart pounded at the sight of her, her dark hair cascading over her shoulders like a waterfall.

"Ah...um... I can't really remember..."

"Is it that hard to answer? Last week? Last full moon?" she

asked, stepping closer. Her scent made his knees weak... cherry blossom. It must be her perfume.

What had she asked him again? Every thought had flown out the window, and as she continued to stare at him with her piercing blue eyes, he struggled even more.

"Lucas..." she reached out a hand to him, and he stumbled backwards, not wanting that physical connection again. Last time she'd touched him, he'd basically dropped to his knees from the impact.

"Is it true that Omegas in your pack shift?"

There! He'd remembered, and he'd managed to get it out.

She blinked. "Yes, some of them do. For a long time, we believed only the Betas and Alphas could shift, but last year, when we had to fight off the Rogues, some of the Omegas stepped up to fight. It was pretty incredible."

"Wow."

He'd heard a little of that fight, but again, it had been in whispers, rumours. Their Alphas made sure their pack stayed pretty clueless about the outside world.

"I heard a bit about the Rogues, but not much."

She laughed, a strange, strained noise. "You're kidding? They almost killed my brother, and managed to kill half our pack, and you don't know anything about it?"

Her tone was angry and her hands were fisted beside her.

He looked away, ashamed at being so dumb.

"I'm sorry. We're so secluded up in Robinvale. We don't get told much."

"You mean your Alphas keep you in the dark, even when it could have been your pack under attack."

He shrugged and went back to his work. What could he say? Do? His world was his world.

Megan suddenly grabbed him, turned him, and yanked his top up.

"Hey." He went to pull it down, not wanting her to see the scars they'd put on him.

"What happened?" Megan's soft voice flowed over him as her palms pressed to the lumpy scars around his belly button.

He froze, her touch turning whatever fear he had of her seeing his scars into jelly.

"Ah... an accident."

And that was the lie he stuck to whenever anyone asked him. Not that one of his Alphas had taken a knife to his birth mark one drunken night in a fit of rage.

You'll never have a mate, he'd screamed as he'd cut Lucas up, destroying any hope of anyone seeing his mark and bonding with him.

Megan's gaze lifted slowly, heat burning inside those eyes like blue flames.

"They cut your mark, didn't they?"

Her lips were turned down, and a muscle tightened in her jaw.

"How did you know that?"

Megan stepped back and lifted her own white t-shirt.

Lucas stumbled backwards, falling into one of the remaining chairs.

Someone may as well have hit him over the head with a lump of wood.

There was his birthmark. A crescent shaped, dark mark curling around Megan's belly button. Her flat stomach and luminescent skin made him want to crawl over and lick her from top to bottom.

"You're my mate," she stated, not an ounce of question in her voice.

He could deny it, he *should* deny it, but he'd always been a hopeless liar.

"I don't have my mark anymore, Megan. No one will believe you."

"Are you serious?!" The look on her face was so angry, he flinched. Her eyebrows were drawn together, and her mouth was tight.

He cleared his throat. "I don't know what you mean."

"We are destined to be! Chosen by Fate to be together, and you're letting your fucking... horrible Alphas take that from you? Grow some balls!"

She stormed off, and he was left staring after her. His wolf howled inside of him and began to fight to get out.

Pain ripped through him as he tried to push him down, not allow the Beta wolf in him to escape.

A groan ripped through his vocal cords as he fell to the ground, silver fur sprouting out of his skin as his body contorted into that of a wolf.

Prickles of fire burned along his skin, but the full moon above his head called to him like a siren.

When he had fully shifted, he relaxed, accepting his fate. There was no going back now. He turned and began to run, his feet clumsy and awkward as he made his way through the throngs of females and into the pack of wolves.

The Alphas, all huge black wolves, threw back their heads and howled to the moon, calling forth the run.

I am so going to be punished for this.

One of the Alphas, probably Bill from his pack, spotted him, and the look on his face was murderous.

Better stay away from him.

The combined pack turned and headed into the forest, running through the overgrown brush.

Despite the danger, the run was thrilling. The fresh, cool air in his lungs. His awkward wolf body stumbling through the woods as though shifting for the first time.

Whack.

Someone slammed into him, throwing him to the ground.

The black wolf who'd hit him kept running, *thank God*, but the warning was clear.

Lucas hung back from the pack, but kept moving with them. The smells of the forest were beautiful. So different to the arid places they would run in around Robinvale.

His legs went out from under him, and a sharp, knife-like pain cut into his back legs.

A whimper went through him, and he looked up, his big black Alpha looming over him, blood-stained teeth bared.

Anger stirred in Lucas, and he pushed up from the ground, despite the intense pain.

He bared his own teeth and growled back. He was half the Alpha's size and was weak from lack of food and shifting, but if they wanted to kill him, they'd have to do it while he was standing.

He'd taken enough from these arseholes. He would not die like a dog in the dirt.

The Alpha in front of him crouched back on his haunches, ready to pounce, and the ground shook with the running of the wolves.

The combined pack ran past them, sweeping Lucas up in the tide as they all moved back to the campsite.

His heart pounded like a bass drum and pain exploded up his leg, but he hobbled back to the clearing, where the men were shifting back to their human selves.

Lucas let go of his wolf, slowly transforming back to his

human body. The shift was painful, like someone scraping his skin with a piece of flint, but he managed.

Just. It took every ounce of will power not to scream aloud.

Blood dripped down his leg, and he raised his gaze to his Alpha, who had blood running down the side of his jaw.

Bastard.

Megan came bolting over to him, her mother Katherine behind her.

"Who did this to you?" she gasped, grabbing at his arm to steady him.

Bill may have torn the muscle from the bone. Lucas couldn't put any weight on that leg, and he didn't want to look down and see the damage Bill had done.

His shoulders ached, and Lucas was pretty sure there was damage down to his back from the original knocks.

"It's okay, Megan."

He'd left his clothes in the clearing where he'd shifted. He'd have to ask someone to get them for him.

Jack walked over as he tugged on his jeans, his face a mask of concern.

"Who did this to you, Lucas?"

His gaze shifted to his Alpha, who was wiping the blood from his face.

A loud growl echoed in the clearing and the crowd parted, Jack facing off against Bill.

"Is this true?" Jack roared, and Lucas straightened as much as he could.

His pack rushed to stand behind Bill, and Jack's back became crowded with his pack.

Twice the number Bill had.

Lucas looked behind him. Omegas, Betas, even their women

had rushed to protect the Alpha they knew had just issued a challenge.

Bill spat on the grass, red glistening on the space in front of him.

"He's my pack, and I decide how he is punished."

Lucas shifted his weight and took a step towards his own pack.

"I should go back, Jack. Thank you. But..."

Jack's arm snapped out, stopping Lucas's progression forward.

"No. You stay with me."

The command was unfightable.

Something snapped inside of Lucas, and he straightened taller. Pride filled his chest, something he had never felt before.

Someone was standing up for him.

Someone wanted him. And that someone was Jack Nox of Greensborough.

"Yes, Alpha."

Bill growled back, the other Alphas coming to stand with him. "No! He's mine. You will not take him from me."

Jack got down on all fours and growled. "Try me."

The shift happened so fast, Lucas didn't even blink, and he still missed it.

Two huge black wolves stood before them, and as one, launched themselves at each other.

Lucas staggered back, his allegiances struggling inside his mind.

"Lucas!" Tom yelled out for him, calling him back over to Bill and Raymond's pack.

Part of him wanted to go, sickness and guilt at causing such a fight eating at him as the two black wolves snarled and snapped, ripping into one another.

Megan's hand slid into his and tugged hard.

He turned towards her and saw the moonlight shimmering in her hair. A beacon calling him home.

He went where she called, and Megan wrapped her arms around his waist, standing behind him so they could both watch as Jack got the upper hand.

He planted Bill on the ground, paws pushing him into the dirt.

Bill whined, a signal that the match was done, and Jack nipped him on the ear before backing off, his fur disappearing as he became the huge Alpha he was once again.

When Bill shifted back, he seemed smaller, the blood on his face fitting for the horrible man he was.

"Go," Jack commanded.

Slowly, defeated, they left. Jack waited until every one of the pack members from Robinvale had gone. Then he turned his back on them and came over to the Greensborough pack.

"Thank you, sir."

Lucas didn't know what else to say.

Jack was puffing, but otherwise looked unharmed.

"What was he wanting to punish you for?"

Wow. Jack fought for me without even asking what I'd done wrong.

"For shifting and running tonight. He told me not to."

Jack's eye brows quirked. "I don't understand."

Megan's huffing came through clear, but he tried to ignore her. He needed to explain.

"The Alphas don't allow us to shift at will, and it's been... Three or four months for me. I couldn't stop my wolf tonight, and I'm sorry I caused such a problem."

Megan squeezed him tightly, and Jack's eyebrows shot up, then they lowered menacingly.

"I'll deal with your Alpha later. No wonder you looked so

weak. They have no right to keep you all from shifting. Are they trying to make you sick?"

He had to be honest there. "I believe they are. They like us dependent on them."

Jack's growl could be heard through the whole clearing, but finally, he shook his head.

"Let's get dressed and back to the cabin to talk. Megan, I think you'd like to speak to us?"

"Yes, Dad."

Jack pulled on his clothes once again, but Lucas had left his too far away.

"I..."

Reagan, the blond Alpha Mate, came running with a bundle of clothes.

"Here, Lucas. Put these on. We need to look at that leg, too. It's nasty."

Lucas looked to Megan for guidance.

"Oh, Reagan's a doctor. Works in our hospital."

Wow. Another reason he was an Alpha's mate.

"That would be great. Thank you."

Reagan tucked himself under Lucas's arm and took some of his weight as they hobbled back to the cabin Jack spoke of.

He pulled on the t-shirt and loose-fitting shorts Reagan had brought him and let the doctor fuss over him.

"Fuck. He did a good job." Reagan said, as he wrapped and cleaned the wound.

Lucas shrugged, his mind fighting the pain with age-old techniques.

"He's done worse before."

"He's done what?" Katherine asked, her voice high pitched and upset.

Lucas looked down as the family stared at him.

"Nothing, please forget I spoke."

Megan grabbed his hand and stared at him, as though trying to give him strength.

Jack's deep voice filled the air. "No, son. I think it's time you told us the whole truth."

Lucas took a deep breath, fear tickling the back of his mind.

"I can't. If they find out what I've told you, they'll make my life a living hell when I go home."

"You're not going back there!" Megan gasped. "Never! You'll come back and live in the Borough with us, won't he, Dad?"

Lucas raised his head, the paralysing fears trickling away to make room for the light filling his heart.

"Damn straight, son. So, spill." Jack's voice boomed around the room, and whereas in the past, an Alpha's voice would have made him cower, instead, he settled. Was made to feel safe, and strong.

"Well, I don't really know everything, to be honest."

"Just tell us whatever you can."

He took a deep breath. He'd never envisioned telling his story to anyone. Where to begin?

"Well, my parents died when I was a teenager, but the Alphas never liked me. They let me finish school because I was smart, but they've always given me twice the workload of anyone else. I don't really know why."

"It's because you smell like an Alpha," Jack said, and Lucas's mouth fell open.

"What?"

That didn't make any sense. His dad had been a Beta, and they'd all told him he was a Beta, too.

Katherine nodded. "You do. I think that's why one of our

Omegas sent you over to us. Your Alphas would have seen all the Alpha qualities in you that they should possess, and don't. Intelligence, empathy..."

"An ability to work like the devil's chasing you." Megan continued.

"Yeah... well..." He swallowed hard, the emotions choking him. They saw him for who he was, which had to be for the first time in his life. "I... like being part of a pack. Helping everyone. They've always taken advantage of that part of me, and yet they hate it, too."

Jack nodded. "Of course they hate it. If you'd known what you *could* become, you probably would have challenged them when you reached maturity."

He shook his head. "No one challenges an Alpha. An Alpha is born, not won."

Jack shook his head. "That's not true. We've recently allowed lots of challenges, including a new Alpha. Our pack is stronger for it, because our Alphas protect their pack, and do a lot of the work. Why wouldn't you want more of that heart leading the pack?"

Lucas snorted. "Yeah, like the Alphas do anything except sit in their castle and point out the jobs for the rest of the pack to do."

The room vibrated with anger, and he let his gaze drop. "I'm sorry. I didn't mean you."

Jack grunted. "It's okay, Lucas. We're just upset that you have been raised to see us, and our kind, in that way. When you move to Greensborough, you will see a very different sort of hierarchy."

Reagan winked at him. "Yeah, and lots of all-male Alpha pairs, so you better be cool with that."

Lucas laughed. "Oh, I don't care about any of that."

"Good."

Then Jack sat forward in his chair, his mouth quirking up. "So,

Megan. Tell me why I just risked my life for a young man I barely know. Do you think you know the answer?"

Lucas looked over at the Alpha's daughter, and Megan sat up proudly.

"Lucas is my mate."

CHAPTER FIVE

Megan couldn't believe she was finally saying it, and she wanted to say it again. Her heart was hammering in her chest after tonight's events, and she didn't want to waste another moment being apart from Lucas.

If those stupid Alphas had their way, he probably wouldn't be here at all, and that only strengthened her resolve to bond with him straight away.

"They destroyed his mark so I couldn't identify him, but everything else is there. The beautiful smell, the instant attraction... um."

Heat coursed up her face in a rush as she told her parents everything. She shouldn't be embarrassed, she knew. What she was feeling was natural and exactly what her mother had told her she would experience.

But explaining it to her parents was strangely awkward.

"Show me the mark," her father said, and she turned to Lucas, encouraging her mate with a smile. He stood up awkwardly on his sore leg and lifted the t-shirt Reagan had given him to wear.

A sigh escaped her lips at the sight of his damaged torso. Desire and disgust fighting for supremacy. His body was so beautiful, so thin and yet muscled. To think someone would hurt him like that, intentionally, was simply horrible.

"What happened?" her mother asked, her gaze trained on the scarring around his belly button.

"Alpha Bill... got drunk one night and took a knife to me. He told me that I didn't deserve a mate and attempted to remove my mark. It's mostly gone, as you can see. There's a tail of the crescent here and here," He pointed to the start and the end of their identical marks, "but he cut the rest off."

"That must have been painful," Reagan whispered, his throat working as he swallowed hard.

Lucas shrugged. "They had me back working within a few days. Just a flesh wound, they said. Nothing serious. And they were right."

"And this is the sort of thing that goes on within your pack?" her dad asked, his voice deep, dark, and angry.

A shiver ran over her skin. She didn't think she'd ever heard her father's voice sound like that.

Lucas nodded once, his eyes shadowed with pain. "Yes."

Her dad stood up and motioned to her mum. "Katherine, let's head out to speak to the leaders. I'm going to see an end to this barbaric crap that's happening in Robinvale."

His eyes slid over to her. "And Megan, we'll be gone a few hours, with Reagan. Perhaps your mate and you would like to finish bonding, so we can take him back to the Borough as your official mate."

The heat of her embarrassment before may have been like a kitchen fire; now, a full wild brush fire spread up her face.

She swallowed hard. "Thank you, Dad."

The other three left, and she turned to Lucas, whose fiery complexion, she was sure, mirrored her own.

"I can't believe they want us to... mate, now."

She giggled and stood up, mindful of his leg. She needed to give him a choice. After years of living under the oppression of his Alphas, the last thing she wanted was to make him feel like he didn't have a choice with her.

"We don't have to, you know. If you don't want to. I know you were reluctant to get to know me, let alone mate with me... Is that still the case, Lucas?"

She sincerely hoped not, but there was no way of knowing how he felt.

She sat down next to him, and he shuffled closer, taking both of her hands in his.

"I always wanted to know you. I still do. I'm sorry I wasn't who you needed me to be yesterday. My past is... complicated and horrible... and I don't want to put any of that on you."

She made a dismissive noise out of the side of her mouth.

"You've been abused by people who were supposed to look after you. That's not your fault. I just..." she gathered all the strength her parents had put into her. She needed to be the brave one here. She'd been the one with the blessed life. "I need to know if you want me. If you don't, you can still live in the Borough—my family will take you in, no questions asked. I'm not something you have to take on. I don't want to be another thing in your life that's been forced upon you."

He drew her closer without saying a word until she was sitting on his lap and he was cupping her face with his hand.

"I want you. I desire you. I would love, more than anything, to be your mate. If you'll have me? Scars and all."

Tears leaked down her face, but she leaned forward as he pressed his lips to hers.

Pleasure curled in her heart at the first touch of his mouth against hers. A moan escaped her throat, and she wrapped her arms around his neck, clinging to him. Not wanting to let him go, ever.

The kiss went on and on, his tongue delving in to meet hers. She thrust her tongue back, wanting to taste him as well. Needing so desperately to know what this felt like. This magical thing that came with love and being a woman.

His rough hands moved down, stroking the skin of her throat, her arms, his touch causing waves of awareness to flow over her body.

Then they moved over her aching breasts. She gasped against his mouth as her nipples hardened and he flicked each one with his thumb.

He tore their mouths apart.

"Where can we go? Do you have a bed?"

She did. But it was two singles in the one room. "Yes, but we may need to be creative."

He grinned and stood up, taking her hand. "Lead the way, my beautiful mate."

She tugged his arm and he followed with a smile. She walked into the room she was sharing with Reagan. Under no circumstances was she making love for the first time in her parents' bed.

"Ah. Let's push them together." Lucas said, and before she could protest, he was tugging and pushing the two beds against one of the walls.

"Your leg!"

He hopped over to her, pulling her down onto the bed with him.

"I've had a lot worse, and believe me, your touch is healing."

Sadness flowed through her at the thought of all he'd suffered while she'd been safe and happy, waiting in Greensborough.

"I'm so sorry you had this all done to you."

She dropped her head as tears gathered, hot and tingly in her eyes.

He lifted her chin again with his roughened finger tips. "Don't think about it now. You are Heaven to me, and I will never forget that. Nor take you for granted. You have saved me."

He kissed her once again, his hands busy lifting the hem of her t-shirt. She moved back to help him remove it.

She grabbed for his top and pulled it off, too, wanting him naked so she could feel his skin against hers. She lifted her hands to spread her palms over his warm skin, loving the feel of his strong muscles beneath her hands.

"I know I'm not very big. I know you're used to Alpha men. But I will grow now that I have the chance to shift, and get stronger."

His words hurt her, though they were meant to be thoughtful.

She looked him straight in the eye. "You are my mate. My destiny. You are perfect in every way. And I have never known any man... so if you're comparing yourself to anyone, your only competition is yourself."

His eyes widened, and his mouth dropped open.

"You've never... why?"

She shrugged, shivering as his fingers traced her nipples and the upper swell of her breasts.

"I was waiting for you. I knew you'd find me, sooner or later."

And it was true. No one else had ever felt right. Even a simple teenage kiss had felt wrong. She'd waited, and she was glad.

His gaze burned with intensity as he stared at her. "I will make sure you never regret your decision to fight for me, Megan, I promise you."

"I know," she said, lifting her arms to pull him closer.

His lips found hers once again and he unclipped her bra, the material falling away. She shivered as he stared at her, cupping her breasts and smiling with a contented look on his face.

"You are an incredibly beautiful woman."

She was glad she pleased him, having had nothing to compare herself to except other women her own age. And often, she'd found herself lacking.

She pushed such negative thoughts aside and stood up. Pushing her shorts off, she left her knickers on, then lay down, wanting to know what it felt like to be his woman.

"Come here. Please."

She held up her arms and he nodded, and stood to strip his shorts off.

His cock sprung up, pointing directly at her. She'd never seen such a display before. It had changed from when she'd seen him naked this evening, after shifting. It was hard, and redder.

He lay down next to her and pulled her knickers off, throwing them on the ground.

She lay stiffly, not sure what to do.

"Touch me, beautiful, please."

He took her hand and wrapped it around the hot shaft of his cock. A naïve squeal rose in her throat, but she pushed it down, wanting to feel more.

It was silky smooth and so different to anything she'd ever touched before. She was rewarded when he groaned and dropped his head, suckling on one of her nipples.

She cried out in shock, then arched her back to get closer, pleasure arrowing down from her breasts to her belly.

He slipped a hand between her thighs and gently pushed them apart with his fingers.

She tried to relax and closed her eyes, using one hand on his shaft and the other hand to hold him to her breast where his mouth was doing wicked things to her flesh.

"Ah..." She gasped and groaned when his fingers slid over her, circling her clit and rubbing her in a way that made her skin tingle, her organ throb.

She squirmed as he began to kiss lower, moving until he lay between her thighs and set his tongue where his fingers had been.

Pleasure exploded in her belly, licks of fire caressing her pussy as he ate around the lips, then moved up and down. Dipping his tongue inside of her, then moving around and up to where she was most sensitive.

"Lucas... oh.... fuck!"

She grabbed at his hair and held tight as a wave of pleasure began to build like a coming storm. His fingers slid inside her and she screamed out, pulses of ecstasy moving through her belly as blinding flashes blew apart her mind.

He moved up, covered her body, separated her legs, then thrust inside her in one long stroke.

Pain splintered inside of her, dulling some of the pleasure, but she floated down slowly, her high too far up to destroy completely.

Lucas didn't move, though he trembled beneath her hands. She had to assume he was staying still to allow her time to adjust.

Eventually, she opened her eyes, and he was staring down at her, the love she saw on his face everything she had ever dreamed about.

"Are you all right, my mate?"

She nodded, lifting her legs to wrap around his slim waist.

"Please keep going."

He dropped down and kissed her, his tongue spearing between her lips as he began to move, thrusting his hips so that his cock matched the movement of his tongue.

She sucked on his tongue, loving the flavour of his mouth mixed with her own, while his hips beat harder and harder against her in a primitive dance she'd only ever heard about.

The swell of the wave began again, this time moving through her as one, long, steady pulse.

She cried out again, his movements turning erratic as he pumped into her, then strained against her.

She gasped, she was almost there.

Then it happened.

He cried out as his seed pulsed into her, the sound so primitive and raw it made her turn her head and bite into his shoulder in response. His orgasm called to hers, her pussy going into instant, sudden, and violent convulsions.

Her orgasm slammed into her with no warning and the strength of a truck. She screamed as it tore her apart, her body squeezing every drop out of Lucas until he finally collapsed on top of her.

She shuddered over and over again, loving every second, every moment of this. Her mating. A time she would never forget.

Lucas lay on top of her, and she held him tight, stroking his back and his hair as his breathing grew steady.

She let herself relax, a giggle rising and lifting her lips into a smile.

What an incredible night.

What a weekend!

She'd known she would meet her mate at this festival, but everything else had been a massive surprise, and the best part was, she was sure that she and Lucas would continue as they had begun.

Her life with Lucas was going to be one unplanned, amazing adventure.

She heard Reagan and her parents come home during the night, but she and Lucas weren't disturbed.

Her family knew she'd found her mate, and tomorrow they would set off home, and her life would be better than it had ever been, with her mate at her side.

EPILOGUE

12 months later.

Megan watched her mate with greedy eyes as he stripped in the clearing, getting ready to shift with the rest of the pack at the full moon.

God, he's beautiful.

A year of good food, love, and acceptance and Lucas was one of the strongest, healthiest members of their pack.

She dropped her hand to caress her large belly, the swell of their child moving and shifting with excitement.

"You're going to love running with your daddy beneath the full moon, aren't you, little one?"

Reagan hadn't told her she was having a boy, but her baby loved this time of the month so much, he didn't stop moving. She was sure her baby was a little Alpha wolf.

Or he could be a Beta like his daddy. She didn't care. So long as he was happy.

The howl went up into the air and Lucas turned to find her,

their gazes locking and love flowing between them for one moment, before he began to shift.

He dropped down onto all fours as his bronzed skin turned into fur. She sighed as she stared at him. Lucas's silver wolf was now as big as the black Alphas.

Upon her encouragement, and he'd needed quite a lot of it, Lucas had challenged for Alpha status a few weeks ago. He'd been awarded the rank in record time.

No one deserved it more. The strength he brought the pack made it so. No one worked harder, or was more of a pack man than her mate.

Even Brad's mate, Stephen, was in awe of Lucas and everything he achieved.

The Robinvale pack had been taken over and reorganised, and Betas from every other pack over the state, including Greensborough, had moved there to help the pack rebuild.

Bill and his other horrible Alphas had been exiled to atone for their sins.

"How's my grandchild today?" her mum asked as she walked up and stroked Megan's belly.

"Wonderful. Won't be long now, I don't think."

And as though her words had called on it, a strong cramp hit her and water flooded her thighs.

She looked down and then up at her mum again, blinking in shock.

Her mum's smile was blinding as she called to Reagan.

Megan started breathing deeply, sending out a silent message to Lucas not to be long on his run tonight.

Because tomorrow they would be parents, and their worlds would change once again.

www.ingramcontent.com/pod-product-compliance
Lightning Source LLC
Chambersburg PA
CBHW071951210726
48292CB00020B/124

* 9 7 8 1 9 2 3 4 4 6 4 7 2 *